The Last Carolina Sister

MICHELLE MAJOR

HQN

HQN

Recycling programs
for this product may
not exist in your area.

ISBN-13: 978-1-335-41997-2

The Last Carolina Sister

Copyright © 2021 by Michelle Major

A Carolina Valentine

Copyright © 2021 by Michelle Major

This edition published by arrangement with Harlequin Books S.A.

For questions and comments about the quality of this book,
please contact us at CustomerService@Harlequin.com.

HQN
22 Adelaide St. West, 40th Floor
Toronto, Ontario M5H 4E3, Canada
www.Harlequin.com

Printed in Spain

CONTENTS

To DCG: For decades (how are we that old?!)
of friendship and for being my safe space.
I appreciate you, lady. Always.

THE LAST CAROLINA SISTER

CHAPTER ONE

WHEN THE POUNDING STARTED, Ryan Sorensen glanced from the television to the front door and then back again, settling deeper into the faded recliner.

Rain beat against the roof of the cottage situated a few blocks from the beach near the town of Magnolia, North Carolina. The Carolina Hurricanes were up by one goal against Detroit with five minutes left in the second period. He was warm, dry and as comfortable as his injured leg would allow.

Nothing good would come of answering an insistent knock on a stormy night.

His jaw tightened as he imagined what his father would think of him ignoring a person potentially in need of help. Ryan had been taught from a young age that he owed the world something, no matter what the world handed him in return. The lesson had led, in a roundabout sort of way, to a bullet in his leg a month earlier and a colleague and friend dying in his arms. It had been one hell of a difficult pill to swallow.

He figured whoever was outside his door would give up eventually. Minutes later the door rattled on its hinges as the pounding increased in intensity.

"Hello?" a female voice shouted over the noise from

the storm. "I'm not going away. I know you're in there. I can see the light from the TV. Hello! I need help. Please."

Resignation snaked along his spine as he straightened from the worn chair with a grunt. The *please* had been a nice touch. Feigning deafness to the knocking was one thing. Outright ignoring a plea for assistance was more than he could manage, even if he wanted to.

He eyed the cane that sat propped against the coffee table, then turned his gaze to the front door. Seven feet max. He could make it that far on his own.

By the time his hand grasped the doorknob, pinpricks of pain radiated up from his calf to make his entire left leg burn. Gritting his teeth, he pulled the door open, unsure of what he expected to find on the other side.

"You're a doctor, right?" the woman asked, and it took Ryan a few seconds to process the question as he looked her over from head to toe.

All five-foot-nothing inches of her, soaking wet with dark, chin-length hair tucked under a faded baseball cap and mossy-green eyes that were almost cartoonishly round. Raindrops clung to her cheeks and lashes, giving her an ethereal sort of look, but the spark in her eyes told him she was no shrinking violet.

He recognized her as his nearest neighbor, even though they hadn't spoken in the week since he arrived to finish his leave of absence in the beach cottage belonging to the hospital chief's family. This was Meredith Ventner, the woman who operated some sort of wayward-animal rescue from the property next door.

Ryan hadn't come to this small town to make friends, and there was enough acreage between the houses that he'd had no reason to introduce himself to her.

Until now.

"Yeah," he said. "I'm here on vacation."

Not exactly the truth but close enough that she'd hopefully get the message he wasn't on duty. Jerk move, but Ryan was in no shape to make a difference to anyone at this point.

Her green eyes narrowed. "Sorry to bother you," she said, not sounding sorry at all. "But I need you to come with me. There's an injured man at my house."

Panic threatened to choke Ryan, and he forced himself not to flinch away from her request.

"I understand Magnolia has a hospital and regular doctors."

"The road leading to town is a mess. Pretty sure it's washed out in some places." She gestured to the deluge coming down past the cover of his front porch. "Plus Joey might need stitches. I don't want to wait."

Stitches. Okay, then. Ryan could probably handle stitches without losing his composure.

"What happened to him?"

She threw up her hands like he'd just asked the dumbest question in the world. "Does it matter? He's hurt. You're a doctor. I learned about the Hippocratic oath on *Grey's Anatomy*. You might want to stop dillydallying because the storm's supposed to get worse before it lets up."

"You do realize you're the one asking for a favor?"

"I already said *please*," she countered.

So she had.

Every self-preservation instinct inside Ryan told him not to get involved with this woman or her injured friend. If it wasn't that serious she could...

Damn it. Who was he fooling?

"I'll get my medical bag," he told her. "But I want more details on the ride over."

"Fine."

She started to step into his house, then paused when he didn't move. "Fine," she repeated. "I'll wait in the truck."

Her tone communicated quite clearly that she thought he was a royal jerk, and he didn't disabuse her of that notion.

Instead he closed the door as she turned away, preferring to be labeled an ass than to have a complete stranger witness the agonizing walk to his cane.

Gritting his teeth against the pain, he collected it and then pulled his medical bag from the hall closet and grabbed a waterproof jacket from the coat hook. It had been raining off and on for his entire stay, suiting his mood to a T. Unfortunately, the conditions also made the wood porch and steps slick, and Ryan had to take it slow to ensure he didn't end up falling on his butt in front of his neighbor.

Insult to injury and all that.

She drove a behemoth of a truck and looked almost comical behind the wheel, like she should be sitting on a stack of phone books to see over the dash.

As soon as he climbed in, after stashing the supplies and cane in the back, she hit the gas. The truck fishtailed for a few seconds, then lumbered down the gravel drive.

So much for a quiet evening with the hockey game.

"I'm Meredith," she told him as she drove, her gaze steady out the front window. The rain made visibility almost nonexistent, but she handled the hulking vehicle like a pro.

"Ryan Sorensen."

"David Parthen emailed me that one of his friends would

be staying in the cottage for a few weeks. He mentioned that you're an ER doc."

"Tell me about the man's who's hurt."

"Joey Granger," she said, almost reluctantly. "He came out tonight to look at a cat he wanted to adopt. Or at least that's what I thought. I guess he had other plans, as well. Stupid ones."

"And he got injured in the process of these stupid plans?"

"Something knocked him off balance, and he fell."

"And…"

"Hit his head on the corner of a table."

Ryan let out a breath. It was like prying a clamshell apart to get the story. There was something more Meredith wasn't telling him, but he decided to concentrate on the part that involved him. "Did he lose consciousness?"

"No," she answered immediately, then added under her breath, "unfortunately."

"Um…"

"I'm sure he's fine. He just got a little woozy with all the blood."

"'All the blood,'" he murmured. "That's encouraging."

The truck hit a rut, jostling both of them.

"You're distracting me," Meredith told him, and something about the accusation in her tone made him want to smile.

In the wake of the quiet routine of his first week at the beach house, the past several minutes felt like walking into the sunlight after hours in a darkened room. He couldn't quite make sense of the situation, and his equilibrium felt shattered.

"We're almost there." She'd gentled her tone, purposely he imagined, and Ryan decided not to question her anymore. The light from her two-story farmhouse glowed ahead of them as the windshield wipers swish-swished a rapid pattern, filling the silence that stretched between them.

She parked at the base of the front-porch steps, five of them. Ryan hated dealing with stairs, but he wasn't about to admit that.

Instead he got out, took his bag and cane from the back seat and followed her as quickly as he was able.

Meredith took the steps two at a time. Bounding up them as he would have done three weeks earlier. Now he went slowly, working to keep his features neutral as pain shot up his leg again.

At least she didn't ask about the cane, although he could tell she wanted to. The stupid stick was like a giant arrow pointing out to everyone that he wasn't right. If only his issues were just physical. What a blessing that would be.

He gave himself a mental shake. This moment wasn't about him. He could fake normal for as long as it took to deal with her friend and his fall or whatever had really happened. Ryan had quickly become a master of faking it.

As he followed Meredith out of the storm and into her house, he tried not to think about anything else. About what the next few minutes might bring and how somehow he knew everything in his world was about to change. Again.

"JOEY, I'M BACK," Meredith called as she headed toward the back of the house, Ryan Sorensen's cane thumping on the hardwood floor as he followed her. Plaintive whines came from behind her closed bedroom door, but she ignored them. She'd put away the dogs and the two cats she could find when she'd left to get Ryan. They were well trained, but since the same couldn't be said for Joey, she figured leaving him on his own was better than inviting him to get comfortable with her overly friendly menagerie of adopted pets.

David Parthen hadn't mentioned in the email about someone staying at the cottage that his friend was injured or unfriendly or hot as all get-out.

She'd nearly forgotten the disaster waiting at her house when he'd opened the door. Heck, she'd nearly forgotten her own name.

Ryan was well over six feet, with broad shoulders and muscled arms under the faded Georgetown T-shirt he wore. He had sandy-blond hair that was long enough to make him look more like a surfer than the big-city physician she'd expected to meet.

Weren't doctors only supposed to be movie-star good-looking on television?

He clearly hadn't wanted to come with her tonight, which had been another shock. Being healthy most of her twenty-seven years, Meredith hadn't had much interaction with doctors. Again, if Hollywood could be relied upon for accuracy, doctors loved jumping in to save the day.

Ryan had needed more than a little prodding.

But he was here now and—

"Did you bring whiskey?" Joey called from where he sat on her couch, still holding the ice pack she'd given him against his head. At least he didn't look any worse than he had when she'd left to retrieve the doctor.

"No alcohol," she said. "You're trouble when you're sober, Joey. I've seen you drunk enough times to know we're not going there tonight."

"Apparently, we're not going anywhere," he muttered. "I feel like you led me on, Mer."

"You said you were coming out for a kitten," she reminded him through clenched teeth.

"I said a *kitty*," he told her, removing the ice pack. "It was a eudanisn."

She winced at the dried blood that matted his hair around the edges of the bandage she'd done her best to apply to the wound.

"I think he means a *euphemism*," Ryan said at her shoulder, his tone both bewildered and amused. "Instead of a kitty, he might be talking about—"

"I know what he's talking about." Meredith focused on her irritation with the fellow townie she'd known since elementary school and tried to ignore the heat she could feel from the doctor standing so close. "That's what led to this whole fiasco."

"She tried to kill me," Joey told Ryan.

"The women of Magnolia should be so lucky," Meredith shot back.

"I could have you arrested." He held up a hand. "Wait. You aren't going to tell Tanya about this, right? She and me aren't exclusive, but she's got a jealous streak a mile wide. Now that I think about things, it was a simple misunderstanding."

"Involving attempted murder?" Ryan asked as he stepped forward.

"Not exactly murder, I guess," Joey admitted. "I forgot about Meredith's temper, which was my bad. After the article last month, I figured I was doing her a favor coming out here. She's lonely, you know?"

Meredith gave a tight shake of her head when Ryan

glanced over his shoulder at her. She should have given Joey a Band-Aid and sent him on his way, washed-out road be damned. As Ryan arched a thick eyebrow, she felt color rush to her cheeks.

"Don't ask," she told him, hoping it didn't sound like she was begging. Although she'd beg, borrow and plead to have tonight a distant memory.

"You the doc?" Joey asked when Ryan turned to face him again.

"Yes." Ryan crouched down in front of Joey. "Tell me about your head. You can leave out the lonely bits."

Joey looked around Ryan's broad frame toward Meredith. "Can I at least get a beer?"

She counted to ten in her head, then asked, "How about a glass of orange juice?"

"Close enough," he grumbled.

"Doc?" she added.

"Nothing for me."

She went around the corner to the kitchen and poured Joey a glass of OJ, then stood by the counter for several minutes, trying to convince herself that her reaction had been a normal one. Didn't most women haul off and deck a man who tried to kiss them? Joey had taken a step back, lost his balance and fallen, cutting the skin above his right eye on the corner of a shelf in the barn.

Now that the moment was over, she couldn't help but think she'd been slightly irrational. Joey had acted like an idiot, but he wasn't a predator or some kind of bad guy. Not the sharpest knife in the drawer, either. But was he really to blame?

The article about Furever Friends that had appeared in the local paper last month was meant as free publicity for a Valentine's Day adoption fair she'd been holding. She'd talked to the reporter, Kate Crane, about the unconditional love of a pet and how animals could help people who didn't have other close relationships in their lives. Meredith had made a few awkward jokes about dogs being better company than men. Still, she hadn't expected the article's focus to turn to her modern-day spinsterhood and how sweet and pathetic it was that she devoted her life to animals in need while she pined for the right man to appear.

Since that time, every red-blooded bachelor in Magnolia seemed to show up at her doorstep ready to sweep her off her feet. As if she were hard up for a date. Okay, that might be true, and she'd possibly tried a few online dating sites, but advertising her singleton status in the news was too much.

A yelp from the family room brought her thoughts back to the present, and she grabbed the glass from the counter.

Joey hissed out a pained breath as she reentered room. "That hurts like a mother."

"A few more seconds," Ryan answered. "The sting will subside as the liquid stitches dry. If you have any problems, your regular doctor will know how to handle them."

"I don't got a regular doctor. I appreciate all your help, but I'm gonna be just fine. Takes more than a little scrape to the head to keep Joey Granger down."

Meredith handed Joey the orange juice as Ryan straightened. "I'll give you my number, then," he told the other man. "Call me if you need anything."

"I need a beer," Joey said after downing the juice. His phone dinged, and he fished it out of his back pocket. "Nice." He pumped his fist after reading the text. "Jack got around the washout. He'll be here to pick me up in a few. I'll make it to Murphy's Pub tonight after all."

"No one should be out in this," Meredith told him. "Not even your nutty brother."

"Come on, Mer. You know a little rain isn't going to stop Jack. Is it cool if I leave my car here overnight? I can pick it up tomorrow."

"Fine," Meredith said. In all honesty, she owed Jack, Joey's twin brother, a debt of gratitude. Joey's lowrider Nissan would never make it back to town tonight. While her moment of panic was gone, she didn't relish a houseguest for the night.

Joey placed the empty glass on the coffee table. "Maybe I'll take another look at the kittens," he told her with a grin. "Now that I understand how things are with you, I won't be so distracted."

No way in hell would Meredith allow Joey to adopt one of her animals at this point. She liked to give people the benefit of the doubt, but he was as immature now as he'd been when he and his brother used to pull the fire alarm in elementary school.

"Be safe tonight, Joey. Both you and Jack need to get a ride home from the bar later."

"Yes, ma'am," he said with a wink, clearly feeling much better now that the doctor had patched him up. The rain died down enough to hear the roar of a modified truck pulling up in front of the house.

Joey stood. "Thanks again," he said to Ryan.

"You should go home and get some rest," Ryan answered.

"I can rest when I'm dead," Joey answered, chuckling to himself. He turned to Meredith. "Sorry about the miscommunication tonight. I know you weren't trying to kill me." He leaned in. "Even if you wanted to."

"Sorry about your head," she said, crossing her arms over her chest. Meredith didn't like to apologize but felt she owed Joey a little something, despite the fact that he'd been an idiot earlier. "Remember to confirm a woman's interest before you try putting any moves on her."

"But I got moves like a jaguar," Joey said, forming his hand into the shape of a claw.

Meredith stepped more fully in front of him and held up a hand. "Joey, stop."

He had the good sense to look embarrassed. "I got it, Mer. There are plenty of willing women interested in what I've got to offer, you know?"

"I know," she agreed, even though she couldn't imagine it. Definitely didn't want to. "Be safe."

He held up a hand. "See ya. Thanks again, Doc."

Meredith blew out a breath as he walked away. A moment later she heard the front door open and shut. Gracie gave an insistent bark from the bedroom.

"Are you okay with dogs?" she asked Ryan, unable to meet his gaze now that they were alone. There was so much about tonight she had no desire to revisit.

"Sure," he said slowly, leaning on his cane. "I still don't understand what just happened."

"Give me a quick second, and then I'll clear things up while I take you home."

She didn't want to talk about Joey or try to explain what had led to her medical nonemergency.

Ignoring the anxiety that pushed at the lid of the box where she kept it trapped, Meredith opened her bedroom door. Three excited dogs tumbled out.

Buster, the Labrador retriever alpha of her small pack despite having only three legs, was the first to run forward to investigate their visitor.

After receiving the requisite loving from Meredith, Gracie and Marlin followed. Her ragtag trio of mutts could be a lot, but Ryan gave them a genuine smile as he lowered himself to the sofa so he could pet each of them.

Normally Gracie, a giant German shepherd mix with only one ear, was hesitant around new people but jumped onto the couch next to Ryan and immediately tried to burrow under his arm. Marlin, her adorable and bucktoothed bulldog, plopped down on one of Ryan's sneakers.

"Gracie, off," Meredith commanded.

The dog's ear popped up, and she reluctantly hopped to the floor.

"I appreciate you coming with me," she said, approaching her dogs and her hot-doctor neighbor. "Joey and I had a misunderstanding that veered a bit south. I didn't try to kill him."

"Good to know," Ryan said, leveling her with a look that said he believed she had it in her.

Maybe she did. Honestly, she rarely let herself get close enough to a man to know.

"I'll take you home," she offered.

His thick brows lowered over his eyes as if he were weighing something in his mind. "Tell me the story of tonight, first."

"It's nothing," she lied.

"You practically broke down my front door, drove me over here like you were some kind of renegade storm chaser and then gave the man who you apparently attacked advice on his dating life that sounded like something my mother would have said. There's a story. I missed the end of the Hurricanes game, so I'd like to know I gave it up for a good reason."

Her mouth went dry at the intensity in his gaze, like he expected her to reveal the dark secret she'd shared with no one. Like he might already guess what she was hiding.

She gave an exaggerated eye roll and plopped onto the chair next to the sofa. "I'll share it, but you're going to be disappointed. It's really nothing."

At least, the version she planned to tell him.

CHAPTER TWO

"SHE MISQUOTED YOU as saying no one loves you like the animals." Ryan tried and failed to hide his grin. "Are you sure it was a misquote?"

Meredith covered her eyes with her hands, then peeked through her fingers. "Did I mention the title of the article was 'Must Love Dog Mom'?"

"Ouch," he said with a laugh, which sounded far too rusty coming from him. He still didn't know what had possessed him to ask Meredith to explain the situation with Joey. Even before the horrible night in the ER that had turned his entire world upside down, Ryan didn't do much hanging out and chatting. Certainly not with virtual strangers.

But he hadn't wanted to leave Meredith's cozy house. It smelled like vanilla candles. The three mutts that had so enthusiastically greeted him when she'd released them from her bedroom made him feel…normal. They hadn't looked sideways at his cane or given a sympathetic nod when he lost his balance for an instant.

They'd only wanted his attention, and he'd been oddly eager to give it. Ryan couldn't remember the last time he'd felt eager about anything.

In truth, he also wanted to know more about Meredith. Every minute he spent with her made her more intriguing.

She was a tiny sprite of a woman with a personality far larger than her petite frame.

"It feels like every guy I've ever known has asked me out in the past month. The article generated a certain amount of social-media buzz as well, so I've been fielding emails and messages to the rescue's Facebook page. I'm so over all of it."

"Not one prospect for Mr. Right?"

She shook her head. "Not even Mr. Right Now."

That news curled through Ryan, refreshing like a cool breeze on a hot summer day, which didn't make sense because Meredith's dating habits were none of his concern.

"Joey didn't bother asking me out. Since I've known him forever, I didn't expect the kiss."

He felt his smile fade. "No one should touch you without permission." She could joke all she wanted, but he'd seen enough women come into the ER after being hurt by a man. Sexual assault wasn't a laughing matter.

Meredith's mouth formed a small o, and her big eyes widened even further, as if he'd shocked her with his words. The moment stretched on for several seconds. Once again, he got the impression there was more to tonight's misunderstanding than she was willing to explain.

She quickly stood, displacing Marlin in the process. "There's a silver lining in all of this. The article has generated more press for me but also for the animals. Adoptions usually slow down this time of year, but I've had more traffic to the website, and our social-media following has grown a ton." Brushing her hands across the front of her flannel shirt, she glanced toward the ceiling. "Sounds like the rain has finally stopped. I can take you home."

Home. Ryan didn't know why that one word made his

chest ache. He nodded and got up from the sofa, grabbing his cane and wishing, for the millionth time, that he didn't need the damn thing.

"I've done all the talking tonight," Meredith said with a bright smile that appeared strained at the edges. "What brings you to Magnolia?"

"Forced vacation," he said, then ran a hand through his hair when she continued to study him, clearly waiting for a better explanation. "I work in a DC hospital and got injured on the job. I won't be cleared to go back for a few more weeks and sitting around in the city was making me crazy. When David offered the cottage, it seemed like a great alternative."

"Does that mean the cane isn't permanent?" she asked, leading him toward the front of the house.

Her dogs stayed behind, obviously content to curl up in the warm house as opposed to braving the dark and wet night. Ryan couldn't blame them.

"No."

She glanced over her shoulder, as if waiting for him to say more but didn't ask questions when he stayed quiet. He might be curious about Meredith, but that didn't mean he planned to spill his guts about the horrible night that had led him to this tiny town.

They walked out of the house, and he took in the canopy of stars overhead now that the sky had cleared. He'd been in North Carolina for a week but hadn't done much, other than go to the grocery store and sit around the house watching television and playing old-school video games on the console in the cottage. Hell, he hadn't even been to the beach, even though it was less than a mile from his front door. Every painful step reminded him of how much he'd lost, not just physical mobility but—

A loud whine broke the silence, pulling him away from the dark thoughts swirling through his mind. Ryan had never been so damn grateful.

He glanced toward the barn situated behind and to the right of the farmhouse. "How many animals do you have here?"

"Anywhere from a half dozen to somewhere in the low twenties, depending on the time of year." A chorus of barking filled the air. Meredith shrugged. "Things with Joey put me off schedule for tonight, so I still have to do one last check in the barn and give out evening meds. They'll settle after that."

"You need help?"

She stared at him as if he'd just offered her a winning lottery ticket. "Seriously? Don't feel obligated. I've already imposed on you enough for one night."

"My schedule is fairly light at the moment," he said, trying to sound casual. The truth was after his time with Meredith, he didn't relish returning to the empty, silent cottage. He'd thought the solitude was what he needed. The noise and bustle of the city reminded him of the way things used to be, and it had just about made him crazy.

What he hadn't counted on was that leaving DC for a few weeks might not allow him to leave behind his memories. The waking hours were palatable, but nights posed more of a challenge.

He'd refused to open the bottle of pills one of his colleagues had given him before he left. A sleeping pill might help with the nightmares, but Ryan didn't like the way he felt in the morning after taking one. Besides, he didn't deserve to anesthetize himself against the nightmares.

After all, he'd survived that night. Why should he be allowed to forget the colleague he hadn't been able to save, even for a few blessed hours of peaceful slumber?

"Then, follow me," Meredith said, placing her hands on her hips as she turned for the barn.

"Do you manage the rescue on your own?" he asked before she could turn the conversation back to him. It was easier to keep her talking than to have to worry about filtering how much he revealed.

"I have a couple of high-school students who come in after school, on weekends and during summer break. I also work part-time at a local vet clinic, and one of the other techs helps out when he can."

"That's a lot of responsibility for one person," he observed.

Her shoulders stiffened under the corduroy jacket she'd put on over her shirt. "I can handle it."

"Do you have family in town?"

"My dad," she said, almost defiantly. "And my two sisters."

"So there's some support. That's good."

She rounded on him so fast he almost bumped into her. "What makes you think I need help out here? For your information, I've managed everything on my own for nearly three years, and I have big plans for this place." Her green eyes sparked with a flame of determination that looked ready to ignite like a wildfire across a dry prairie. He liked her spunkiness even though her intensity felt misdirected.

"That's great, and forget I said anything. You've got it all under control."

"Exactly." She spun to face the barn again and heaved the heavy door open, then cursed under her breath.

He set down his bag and followed her into the barn, which was large and drafty, and immediately saw an issue outside of her control. A puddle of water, almost two feet in diameter, had formed in the middle of the aisle where a steady leak came from the structure's ceiling.

"We need a new roof," she explained as she grabbed a bucket from near the first stall and set it in the middle of the wetness.

Drip, drip, drip.

"I imagine you won't take care of that on your own," he said, trying to lighten the moment and earning another narrowed stare.

"As a matter of fact," she said, "it's on my list. The materials will be delivered next week."

Ryan opened his mouth to respond, then shut it again.

And he got accused of being too stubborn and independent? She had him beat by a mile.

She pointed to a hose hanging from the far wall. "Could you give fresh water to the animals on that side of the barn? All of the dogs over there are social. Try not to let any of them escape."

"Got it." He resisted the urge to salute, figuring she wouldn't find that amusing, either. The barn smelled like hay and animals, and the scent was more appealing than he imagined. There were two dogs in each of the first two stalls and one on its own in the last. All of them wagged their tails and sniffed when he retrieved and then returned their water bowls, his progress slower than he'd prefer due to the cane.

He could hear Meredith talking, her voice gentle, to

the animals in the other pens as she distributed meds and settled them for the night. At the end of the barn were two larger stalls, one housing the horse he'd heard earlier and the other with three goats huddled in the corner.

"You rescue farm animals, too?"

She nodded and smiled into the stall that held the goats. "Not often, but when there's a need in this area, the humane society out of Raleigh will give me a call. These three were abandoned when their family moved. They're sweet but naughty."

"I didn't realize goats had actual personalities."

She laughed softly. "All animals have personalities, most of them more appealing than humans you meet."

"Based on some of the characters I've run across in the ER, I can only imagine."

"You must think I'm a silly, crazy pet-rescue lady, when what you do has life-or-death stakes. Most people do."

As they watched the animals, he shifted closer to her, not so they were touching but enough that he felt the startling connection like a physical force between them. "I don't think you're silly, Meredith." Her name on his lips felt right. "I'd considered crazy with the way you showed up on my doorstep, but now I get that it's passion. You're passionate."

The moment the word slipped off his tongue, he regretted it. She glanced up at him, and he took a step away, not wanting to spook her. Her gaze had sharpened but held the tiniest speck of vulnerability, like she needed someone to tell her she wasn't silly or crazy.

He wanted to say a lot of things in this moment that wouldn't be smart for either of them. Ryan had come to Magnolia to recover on his own, not to make friends and definitely not to acknowledge an unexpected attraction to his gorgeous, spitfire neighbor.

"I should be getting home." He made a show of yawning.

"Right," she agreed, calling out good-night to each of the animals by name as they passed.

The damp air of the barn made Ryan's lower leg stiffen, and he did his best not to be too obvious about how much he had to rely on his cane as they walked to her truck.

He noticed each time Meredith's gaze tracked to his bum leg, but thankfully she didn't ask any more questions. It was as if they'd both used up their allotment of words for the day, and by mutual agreement they drove the short distance between the two properties in a companionable silence.

"Thank you again, Doc," she said when she pulled to a stop in front of the cottage. "I owe you."

"Just promise me you won't trust any more idiot men who tell you they're interested in your kittens," he said, then opened the door.

She grinned. "Cross my heart," she said as she traced the shape over her thick jacket.

Ryan's heart thumped in his chest. Despite a job that must entail hours of manual labor, her fingers were slender and elegant. Noticing them made him wonder about the rest of her body, which was not a path he had any intention of letting his mind wander down.

"Good night," he told her and closed the car door with more force than was probably necessary. Time to remind himself that their little adventure tonight had been an aberration, not the start of anything more.

He waited until her taillights disappeared around the curve in his driveway and then limped up the steps to his front door.

"WHAT'S WRONG?"

Meredith pasted on a smile as she glanced across the table at her two sisters the next afternoon.

"Nothing. What could be wrong? We're having cake in the middle of the afternoon. Life is good."

Avery and Carrie shared a look. "Something's not right," Carrie murmured, studying Meredith as she scooped up a bit of lemon-lavender cake.

They were at a table in the back of Magnolia's popular Sunnyside Bakery, together for a tasting to decide which flavor of cake Avery would serve during the reception of her upcoming wedding to local firefighter Gray Atwell.

Meredith didn't appreciate the scrutiny and still couldn't believe these two women were able to read her so easily. All three of their worlds had been turned upside down last summer when famed local artist Niall Reed had died and named them his beneficiaries. Carrie had been Niall's legitimate daughter, but his will revealed that both Avery and Meredith had been born after affairs with each of their mothers.

Avery Keller, the oldest of them, grew up in San Francisco, the only child of a single mother. She'd driven across the country for the reading of the will with no intention of staying in Magnolia. But she, Carrie and Meredith had formed an instant bond.

Having both grown up in Magnolia, Meredith had known Carrie Reed most of her life and had resented her elevated status in the community for almost as long. Compared to Carrie, who lived with her eccentric father and snooty mother in the biggest house in Magnolia, Meredith's childhood seemed less than ideal. Her mother had taken off when she was only five, divorcing the man Meredith believed to be her father and deserting Meredith and her two older brothers, Theo and Erik.

Carl Ventner was a former Marine, craggy and stoic. As the only girl in the house, Meredith had learned to become one of the boys as a means of survival.

Until Avery and Carrie, she hadn't had female friends and was still getting used to the idea of sharing confidences or her feelings. Heck, she still had trouble admitting she had feelings a lot of the time. But for the sake of her sisters, she kept trying.

"I punched Joey Granger last night," she said, picking at an icing flower petal on the edge of one cake slice.

"I don't know him, but I'm sure he deserved it," Avery said without missing a beat.

The tight ball of anxiety lodged in Meredith's gut loosened ever so slightly.

"Why were you with Joey?" Carrie asked. "I thought most of the sane people in Magnolia steered clear of both the Granger brothers."

Meredith shrugged. "He called and wanted to come out to the rescue to look at a kitten."

"A kitten," Carrie repeated with a scoff. "Such a ruse. I'm sure he was there thinking he had a chance with you because of the article." She tucked a strand of chestnut-colored hair behind one ear, her eyes widening as she looked at Meredith. "Don't tell me you didn't realize it."

"It was a busy day, and I wasn't thinking along those lines. That stupid article is the bane of my existence right now." She pointed her fork at Avery. "I like the chocolate better than the lemon."

"Try the carrot cake," Carrie suggested, pushing her plate toward Meredith.

"Do we need to kick this Joey Granger's butt?" Avery demanded. "If any man thinks he can take advantage of my baby sister, he'll have to deal with me."

Meredith grinned, and this time it was real. Avery was tall and slim and looked like she'd just stepped out of a Talbots ad. With shiny blond hair, clear blue eyes and an air of big-city sophistication that hadn't been dulled by her move to Magnolia, Avery didn't look like a threat. But Meredith knew looks could be deceiving and had no doubt that either of her sisters would have her back if she needed it.

"Carrot cake is definitely my fave," she said after taking a bite. "And I handled Joey." She cringed. "Maybe a little too enthusiastically. I had to ask my new neighbor to come over and stitch a cut above his eye."

"I'm going to have a talk with Joey just on principle," Carrie said.

"It's fine," Meredith lied. "I probably overreacted. I wish I'd never said anything about dating to Kate."

"You've wanted to meet someone," Avery reminded her.

"The results of me trying to date have been dismal," Meredith countered around another bite. "How does Mary Ellen make everything taste so good?" She took a small sip of water. "I'm done with dating or even trying to date. Men aren't worth the trouble."

Avery and Carrie shared another look. Both sisters had recently fallen for men who adored them. While Meredith was happy for them, she couldn't help but wonder why she'd never been lucky in love. Unfortunately, the answer always came back to the fact that there was something undeniably broken in her. She was like a man repellent.

"Tell us about the neighbor," Carrie prompted. "There's been lots of murmuring around town regarding the Parthen cottage's new occupant. He's quite the mystery man. Apparently, he came into the hardware store a few days ago, and Lily said he was crazy handsome and just as unfriendly."

Avery raised a brow at Meredith. "But he helped you?"

"I didn't give him much of a choice," Meredith admitted. "I wouldn't say he's unfriendly, but I get the impression he wants to keep to himself. He said he's here on a vacation, but he doesn't seem very relaxed for a guy spending a month at the beach. The dogs liked him."

"That's a mark in his favor," Avery observed.

Carrie nodded in agreement as she glanced at the diamond ring on her left finger, a dreamy smile tugging at the corners of her mouth. "Daisy and Barnaby absolutely worship Dylan. Those two will hardly look at me if he's around. It's annoying and cute at the same time."

Dylan Scott, Carrie's first love, had returned to Magnolia just before Thanksgiving last year. Although he and Carrie had started off as enemies, they'd quickly rekindled their love affair from a decade earlier.

At first, Meredith wasn't sure whether she trusted Dylan with her sister's heart, but he'd adopted both a dog and a kitten from her rescue. To Meredith, there was no better measure of a person's character than how they treated animals. Dylan had won her over just as he had Carrie. Well, not exactly in the same way, but she approved of him.

"I'm sure Ryan Sorensen will be happy not to have anything more to do with me or my animals while he's in Magnolia. He helped me in the barn before I took him home. The goats freaked him out, I think."

Both Avery and Carrie stared at her for several seconds.

"You let him help with the animals?" Carrie asked finally.

"He refilled water dishes," she said with an eye roll. "Not a big deal."

"You'll barely allow a capable volunteer into the barn," Carrie pointed out, none too helpfully from Meredith's point of view.

"I've asked for both of you to go on retrievals when I get calls about animals that need rescuing."

"But once they're on the property, you do it all."

She threw up her hands. "Not true and stop making this a big deal. I'm very willing to accept help when I need it."

"Uh-huh," Avery murmured, stabbing another piece of cake. "I want to meet your new doctor."

Meredith felt color rise to her cheeks as she pushed back from the table. "He's not *my* anything. I barely know the man." She wasn't about to admit how images of said doctor had invaded her dreams last night. "Go with the carrot cake and a buttercream icing for the main cake. Gray's groom's cake should be devil's food. Your soon-to-be-husband has a thing for chocolate."

"He does," Avery agreed with a chuckle. "Way to make this decision easy for me, Mer. Thanks."

Carrie winked. "When do we get to meet the hot doc?"

"Stop." Meredith stood and sliced the air with her right hand. "Or you two are on your own with the florist."

Avery's grin widened. "See you there tomorrow at two?"

Meredith let out a long-suffering sigh in response. "I've got to get back to work. Thanks for the sugar rush."

On her way out, she passed Mary Ellen Winkler, Sunnyside's talented owner. "Everything okay, sweetie?" the older woman asked as she wiped a hand across the unicorn-patterned apron Meredith had given her last Christmas.

"Sisters are annoying," Meredith grumbled. "But your cake flavors are amazing."

Mary Ellen pulled her in for a quick hug. As a rule, Meredith didn't like physical displays of affection, but she made exceptions for her irritating sisters and Mary Ellen, who'd been as much a mother to her over the years as her own mom.

"Thank you, dear. And, yes, family will drive you crazy, but we wouldn't have it any other way."

Meredith swallowed around the emotion that rose in her throat at those words. Her relationship with her dad and brothers had been strained since the revelation that Niall Reed was her biological father. She wanted to make things right but didn't know how. Avery and Carrie might drive her crazy, but Mary Ellen was right. She couldn't imagine her life without them.

She squeezed Mary Ellen's plump shoulders and pulled away. "Pay no attention to my mood," she advised. "Lousy night's sleep. I'll snap out of it soon."

"You push yourself too hard."

"I'm fine."

Mary Ellen frowned but didn't argue, and Meredith walked out of the bakery before the other woman could say anything more. She'd been anything but fine for years but could pretend with the best of them. No way she'd stop now.

CHAPTER THREE

TWO DAYS LATER, Ryan was getting out of his Jeep as shades of pink and orange streaked across the sky above him.

A hand-painted sign that read *Furever Friends* hung above the doors of the barn. The lettering matched the font of the sign at the edge of Meredith's winding driveway.

When he'd been here the first time, darkness had prevented him from getting a true sense of the property other than the outline of the main house and the barn.

In the soft light of early evening, he got a better idea of her operation. The house and the barn looked to be many decades old, the house painted a pale yellow while the barn was a traditional, faded red. Both structures were in need of some updating, although it was clear they were cared for. A brown tarp had been draped over a portion of the barn's roof, and in some spots, it looked like the sagging gutters of the house had been reinforced with zip ties.

The property was clean and tidy, and several large fenced enclosures were situated behind the barn.

It was also strangely quiet compared to the other night. He could see a half-dozen dogs milling about one of the outdoor pens, but they didn't seem concerned with his presence.

Meredith's truck was parked to the side of the house, so

she must be around somewhere. He thought about getting back in his Jeep but couldn't bring himself to do it.

Something had changed after his encounter with Meredith. He'd arrived in Magnolia mentally and physically beat down, ready for a month to finish his recovery. He hadn't planned to leave the house or speak to anyone other than what it took to buy what he needed in town. The physical-therapy exercises were easy enough to manage on his own, and he figured the silence would help clear the images swirling around his brain.

He liked the quiet, but it hadn't stopped his mind from revisiting the horrific minutes of the shooting over and over, like a movie he couldn't stop from playing on repeat.

But after the adventure with his feisty neighbor, Ryan had slept through the night for the first time in weeks. He told himself it was simply a change in his routine.

Yesterday he'd walked to the edge of the path that led to the beach but stopped before his feet sank into the soft sand. He wasn't yet willing to push his leg quite that much. Then he'd gone into town to order supplies from the hardware store for the raised garden he planned to build for David's wife, a thank-you gift for allowing him to use the cottage.

He'd read a book, done more rehab exercises and played video games, falling into bed exhausted at ten. Then he'd stayed awake staring at the ceiling until almost two in the morning. He hated the long nights.

Maybe the correlation between sleep and Meredith had been a coincidence, but Ryan was desperate enough to explore the option.

The barn doors were open a foot on either side, so he headed there, figuring it might be close to feeding time for her menagerie.

The overhead lights were on inside, and dust motes floated through the air. He could hear animals milling about in their pens but didn't see Meredith. To his left, a door was ajar, and he could make out the corner of a desk and a woman's boot-clad legs crossed on top of it. He wondered if she hadn't heard him come in.

He started to call out a greeting, but something stopped him. Instead, he approached and pushed the door open. Meredith sat behind the desk fast asleep, her feet propped on a pile of what looked like textbooks. Was she in school in addition to her job at the vet clinic and her work with the rescue?

Heat pricked along the back of Ryan's neck at the fact that he'd had the luxury to take a month off from work after his injury. Okay, maybe he needed to cut himself a little slack. Taking a bullet from a deranged gunman in the middle of a crowded ER would be considered traumatic under any circumstances. But somehow he felt like he paled in comparison to Meredith in the dedication department.

He didn't want to startle her, so retraced his steps, then purposely banged on the barn door as he reentered and called out her name.

A moment later she emerged from the office, blinking as if to clear her head and wiping a hand across her cheek. "Hey."

She looked tousled and sleepy and damn near irresistible.

Ryan shoved his hands into the front pocket of his jeans. He'd covered his injured leg with the medical boot today so he could leave the cane at home. Already, his calf muscle throbbed, and he focused on the pain to take his mind off his awareness of the woman standing before him.

"I hope I'm not interrupting. I was coming back from

town and thought I'd stop in and say hi. Be neighborly and all that. Figured you might be able to use an extra volunteer to scoop kibble or..." he pulled out a hand and waved it in the general direction of the stalls "...whatever needs doing around here." *Whatever needs doing?* Damn. Who spoke like that? He sounded like his paternal grandfather back on the farm in Virginia. This could be the first time in Ryan's life he'd ever babbled.

Meredith inclined her head as she studied him but didn't answer.

"You mentioned having a teenager who helps after school so you could be covered," he continued, unable to stop speaking, "but I'm willing. If you need...anything."

"Shae isn't here today," Meredith said finally. "She has a physics test tomorrow, so I sent her home to study."

He nodded. "Physics is rough." Thank you, Captain Obvious, he chided himself. For the love of all that was holy, why couldn't he pull it together? He hadn't taken a pain pill today so had no excuse for his discombobulation.

Meredith crossed her arms over her chest and turned away for a moment to survey the barn's interior. The temperature had made it to the mid-sixties today, but it was cooling as the evening wore on, and the air in the barn retained a slight chill. She wore a thick flannel shirt and twill cargo pants that highlighted her curves.

Curves he should not notice.

"You can start on the same side as the other night," she said when her gaze returned to his. "The dry food is in the bin just past the first stall. You'll find instructions on the outside of every pen."

He released the breath he hadn't realized he was holding. "Got it."

"Thanks," she said, and the simple word fell over him like a warm blanket.

He liked feeling useful, having a purpose, even if it was something as simple as feeding dogs.

"I'll take everyone on the left," she continued. "Some of them have more complicated meal plans. If you finish with the dogs, the litter boxes in the cat room need attention." She pointed to a door at the far end of the barn. "Unless you can't handle scooping poop."

"I can deal with poop," he assured her and headed for the first stall.

The dogs were even happier to see him now than they'd been before bedtime. Ryan knew it had more to do with the promise of dinner than his presence but smiled at their enthusiasm.

Although Meredith didn't bother with conversation as they worked, he could once again hear her soft murmurs to the animals. He filled the food bowls according to the handwritten instructions affixed to each stall and ended up talking to the dogs as they gathered around him.

After all of the dogs on his side of the barn had been fed, he headed for the cat room. There was a scooper and a garbage can just outside the door, so he picked up both and let himself in.

The room was probably ten feet by ten feet and filled with cat trees, toys and a few random pieces of wood furniture. Several of the animals slunk toward him, curious as to the newcomer in their space, while a few of the others watched from perches or darted into tunnels to hide.

Ryan had grown up with dogs and cats, but they were the kind that stayed in the yard when the weather allowed and often seemed more feral than family pets.

He finished the business at hand, then placed the scooper and can outside the door. Meredith was a silhouette at the opposite end of the barn, so he closed himself in with the cats and took a seat in the ladder-back chair positioned in one corner. Immediately, a sleek black cat climbed into his lap and began to purr. Two more animals, a tabby and one that had distinctive orange stripes, came closer to sniff at him. The orange one let out a series of meows and placed its front paws on Ryan's leg.

He ran a hand along the black cat and reached forward to scratch the orange one. Although he felt silly, he couldn't help but talk to them, much as he'd heard Meredith do as she went about her duties.

Two older kittens began to tussle on the floor in front of where he sat, rolling around like they were the main attraction in some feline wrestling federation.

He grinned at their show, so engrossed that he didn't notice Meredith enter the room until the cats abruptly stopped and the striped one trotted over to her.

"You scoop and socialize?" she asked as she bent to lift the smaller kitten into her arms. "Be careful or I might try to hire you for real."

"Okay," he answered without hesitation, then shrugged when she gaped at him. "I like having something to do."

Her full mouth turned down at the corners. "I thought you were on vacation."

"Like I said, it was forced." He shifted, and the black cat stretched out its two front paws, purring even more intensely. Ryan let the rhythmic sound soothe him as his mind raced, determining how much to share about his story.

"Are you in hiding?" One delicate brow rose in question. "On the run from something?"

Only myself, he thought but, of course, didn't say that out loud. "I'm on medical leave because of my leg."

She stayed quiet.

"My hospital is located in an area with a lot of gang violence." Anger bubbled up inside him as images flashed across his brain, but he concentrated on the feel of the cat's silky fur. The therapist his boss had forced him to talk to in the aftermath of that night had said to use his senses to ground him when the memories threatened to overwhelm him.

"A few weeks ago, we had a couple of kids—teenagers— brought in. They'd been in a fight, and both had been stabbed. One of them was bleeding pretty badly, and they came in with several friends, so the scene was chaotic for a few minutes." He blew out a breath. "Which is all the time it took for a rival gang member to walk in and start shooting."

The cats startled at Meredith's shocked gasp. "You were shot?" she asked in a hushed tone.

He gave a tight nod. "The bullet tore through my calf. It could have been—should have been—worse. One of the nurses, Kevin Hagler, tackled me to the floor as the guy started to shoot." He thought about ending the story there. He'd given her more about that night than he'd shared with anyone else in his life. But now that the words spilled from his mouth, he couldn't seem to stop them. "Kevin wasn't so lucky. Two bullets ripped through his chest. He died within minutes."

"I'm sorry," she whispered.

"He had a wife and a three-year-old son." Ryan's hands curled into fists, and the cat nudged him. "He should be here right now, but he's not. One of the kids who'd come in with a knife wound was also killed, along with the fool with the gun. None of that needed to happen, you know?"

Meredith swallowed, unsure of how to respond to everything Ryan had just revealed.

She wished Carrie were here. Carrie had an innate kindness and always seemed to know the right thing to say, pretty much in direct contrast to Meredith.

Which was why she spent more time with animals than people.

"That's about the best reason for wanting to scoop cat poo I've ever heard," she said and immediately cringed. Should have kept her stupid mouth shut.

To her surprise, Ryan's mouth curved into a slow smile that ended with a burst of shocked laughter.

"I'm bad with people," she blurted.

"No, you're right." He lifted the cat off his lap and placed it on one of the nearby perches. "I'm in Magnolia because I was going stir-crazy taking time off in the city. I feel just as useless here, and until my leg heals, I can't go back to work. Working with the animals…I don't know how to explain it but…"

It was her turn to laugh. "You don't need to explain it to the town's crazy rescue lady. I understand what animals do for a person."

She bit down on the inside of her cheek when his eyes narrowed. It was all well and good that he'd shared his story, but Meredith had no intention of traveling back in time to reveal the event that had inspired her on this journey.

"I can't pay you," she told him, "but if you want to help while you're in town, I have no problem with that. Shae is my main helper but she's a senior, so she's busy right now.

You'll have to stick with some of the easy stuff until I can train you on working with the animals that need a higher level of care." She ran a hand through her hair, suddenly self-conscious.

Why would a doctor, even one with a story like Ryan's, want to spend his time dealing with the menial tasks around the rescue? He sat forward, looking every inch a successful, educated, powerful man, and she stood there well aware of her college-dropout status and the fact that she was hanging by a thin financial thread as she worked around the clock to keep her small organization running.

"I can help with the roof, too," he offered. "I mean, I'll do whatever needs to be done around here, but I can handle bigger projects if you want."

She imagined he could handle himself with just about anything. Meredith wasn't sure what possessed her to offer him any work. Not that the place couldn't use an extra set of hands, but normally she liked to manage as much as possible on her own.

Maybe it was the fact that she was tired and over-whelmed, burning the candle at both ends as she managed her vet-tech job with the rescue and the workload of her online classes.

Or perhaps she understood that Ryan needed something on his journey to healing that her motley crew of furry and, occasionally, feathered creatures could offer. She'd always been a sucker for a wounded soul, two- and four-legged alike.

"One step at a time," she answered even though she desperately needed any help he was willing to give. No sense revealing her desperation from the start. That would give him too much power, and Meredith never gave away her power.

He stood and massaged a hand along the back of his neck. "I get that I told you my history, but I'm not really looking to advertise the reason I'm staying in Magnolia."

She gave him what she hoped was a reassuring smile. "Your secret is safe with the cats and me."

"Thank you."

The intensity in his gaze seemed to steal her breath, and the silence between them felt charged. Then her stomach growled.

"I haven't eaten since this morning," she admitted. "The clinic was slammed, and I needed to run back here on my lunch break to administer meds."

"You're in luck," he said with a wink. "I hit the grocery before stopping here and got a slab of flank steak that's way too big for one person. Do you have a grill?"

She blinked. "Yes."

"Want company for dinner?"

"Um...I..."

His gaze went unreadable. "I'm overstepping. Sorry. All the quiet at the cottage is making me weirdly social. I came to Magnolia for peace and quiet and all that."

He looked so uncomfortable, and it made her wonder if despite his looks and his important job in the city Ryan wasn't just as lonely as her.

Meredith felt ashamed of her loneliness most of the time and never admitted it to anyone. Even though their relationship had been strained since the revelation about Niall, she knew her father—the man who'd raised her—loved her. Her brothers loved her, too, and now she had two sisters in her life. She'd lived in Magnolia forever and knew the majority of people in town by name. So what if she didn't have a man in her life? She'd given dating a try, and it didn't work for her. She wasn't cut out to open herself up in that way. Still, there was no excuse for the feeling of emptiness that had recently taken up residence in her chest.

No one would understand.

Except she had a feeling Ryan Sorensen might.

"I love steak," she said simply, and the smile he gave her made her toes curl in her work boots.

If Meredith was going to be lonely, might as well do it with a hot man to cook for her. As long as she remembered it was only for one night.

CHAPTER FOUR

"THE HANDSOME DOCTOR cooked for you?" Avery asked, her tone incredulous.

"He grilled," Meredith muttered. "I made a salad for a side dish. So no one actually did any cooking."

"But you had dinner with him," Carrie pointed out. "In your kitchen."

Meredith tried to will away the heat she could feel rising in her cheeks as her two half-sisters stared at her. "That's where people normally eat dinner. I do like to eat, you know. Hand me those extra towels, Carrie."

Carrie passed over the stack, and Meredith lowered to her knees so she could finish drying the far corner of the living room floor. She had a scheduled day off from the vet clinic, but instead of using her time to finish the paper due tomorrow or to get caught up on office work at the rescue, she'd met Avery and Carrie to clean up a mess in Niall's old house.

During the recent storm, two of the drains on the back had clogged with leaves and sticks, causing water to flow in under the sliding door. Carrie had stopped by earlier that morning to check on things and found the damage, so they were here trying, once again, to fix a mess left in Niall Reed's wake.

"We know you like to eat," Avery said as she moved an

end table out of the way. "But you don't like people. Particularly men."

"I like people just fine," Meredith countered. "At least people who aren't idiots. I have no problem with men. Gray and Dylan happen to be two of my favorites."

"This Dr. Sorensen must be special," Avery continued as if Meredith hadn't spoken. "When do we get to meet him?"

"I'll stop by the hardware store and pick up a few sandbags to use until the rooter company can get to us," Meredith said, ignoring her oldest sister's question. It was still hard to believe a year ago she hadn't known Avery Keller existed in the world and that she'd thought of Carrie as nothing more than Niall's spoiled daughter.

She couldn't imagine her life without either of them in it. But that didn't mean they couldn't annoy the heck out of her without even trying.

"Gray is going to come over after his shift and redo the weather sealing on the door," Avery said, glancing around the nearly empty room. They were getting ready to schedule an estate sale, so most of the furniture had been moved to the garage.

"I'll get what he needs for that, as well." Meredith could never have imagined a scenario where she'd be standing in the center of this historic house, let alone being a partial owner of it. Growing up, she'd been keenly aware of her family's modest financial situation in comparison to Niall Reed and his elevated status in Magnolia.

She hadn't understood why at the time, but her father had never bought into the view of Niall as generous town benefactor. Carl's animosity toward the man had trickled over to Meredith and how she viewed Carrie, Niall's beloved daughter. To Meredith, the shy but poised girl a year older than her had seemed like a spoiled princess. Meredith's stomach tightened with embarrassment at the thought of how she'd picked on Carrie.

It had come as more than a shock when Niall's will revealed that Avery and Meredith were his illegitimate daughters. He'd also divided up the three major assets he'd owned—the big house, the downtown art gallery and adjacent buildings, and the farm where Meredith housed her rescue—between his three heirs.

Although Meredith had rented the property from Niall for two years prior to his death, he'd given no indication that he was her biological father. But the revelation helped explain why Carl Ventner, the man who she still considered her dad in all the ways that mattered, had been so angry after she'd approached the town's famous resident about leasing the farm.

Meredith assumed that her dad's disappointment in the arrangement she made with Niall Reed stemmed from his skepticism about her ability to make the rescue organization that was her dream into a viable business. She understood on a fundamental level that she could in no way measure up to either of her older brothers.

Erik sold insurance down in Wilmington and had his own family, a wife and two rambunctious boys. Theo had followed in their father's footsteps and joined the Marines, although he was no longer active duty.

By contrast, Meredith was the baby of the family and a college dropout. She'd done her best to keep up with her boisterous brothers, especially after their mom left the family to start a new life in Florida. But she'd always felt like she didn't quite belong. Once the truth of her connection to Niall had been revealed, she'd understood why.

"We should be able to get the house on the market by the beginning of May," Carrie said, bringing Meredith's wayward thoughts back to the present moment.

Avery nodded. "We need a quick sale to cover the taxes on the farm."

Meredith's stomach clenched at the mention of the farm's debt. She gathered the wet towels and straightened.

"If things go as well as I expect with the exhibition in New York," Carrie told them, "I should be able to pitch in with—"

"No." Meredith held up a hand. "You can't use the money you make from your art to fund the farm."

Carrie tucked a strand of dark hair behind her ear. "Not all of it but—"

"Not one cent," Meredith insisted. "That's your money from your talent. You have no obligation to support me."

"Come on, Mer." Avery shook her head. "We've gone through this before. Everyone knows how hard you work to make the rescue a success. And it is. You do amazing things to socialize and rehome those animals. Niall left us all in a bad way with his financial mismanagement. We need to work together to straighten out the mess."

"I don't think of it as an obligation," Carrie said gently. "Without you and Avery supporting me, I would have never started painting again. You practically bullied me into picking up a brush."

Meredith winced at Carrie's words, although she knew her sister meant them as a joke. She understood as an adult—in the way she hadn't as a child—that her animosity toward Carrie when they were younger had been a result of Meredith's insecurity and prejudice. Carrie had done nothing to deserve Meredith's spiteful ire, and although they were now close, Meredith still felt twinges of shame at her previous behavior.

"I mean that in a good way," Carrie added, obviously sensing Meredith's reaction.

"I'm a grown woman." Meredith dumped the towels into the laundry basket that sat near the doorway. "I should be able to support myself. Otherwise, I'm no better than Niall living off other people's goodwill."

Avery sniffed. "It's not the same thing, and we all know it. If Niall had managed his finances and his career the right way when he was alive, none of us would be in this situation. You do important work for those animals. No one is a better advocate. I never thought about adopting a dog, but then you practically forced me to foster Spot. I couldn't imagine my life without her."

Meredith cringed again as she shook her head. "I bullied Avery. I forced you. I'm not a nice person."

"You have a huge heart," Carrie countered.

"Nice is overrated," Avery added. "Especially in the South. We don't need any more women blessing our hearts all over town just to talk smack behind our backs. Your candor is refreshing."

"You're really taking this public-relations role to heart," Meredith said with a snort. Since moving to Magnolia, Avery had begun working with the town council to develop a marketing campaign that would support local businesses and help the community flourish without Niall as a draw.

For too many years, the town had relied on his fame to bring in visitors and keep Magnolia on the map. Unfortunately, when his popularity and fortune waned, nothing in town changed. By that point, Niall had greased so many palms to ensure the town would remain a bastion to his former glory that no one raised a voice in dispute. The man's ego had known no limits.

"We help each other," Carrie reminded her. "In whatever way we can."

"I talked to Douglas Damon the other day." Meredith crossed her arms over her chest as she thought about the conversation with their attorney. "He said that Realtor Avery met with last summer still has a developer out of Raleigh interested in buying the beach property."

"Is that what you want?" Avery asked gently. "To sell the farm in addition to the house?"

Meredith swallowed back the lump of emotion that balled in her throat. She couldn't imagine doing anything else but running her animal rescue, and the farm—as dilapidated as it was in many areas—felt like the home of her heart. But the stakes hadn't been so high when she'd been renting the property from Niall. He'd given her such a break on rent that it had barely mattered if she made money.

She'd been able to focus on the animals and nothing else.

The truth was she wanted more. She wanted to make her rescue a viable business, to grow it and expand and add more training classes and education and outreach. She had a deep yearning to make a difference in the lives of shelter animals, to give them the best chance she could at having lives where they were loved and appreciated.

But the responsibility of what she wanted was breathtaking in scope. And every failure or stalled path or unpaid bill reminded her that she was woefully unqualified to make her dream a reality.

It would be easier to sell the whole thing. She could take her bit of whatever profit they made and pay off her debts, focus on her job and school, volunteer for animal shelters the way normal people did. She could give herself a break and in the process, admit what she guessed everyone around her already knew.

Meredith Ventner was a failure.

"No," she whispered and then cleared her throat when the word came out as a croak. "I don't want to give up."

"You don't have to," Carrie told her. "We want to support you."

"I've applied for two more grants," Meredith answered. "I can do this on my own. I know I can."

She ignored the flash of hurt in Carrie's clear eyes. "That's great. I'm sure you have a strong chance at winning them."

"You're becoming quite the legend around the area," Avery added. "Gray said you're the go-to expert whenever they encounter a pet-emergency situation. Magnolia's official animal whisperer."

Meredith forced a smile. "They don't mind that I'm a bully."

"Stop." Carrie reached forward and wrapped Meredith in a tight hug. She normally didn't like being touched in that way but had gotten used to Carrie's easy physical affection. Took comfort in it, even. "You're the sweetest person I know."

Avery choked out a laugh. "That might be a stretch even for you, Care-bear."

"I bet Dr. Hotstuff thinks you're sweet." Carrie wiggled her delicate brows.

"Do not call him that," Meredith said, her cheeks instantly flaming once again. It was like an allergic reaction every time she thought about Ryan. "It's ridiculous."

"Dr. Dreamboat?" Carrie suggested with a wink.

"Dr. Hunky Housecall?" Avery added.

"I hate you both," Meredith said through clenched teeth. "Tell Gray I'll leave the supplies for the door in Niall's garage." She headed for the front door.

"We want to meet him," Avery called after her.

"He's not important," Meredith yelled over her shoulder, even though they all knew it was a lie.

She couldn't explain what made Ryan different. Normally she stayed far away from men who were strong, handsome-as-sin and successful. In truth, she stayed away from men in general.

That had been a hard lesson but one that a single incident in high school should have taught her. Men could not be trusted with her body or her heart.

It had taken a couple of years of self-destructive behavior before she finally pulled out of the emotional tailspin of that horrible night. Since then, her only real relationships with men had been casual work friendships, strictly platonic. She'd tried setting up an online profile, but the only men who'd responded were twice her age or not at all her type or both. It was easier to remain single, and until that stupid newspaper article, no one had questioned her on that choice.

But in the past month, the floodgates had opened, and she needed them closed again. She'd decided she liked being alone, which didn't in any way explain why she also liked Ryan's quiet presence at the barn.

They'd had a relaxing dinner together two nights ago, which had been a revelation unto itself. She was surprised how easy it was to talk to him about the animals and the town and what it had been like growing up in Magnolia— an edited version, but one that had reminded her of happier times. She might not have felt like she fit in, but her craggy Marine father and alpha-pup brothers had loved her. They'd done their best to take care of the lone female left in the family, and it had been Meredith's choice to try to turn herself into the ultimate tomboy so that she would better acclimate to all the testosterone floating around their small house.

Ryan told her he'd grown up in a suburb of DC with a younger sister. He hadn't given a lot of details about his family, but Meredith could tell they were close by the affection in his voice. She'd peppered him with questions about living in a big city, so different than her experience.

At first he'd seemed reluctant to discuss his life in the capital, and she could tell that the shooting that had left him injured had done damage to more than just his leg. She didn't ask about that trauma. Meredith recognized when a person didn't want to share. She'd practically written the book on suppressing feelings, so wasn't about to push someone to open up.

He'd left after helping her with the dishes, and she'd gone to bed that night with an unexplainable smile on her face.

But she hadn't seen him since, although she'd expected him to show up at the barn to help with the animals, at least. He'd seemed to enjoy working with them.

She wasn't about to admit to her sisters that with one simple dinner, she'd managed to chase him away.

Heck, she could barely admit it to herself, although she could see no other explanation. Not that he owed her one.

She pulled into a parking space in front of the hardware store downtown, noticing that it was one of the few open on that block of Main Street. Six months ago it felt like Magnolia was quickly becoming a ghost town, but things had changed since Niall's death.

It was as if the whole town had woken up from a fog. Avery had arrived in town with a chip on her shoulder the size of a boulder, but once she decided that the best way for the three of them to make something of the legacy Niall had left them was to turn around Magnolia's fortunes, they'd all rallied around a common goal.

And their energy seemed to be just what Magnolia had needed to shake off the past. If only it were that easy for Meredith.

She said hello to Lily Wainright, who managed the store now that her father had retired, and began to gather the supplies Gray would need for the door. Stifling a yawn, she hefted several sandbags into the cart and maneuvered it toward the front entrance.

"Hey, Pup."

Meredith stopped in her tracks at the sound of her father's deep voice. He'd nicknamed her that when she was just a girl, always trailing after her older brothers like an enthusiastic puppy. She hadn't heard the pet name on his lips since before her relationship to Niall Reed had been revealed.

"Dad." She bit down on the inside of her cheek as emotions roared through her. "You're back."

Carl Ventner massaged a hand over the back of his neck as he nodded. "I have some work to do on the house before the weather turns hot and humid. Besides, it's getting lonely up at the cabin, and your brother doesn't need me underfoot all the time."

I need you, Meredith wanted to tell him but didn't speak

those words. "If you want any help with house projects, let me know."

He gestured to the supplies piled in her cart. "Looks like you've got your own to-do list."

"This is for..." She trailed off. It had been almost two months since she'd seen her dad, and the last thing she wanted to do was remind him that he wasn't truly her father.

As if either of them could forget.

Although Carl had raised Meredith as his own, he'd known about his wife's affair with Niall Reed almost from the start. It was Anna's dissatisfaction with being a wife and mother that had led her first to be unfaithful and then to desert her family for a new life several states away. Meredith and her brothers hadn't known anything other than her mother left them behind without a backward glance.

They were all fiercely loyal to Carl and to each other, and it had rocked the foundation of their family when the truth came out. At first, Carl had been angry on his daughter's behalf. He thought Meredith should react the same way. And while she was spitting mad at the deceit that had unknowingly colored her whole life, she'd also been curious about her history and her sisters.

Something had snapped in her dad when she'd told him she wanted a relationship with Avery and Carrie. In his mind, her decision was a betrayal, and it had caused a deep rift in their relationship.

He'd spent the past half a year traveling between Erik's home in Wilmington to the hunting cabin he owned outside of Asheville, with very little time in Magnolia. He looked the same as ever, although maybe he'd lost a few pounds over the winter. Probably eating nothing but canned chili and frozen dinners up at the cabin.

He stood just shy of six feet with a stocky build and the same short military-issue haircut he'd sported for her entire life. He wore an old flannel shirt tucked into faded jeans and looked like he hadn't shaved in a few days, which was unlike him.

Meredith missed him terribly, but she didn't quite know how to react. Was he back in Magnolia to stay? Had he forgiven her? If she mentioned anything about Niall or her new sisters, would that send him into an emotional tailspin once more?

"Gray Atwell is helping me with a project," she told him, which might not be the whole truth but also wasn't an outright lie. Lies had already done too much damage in her life.

"He's a good kid," her father said with a nod. "I heard he's getting married in a few weeks."

Meredith nodded, then forced a smile. "To my sister, Avery."

Carl's jaw tightened. "You look tired, Pup. You been burning the candle at both ends again?"

"I can barely keep the candle lit at one," she answered with a small laugh. She pushed her cart out of the way when a man carrying a ladder struggled to move around her. "I'm a roadblock here, so I should go. I'm glad you're back, Dad."

The word settled like a stone between them, and Meredith cursed the tears that stung the back of her eyes. Carl Ventner would always be her father, but she had no idea if he felt that way any longer.

"I'll stop by if that's okay? Check on you."

"Sure."

"Maybe we could grab a bite to eat. I haven't been out in town for a while."

"Okay," she agreed, wondering if this was how things

were going to be. They'd both ignore the past and pretend like the last few months hadn't torn them apart. Meredith knew it wouldn't work, not with how close she'd grown to Avery and Carrie. But she wasn't going to mention that in the middle of the hardware store.

"We'll talk soon," her father promised, then headed down one of the aisles.

Although Meredith could feel the weight of Lily's gaze on her as she paid for her items, she kept her eyes focused straight ahead as she wheeled her cart into the afternoon sunshine.

Moving forward was the only way she knew how to handle her life when it felt like the past was constantly nipping at her heels.

CHAPTER FIVE

RYAN STRAIGHTENED FROM the kitchen table later that afternoon at the sound of a car coming down the driveway. He rubbed two fingers into his chest when his heart began to thump against his rib cage.

Anticipation was a dangerous emotion, hope even more so. But he couldn't quite extinguish the unexpected hope that his neighbor had stopped by to check on him.

Meredith didn't owe him a visit or anything else. He hadn't even been back to the animal rescue since the evening they'd had dinner together.

He couldn't explain his reason other than he'd enjoyed himself too damn much. His stay in Magnolia wasn't for pleasure or to ease his survivor guilt. He didn't deserve that. After all, he was still alive, and it seemed only fitting that every day remind him of the fact that he'd been spared when others—people who had way more to live for—hadn't been so lucky.

He had to stay away from anything that felt like happiness. Ryan wasn't ready to allow himself any happiness. He couldn't imagine a time when he might be.

He didn't want to examine the disappointment that crashed through him at the sight of an unfamiliar vehicle—not Meredith's truck—pulling to a stop in front of the cottage as he opened the front door. A few scoops of kibble and one steak dinner and he was somehow smitten with his too-cute neighbor? Ridiculous.

A man got out of the fancy SUV and waved as he headed toward the house. He looked to be a few years older than Ryan, flecks of silver running through his dark hair.

"Hey there. You must be Ryan."

"Yes." Ryan continued to stand in the doorway but didn't open the screen to invite the stranger in.

"I'm Paul Thorpe," the man told him with a smile. "Chief of staff at Magnolia Community Hospital."

Ryan's gut clenched, but he made sure his features didn't give away his reaction. "You're young to make chief."

Paul shrugged. "I've worked at the hospital for my whole career, and until recently, we weren't a big draw for younger health-care workers. Things are changing around here, and your reputation precedes you, Dr. Sorensen."

"Ryan. I'm on vacation at the moment, and no one calls me Doctor around here." Which wasn't exactly true. Both Meredith and her would-be suitor had called him Doc, and it hadn't bothered him. But the way Paul Thorpe said his name was loaded with implications Ryan preferred to ignore.

"Vacation," the other man repeated. "Interesting. Okay, then. Would you mind if I came in for a few minutes?"

Ryan shook his head. "Not a good time."

Paul's warm hazel eyes narrowed. "David Parthen speaks highly of you, and I've read the articles about your heroism during the active-shooter event."

Event. What an inconsequential word for five minutes that had destroyed so many lives. "I wasn't the hero," he said, then stepped out onto the porch, careful not to reveal his limp. He was suddenly burning up, and he needed to feel the cool breeze. "Somehow I don't think this is a social call."

"We're starting a mobile health clinic to service the area," Paul told him without preamble. "There are a lot of longtime residents in rural communities who don't like coming to a medical center for treatment. We want to be able to offer preventative care to those folks as well as urgent-care services."

"Good for you." Ryan pressed two fingers to his forehead. Damn it, he once again sounded like a royal jackass. "It's an important resource, but I'm not sure what it has to do with me."

"My girlfriend spearheaded the initiative, and we've raised enough money to outfit a van with the necessary equipment and started distributing flyers to local churches and stores. Until we secure funding, the doctors and nurses who staff the clinic will have to work on a volunteer basis. David suggested that you might have some time on your hands during your..." Paul glanced at Ryan's left leg "... vacation."

Ryan reached out a hand to grasp the wood railing. He hoped the action seemed casual and not like he needed to ground himself from the flurry of emotions that swirled through him at the thought of practicing medicine in any capacity. "Not sure my schedule will allow time for that." His voice remained steady, even though he guessed Paul Thorpe recognized the lie for what it was.

"Think about it," the other man said without missing a beat. "I also was hoping to talk to you about potential sources of funding for the project."

Ryan's gaze sharpened. Either David had blabbed way

more than was appropriate, or this local doctor had done his homework.

"I'm not connected to the foundation," he said simply.

"You're on the board of directors," Paul reminded him as if Ryan could forget.

"In name only," Ryan clarified. It was odd to be discussing the charitable organization started by Duffy Howard, his grandfather—who made his money in the early days of the technology boom—standing on this dilapidated porch in a Podunk town. Very few people in DC knew about his connection to the Howard Family Foundation, which was exactly how Ryan wanted it. His father was a carpenter by trade, living a quiet life before meeting and quickly marrying Gillian Howard, the only daughter of one of the richest men in the country. Peter Sorensen refused to take anything from his in-laws and insisted that both Ryan and his sister, Emma, make their own way in the world without relying on family connections.

The difference between his maternal grandparents' wealth and the modest way his father dictated their family live had been a source of friction in the house all through Ryan's childhood. He could remember a huge, enclosed trampoline being delivered for his tenth birthday and his dad forcing him to donate it to a local community center. His mom had tried to support her husband's wishes, but Ryan knew that the tension with her parents and extended family took its toll.

He also understood that the kind of wealth his mom's family had made him different from most other people and that despite having worked hard to make his own way, it was easier for others to assume he'd grown up with a silver spoon feeding him every advantage in life.

"We've put together a strong, necessary program in the mobile van." Paul looked out over the rolling grass that surrounded the cottage. "We already qualify for the health-care grant the Howard Family Foundation offers each year, but it always helps to have someone on the inside put in a good word."

"I'm not an insider," Ryan answered automatically.

Paul sighed and pulled a business card out of his back pocket. "Just consider helping out in whatever way you feel comfortable." He handed the crisp white card to Ryan. "My cell number is on the back along with the hospital's website. There's a schedule of where the mobile medical center will be over the next few weeks. Right now, we only have the staff to take it out once a week. We need more volunteers." He took a step closer. "We could use you, Dr. Sorensen."

"I'll think about it," Ryan said grudgingly. He didn't want to think about medicine or people in need or his family or all the ways he'd failed when a friend had needed him most.

He wanted to escape, but that didn't seem possible.

Paul Thorpe clapped him on the shoulder as he headed for his SUV again. "This is a great community," he called. "Getting involved could take your mind off things."

Ryan pocketed the business card and turned for the house without answering. What did that man know about his mind? If the good doctor had any idea of the internal torment that played over and over in Ryan's mind like a needle stuck on scratched vinyl, he'd grab that card back and rip it into a dozen scraps of paper.

Ryan had gone into emergency medicine because he wanted the challenge and variety of working on the front line.

He liked the adrenaline and the pace and the way he could take care of people without having to really know them.

He knew what that said about his lack of depth, his lack of heart, some people would say. Up until now, he could manage around that. He was a skilled physician. As long as he kept things moving and coordinated all the aspects of his emergency department, none of the rest of it mattered.

It would in a town like Magnolia. He'd grown up in a small town. He knew the drill and had no desire to get involved with anyone here.

Not entirely true. He had far too much desire when it came to Meredith Ventner, which was why after one dinner, he'd thought it best to keep his distance.

It was the smart decision for both of them.

But as he closed the front door to the house and listened to Paul drive away, the walls seemed to be closing in on him. He'd had his first panic attack a few days after the shooting, so he knew what was happening.

The hospital counselor they'd forced him to talk to had given him physical and mental exercises to deal with the anxiety. Breathing, meditation and visualization were the counselor's preferred methods of mitigating panic.

Ryan tended to think whiskey worked as a more effective cure, but acid burned in his stomach at the thought of another night drinking himself into oblivion and the throbbing headache that would greet him the following morning.

He closed his eyes and focused on the breath moving in and out of his lungs. Even after several minutes, anxiety continued to pummel him. Grabbing his keys from the counter, he headed out the front door again, the screen banging behind him.

He got in his car without a clear destination in mind.

Maybe he'd drive down the coast. Maybe he'd find a local bar and drink himself silly in a new place.

But minutes later he parked in front of Meredith's barn. Dust swirled around the tires as he climbed out of the car. He'd left home without his cane again, and his leg protested the speed of his movements.

He welcomed the pain. Lately it was the only thing that let him know he could still feel anything.

Meredith appeared in the barn's open doorway a moment later.

"Hey." He raised a hand in greeting. "I was wondering if you could use some help."

An emotion he couldn't name flashed in her gaze, and disappointment cascaded through him as she gave a barely perceptible shake of her head.

"We can always use more help," a voice said from behind him. He glanced over to see a teenage girl with long blond hair and wire-rimmed glasses. "Meredith is finishing up her weekly obedience class, so I can get you started." The girl looked toward Meredith. "That's okay, right?"

"Have him exercise the dogs," she called. "We have about ten more minutes of class." She disappeared again without meeting his gaze.

Ryan hadn't noticed when he pulled in but now realized that his car wasn't the only one in the parking lot. Four other vehicles were parked in a row along the barn's exterior.

"She does dog training, too?" he asked as the girl approached.

The teenager nodded. "Right now, it's only for people who adopt from us. But she could definitely get more clients if she wanted them. Heck, Mer could star in her own reality show. She's that good."

Ryan smiled at the adoration clear in the girl's tone. He certainly understood why she'd be in awe of Meredith.

"I'm Shae." The girl stuck out her hand. "You must be the neighbor who stopped by to help."

"Ryan." He lifted a brow. "How was the physics test?"

"Impossible," she answered with a grimace. "But I still got an A."

"That's impressive."

She led him toward the far side of the barn. "I want to study some kind of science or engineering in college. Or maybe veterinary medicine. I could come back here and work with Meredith once she expands."

"What kind of expansion does she have planned?"

"Big-time stuff. More training classes and education. She plans to renovate the barn and start a therapy-dog program. It's going to be awesome if it works."

The image of Meredith asleep at her desk with textbooks piled in front of her appeared in his mind. "She's going to need a lot more help to make all of that a reality."

"Mostly she needs money," Shae told him. "Niall left everything in a pretty bad way. I didn't know the guy, but my mom says he was a big deal back in the day. It's cool to inherit a place like this, but not if the cost of it runs her into the ground."

Curiosity thrummed along Ryan's nerve endings. In the time they'd spent together, Meredith had revealed a few things about herself but nothing as personal as her history with this property.

"You can toss them the ball." Shae handed him a plastic lacrosse stick with a tennis ball cradled in the pocket. She greeted the half-dozen dogs dancing around them as they entered the gated pasture. "Sometimes they lose the balls, so there are extras in the bin inside the barn if you need more."

"Who was Niall?" he asked as he chucked the ball as far as he could. The dogs gave chase without a moment's hesitation.

"Niall Reed."

"The artist?" Ryan wasn't overly familiar with the painter, although he'd heard of him. Schmaltzy landscapes that made better greeting-card illustrations than real art as far as what Ryan had seen.

"He was Meredith's dad. I mean, she has her other dad still but found out about being Niall's daughter after he died last year. Along with her two sisters. It's kind of complicated."

"I guess," Ryan agreed. "And she inherited this place from Niall?"

Shae looked uncomfortable, as if she realized she might have already shared more than her boss would want her to. "I don't really know the details. You can ask Meredith. I need to go check on the cats before I head home for the night. Nice to meet you, Ryan."

"You too, Shae." The small herd of dogs came barreling back toward him, an Australian shepherd in the lead. The dog dropped the tennis ball at his feet, so Ryan scooped it up and sent it flying again.

He tried to figure out how to learn more about Meredith's background without appearing overly interested. For the life of him, he had no idea why he was interested in the first place.

What he did know was that fifteen minutes hanging out at the rescue and all his anxiety about the conversation with Paul Thorpe had disappeared. It was virtually impossible to stay in a bad mood while surrounded by dogs that were so clearly thrilled by any attention he gave them. He hadn't owned a pet since he'd moved out of his parents' house for college. His current life didn't seem conducive to taking on a pet, but he wondered if that was an excuse he used for his unwillingness to commit to anything other than his job.

He glanced toward the main entrance to the barn when he heard the first car pull away. There was a better than average chance that Meredith would have sent him away if Shae hadn't intervened.

But he didn't want to be sent away. He might not understand why being at the rescue calmed him, but there was no use denying it. And he was going to need a way to stay busy so he wouldn't feel guilty about ignoring Paul's request for help with the mobile medical unit. If that kind of busy included scooping poop and chucking balls all day, then so be it.

MEREDITH FELT RYAN'S approach behind her as she stood with Trinity Marshall and Biscuit, the goldendoodle Trinity and her daughter had adopted a month earlier.

Or maybe she realized he was heading her way due to Trinity's reaction. The woman's pale blue eyes widened, and she automatically fluffed her already expertly styled hair.

"No wonder you're so dedicated," Trinity said with a soft laugh, "if that's the kind of volunteers you attract."

"My dedication has nothing to do with him." Meredith kept her features neutral as she turned toward Ryan.

"They lost the ball," he said, holding up the empty lacrosse stick. "Shae told me there are more in the barn."

"My sweet Biscuit loves to play fetch," Trinity said, stepping forward and introducing herself to Ryan.

After an awkward moment of silence, they all glanced down at the dog, who was sprawled on his back in the dirt, private bits on full display. Biscuit loved eating leather shoes and surfing any available trash can. Chasing balls wasn't high on his list of favorite pastimes.

"He's a handsome boy. Seems like a real live wire," Ryan said, and Meredith struggled to keep a straight face.

Trinity beamed. "I adopted him after my no-good husband left me for his massage therapist. Biscuit is way better company than Troy ever was, and Meredith's helping me train him to be a perfect gentleman."

"Well, Biscuit's lucky you found him." He crouched down to scratch the dog's belly, and when he winced, Meredith noticed he wasn't using his cane today. Biscuit stretched, then flipped over and nudged Ryan's hand.

"I'm the lucky one," Trinity said. "Let me know…" she eased closer to Ryan "…if you're ever interested in getting together for a game of fetch."

A laugh burst from Meredith, and she quickly coughed and clasped a hand over her mouth to disguise it. Trinity overlooked it, her attention laser focused on Ryan.

He definitely noticed, quickly straightening and taking a step away. "I'll keep that in mind, but I'm going to go find another tennis ball."

"If not fetch," Trinity said to Meredith as he moved away, "maybe he'd be interested in a round or two of hide the sausage."

This time Meredith didn't bother to conceal her laugh. Based on the way Ryan's shoulders stiffened, he'd heard Trinity's not-so-subtle whisper.

"Keep working on Sit and Stay this week with Biscuit," she told her lustful client. "He's got to learn basic obedience." She put a hand on Trinity's sleeve. "And no more sexual innuendos with my volunteers, especially when I know you don't mean it."

Trinity pouted. "If Troy can poke his business in indiscriminate honeypots, why can't I do the same?"

"Because you want more for your honeypot," Meredith said, shaking her head. "You deserve better."

"But you said he's a doctor." Trinity gestured to the barn. "What's wrong with being interested in a doctor?"

"Nothing," Meredith said quietly, "if you're getting to know a person for the right reasons."

"I should pay you extra for the pep talks." Trinity gave her a watery smile. "Come on, Biscuit. There's a new season of *90 Day Fiancé* starting later. We don't want to miss it."

Meredith watched Trinity load the dog into her car, then turned toward the barn. There was absolutely nothing wrong with being interested in a doctor, she told herself, but she wished she wasn't the one so affected by Ryan. She needed to think rationally and ignore her impulses. She'd given up men for a reason and, despite the newspaper article that claimed otherwise, Meredith wasn't pining for love. Definitely not with a guy who was only in her life for a few weeks. Too bad logic and reason seemed to be in short supply at the moment!

CHAPTER SIX

"I'M SURPRISED TO see you here." Meredith carried a bucket of feed toward the far end of the barn, hoping her tone sounded casual and not at all like she'd been hurt when he hadn't returned after their dinner. "Let me guess. You missed the goats."

Ryan stood in the center of the goat stall. The two larger animals headed toward the door as she approached, but Rachel stuck close to Ryan like she was afraid he might disappear at any moment.

Meredith knew the feeling.

"Among other things," he said, his voice a low rumble that made her stomach flip and tumble.

She gave herself a mental headshake. No way was she going to allow him off so easily.

"I guess you've been busy the past couple of days?" She lifted a brow. "Or maybe grilling steaks took a lot out of you, huh?"

He cringed. "I should have called or stopped by before now."

"It's fine." She reached over and dumped the pellets into the feeding trough. "You don't owe me anything. Go ahead and put some more hay into their pen. I've got to check on one of the dogs." She started to turn away, embarrassed at the blush that rose to her cheeks when his gaze remained steady on her.

"Meredith."

She forced herself to look at him, her breath catching at the warmth in his gaze.

"I had a really good time with you the other night." He sighed. "Too good. I didn't come to Magnolia to make friends. My purpose here is to get my mind right while my leg heals. No distractions."

"I'm a distraction?"

His mouth pulled up at one corner. "You have no idea."

She mulled over those words. Other than potential adopters who came to the rescue or those she dealt with at adoption fairs or outreach events, Meredith didn't spend much time with people she didn't know well.

Outside of her work colleagues, her sisters and their significant others, she didn't have friends. Between the disappointment of the responses to her online profile and the lack of interesting guys in Magnolia, she almost never dated and wasn't in the market for a man, despite what the Valentine's article would have people believe.

Although she sometimes talked a big game with Avery and Carrie about wanting a man, mostly she kept her distance from the opposite sex. So for a man like Ryan Sorensen to consider her a distraction…well, it was difficult to fathom.

"Why are friends off-limits for you while you're here?" She crossed her arms over her chest as she waited for him to answer.

He took a step toward the stall's entrance. "Do you want to be friends?"

No. The word balanced on the tip of her tongue. She

shouldn't want to be anything with him. Tall, dark, handsome and just passing through. For Ryan, Magnolia was a short-term stop until he could return to his big-city life. Maybe that's what made her bold when it came to the attraction that simmered between them.

It was harmless, or at least she could convince herself of that.

"It's kind of useful to have a friend who can grill a perfect steak. Do you have any other skills worth noting?"

His eyes widened a fraction, and she marveled at her own daring. Meredith Ventner didn't flirt with men, but this banter with Ryan was like a release. Pressure had built inside her for so long she felt like a dam close to bursting.

Why not let off a little steam? Something told her Ryan was just as broken as she was, if in a different way.

"A few," he said, and his tone was sexy as heck until he yelped and grabbed at the back of his pants. "She bit me," he said, pointing to Rachel.

"Probably just a love nip." Meredith tried and failed to suppress a laugh. "She got jealous."

"That's crazy talk. Goats don't get jealous." He turned fully to the animal. "If we're going to be friends, there are boundaries, Miss Thing. No teeth."

The goat gave a plaintive bleat, making Meredith laugh even harder. "You like boundaries." She tapped one finger on her chin. "Good to know."

He let himself out of the pen, and the goat headbutted the door. "With farm animals," he clarified.

"Meredith, do you need help with feeding tonight?"

They both turned as Shae approached.

"What's so funny?" the girl asked. "Your smile is creeping me out."

Meredith sniffed. "I have a creepy smile?"

"I mean…no…" The teenager shook her head. "You just don't do it very often."

"I smile plenty," Meredith protested, hating that Ryan had to hear this conversation. Hating even more that Shae was probably right. "All the time, in fact."

"Okay," the girl answered, holding up her hands. "Don't bite my head off about it."

"Speaking of bites, Rachel bit me," Ryan offered.

"Aww." That revelation earned a cheeky grin from the girl. "She likes you."

"She likes him a lot," Meredith confirmed.

"I wouldn't advertise love bites to potential adopters," Ryan cautioned, rubbing the back of his leg.

"Good point." Meredith checked her watch and sighed. She still had so much work to do in the barn, as well as a paper to finish for her accounting class. It was going to be a late night, but that was her problem, not Shae's. "I can handle things from here. Thanks for your help today."

The girl nodded, then winced. "I think I forgot to tell you that the honor choir is performing in Asheville this weekend, so I won't be around. Sorry for the late notice."

Meredith had an adoption event and two obedience classes scheduled, as well as plans with her sisters to continue cleaning out Niall's house. She'd been counting on Shae as backup. "No problem," she lied. "I'll see if Tom wants to pick up some hours."

"I think his band has a gig in Charleston, so he'll be gone, too." Shae looked stricken. "I'm really sorry. Maybe—"

"It's fine." Meredith forced a smile. See, she smiled all the time. "I'll figure something out."

With a nod, Shae turned and headed back down the barn's center aisle.

"I can help you this weekend," Ryan offered when they were alone again. "My schedule is open."

She studied him, trying to ignore the way her spine tingled at the thought of spending the weekend together.

"What's the deal, Doc?" she demanded. "I had that same offer from you earlier this week, and then you ghosted me." She cleared her throat. "I don't matter, but the animals do, and I can't let someone into our lives who's going to flake on them."

"I won't flake," he promised.

She lifted a brow. "Was it your injury? Did you need to rest after—"

"My leg is fine."

"You aren't using the cane today."

"I don't need…" He shook his head. "I forgot it."

"You'll hurt tonight."

"I'll be fine."

"I'm sure you will."

"I'm sorry I went MIA for the past couple of days." He ran a hand through his overly long hair. "I had some things I needed to take care of at the cottage."

"Did those things involve a fifth of Jack Daniel's?" she asked, then turned and started down the aisle.

"What's that supposed to mean?" He caught up with her in a few strides, and she couldn't help but notice that his limp was more pronounced than it had been when he'd arrived earlier.

"Magnolia is a small town. There are no secrets." She laughed at the ridiculousness of that comment given her own life. "Or at least, there are very few well-kept ones.

Dennis from the liquor store stopped by here a few days ago. He was on his way back to town from your place. Said that the guy staying at the Parthens' cottage had paid an extra fifty to have a few bottles delivered. He wanted to warn me you might be having a party in case I heard the noise."

She felt the tension coming off him in waves, but he didn't answer.

"Party of one?" she asked casually.

"I don't see how that's any of your business," Ryan muttered. "Or the delivery guy's business for that matter."

"It's not," she agreed. "But as shorthanded as I am at the moment, I won't have someone around the animals who's been drinking."

"I haven't—"

She held up a hand. "And I don't have time to worry if you're going to show up or whether you're too hungover to get out of bed on any given morning. If you want to spend your time in Magnolia drinking yourself into oblivion, that's your business as long as you don't get behind the wheel. But it isn't going to affect me."

He followed her out of the barn. Meredith hadn't looked at him during her tirade. In truth, nothing Ryan did in Magnolia was her business. She shouldn't care, but somehow she did, anyway. After Dennis stopped by with his tidbit of information, she'd been distracted and ornery, hating the thought of Ryan drowning the demons that obviously plagued him in brown liquor.

Hating that she cared.

Meredith had long ago forced herself to stop trying to rescue men hell-bent on destruction. The surliest, most ill-behaved animal she could think of was still better than wasting her time on a man with issues.

Especially issues that involved copious amounts of alcohol.

She looked up, where fluffy clouds filled the early-evening sky. The first spikes of pink were just beginning to color their edges, and she hoped that the forecast had been correct about cloudy conditions but no rain.

The barn roof wouldn't withstand another deluge, and the materials weren't set to be delivered until early next week. It needed to stay dry until then.

Ryan shifted next to her, and she glanced at him, not sure what she expected to see. Would he be glaring at her for shoving her nose into his business like some sort of overeager dog with no personal boundaries?

She should have just sent him on his way. Her plate was full without the addition of a man who had his own heaping pile of emotional issues.

Instead of anger in his honey-tinged gaze, he was looking at her with a mix of astonishment and admiration.

"You're right," he said, his voice barely above a whisper. "I'm a mess."

Oh, no. Anger she could deal with. Honesty punctuated with a healthy dose of vulnerability… That was more than Meredith expected.

"You can't be a mess on my time," she told him, keeping her tone stern. What she really wanted to do was draw him into her arms. She knew the weight of trying to anesthetize herself until the pain subsided and where that left her in the cold light of morning. Her heart ached for whatever this man was fighting so hard to ignore.

But giving up or giving him a pass on his negative habits

wouldn't do either of them any good. She'd been hurt when he didn't show up after their dinner together. She'd taken his absence personally, a silent critique of her company. It was only after the visit from Dennis that she realized Ryan might be even better than her at disguising his issues.

"I have pills, too," he said into the silence that stretched between them. "For the pain and to help me sleep. Sleep has been a wily bastard."

She couldn't hide her reaction to that news so didn't bother to try.

"Are you mixing the pills with alcohol?"

He gave a sharp shake of his head. "I'm telling myself that a few drinks are a better option than popping pills. Hell, I'm worse-off than I even imagined. I can't believe you called me out on it."

She shrugged. "Like I said, your business is your own, but not if you're going to be taking care of my animals."

"So if I walked away right now…" he turned to her more fully "…it wouldn't bother you?"

Not one bit. That's what she should answer. She should, in fact, encourage him to walk away, because she knew that having him in her life would only complicate things more.

"I want you to stay," she answered instead, then quickly added, "I need another set of hands around here, and the animals like you."

One side of his mouth curved. "The animals?"

"Don't make me put you back in the stall with Rachel."

"Point taken."

"But it's not worth it if you can't stay sober."

His chin snapped up like she'd smacked him, then he nodded. "Yeah, I get that. I'll keep it together."

She studied him more closely. "Just like that?"

"As long as you promise to keep me busy."

Oh, the ways she'd like to keep him busy.

"It's a deal." She held out her hand to shake on it but realized her mistake as soon as his fingers wrapped around hers. The part of her that had been lonely for so long wanted to pull him closer, another lost soul in need of solace.

He let out what sounded like a relieved breath and pulled his hand from her grasp. "Where do you want me?"

"Good lord." She let out a shaky laugh. "Do you have to make everything sound like a proposition?"

He reached out and tapped one finger against her forehead. "You have a dirty mind. I like it."

She rolled her eyes. "We'll start in the office, and I'll show you the care schedule. Do you have plans for dinner?"

"Does frozen pizza count?"

"It's fish taco night at my favorite Mexican place in town. The Bean Bandito is totally worth the crowd. Let me grab some paperwork, and then we'll head to town, and we can go over what will need to be done so you won't have to rely on me during your time here."

"We've got a deal," Ryan said.

Meredith couldn't help wondering where all of this might lead.

"Maybe it's in comparison to the frozen dinners I've been eating, but these are the best tacos I've ever had." He grabbed a chip from the basket in the middle of the table. "And I go to Mexico every year."

"Every year?" Meredith seemed genuinely surprised.

"I usually take a week or two to volunteer at a health clinic and then spend a few days deep-sea fishing off the coast."

"Do you like to travel?" She took a long pull on her beer, pursing her lips from the tang of the lime that she'd squeezed into the bottle. Ryan could watch her mouth all night long.

"Sure, although my job doesn't allow much time off."

"I can relate to that," she admitted. "I haven't been on vacation since I was a kid."

"Seriously?"

"At least not anywhere exotic. It's not a big deal. My dad has a cabin in the mountains, so I sometimes spend time up there. But it's hard to find someone I trust to manage the rescue."

"You need to hire a full-time employee," he told her.

She gave him a wry grin. "In my dreams. Actually, I just submitted a grant application that would fund a full-time staff person." Her green eyes widened as she looked from him to the half-empty bottle of beer on the table. "What's in that stuff? I can't believe I told you that. Forget I mentioned it."

He was fascinated by the emotions that played across her delicate features—hope, embarrassment, frustration—and the way her cheeks bloomed with color. "Why should I forget? You need real employees—probably more than one."

"Plenty of rescue organizations function with just volunteers." She shrugged. "Furever Friends isn't even that big. I should be able to handle it on my own. I don't need to get ahead of myself. If I was smarter or more organized—"

Without thinking, he reached out and grabbed her hand as she nervously picked at the beer bottle's label. "In addition to the part where I don't drink myself into oblivion as part of my work agreement, I'd like to add a clause that you don't devalue yourself or your accomplishments."

She yanked her hand away from his. "You don't know me well enough to make that request."

"You called me out on my drinking, and I didn't complain."

"Because I'm right," she said with a sniff.

"So am I." He inclined his head. "I don't know you well—"

"You don't know me at all," she countered, sounding grumpy. He liked her grumpy. He liked her far too much.

"Be that as it may, it's obvious that you don't think you deserve success. Even I can see that. Everyone sees it."

She glanced around, as if everyone in the crowded restaurant were staring at them. "People see what they want to, and when you've spent your whole life in the same town... well, they see the Meredith they've always known. I'm the crazy dog lady, not a successful business owner or an activist."

"I don't think that's the only reason," he insisted, shocked when the color drained from her face. "What did I say?"

"Do you know about my father?" She leaned forward across the table. "Who told you? Never mind. It doesn't matter. Niall Reed doesn't define me. Carrie is the artist. I'm not going to milk some convoluted connection to him into support for the rescue."

"Hold on." Ryan held up his hands, mind racing. "I wasn't suggesting anything of the sort."

Suddenly she placed her elbows on the table and leaned forward, resting her head in her hands. "No wonder you ghosted me. I've had a half a beer and I'm a bigger mess than you probably are after a half a bottle of Jack."

He wished he could deny that he'd made it that far into a bottle on his own. "You aren't a mess."

"A hot mess," she said on a shaky breath.

"Hot, yes," he agreed.

That got her attention. He could tell by the way her full mouth pressed into a thin line.

"You should meet my sisters." She sighed, and he could feel the heaviness of it across the table. "They're amazing. They both have their lives together, and they're gorgeous and talented, and awesome men love them. They are nothing like me."

"You seem to be doing just fine," he assured her. "Stick with me, kid. I'm a dumpster fire of a mess. I've got emotional problems for days, my leg is constantly aching, and I blame myself for a friend's death."

She lifted her head to study him. "You're a successful doctor. I'm a college dropout."

"I'm a doctor who can't walk into a hospital without feeling like I'm going to hyperventilate. The medical degree does me little good if I can't manage my mind."

"You'll get there."

"Why are you so generous with other people and hard on yourself?"

"Habit," she answered without hesitation. "Although, I doubt many people around here would describe me as *generous*. That's almost funny."

"Meredith."

They both looked over as a woman approached the table. She had dark hair pulled back into a tight bun and picked at the front of the UNC sweatshirt she wore.

"Hey, Kat." Meredith smiled although it didn't reach her eyes. Her shoulders straightened. Ryan could almost see her rebuilding her armor. It disappointed him in a way he couldn't understand. It was clear that Meredith struggled with being vulnerable, and he liked that he got to see some of her walls come down.

"I figured you'd be here for taco night," the woman said, then flicked a glance at Ryan. "So the article was true? You really are looking for love?"

Ryan had to force himself not to laugh in disbelief at the woman's boldness.

Meredith seemed to take it in stride, as if she expected nothing more or less. "This is Ryan Sorensen," she explained evenly. "He's staying at the Parthens' cottage and is going to be helping me around the rescue while he's in town."

"Welcome to Magnolia," the woman told him before her attention focused back on Meredith without waiting for his response. "That's what I want to talk to you about. I think there's a dog in a bad way out by our property."

He felt rather than saw another change come over Meredith. Gone were both the vulnerability and the resigned small-town resident. Everything about her sharpened, her focus resolute. "Tell me everything you know, Kat."

CHAPTER SEVEN

"YOU DON'T HAVE to go with me," Meredith repeated even as her truck sped farther from the beach and closer to the address she'd plugged into her GPS. "This doesn't involve you."

"I work for the rescue," Ryan said. "I'm your wingman."

"You don't work there," she countered, even though she found the thought of this man as her backup strangely appealing. "I agreed that you could volunteer. An actual dog rescue is well beyond what I'd expect of anyone."

"Don't tell me you go on these kinds of missions alone?" He let out a harsh laugh. "Do you know the kind of trouble you could get into if you ran across the wrong type of person?"

"I know," she said quietly. Her stomach pitched and tumbled. It wasn't only a dark night that brought trouble. Trouble could also find a person at a party with a boy she'd known for most of her life. She wanted to say more, to reassure him that she no longer took chances—either with her physical or emotional well-being. But too many feelings coursed through her, and she couldn't trust her voice not to reveal her personal history.

"You didn't sound surprised when that woman told you about the dog," Ryan said a moment later.

She felt his gaze on her but kept her eyes glued to the

road. After Kat had approached with her plea for Meredith to investigate the Brons' property, they'd quickly paid the bill and returned to the rescue so Meredith could pick up her truck and several crates, not knowing exactly what she'd need. Kat had mentioned one pregnant-looking animal, but there might be others.

She'd expected Ryan to head home, but he'd helped her load the wire crates into the truck bed, then climbed in next to her. Every few minutes, he massaged a hand over his left thigh, and she couldn't tell whether the movement was to ease a physical ache or simply habit.

"Backyard breeders are far too common around here, especially out in the country where people have more land. It's what made me start the rescue." She flicked a glance in Ryan's direction and found him watching her with an intensity that made her toes curl in the thick hikers she'd changed into at the house.

"Tell me your origin story," he said with a half smile.

She laughed softly. "It wasn't long after I got hired at the vet clinic. A woman brought in a puppy for a checkup, and the wee baby was in bad shape. He was barely six weeks old, too early to be separated from his mama and showed signs of dehydration and infection." Meredith's heart still tightened at the pitiful shape of that first pup. "He didn't survive the night, and the owner was mad that she'd paid good money for a sick dog. She told the vet about how she'd bought the puppy after seeing a sign for discounted purebred German shepherd pups on one of the back roads outside of town."

"I'm guessing those puppies weren't purebred?"

"That's how they were advertised, but the vet didn't think so. Some people get into the bloodlines of dogs because of a dedication to breed standards or specific personality traits."

"If you ask me," he said, looking out the window into the blackness surrounding them, "breed standards shouldn't be how dogs are judged."

"There are different schools of thought, but responsible breeders take care of their animals. People may have legitimate reasons to seek out a reputable breeder, but that isn't what we were dealing with in the case of the puppies. The vet called local law enforcement, and I volunteered to drive out to the house with them."

She shook her head at the memory. "There were over three dozen dogs in squalid conditions. I'd heard of puppy mills and backyard breeders, but I'd never seen anything like those mistreated animals. It made me sick to my stomach. We seized the dogs, but the local shelter didn't have room for all of them. I ended up with five at my house. I managed to nurse them back to health and find new homes for them. I knew I could do more, so I started Furever Friends shortly after."

"You created a solution," he murmured. "That's impressive."

"Not really," she protested automatically. "It wasn't exactly splitting the atom, but I filled a need. Once I rented the property near the beach from Niall—"

"Your father," Ryan confirmed.

She bit down on the inside of her cheek. "I don't think of him that way, but technically, yes. After I had more land and the barn, word spread that I would take on animals in need, and things expanded."

"Why not bring in animal control or local law enforcement tonight?"

The car bumped over a rut on the gravel drive she'd turned onto. "It slows down the process," she said, then blew out a breath. "Obviously I can't seize a dog, so this is more of a wellness check. Kat said Matthew Bron is out of town. I've never met the guy, but my brother Erik was in the same grade as his girlfriend. I'm hoping I can talk her into doing what's right for whatever dogs they have on the property without calling in animal control or the sheriff."

A house came into view, and Meredith automatically scanned the property.

"And you think she's going to hand over the dog or dogs?" He frowned and rolled down the truck's passenger window. "It seems unlikely if the animals are a source of income."

"I'll work it out," she told him and hoped she sounded more convinced than she felt. In truth, it would have been smarter to call law enforcement, but the thought of animals in need made her act impulsively. The story of her life. But if she could save even one dog tonight, she had to try. She knew from experience that every hour counted.

She parked about a hundred yards from the house, near a detached garage. To her astonishment, Ryan didn't argue. He got out of the truck and followed her to the side door of the garage, using his phone to shine a light into the dark interior.

"I don't see any movement," Meredith said quietly.

"Do you think we should knock on the door before someone comes out with a shotgun?"

Meredith glanced over her shoulder at him. "That only happens on TV."

He gave a disbelieving grunt. "We'll see."

She turned at the sound of a plaintive whine. "Did you hear that? It's around back."

"Hey! What's going on out here?"

They both froze at the sound of a woman's angry yell.

"Kris, it's Meredith Ventner. Erik's sister."

"I know who you are. What the hell are you doing lurking around the garage?"

Meredith squinted as Kris Dulles walked toward them with the bright light of a heavy-duty flashlight trained on Meredith's face.

"I heard you have a dog in trouble on the property. Can you stop shining that in my eyes?"

Kris moved the beam of the flashlight from Meredith to Ryan. He lifted his arm to shield his face. "Matthew's dogs are none of your business. You bring your boyfriend with you?"

"He works with me at the rescue," Meredith said, annoyed. Why did everyone assume Ryan was her boyfriend? Why was the idea of that so darn appealing? "How many dogs does Matthew have?"

"Just one at the moment." Kris lowered the flashlight and gave an irritated sniff. "Praise the damn lord, since Matty took off a couple weeks ago. I ain't got time to deal with his animals while he's probably partying his butt off with some random woman."

"That's not fair to you." Meredith made her tone sympathetic, sensing an angle she could exploit to get the dog to safety. "You're way too busy with your own life, right?"

"Yeah." Kris frowned as if mulling over Meredith's assessment of the situation, then nodded. "Damn straight."

The woman wore a snug tank top with a flannel shirt over it, cropped jeans and flip-flops. Her dark hair fell almost to the middle of her back, and she had smudges of mascara under her eyes. Meredith had no idea what Kris did for a job, but she knew that she still ran with a crowd that liked to shut the local bar down on weekend nights. Another whine sounded from the back of the garage, making the fine hairs on the back of Meredith's neck stand on end.

"Can I see the dog?" Meredith asked and felt Ryan's fingers brush her hand. The featherlight touch felt both comforting and supportive. "I might be able to help give you a break."

"Sure." Kris started for the back of the garage. "You could have just knocked on the damn door, Mer. Scared the pants off me when I saw a couple of dark figures outside."

"Sorry," Meredith said, not having to work at sounding contrite. Once again, she'd let her instinct override good sense. "I wanted to take a look around before bothering you."

"That's some convoluted-ass reasoning." Kris sniffed. "You're lucky Matty's out of town. You might have ended up with the barrel of a gun in your face instead of my flashlight."

"Exactly," Ryan muttered, and Meredith elbowed him— gently, of course—in the ribs.

As they came around the back of the garage, their movement triggered a motion light, and Meredith got her first glimpse at the animal Kat had told her about.

It was a yellow Lab—or some indiscriminate mix that looked like a Lab. The dog watched them from where she lay, chained to a metal stake in the ground. The ground was bare dirt under and around her, and the stench of urine and feces carried to them on the night breeze.

All thoughts of contrition fled her mind as she moved

toward the animal. "What the hell, Kris?" she demanded. The dog's stomach was round and even in the dim light Meredith could see her frightened, panting and wide eyes.

"It looks like she could go into labor any day." Meredith blew out a breath, trying to control the anger and frustration coursing through her. "She's in bad shape." She turned to the woman standing at her side. "How many litters has she had in the past year?"

Kris shrugged. "I told you, the dogs are Matthew's business. I don't pay no attention."

"How many litters?" Meredith demanded. "Give me your best guess."

"Two or maybe three," the woman said with a sigh. "What's it matter?"

"A dog needs time to recover." Meredith fisted her hands at her sides. Why hadn't she known about this place before now? How many more substandard operations were there around Magnolia? She couldn't stand the thought of any animal suffering, and this dog was clearly distressed and malnourished.

"The dog don't complain," Kris said. "She barely makes a damn sound. Matthew had another bitch in here, but that one was a fighter, so he had to get rid of her. He's been selling off all of them. She's the last."

Meredith felt Ryan move closer, and the heat from his body gave her a strange bit of comfort. "Got rid of her how?" he asked, his voice tight.

"I don't ask questions." Kris placed her hands on her waist. "But what I can tell you is this dog is our private property, and her puppies are gonna be worth some money."

"I could come back with law enforcement," Meredith said casually. "I don't want that, Kris. Do you?"

"Matty's gonna be real mad if I let that bitch go," the other woman said. "Whenever that jerk comes crawling back to me."

"How much do you think she's worth?" Ryan asked.

Meredith glanced over her shoulder at him and then back at Kris, whose eyes had taken on an almost predatory gleam. "She normally pumps out five to six pups, so that's a decent amount of income."

"I thought you didn't pay attention to the breeding operation," Meredith reminded her.

"It's a guesstimate."

"I've got seven hundred dollars cash." Ryan pulled his wallet from his back pocket. "It's yours right now if we can take the dog."

Meredith felt herself gawk as much as the other woman. "Why do you carry that kind of cash?" she asked.

He gave her an arch look. "Does it matter at the moment?" He took several crisp bills from his wallet. "This is between us. Tell your boyfriend that the dog ran away. Tell him whatever you want."

Kris licked her lips, clearly wavering.

"No cops need to be involved," Meredith added. "At least for tonight. But you'd better find a way to encourage Matthew to get a different hobby other than dog breeding. Because I'm going to be watching you, Kris, and next time it won't be just me who shows up at your door."

"Why are you still bothering with all these strays?" Kris crossed her arms over her ample bustline. "I thought once you were outed as Niall Reed's daughter that you'd start living the life of luxury or something."

"This is my *'or something,'*" Meredith answered. "Are you going to take the money or not?"

She held her breath as Kris stared at the outstretched hundred-dollar bills. For a moment Meredith thought the woman was going to walk away, fear over the potential repercussions from her boyfriend outweighing her greed.

There was no way Meredith was leaving this property without that sad, neglected dog in her truck, so if Kris wouldn't—

In a flash, Kris reached out and plucked the money from Ryan's hand.

"Not a word of this to Matty," she said, flipping through the bills, her chest rising and falling like she'd just sprinted around the track at the high school. "I'm telling him that dumb bitch just disappeared."

Meredith's temper spiked at the venom in the woman's tone. "Seems to me," she said through clenched teeth, "that you've got the market cornered on dumb bi—"

"No one is going to talk to Matthew," Ryan interrupted, wrapping a hand around Meredith's upper arm. "You made the right choice."

"That makes one of us," Kris said, smiling at Ryan. "If you ever want to drop the crazy dog-lady baggage, let me know." She shot a glare at Meredith and then turned on her heel and stalked back toward the house.

"Five minutes alone in a room with her," Meredith muttered. "That's all I'm asking for."

"Eyes on the prize," he reminded her. "Let's get the dog loaded up and back to the rescue where you can take care of her."

"Right." Meredith shook her head, frustrated that she'd almost let her anger get the best of her. Her firecracker temper had been a problem most of her life. She'd inherited it from her mom, according to her father, which didn't sit well with Meredith. She didn't want anything to tie her to the woman who'd left her behind without so much as a call or a birthday card in the years that followed.

"Why do you carry so much money in your wallet?" she asked as she eased toward the animal.

"Habit," he said.

"I thought only drug dealers or gangsters carried that kind of cash."

"I'm not either of those."

"You're a good negotiator," she told him. "Thank you."

"The money did the talking for me. You can thank the Benjamins."

"I can pay you back."

"No." His voice was solemn. "I'm happy to help get the dog out of here."

The animal didn't move as Meredith approached. "Poor thing," Meredith murmured. "I hope we're not too late for the pups she's carrying."

"Do you think she can walk?" Ryan's voice sounded shaky, and her heart melted to think that he seemed as invested in this dog's health and survival as she felt.

"Probably, but we'll have to coax her to get up." Meredith knelt down, ignoring the cold that immediately seeped into her skin through her jeans. "Hey, sweetie, can you come with us?" The dog continued to look away into the night, like she was mesmerized by something that only she could see. Meredith pulled a plastic sandwich bag of mini liver treats from her coat pocket. She dumped a few into her hand and held out her palm for the dog to sniff.

No response, not even a tail flick.

"She's got to be hungry," Ryan said. "Come on, girl."

He made a kissing sound and patted his leg, but the dog stayed put.

"She's given up," Meredith said, trying not to let tears clog her throat. "I hate it the most when they give up."

"I'll carry her," Ryan offered. "She can't weigh more than fifty or sixty pounds."

"It's risky." Meredith shook her head. "We don't know how she's been abused. She could bite."

"I'll take the chance," he answered without hesitation.

She looked up at him. "Why?"

"Because she needs a chance."

"Let me try to distract her." Meredith reached forward and dropped the treats on the ground in front of the dog. She smelled them but didn't try to eat them. Then she lifted her snout and sniffed at Meredith's fingers, snuffling softly.

"That's a girl," Meredith said, keeping her voice soothing. "A sweet, sweet girl." She continued to murmur to the dog as she stroked under her chin and then around her head. The dog whined and tried to scoot closer when Meredith drew back her hand.

"My friend Ryan is going to lift you," she told the animal as if the dog could understand her.

"So don't bite him," Ryan added, his voice pitched just above a whisper.

The dog let out a rumbly growl as Ryan bent and reached for her but allowed herself to be lifted without a struggle. Or a nip, much to Meredith's relief.

As soon as Ryan had the animal balanced in his arms, she led the way back to her truck.

"Normally, I'd put her in one of the crates," she said. "But I think she'd be more comfortable in the back seat. I can spread out a blanket."

"Should I sit with her?"

"Probably. Who knows if she's ever ridden in a car before?"

They got the dog situated on the seat, and Ryan climbed in on the other side. Meredith started the truck and pulled away from the property slowly, trying to jostle the dog as little as she could manage.

"Congratulations," she said on a shaky breath once she got to the main road. "You just took part in your first animal rescue."

He chuckled under his breath. "Do I get a merit badge?"

"You get my unending gratitude." Meredith lifted her gaze to the rearview mirror. She met Ryan's gaze, and the intensity in his eyes made her heart thump wildly in her chest.

They drove the rest of the way to the farm in silence, and she worked to process the avalanche of emotions tumbling through her. She didn't understand what was happening between them, but she liked it. She liked it far too much.

CHAPTER EIGHT

RYAN WOKE BEFORE seven and lifted his hand to his forehead. Unlike too many mornings following the shooting, there was no pounding behind his eyes. Since Meredith had confronted him on cleaning up his act, he'd done exactly that. Helping her to rescue the pregnant dog, which they were calling Sugar because of her sweet disposition, had invigorated him in ways he couldn't explain. He'd spent the past two days working at the rescue, both with the animals and taking on maintenance projects around the property. He'd done his best to keep a bit of distance with Meredith, embarrassed to reveal how much she and her animals were coming to mean to him.

He forced himself out of bed and, despite the ache in his leg, began the series of exercises the physical therapist had given him. Exercises he hated because they made him feel weak and less than he wanted to be. A painful reminder of what he'd lost and how uncertain it was that he'd be able to regain it.

His leg would heal eventually, although whether he'd ever be able to withstand the rigors of life in the ER again remained to be seen. Okay, maybe he was being melodramatic. He'd function, although maybe not at the level he had before. But for Ryan that loss felt like a complete failure.

He'd always performed at his peak and the thought of

being capable of giving anything less than that was a hard pill to swallow.

A good man had died the night of the shooting, with Ryan powerless to stop it. He was the doctor, so if he couldn't save a friend and colleague, what value did he offer?

His father had constantly drummed the message into Ryan and his sister that they couldn't rely on the money and privilege that came from their grandfather. *To whom much is given, much is expected* was the adage that defined most of Ryan's life, looming like a shadow over every decision he made.

Until everything he counted on had been stripped away.

He grunted in frustration when his leg gave out during another round of squats, but he didn't stop. Sweat dripped between his shoulder blades, and the ache in his leg morphed into a fiery burn.

But he felt strangely good. Alive.

The sun shined brightly in the morning sky by the time he ate breakfast, showered and headed for his car. The temperature hovered near sixty degrees, and tiny shoots of green grass pushed through the dirt. Birdsong echoed all around the property. Spring was coming to the coast, and for the first time since he'd arrived in Magnolia, Ryan welcomed the thought of a new beginning.

He still wasn't ready to think about returning to his old life, but at least he felt like living again.

As he drove toward the neighboring property, he rolled down the windows to enjoy the fresh air. There was no point in examining too closely the way his chest tightened every time he thought about Meredith and her motley menagerie of furry beasts.

The existence he knew had been turned on its head by

a staccato fire of bullets, and if he spent too much time considering where that left him, he'd end up right back at the bottom of the liquor bottle still stashed under the kitchen sink.

A chorus of dog barks and a few friendly whinnies greeted him from the animals roaming in the pasture behind the barn as he got out of his car. Apparently, he wasn't the only one enjoying the beauty of the changing season.

The wide plank door had been left open, and he watched dust motes dance in the air of the barn's entrance.

"Hello?" he called as he entered. Meredith must be nearby because under the smell of spring and the dusty-barn scents, he caught whiffs of warm vanilla, which he would forever associate with his temporary neighbor.

"I'm in the office," she answered. "Hurry!"

The breathless command made the hairs on his arms stand on end. He moved as fast as he could without the help of his cane, then came to an abrupt stop at the open office door.

"Puppies," he whispered.

Meredith turned her attention to him. Her wide smile and the tears shining in her beautiful green eyes made him feel like he'd just been bathed in some kind of fairy dust. "She just finished," she said in a hushed tone.

The dog was curled in a corner of the whelping box Meredith had placed along the far wall of the office. Five tiny, wriggling creatures were tucked next to her, and the dog vigorously licked at her pups while they nursed.

"Are they healthy?" He wanted to step forward but felt rooted in place by the odd intimacy of the scene in front of him.

"I think so." Meredith's hands were clasped together in

front of her in prayer position. "One of the vets is going to stop by in a bit to check on both mama and her pups."

She straightened and moved toward Ryan, taking his hand and squeezing. "We got her out of there at exactly the right time. Thank you again."

"You're crying," he said, sweeping his thumb across her cheeks. "What's wrong?"

She sniffed and tried to turn away, but he held her fast. "It's so stupid, but I only cry when I'm happy. Happy tears freak people out."

"I'm not freaked out by you, Meredith." She amazed and intrigued him with her prickly outer shell that hid so much warmth and heart. He'd never met anyone like her.

"You just don't know me well enough yet," she said on a small laugh. "Give it time."

"I'd like to." Unable to resist, he leaned in and brushed his mouth over hers. She tasted both sweet like vanilla creamer and salty from the tears. He felt immediately addicted to the combination. She sighed against him, and all of his resolve to keep his distance crumbled like his willpower was nothing more than a child's sandcastle.

He cupped her face in his hands, marveling at how a woman with so many sharp edges could have skin as soft as satin. She didn't seem sharp in his arms. She seemed warm and pliant, splaying her hands over his chest.

The sensations swirling through him were a cacophony of pleasure, but he didn't push for more. Oh, he would have liked to. His body screamed at him to lift her in his arms and find the nearest horizontal surface. To snake his fingers up and under the bulky sweater she wore to discover for himself the feel of the rest of her body.

A loud yip sounded out of nowhere, disrupting the

quiet and breaking the connection between them. Meredith pulled him into the main barn and shut the office door as her three dogs came barreling toward them.

"How'd you escape?" she asked as she bent to greet the trio.

His mind still reeling from the pleasure of kissing her, Ryan forgot to brace himself for impact. When Buster shoved against him to say hello, he stumbled back a step. After the grueling workout this morning, his muscles were shaky and protested the sudden movement.

A moment later he landed on his butt in the dirt, all three dogs taking his lowered position to their level as an invitation to climb all over him.

"Off," Meredith commanded. Buster and Marlin immediately moved away. Gracie took the opportunity for a few more sloppy face kisses before settling back on her haunches.

Embarrassment heated Ryan's cheeks as Meredith held out a hand to help him up. Talk about a mood deflater.

"I've got it," he muttered as he made his way to standing again.

"They get overexcited," she explained, sounding apologetic.

"I'm fine." He wanted to stalk away but forced himself to pet the dogs like the humiliation of being toppled by one of them was no big deal. How the hell was he supposed to function like a normal man—let alone seduce a woman—if he couldn't even stay balanced on his own damn feet? The thought that he'd had earlier of carrying her off for some sort of lusty tryst seemed almost comical now. He couldn't carry his own weight, let alone pick her up.

She inclined her head and opened her mouth like she wanted to speak, but a long shadow fell over the two of them.

"Hope it's okay that I let them out," a deep voice said from the barn's open doorway.

Ryan saw Meredith's eyes go wide with a mix of trepidation and vulnerability he didn't understand. Then she plastered on a smile and turned away from him.

"Hey, Dad," she said to the man who approached. He was just under six feet with salt-and-pepper hair, broad shoulders and a tense expression in his dark eyes that matched his daughter's. "What are you doing here?"

Now that her trio of mutts had gotten the loving they wanted as a greeting, they headed out into the morning sunshine to do whatever it was dogs did when left to their own devices.

"Harry Myers called me because he'd heard something about you being out at Matthew Bron's place. Tell me he was wrong, Pup."

Ryan bit back his smile. Of course Meredith's nickname would be Pup. But she looked more like defensive Cujo at the moment as she squared up against her father.

"He wasn't there, but he left behind a pregnant dog that was in bad shape," she said as if that explained everything.

No wonder she wasn't easily intimidated. Meredith's father looked like he could scare the piss out of a hardened criminal, but she hitched her chin and didn't flinch as he stared her down.

After a tense moment, the older man blinked and turned his attention to Ryan, the hint of a smile playing at the corner of his mouth. Ryan could tell the man respected his daughter's spunky attitude, and he immediately liked him for it. His own father hadn't been nearly as understanding when his sister asserted her will. There had been way too many angry yelling matches between Emma and their overbearing father.

"I'm Carl Ventner," the man said, his handshake firm and no-nonsense. A handshake that fit him perfectly.

"Ryan Sorensen." Ryan cleared his throat. "I'm the temporary neighbor, so I've been stopping by to volunteer with the animals."

Carl studied him, then nodded. "You're the doc staying at the Parthens' place?"

Ryan ran a hand through his hair. "Is there anyone in Magnolia who doesn't know who I am even before meeting me?"

"Probably a few," Carl told him. "I had an appointment with Doc Thorpe yesterday morning. He mentioned you might be helping out with the mobile clinic."

"You didn't tell me that." Meredith's voice carried a hint of accusation.

"Because I didn't agree to it," Ryan said with an exasperated sigh.

Her father ignored his words, just as Paul Thorpe had. "A lot of folks around here will benefit from medical care coming to them, especially some of the older vets."

"It's a worthwhile project," Ryan agreed. "But I'm not involved. In fact, I'm on medical leave from my hospital in DC, so—"

"Let me guess." Carl let out a derisive snort. "Skiing injury."

"Dad." Now Meredith sounded scandalized.

"Bullet through my calf thanks to a hospital shooter," Ryan said, feeling his face burn at the man's insinuation.

Carl's expression gentled, and the sympathy was almost as

galling as the judgment from moments earlier. "Well, if you can find a way to help out even a little, we'd all appreciate it."

"I'm keeping him busy here," Meredith said, stepping between Ryan and her father like some sort of bodyguard.

Carl met Ryan's gaze over her head, one brow lifting almost imperceptibly. "Is that so?"

"He's feeding animals and scooping poop," she clarified with a shake of her head. Several strands of hair had come out of the clips that held it back. He wondered if it had happened naturally or if he'd tugged them loose while kissing her. He wanted to reach out and take them between his fingers but fisted his hands at his sides instead.

"One of the goats has taken quite a shine to me," Ryan offered, earning a smirk from Carl and a glare thrown over Meredith's shoulder.

Carl focused on Meredith once more. "Tell me about Matty Bron and the dog."

"See for yourself." Meredith cracked opened the door to her office, and her father peered in.

"That poor girl looks like she's been run through the mill," he said, whistling under his breath.

"An unofficial puppy mill." Meredith shifted closer to her dad. "I couldn't leave her there."

"Why didn't you call the sheriff?" Carl placed a hand on her shoulder. "Micah would have gone out there with you. We both know it's too dangerous for you to be flying out into the dark on your own."

"I wasn't alone," she answered stiffly. "Ryan came with me. Like I said, Matthew wasn't even around. His girlfriend wants nothing to do with any animals, so she was happy to take the money Ryan offered her and ignore us loading her into the truck."

Carl looked over his shoulder at Ryan. "I appreciate you having my girl's back."

Ryan nodded. "Anytime."

For some reason, Carl's words seemed to rub Meredith the wrong way. "So I'm your girl, now?" She shifted away from her father, hands on her hips. "At least until you disappear again?"

"I didn't disappear," Carl said, a muscle ticking in his jaw. "You knew where I was the whole time."

"I'm going to fill the water buckets in the pens out back," Ryan said before Meredith could offer her father a snippy response.

"Nice to meet you, Ryan." Carl inclined his head. "I hope you give Paul a call about the mobile clinic."

"I'll consider it, sir," Ryan affirmed, even though he had no intention of practicing medicine during his stay in this small coastal town. "Let me know if you need me," he said to Meredith, disappointment spearing his chest when she wouldn't make eye contact with him.

As he walked away, Ryan wondered if instead of working with the local doctors he should actually make an appointment to have his head examined. He'd purposely structured his life so the only complications in it were the ones that came through the emergency-room doors. It was no accident that he didn't date seriously or have any close friends to speak of. He liked his world simple, but suddenly all he could think about was getting involved in every tangled aspect of Meredith Ventner's small-town life.

As Ryan moved away, Meredith turned from her father and walked into the office to check on mama and her puppies once more.

"This is the only dog you took from Matthew?" Carl asked as he came to stand next to her.

"Rescued," she clarified. "It would have been a disaster for her to give birth in those conditions, but the puppies seem healthy at the moment. We need to make sure she stays hydrated. Thomas should be here any minute to take a look at her. She might do well with a course of antibiotics, too."

"I worry about you putting your own safety at risk. Matthew Bron isn't safe."

"He's out of town."

"But if he'd been there..."

"If I thought there was real trouble, I would have brought in one of the sheriff's deputies or animal control. I'm not an idiot, Dad."

Her father let out a long-suffering sigh. "I know that."

"Ryan paid Matthew's girlfriend for the dog. She was happy to let the animal go. I don't know what will happen when he gets back, but I'll deal with it then."

"So you've got a doctor working for you during his vacation? That's a little odd."

Meredith blew out a breath. She hated the tension between her and her father but didn't know how to breach the expanse that had grown wide between them since she'd found out about Niall.

"He's volunteering, and I'm not asking a lot of questions."

"I worry about you, Pup. Even with everything else, that hasn't changed."

Sadness threaded through her father's words, just about breaking her heart. "I'm fine," she whispered.

She was just about to hug him when he cleared his throat. "How are the other two?"

"My sisters?" she countered, although they both knew who he was talking about. "Avery and Carrie are great. In fact, Avery's wedding is right around the corner. She's marrying Gray Atwell. They're really happy together."

"I heard something about that." Carl scratched a hand along his jaw. "He's a good man. Theo played football with him."

Silence descended between them again, although somehow it wasn't quite as tense as a few minutes earlier. Sugar let out a sigh as her puppies nursed. In the distance, Meredith heard barking as a car pulled down the driveway. "Thomas is here," she said, turning.

"I'd like to meet them," her father blurted, looking ten kinds of uncomfortable as he stared at a place beyond her shoulder. "Your...um...sisters. Half-sisters."

"Why?" The word fell out of her mouth before she could stop it. The thought of her two different families crossing paths set off a string of warning bells in her brain.

"Because they obviously mean something to you," her dad said, then blew out a breath. "I thought I was over all the anger at your mom. I know it was tough, but the boys and you and I did okay, right?"

"More than okay," she said, emotion clogging her throat.

"This business with Niall brought it all up again, and I didn't handle myself all that well. I can't say I'll be perfect going forward, but I want to try to be better. If you'll give me another chance, Pup?"

Now Meredith did throw her arms around her father—this tough, craggy man who was her dad in every sense of the word, no matter what story DNA told them.

"All the chances," she said. "I'm sorry this has been hard on you. I never wanted that."

"I know." He rubbed a hand across her back but released her when the chorus of dog barking grew louder.

Meredith stepped away and swiped a finger at the corner of her eye.

"I'm going to head out. Meeting a few of my buddies for breakfast in town," he said. "Talk to your sisters and invite them to the house for dinner one night. We'll figure it out as we go along."

She nodded, then schooled her features as the senior vet in the practice where she worked approached them.

"Morning," Thomas said, greeting her father and turning to Meredith. "You okay?"

"Yeah. But I'll be better after you give the puppies and their mama a clean bill of health."

Her father headed for the barn's exit as she and Dr. Meninger entered the office. Meredith was exhausted, both physically and emotionally, but also felt more hopeful than she had in a long time.

CHAPTER NINE

"WHY WOULD THEY want a stranger at their engagement party?" Ryan asked later that week as he parked a block down from the Reed Gallery in downtown Magnolia.

"You seem nervous, Doc." Meredith grinned at him. "Does the thought of true love make you nervous?"

"Terrified," he said without hesitation, and the honesty in his tone made her smile falter.

"You'll be fine," she assured him, flipping down the sun visor on the passenger side and giving herself a quick once-over in the small mirror. "Damn, I should have at least slapped on some lipstick."

"No."

She glanced at him. "Not a fan of makeup?"

He shrugged. "I don't have an opinion of makeup other than to say you don't need it. You're beautiful just the way you are."

Before she had time to register the compliment, he was out of the car and slamming shut the door behind him.

Meredith looked at herself in the tiny mirror again. Same freckled cheeks, same blunt-cut dark hair that could do with a trip to the beauty salon. She'd been described in a lot of ways over the years. Never as *"beautiful."*

Warmth expanded through her chest, and she exited the

car while smoothing a hand over the simple sheath dress she'd chosen for Avery and Gray's celebration.

"Everyone in town is curious about you," she told Ryan as they crossed the street. "And we hired an awesome caterer, so you're guaranteed to get an amazing dinner."

"Why would anyone be curious about me?" he said, sounding grumpy about the idea.

"I thought you grew up in a small town." She nudged him with her elbow.

"People knew my family," he answered. "We were part of the community. Nothing more."

Something about the way his words sounded forced made her doubt that he was telling her the whole truth, but he proved her point just the same. "In Magnolia, you're a new, shiny penny. They need to know where you fit."

"Nowhere," he said, his voice barely above a whisper.

"Rachel the goat would beg to differ," she said, deciding to try to lighten his mood. In truth, she was just as nervous about bringing Ryan with her tonight. Not that she considered this a date. Since that one moment in the barn, he hadn't tried to or even seemed interested in kissing her again. She chalked it up to a momentary lapse in judgment or getting caught up in the excitement of the pups being born. She told herself that she didn't want another kiss. Didn't fantasize about the way his mouth felt against her and the heat and strength of his body a hundred times a day. Maybe more when she went to bed at night.

She appreciated his help around the property and wouldn't take the chance of ruining their friendship and a great working relationship with her wayward thoughts of ripping off his clothes and having her merry way with him. Even if he was going to be gone in a few weeks.

But her sisters begged her to bring him along tonight, and Meredith had finally agreed. It would be nice not to be the third—or fifth—wheel. As glad as she was for both Avery and Carrie, sometimes it felt like their bliss made her loneliness stand out in stark contrast. Even if he didn't want to kiss her again, having Ryan at her side made her feel less alone.

"Your goat has bad manners," he said with a chuckle, and she noticed that his broad shoulders relaxed the tiniest bit but didn't stop to examine why that felt like such a win.

All the animals liked him, but Rachel had fallen head over hoof for Ryan. She'd seemed to imprint on him like something out of an interspecies romance.

Meredith had first noticed it when the goat had started incessantly bleating the morning after the puppies were born. She and Ryan had been working on a plan for the roof since the final materials were due to be delivered. They'd rushed into the barn, Meredith's heart hammering in terror about what could have alarmed the animal so much. The pups had been sleeping peacefully, curled up against their mama, and all the other animals remained calm. When Meredith opened the door of the goat pen, Rachel pushed her way out, then went to stand next to Ryan.

For the rest of the day, every time the animal was separated from him, she complained vocally, but as long as she could follow him around or keep an eye on her new favorite human, she seemed content.

Meredith was embarrassed at how much she had in common with the goat. Being near Ryan had the same calming effect on her soul.

"You have a way with the ladies," she said, then laughed at his affronted glare.

"The four-legged, furry ones," he clarified, making her laugh harder.

"If you're having this much fun before you've gotten to the party," a voice called, "I can't wait to see what comes next."

Meredith waved at Malcolm Grimes, Magnolia's charismatic mayor, and one of her father's oldest friends.

"Hey, Mal." Meredith gave the mayor an easy hug. He'd been a fixture in her life since she could remember, long before he'd entered local politics. Mal had also been a support to Meredith and her sisters, even hiring Avery as the town's marketing director once the three of them successfully helped reinvigorate the town's economy. "Ryan, this is Magnolia's famous mayor, Malcolm Grimes. Mal, this is Ryan Sorensen—"

"Staying out at the Parthens'," Mal said with a nod. "I've been hoping to meet you, Doctor."

"You and most of the rest of the town." Ryan's expression was an entertaining mix of bewilderment and exasperation. "I didn't realize I was so interesting."

"Slow news cycle," Mal told him with a wink, then looked at Meredith. "Why are you grinning so big, Pupsqueak?"

Meredith rolled her eyes at the nickname. Seriously, she needed to go someplace where everyone hadn't known her since she was in diapers. A handsome doctor calls her beautiful, and minutes later he's being reminded that people seem to associate her with dogs and short people. "One of the goats has a crush on the doc," she told Mal.

The mayor smiled and hitched a thumb at the gallery's picture window. "Love is in the air."

"Not with me and a farm animal," Ryan corrected.

"Good to have boundaries." Mal looked like he was trying to keep from laughing out loud. "I was hoping to talk to you about the mobile clinic."

Meredith felt the instant change in Ryan. All the humor disappeared to be replaced by an uncomfortable stiffness. She didn't know how much Mal or Dr. Thorpe or anyone in town knew about Ryan's history and what precipitated his stay in Magnolia, but it was obvious that the thought of being involved in practicing medicine at any level bothered him.

He was a grown man and a successful doctor so clearly he could fight his own battles, but she still felt protective of him, the same way she would with a pit bull who'd been through a trauma and was being pushed to socialize beyond what the animal could handle.

Okay, not exactly like that. Meredith didn't think of Ryan like one of her rescues in any way.

But she felt protective, nonetheless.

"No business talk tonight," she told the mayor before Ryan could answer. "He's here to celebrate Avery and Gray, same as the rest of us. You can stop out to the rescue with a donation if you want to harass him about the mobile clinic."

Mal blinked, then looked between the two of them. Finally, he gave Meredith an exaggerated salute. "Yes, ma'am. I've got my marching orders."

"Your orders are to give the best toast to my sister and her fiancé that this town has ever heard," she said, then entered the gallery when Mal held open the door.

The good news was that defending Ryan had distracted her from her own nerves. He followed her into the gallery's main room, leaning forward to whisper "Thank you," his breath tickling her ear and making her nerves flutter for an entirely different reason.

She greeted a few people and then was enveloped in a

double hug, sandwiched between Avery and Carrie. Her heart pinched even as she squirmed away. "No touchy-feely garbage," she told her sisters, then stuck out her tongue when they both laughed and hugged her again.

"Everything's perfect," Avery said, joy written all over her face. "You had Angi make all of our favorite foods, and the cupcakes are perfect. Violet was actually squealing when she saw the arrangement."

"That was the easy part," Meredith said, feeling color rise to her cheeks. "Carrie took care of all the sentimental bits."

She and Carrie had planned this night together. Carrie had handled decorations, including personal-photograph displays and flowers while Meredith handled the food and drinks.

"We're a great team," the willowy brunette said. It was still difficult for Meredith to believe that she counted Niall Reed's precious daughter as her sister and one of her two best friends in the world. Growing up, neither of them had known about their connection. All Meredith understood was that Carrie's life had seemed so charmed, with her glamorous mother and famous father who lorded his privilege all over town. Carrie always seemed to have the best of everything—from frilly dresses and elaborate birthday parties as a kid to a brand-spanking-new car on her sixteenth birthday.

Meredith had never yearned for fancy dresses but growing up motherless in a household filled with a ton of testosterone, she'd been insanely jealous of Carrie. Coupled with her father's animosity toward Niall, which Meredith hadn't understood but supported with the blind loyalty of a dutiful daughter, she'd been rude and sometimes outright cruel.

When she'd first learned about Niall's will and the truth of her biological father, she'd wanted to deny it. She'd become as angry and bitter as her mother in the hazy memories Meredith had of her. Now she couldn't imagine her life without the connection she felt with Avery and Carrie. The solidarity that had grown between them gave her the sense of having truly found her place in the world.

"And this must be the newest member of Team Furever Friends." Avery offered Ryan a friendly smile and her outstretched hand. "I'm Avery Keller."

"Soon to be Avery Keller Atwell," Carrie added with a brow wiggle. "I'm Carrie."

"Ryan Sorensen."

Meredith glanced at Ryan, surprised to see the open smile he offered both of her sisters. When she'd introduced him to both her father and Mal, he'd been cordial but slightly standoffish. There was none of that with Avery and Carrie. "I owe Meredith for letting me help out around the rescue. I'm on a leave of absence from work, but the slow pace of vacation life was driving me crazy. It's nice to be busy again."

"And Rachel loves him," Meredith answered, somehow embarrassed by his gratitude. Her sisters were obviously eating it up like candy. They beamed at Ryan, then looked at her with twin expressions of approval.

"She's obviously a goat with good taste," Avery said.

"I heard you're into '90s television," he said.

"Without a doubt."

"My sister and I didn't miss an episode of *Friends*," he told them. "When Rachel kissed Ross after watching the prom video...pivotal moment."

"Oh, yes." Avery pumped her fist in the air. "I knew we were going to like you, Ryan."

"Oh, yes," Carrie repeated under her breath so only Meredith could hear.

"Enough of the fawning all over him." Meredith made a show of not smiling to mask her fascination with this charming version of Ryan. "He's a big-city doctor so his ego doesn't need any stroking. I've got him scooping poop and walking dogs. I don't want him to realize he's over-qualified."

Ryan laughed softly, the rumbly sound reverberating through her. "There's a certain Zen to poop-scooping if you ignore the poop part."

"Holy crap," Avery muttered, slapping Carrie lightly on the arm. "He's actually perfect for her."

"Stop." Meredith's cheeks flamed with embarrassment. "Let's go check out the food."

Without waiting for an answer, she stalked away from her sisters. She knew almost everyone in attendance, from Josie Trumbell, who owned the dance studio next door, to Lily from the hardware store and her boyfriend, Garrett Dawes. Almost all of them stopped her to say hello, darting speculative glances between her and Ryan, especially once they realized the mysterious doctor staying at the beach cottage was the man at her side.

"I'm sorry," she told him when they finally reached the buffet table. "This was probably a mistake. I didn't real-ize how obnoxious every single person I know could be."

"Your friends seem nice," he said, grabbing a stuffed mushroom and popping it into his mouth. "Your sisters are fun. It's crazy to think the three of you haven't known each other forever. Your connection feels really tight."

She glanced from the display of food to Ryan, then back again, her mind reeling at the thought that he didn't seem to be the least bit upset by the attention on the two of them. She couldn't quite understand it. Meredith hadn't dated anyone seriously—and barely casually—since she'd dropped out of college and returned to Magnolia. Other than last month's article about her pathetic dog-mom status, no one had any reason to believe she was interested in falling in love.

In fact, she assumed she'd been relegated to the role of crazy animal-lady spinster in most people's view.

So was it just conjecture or assumptions because she'd brought Ryan tonight, or was there more to it? She felt a spark with him that she couldn't explain. Were people picking up on that?

Did he sense it like she was some sort of lovestruck schoolgirl? No better than Rachel, the enamored goat?

"This food is awesome." He'd grabbed a plate and begun filling it with appetizers, giving no sign of distress. Did he not notice the pointed looks people gave her when she introduced him, or was he so used to women crushing on him that Meredith's infatuation didn't faze him?

Or maybe he was just that hungry.

"I hired Angi Guilardi to cater it. Her family owns the Italian restaurant across the street. She's always been a waitress there but happened to mention that she wanted to start her own catering company. I thought I'd give her a chance."

"You do that a lot."

She made a face. "Hire caterers?"

"Give chances. To people or animals. Any creature who needs a bit of help."

"It's not exactly altruistic," she protested, feeling uncomfortable with the way he'd looked at her as he said the words. Like she was a good person. "Angi is a great cook. You scoop poop like it's a meditation practice. I'm just looking out for what's best for me."

"Not true."

Before she could argue further, he held up a cheese puff, and she automatically opened her mouth to take it from him. His finger brushed against her bottom lip, sending a flood of sensation through her. Then her taste buds registered the burst of flavor as she bit down on the flaky pastry with the smoked-cheese center. It was the perfect combination of savory and spicy with just a hint of sweetness.

Ryan smiled as her eyes widened. "You gave the right chef a chance," he said. "And let me be clear, Meredith. I realize people are making assumptions about us, and I don't care. It's flattering that anyone would believe you'd give me the time of day. It doesn't have to be true. I'm happy to pretend."

She grabbed a napkin and dabbed it at her mouth. "Flattering? That's rich. Like I'm such a catch. Broke and overworked and often smelling as bad as the animals I rescue. No one would think for a minute that I could capture the interest of a man like you."

He leaned in closer. "Then, let me fill you in on something that everyone except you can see—you already have."

Heat flooded her cheeks, and she willed herself not to melt into a puddle of goo at his feet. Dylan Scott, Carrie's fiancé, who'd also been friends with Meredith's older brothers growing up, approached at that moment. She welcomed the distraction.

The next two hours were filled with introductions, conversations and a lot of smiles as the party went into full swing. Gray's daughter, Violet, and several of her friends entertained the crowd with an impromptu dance recital. Meredith tried to appear normal on the outside, but inside it felt like all of her nerve endings tingled with awareness.

Every small glance Ryan threw her way, each time he managed to casually brush his hand against hers made her body buzz so that by the time they drove back along the dark road that led to the beach, she had to work not to obviously tremble.

"Should I turn off my lights as I approach so I don't send the dogs into a frenzy?" he asked, and the only word Meredith could process was *frenzy*. Like the frenzy swirling inside her.

"No, it's fine," she told him, then cleared her throat. "But…um…would you like to come in for a minute?"

Oh, lord. Did she just extend that invitation? Her heart pumped so heard she thought it might bruise her ribs. Did she even have clean sheets? She'd been rushing to get ready before he picked her up earlier. Why couldn't she remember if she'd put on decent panties?

"Meredith."

She swallowed, then turned to find him looking at her with a speculative gleam in his eyes.

"Did you answer?" she asked on a rush of breath.

"Yes." He lifted his hand to her face and tucked a lock of hair behind one ear. "I answered *yes*. But if you want to change your mind—"

"No." She reached up and covered his hand with hers. "I'm just…I don't usually…it's been a while."

"We don't have to do anything. No pressure. Let's just take it one moment at a time, okay?"

She licked her suddenly dry lips and nodded. "Okay."

CHAPTER TEN

MEREDITH TRIED TO ignore the trembling in her fingers as she poured two glasses of lemonade fifteen minutes later. She'd entered the house with Ryan at her side, nerves fluttering like the whisper of hummingbird wings, only to be greeted by the dogs and Mo, her tailless cat.

As always, her menagerie's enthusiastic unconditional love had the immediate result of relaxing her. She and Ryan followed them into the backyard and watched as the dogs investigated the fenced-in area like it was brand-new, did their business, then trotted back toward the house ready to take up residence on their beds once again.

The calm she felt from that evening routine lasted just until Ryan leaned in and placed a quick kiss on her mouth after they returned to the kitchen. It was tender and chaste, but desire howled to life inside her, and that roar scared the hell out of her.

Confusion flashed in his eyes when she pulled away before he quickly replaced it with acceptance.

He took the glass from her and put it on the counter. "What's going on?" He touched a finger to her lips when she would have answered. "Don't tell me *nothing*. Please. You don't have to lie."

She tried to process that concept. She'd been lying for

so long—to herself and everyone around her. Did she even truly understand the full truth anymore?

Yes.

The word blew through her like a gust of wind, rattling the windowpanes of the fortress she'd built around her heart. Of course she knew the truth. She was broken. Not bent. Not fixable. Broken.

How could she explain that?

For several seconds all she concentrated on was pulling air into her lungs and then blowing it out again. The wind still whipped around inside her, hurricane-force now, and the door to her protective inner fortress slammed open with the force of it.

"I'm not very good at sex," she said on a rush of breath, then cringed at how that sounded. "Sober sex," she clarified but quickly realized that was even worse.

"What makes you think that?" Ryan asked, his voice so gentle it felt like a caress.

"It's the only... I've never... I don't do men sober," she finished, feeling her cheeks heat with shame. This could be the most embarrassing conversation of her life, and she'd had some pretty awkward talks. Her body screamed at her to shut her damn mouth and just kiss the man. Might as well run the hot doctor off for good, her mind argued. Nothing could come of it, anyway.

"Then, let me clarify for you," Ryan said, his tone still achingly soft, "I'm not looking to be done."

Meredith groaned and turned away. "I've screwed everything up. You see why I don't date, right?" She stalked to the edge of the kitchen, then started back again. "This is stupid. I'm stupid. We should just agree that—"

"What happened?"

She paused midstep and glanced at Ryan, his gaze somehow curious and too aware at the same time.

"There are a lot of amazing women in the world," she said instead of answering. "Ones that don't come with loads of baggage. Ones who can sleep with a guy without freaking out."

"You don't have to tell me if you don't want to, but I'd like to understand."

"Have you ever heard the expression *dog with a bone*?" she muttered, and one side of his mouth quirked.

"Coming from you, I take that as a compliment. You can tell me."

She crossed her arms over her chest and glared at him. "Nothing happened. Not really." She focused her gaze on a spot just over his right shoulder and tried not to grind her teeth into dust as the emotions from that night came flooding back. "I made some stupid choices and got myself in a bad situation with a boy. It was a long time ago, so it shouldn't matter."

"Did he hurt you?"

Meredith bit down on the inside of her cheek until she tasted blood. What was pain, really? "I don't remember," she whispered, miserably. "I mean…it was my first time, so after…yes, it hurt. But during…when we…I was drunk and maybe he'd put something in my glass…I still can't remember."

The silence stretched between them like a heavy fog. She concentrated on the familiar scent of her house to ground her, the sound of a dog snoring quietly in the other room.

"How old were you?" Ryan's voice had taken on a different quality, soft but also strained. She could only imagine what he must think of her.

"Sixteen." She tried to move the muscles of her face into a smile, to laugh it off like it was no big deal, but her recalcitrant mouth refused to budge. "My brothers had both left home, and I wanted to prove that I didn't need them to be popular or have fun. I was hanging out with a wild crowd, older and into partying. I thought it made me special when, in reality, it made me an idiot."

"I doubt you were ever an idiot," he said. "You couldn't consent if you were drunk, Meredith. That's not something to take lightly."

"I know what you're implying, but I don't think it applies here. No one forced me to do those shots or down that liquor. No one held a gun to my head when a boy I barely knew handed me a drink laced with who knows what. I made those choices." She pressed two fingers to her chest, the keening ache there making her feel like her rib cage might split apart. "I deserved—"

"Don't say it." Ryan took a step closer, reaching for her.

She tried to shrug away, but the attempt was half-hearted at best. She liked him touching her, craved the heat and comfort of his body.

"What happened wasn't your fault," he said. "Did you go to the hospital after?"

The word *hospital* triggered the realization inside her that he probably understood that night more than most people could. She didn't want to imagine how many women he'd seen in the ER after they'd been truly violated. Knowing she wasn't alone offered little comfort.

She shook her head. "He called me the next day. Said he'd had a great time and asked if I wanted to hang out that night." Her jaw tightened. "Like everything was normal, which made me think the situation was normal."

"Did you see him again?"

"Only at school, but something changed in me at that moment. I believed I was the person he assumed me to be. A girl who got drunk and slept with a guy she barely knew in somebody's smelly basement bedroom." She raised her gaze to his. "That's what I became for a while after. It was like I needed to prove that he'd been right about me, which was the dumbest thing ever." She shook her head. "I went down a bad path."

"You have to give yourself a break." His hands tightened around her arms like he could will her to believe him by the strength of his hold.

"I garnered quite the reputation my senior year of high school and then partied my way through freshman year of college." Her throat felt like it was coated with sandpaper, but she forced herself to keep speaking.

To her surprise, it wasn't difficult. Now that she'd started to share her past, the details rushed forward like a caged bull stampeding out of its pen. Underneath the shame of sharing her mistakes ran a steady trickle of relief at not having to carry this hidden truth alone. No one, not even her sisters, understood the full extent of her shame. "I flunked out of school." She managed a wan smile. "That's why I'm working so hard to get my degree online now. Because I partied away my first chance."

"Everyone has regrets."

She laughed without humor. "Not like mine."

"Everyone," he insisted.

She wanted to believe him but couldn't let herself. She wanted to ask about his regrets but was so afraid that he'd list off something like not making the dean's list one semester or only saving a hundred lives instead of a thousand, and then she'd just feel worse.

If that were possible.

"So now you know," she said, stepping away from him when all she wanted to do was lean in. "I'm damaged goods."

"Don't say that."

Her heart hammered inside her chest and panic skittered across her spine as she thought about everything she'd just shared.

Mind racing for a way to regain her emotional equilibrium, she moved to the cabinet and pulled out a bottle of wine that hadn't been opened when she'd hosted Thanksgiving dinner. She held up the bottle and gave him an exaggerated wink. "Since we both understand that I'm an emotional train wreck with all kinds of intimacy issues, why don't we get drunk and scr—"

"Stop." He grabbed the bottle from her hand and placed it on the counter, then handed her one of the glasses of lemonade she'd poured earlier. "I'm in the mood for a distraction. You like action flicks?"

She glanced back and forth between the glass in her hand and the man standing in front of her. "Sure," she said after a moment.

"Let's see what's on late-night."

"You want to watch a movie?" She placed a hand on his arm. "My crazy story was an out for you, Doc. A warning. Don't get involved with the nutty dog lady."

He chuckled. "Oh, sweetheart, that's cute. Remember, I work in an urban ER. You can't come anywhere near the crazy I've seen. Besides…" He dropped a quick kiss on her forehead. "Nothing you told me tonight makes me want you any less. In fact, what you've been through and battled back from only makes you more fascinating as far as I'm concerned. We've got time, and whatever happens between us is going to be 100 percent sober and 110 percent consensual. I can damn well promise you that."

"Oh." She exhaled the soft sound, and about a million pounds of shame went with it.

He laced his fingers with hers and drew her toward the family room. Marlin had taken up residence on the old love seat, and she and Ryan sat on the overstuffed sofa, so close that their thighs grazed against each other. She placed her glass on the coffee table and picked up the remote.

She found an old Sylvester Stallone movie, laughing at Ryan's excitement. "This is a classic," he murmured when the opening credits rolled. Like it was the most natural thing in the world, he put an arm around her and gathered her close.

Meredith had to swallow back the emotion that rose up into her throat. She'd carried the secret of the summer night that had changed her whole life, who she was on a cellular level, for so many years. It still boggled her mind that she'd shared it with Ryan. And somehow the revelation shifted something inside her again. As if there had been tiny pieces of her floating in the air for all this time. They were with her but not part of her.

Ryan's reaction allowed her to begin to gather those bits and reposition them within her. She might be broken, but for the first time she wondered if maybe she didn't have to stay that way. Maybe there was a way to once more become whole.

RYAN BLINKED AWAKE SLOWLY, unable to say where he was or what time it was but aware that he wanted to go right back to sleep and return to the amazing dream he'd been having.

He felt something press against his jaw, light and soft like the flicker of butterfly wings.

"Are you awake?" a voice asked, and he heard both humor and desire in it.

"I hope not," he answered automatically, earning a breathy laugh that tickled his skin.

Suddenly he realized he wasn't dreaming. His eyes adjusted to the dim light of Meredith's family room, and he became conscious that the butterfly wings were from the woman at his side. She kissed his cheek, and he quickly turned his head to capture her mouth with his.

She moaned against him and shifted. His still-fuzzy brain took a moment to process the situation, but when he did it was the most natural thing in the world to lift her into his lap so that she straddled his hips.

"Good call," she said, pulling back to look at him. "You fell asleep and missed the end of the movie."

"Rambo won," he told her, still trying to wrap his brain around what was happening.

"Yeah." A smile tugged at one side of her mouth. "He won."

"You should have kicked me out."

She shrugged. "You looked so peaceful, and I needed to check on the puppies." Her green eyes darkened a touch, reminding him of the color of the ocean in winter. She cupped his cheek with a soft hand. "So we're clear, I'm not kicking you out now, either."

"We don't have to—"

"What if I want to?" she asked with a small smile that was both flirty and the tiniest bit hesitant.

His body went from zero to hell yes in an instant. He did his best to tamp down the need surging through him so that his brain didn't short-circuit. He couldn't remember the last time he'd wanted a woman the way he did Meredith. Everything about her captivated him. But she'd shared some heady stuff with him earlier. He'd seen enough women hurt by men to know that scars weren't always physical. He didn't want her to feel pressure to take a step she wasn't ready for. They might have only known each other a short time, but she was already precious to him.

"There's no hurry," he told her, even though it was a struggle to get out the words. "We have time."

"How much?" She shifted against him, and he lost all ability to process coherent thought for a moment. Her smile widened as if she liked the torture she put him through. "How much time?"

"Time," he repeated, his mind still trying to catch up to her words. "All night."

Her laugh was husky and did crazy things to his insides. "How long until you leave?"

A five-alarm fire couldn't force him to leave this moment. He started to tell her exactly that and then realized what she was really asking. When was he leaving Magnolia?

"I have another three weeks until I can be reassessed and cleared to go back to work."

He couldn't tell if relief or disappointment flashed in her gaze, but she replaced it with a smile before he could react.

"That's good," she said, then leaned in and kissed him again.

Did she mean good because it was enough time or good because they had a built-in end date to whatever happened between them?

"I should be able to get you out of my system in that

time." She paused, and her eyes widened as she pulled away. "I didn't mean it like—"

He wrapped his arms around her waist. "I'm yours for however long you'll have me."

"I'm bad at this," she muttered with a shake of her head.

"You're amazing," he countered and pressed his mouth to hers. He hadn't been lying. He'd take whatever time she'd give him, although the fact that they both knew it was temporary probably made it easier. At least it did for him, even though he shouldn't admit it.

But Meredith made him feel too much, made him want things he'd told himself he wasn't cut out for in life. As a kid, trying to balance the privilege of his family's wealth with the conditions his father had set on proving his worthiness had messed with his sense of self.

His desires had never been a priority. He'd been taught to put his professional goals ahead of personal ones until he didn't have any of the latter. Ryan knew his existence would always revolve around his career. He didn't want to settle down or have a family of his own.

In fact, he'd never even considered it. So it made no sense that he couldn't stop thinking about a future with Meredith.

But then the tip of her tongue touched his, and all the thoughts of the future disappeared, blotted out by the blinding pleasure of this moment.

CHAPTER ELEVEN

As she held tight to Ryan's broad shoulders, Meredith savored the sensation of his strong arms wrapped around her. She breathed in the scent of him and tried not to feel shock at the fact that she wasn't freaking out. The intensity of her desire outweighed her potential nervousness, and he was being so damn sweet.

Even when she thought about it, the anxiety didn't come. As if sharing the story of what had happened to her released the necessity for panic. The bottom line was she trusted this man. She trusted him not to hurt her, to respect her boundaries. That trust enabled her to let down her guard.

Maybe she'd regret it.

Maybe she should down a few slugs of vodka just to make sure she could go through with this.

No.

She wanted this. She wanted Ryan.

He walked into her bedroom with her legs wrapped around him, the first man to enter her private space. She was secretly glad that she'd gone with a queen bed when buying her furniture at a secondhand store after moving into the house.

The bedroom was her favorite space, but every bit of Ryan's focus remained on her and not the decor of the room.

"You still doing okay?" he asked as he lowered her

gently to her feet. She curled her toes into the vintage rug and nodded.

"I'm thinking about my dresser."

He stared at her a moment, then let out a loud crack of laughter. "I must be more out of practice at seduction than I realized." He flicked a glance over her shoulder. "It's a fine dresser but..."

"Why do I blurt out the dumbest things to you?" She covered her face with her hands. "I was thinking about how I'm not panicking and then the fact that I've never had a man in my bedroom and then..." She shook her head. "I'm doing it again."

"I'm the first man who's been in your bedroom?" He gently gripped her wrists and pulled her hands away from her face.

She nodded. "Once I came back from college, I decided I was done with the fast lane. I haven't even gone for a Sunday drive since then."

"I like the driving image," he told her with a grin. "I also like that I'm the first man to see your room. Nice quilt."

"My grandma made it." She swore under her breath. "Okay, now I've brought up furniture, panic attacks and my grandmother. Somebody muzzle me."

"What do you want, Meredith?" The pads of his thumbs traced small circles against the sensitive skin on the inside of her wrists. "Right now. No past or future. This moment. You and me. What do you want?"

"Take off your shirt," she told him before she lost her nerve to see what he looked like beneath his clothes.

His sexy half smile made her toes curl. "That a girl," he said softly, then stepped back and grabbed the hem of his shirt, tugging it up and over his head.

Well, that had to be one of the best ideas she'd had in ages. She knew Ryan was fit, but seeing all those muscles under his smooth skin and the smattering of hair covering his chest was something else entirely.

"Wow," she murmured, drinking in the sheer maleness of him. "Wait. Are you blushing?"

His big shoulders rose and lowered in a self-conscious shrug. Her mouth went dry. "Believe it or not, I'm not used to stripping down with an audience."

"You might consider it more often." She flashed a cheeky grin. "Could be an untapped source of alternative medicine, not to mention a great side hustle."

"Sexual healing," he added and began to hum the old classic as he moved toward her.

"You're one hot doc," she said as she smoothed her hands up the front of his body. "Figuratively and literally."

"What next?" he said, nipping at the side of her neck. "Tell me."

"I'd rather show you." She pulled away and unzipped her dress, then slid the soft material down her hips. Her heart beat so wildly it was difficult to keep her focus steady. She felt as exposed as she ever had, standing in front of him wearing only a bra and panties. So much for the few seconds of thinking she'd make a good exhibitionist. "Show's over," she muttered, reaching behind her to flip back the quilt and sheets. "Hit the lights, Doc."

"Easy there." He took her hand before she could dive under the covers and tugged her forward. "What's the hurry?"

"I'll lose my nerve," she said, then groaned as he pulled her fully against him. Damn, he felt so good—warm and strong. She wanted to devour him. "We can slow down when we get to round two."

"This isn't a race," he said, then kissed her deeply. "Although it's going to be hard to savor it with how much I want you."

Goose bumps pricked her skin as he slid his hands around her, flicked open the clasp of her bra and kissed the sensitive skin below her ear. The fabric slid to the ground, and Ryan followed it, his gaze heavy-lidded as he knelt in front of her.

"Your leg," she managed before her voice broke off. He curled his fingers into the waistband of her panties and pulled them off. She felt achy and hot in parts of her body that had been dormant for years.

"It's fine," he promised against her belly. His whiskers tickled her skin, triggering more goose bumps. "This is about you, Mer. I want to make you feel good. All you have to do is say the word and I'll stop. You're in control here. Always."

"For the love of God," she said, her voice hoarse, "don't stop."

Then his mouth was on her, and all the anxiety and worries flew out of her mind because she could only feel. And it felt right. Her muscles went liquid as he touched and tasted. She lost herself in the sensations swirling through her. The pressure built like a flood of water behind a dam until she couldn't take it anymore and cried out her release. She felt rather than heard his groan of pleasure, like the moment was as good for him as her.

But now she wanted more. She wanted him.

Another wave of yearning pummeled her as he rose to his feet and lifted her onto the bed. She wanted him so much it should have scared her. Instead her mouth went dry as she watched him move.

He took a condom out of the wallet he'd fished from his back pocket, then took off his jeans and boxers. Meredith propped herself up on her elbows, too sated to be self-conscious of her body, and took a moment to admire him.

"You're beautiful," he whispered as he rolled on the condom.

"Back at you." When he turned, she noticed the angry red scar that ran almost three inches down the back of his calf. She hated that mark, not because it marred his physical perfection. It was a reminder that he'd been through something no person should have to endure.

Then he joined her on the bed, hard and solid and exactly what she needed. She pushed all thoughts of either of their pasts to the back of her mind and concentrated on now. The past wasn't going to ruin this moment. She wouldn't let it.

They kissed and touched, a melding of hands and mouths until she pulled him closer.

She gasped with pleasure as he entered her and held on tight to his shoulders. He kissed her, and she could tell the need inside him matched her own. They moved together, and it was everything she hadn't realized she wanted or needed. Heaven help her, she wanted it all. Ryan gave it to her, wringing more pleasure from her body before he shuddered with his own release.

As their breathing returned to normal, questions flitted through Meredith's still-hazy brain. Had she made a terrible mistake? What now? What next? Then Ryan wrapped an arm around her and pulled her to him like it was the most normal thing in the world.

She should have protested, but exhaustion and satiated

pressure quieted the voices in her head. Curling against him, cradled in the crook of his arm, was where she wanted to be.

"Thank you for letting me in," he said softly into her hair.

Meredith sighed in response, allowing sleep to finally claim her.

RYAN WAS HALFWAY to town the next afternoon when he spotted the mobile health-care clinic. He drove past, his gut tight, then turned around at the next intersection. As he pulled to a stop across the street, he could see the line of people waiting outside the converted van, most of them either checking their phones or talking to a neighbor in the line.

Ten minutes passed, then fifteen, and still he sat in his car, unwilling to get out but somehow unable to drive away. He thought about the night of the shooting and everything that had been lost in those few, tragic minutes. Sweat beaded between his shoulder blades, despite the fact that the temperature had cooled by several degrees, and billowy clouds tumbled by overhead, the smell of rain ripe in the air.

Would those waiting in line leave if the skies opened up?

It was impossible to know the type or severity of the ailments people were being treated for from this distance, and Ryan hated the way curiosity plucked at his nerves, but he hated the nerves even more.

Finally, he got out and walked toward the clinic when he saw Paul Thorpe exit the van. The other man gave a cautious wave as Ryan approached. "Didn't expect to see you here," Paul said.

"I was heading to the hardware store." Ryan shrugged.

"Thought I'd at least check out your operation since I was driving right by."

"I'll give you the grand tour," Paul said, then greeted a few of the waiting patients as he walked by.

Ryan followed him up the two steps into the van, relieved when his knee didn't protest. The interior held a postage-stamp waiting area and exam room on either end. The walls had been fitted with rows of cabinets, and healthcare posters hung on the pale-yellow walls.

"Get some rest, Stan," Paul told a man who exited one of the exam rooms, buttoning a faded flannel over a dingy undershirt. "Your prescription should be ready within the hour, and the meds will get you back to normal in no time."

"Thanks, Dr. Thorpe." The man drew in a clearly labored breath. "I feel better already."

As Stan exited the van, Paul motioned Ryan forward so he could see the exam room. He smiled at the woman wiping down the table and surrounding surfaces with a sanitary wipe. "Aimee, this is Dr. Ryan Sorensen. He's visiting Magnolia for a few weeks from DC, where he heads up one of the busiest ERs in the region. Ryan, meet Aimee Baker, our managing nurse extraordinaire and...well...she's my... I mean...we're..."

Ryan turned to Paul and noticed the dignified doctor's cheeks had turned an almost-violent shade of pink.

"We're dating," the pretty nurse with a mass of blond curls and a bright smile told Ryan.

"She's the best thing that's ever happened to me," Paul confirmed, then let out a sigh. "Turned me into a complete fool for love."

"Good for you," Ryan said, not sure whether to cringe or

chuckle at the other man's obvious infatuation. He glanced at Aimee. "Both of you, of course."

"It's nice to meet you, Dr. Sorensen."

"Call me Ryan."

"Aimee was instrumental in getting the funding for the clinic. Now she coordinates the schedule and appointments. She's beautiful and a nursing superhero."

"Hardly." Aimee laughed and placed a hand on Paul's arm. "But I appreciate it." She lifted onto her toes to quickly kiss the doctor's cheek. "Andrew Ramirez is up next. He's here to have his sutures removed."

Paul nodded. "Give me five minutes to show Ryan the setup."

Aimee nodded. "I'll get him set up in the other exam room."

"Is it just the two of you?" Ryan asked when the nurse shut the door behind her.

"For the most part," Paul said with a nod. "Aimee practically does the work of a full staff on her own. I know I sound like a lovestruck teenager, but I can't help it. This place couldn't manage without her, and I'm not sure how I made it so long on my own. You have anyone special in your life, Ryan?"

An image of Meredith appeared in his mind, but Ryan shook his head. "Relationships aren't my thing."

"You sound like I did before Aimee. All it takes is meeting the right person."

"I'll take your word for it." Ryan massaged a hand along the back of his neck. He needed to change the subject away from his love life. He'd be leaving Magnolia soon and had too much baggage to think about anything but a temporary relationship, despite what his heart wanted. "How do you have time with your regular shifts at the hospital?"

"This is my day off," Paul admitted with a rueful smile. "Our current budget doesn't allow for two paid staff members."

"I don't get why you have such a crowd. People in Magnolia don't believe in regular doctors?"

Paul shrugged. "Some do, some don't. A lot of folks around here get nervous going to the doctor. The mobile unit feels like less of a commitment. Urgent care on wheels."

"What happens when they need more intensive care?"

"I make a referral, same as any doctor with a private practice would do."

Ryan thought about how many patients he'd seen at the ER with life-threatening illnesses or diseases that had progressed to advanced stages because they hadn't gone for treatment until things became too hard to ignore.

There were plenty of reasons a person might not go to the doctor. Fear, finances, time off from work.

As if reading his mind, Paul said, "Our patients feel like they can come here and it's not as nerve-racking as the hospital. We can't treat everyone or every diagnosis, but we make a difference." The man stifled a yawn. "Sorry about that. My shift ended last night at ten, but I didn't get home until after midnight."

"You need more help," Ryan said absently.

Paul grinned. "Agreed. Do you happen to know any available medical professionals?"

Ryan rolled his eyes as the not-so-subtle hint in the other man's tone. "You said you only run the clinic two days a week, right?"

"At the moment. We're applying for more funding, so I might get enough money to actually pay for another doctor or nurse practitioner."

"I'll take the next shift," Ryan offered suddenly. He waited for the panic to overtake him and breathed a relieved sigh when his heart continued to beat at a normal rate.

"Change of heart?" Paul frowned at him. "Not trying to look a gift horse in the mouth, but I thought you were determined not to get involved. Was my tour of our little facility that impressive?"

"I need to stay busy while I'm here," Ryan said, and it wasn't a complete lie. "I've been getting a little too cozy with my friend Jack Daniel's, so..."

"We're way more entertaining than liquor," Paul told him with a laugh.

They discussed the specifics of what a typical day entailed, and Ryan agreed to meet Aimee at the scheduled location later that week. While Paul saw the patient, Aimee took down his email address so she could send over paperwork and gave him more details about what to expect.

After his time at the mobile clinic, he headed for town again, wondering what Meredith would think of his involvement. In truth, she'd been a motivating factor for him. Or more specifically, his feelings for her had.

One night together, and he felt like as much of a lovesick schoolboy as Paul. He'd left her house early that morning after their night together, and it scared the hell out of him how hard it had been to get in his car, even though he knew he'd see her again later that night.

Ryan was a solitary man. He liked his freedom and independence and the ability his career gave him to not make deep connections. Now he was counting the hours until he could return to her farm, emotionally dependent on a woman and a ragtag crew of rescue animals. His colleagues would have cracked up at the change in him.

Ryan didn't like the thought that he was changing. He'd be going back to the city in a few weeks. Magnolia was a detour on the path he'd laid out for his life. He couldn't allow it to be any more than that.

He wouldn't allow it.

Volunteering at the medical clinic hadn't been in his plan, but maybe it would remind him of his real life. A reminder he needed so he didn't become too close to Meredith. Sex was one thing. Anything more was off the table.

CHAPTER TWELVE

"LUNCH WITH MY dad was a terrible idea." Meredith pressed a palm to her chest. "I think I'm going to have a heart attack."

"Panic is more like it," Avery told her with a pat on the head. "Don't worry. Your dad is going to love us."

Carrie made a sound somewhere between a laugh and a snort as she lowered herself into the chair next to Meredith at the adoption booth. "I doubt he's going to love me, but I'll do my best."

"Don't be silly." Avery bent to scratch the furry head of the three-year-old beagle mix that sat at her feet. "You're as lovable as sweet Molly here."

"Thanks for comparing me to a dog," Carrie muttered.

"Dad loves dogs," Meredith told her, doing her best to control her breathing. "There are worse things he could think about you."

"Niall had an affair with your mother while he was married to my mother," Carrie reminded her. "I'm guessing Carl already thinks the worst of me."

"How many times do we have to go through this?" Avery shot them both a look as she urged Molly to her feet to greet a family who approached the booth. "The fact that Niall was a world-class cheater, scumbag, low-life jackass has nothing to do with any of us."

"She's right," Meredith said and smiled at the young girl who skipped up to pet the dog. Her sisters had come with her to a popular farmer's market in a neighboring town to help staff the Furever Friends' adoption booth.

Once spring arrived on the Carolina coast, Meredith made the rounds of festivals, craft fairs and local markets, bringing as many adoptable dogs as she could handle each time. She also had information on the training classes she ran, as well as an online portfolio of the other animals available through the rescue.

It was great outreach and almost always ended with a successful day of adoptions. She'd been up since five that morning, exercising and then grooming the dogs to make sure they felt relaxed and looked their best when they met potential families. Her absolute favorite part of what she did was matching animals with forever homes, and she liked to think she had a particular talent for it.

Sometimes animals picked their owners, and sometimes it went the other way, but often she could help discern a potential adopter's temperament and what animal might be a good fit for their home.

This morning had been busy, and already two of her recent rescues, Rufus and Roscoe, had been adopted by a couple where the husband was newly retired. According to the wife, he needed more company, and the two friendly mutts would do the trick. It helped to have another person with her at each event so they could keep things moving with processing paperwork and facilitating meet and greets with dogs and interested families.

Today both Avery and Carrie joined her because they were driving to Meredith's father's house for lunch after the market ended. She'd tried to convince him to meet them at a restaurant—neutral turf and all that—but he'd insisted on the sisters coming to him.

She'd hoped that a morning spent with her sisters and her animals would serve to relax her, but so far her nerves jangled like chimes in a windstorm. She pushed back from the table and stood when the girl's father approached, and she shared what she knew of Molly's history.

Unlike many of the dogs in her care, the beagle's life had been mainly happy. She'd had the same owner for the first few years of her life until the family had decided to move across the country and chosen not to take their family pet with them.

It still boggled Meredith's mind that any person could commit to an animal and then simply walk away, but that was what made her especially dedicated to finding good homes for all of her furry charges. After all, Meredith's mother had left her three children without looking back once to start a new life.

Meredith understood what it felt like to be abandoned.

She watched as the family and the small dog began to bond, and as always, bearing witness to one of her animals getting a second chance made her chest pinch with happiness. She helped the parents apply to adopt the dog and scheduled the home visit that she always did for her animals, while Avery and the daughter took Molly for a walk and Carrie talked to other potential adopters.

Before the market hours were over, every one of the seven dogs she'd brought with her had gone home with new families. It didn't always work out so well, but Meredith was grateful every time she placed an animal. They stayed until the end, and she scheduled appointments for two other people to come to the barn to meet her available cats.

She hadn't yet made public the litter of tiny puppies in her care. Puppies were easy to place, and the fee for adoption would be higher in order to help offset the cost of vet bills for the mama. The vets in her practice gave her a great discount, but expenses still added up.

As if reading her mind, Carrie glanced over from the passenger seat of Meredith's truck as she pulled onto the road that led to her childhood home. "Have you heard anything about the shelter grant?"

Meredith grinned with pride. "As a matter of fact, an email from the foundation's operations director came yesterday. I'm on the short list of applicants."

Her sisters screamed in unison and with such enthusiasm that Meredith swerved on the empty road. "Keep it down," she yelled with a laugh. "I don't need my dad pulling us out of a ditch."

"Why didn't you tell us?" Avery leaned forward from the back seat and swatted Meredith on the shoulder. "This is big news. Headline news."

"It's not a done deal." Meredith felt color rush to her face. "I didn't want to jinx anything."

The truth was she'd hardly been able to believe it and was afraid her sisters would be just as incredulous that her little operation had been short-listed. Sometimes giving an out-loud voice to her greatest dreams was hard because she'd just feel like such a fool if she didn't achieve them.

"We're good-luck charms," Avery said, sounding affronted. "Rub my belly. I'm your own personal Buddha."

Carrie tossed Avery a *Shut the hell up* look over her shoulder, then reached across the console to squeeze Meredith's arm. "What happens next?"

"A site visit." Meredith blew out a breath. "Which means

I have to get the roof fixed and make sure the place looks as good as I can make it. I checked out the websites for the other organizations that are finalists. Two of them have pretty elaborate operations. Nothing like my patched-together property."

"Of course they're going to pick you." Avery was calmer, but her tone held no shred of doubt. "Especially if they meet you in person."

Meredith barked out a laugh. "Is that a joke? We all know that charming humans isn't exactly my strong suit."

"They'll see you with the animals," Carrie explained patiently, like she was talking to a toddler. "Everyone who sees you with your babies understands what they mean to you."

"Do you think so?" Meredith hated the catch in her voice, but she couldn't deny that she needed the reassurance. It felt as if there was so much at stake with this grant. A big influx of funding could change everything. She'd managed on a shoestring budget, relying on hope and prayers for far too long. As her confidence grew, so did her desire to do more, to be an even bigger advocate for the animals and within the community.

Winning the grant would go a long way to turning her dreams into a tangible goal.

"Carrie's right," Avery piped up from the back seat. "You might not be likable to people, but animals love you."

"She doesn't mean that the way it came out," Carrie said quickly.

Meredith made herself smile. "If she's right, I don't care about the people. As long as I can do more for the animals who don't have anyone else."

With her normal sensitivity to other people's emotions,

Carrie steered the conversation toward wedding plans for the rest of the drive. Meredith half listened as Avery reviewed the details for the big day.

Part of her continued to ruminate over Avery's words. She might say she didn't care about people because that's what everyone expected of her. She had a reputation as being harsh and brash, a pull-no-punches ballbuster. Her sisters might understand that a lot of her bluster was a defense mechanism, but very few other people recognized her softer side.

For so long she'd been resigned to that because it kept her safe, but lately *safe* had become a synonym for *stifling*.

Lately. As in, since Ryan Sorensen's arrival in Magnolia.

Maybe if she got the grant and finally felt legitimate, she could let down some of her guard with other people, as well. After all, Ryan was only in town temporarily. He was a decent candidate as a starter guy but nothing more.

Too bad her heart didn't want to believe that.

"THIS IS WHERE you grew up?" Avery asked as Meredith turned off onto a short cul-de-sac ten minutes later.

"Not quite the big house on the hill Carrie's used to." Meredith tried, and probably failed, to keep the bitterness out of her voice. In truth, she'd loved her family's small, cramped house as a girl. It had been tough after her mom left, but as she got older, she began to take on more of the domestic chores around the place. Her father hadn't demanded that of her, but it had become clear that he and her brothers could care less about adding homey touches to their living space. Meredith had been a tomboy on the outside with the secret heart of a pint-size domestic goddess.

"It's lovely," Carrie said as she gazed out at the brick

rancher with cream shutters flanking each window and a row of cheery lilac bushes in the front yard. "The house looks happy, which is always most important. No one would ever say that about Niall's house."

"Or the urban apartments I grew up in," Avery added. "This place is cute. Very Norman Rockwell."

"Anything but that comparison." Meredith led her sisters toward the front door. "It reminds me way too much of Niall."

"How long has your dad lived here?" Avery asked, turning in a small circle on the cobblestone walk.

"Thirty-five years," a deep voice said from the doorway.

Nerves catapulted through Meredith as she felt the weight of her father's steely gaze, first on her and then as it switched to each of her sisters. Carl Ventner was a big teddy bear at heart but had quite the growl before a person got to know him.

Maybe Meredith took after the father who'd raised her in more ways than she realized.

"It's lovely," Avery called, the hesitancy in her voice surprising Meredith. Normally Avery made a point of sounding confident in everything she said or did, even if she wasn't feeling that way on the inside.

But Meredith understood. Her dad could be all kinds of intimidating.

"Hey, Dad. I like the new bird feeder." She gestured to a wooden house hanging from one of the low branches in the elm tree that she remembered helping him plant years earlier.

"I had a little time on my hands," he said with a shrug.

"The angles of the roof are great." Carrie approached the feeder with a smile. "One of the vendors was selling something like this at the farmer's market this morning, although it wasn't half as well crafted. You could definitely make money selling them if you wanted."

"Do I look like I need money?" Carl demanded, and Meredith watched his hand grip the doorway tighter. "Just because I don't own some throw-back mansion in the fancy neighborhood of town doesn't mean I can't take care of myself and my property."

"I didn't intend to suggest otherwise," Carrie said softly. "I'm sorry for any offense caused."

"Dad, the place looks great." Meredith shot Carrie a sympathetic glance, then hurried forward to hug her father. It was awkward when neither of them particularly liked physical displays of affection, but she took the opportunity to whisper *Be nice* into his ear.

"You girls come on in," Carl said after nodding at Meredith, then switching his gaze to Carrie. "I'm not interested in selling my wares at the moment, but if you have an available tree branch, I'd be happy to make a bird feeder for your house."

"Thank you." Carrie's smile was warm. "I know my stepson would love it, too." She walked forward and took Carl's big hand in hers. "He's fifteen so tries to act like he's all grown-up, but he's a kid at heart."

Meredith breathed a soft sigh of relief as her father's stiff shoulders relaxed. She could have told him it was impossible to remain standoffish around Carrie once a person got to know her. Neither Niall nor Carrie's mother had been warm or anything near what might be described as kindhearted, but Carrie had the gentlest heart of anyone Meredith had ever met. Which still left Meredith occasionally feeling the weight of residual guilt from how she'd treated

Carrie when they were younger. She was beginning to accept that she couldn't change the past, only what she wanted from her future.

"That's the boy Dylan Scott took in, right?" Carl asked in his gruff tone. "I was sorry to hear about his loss. Dylan's uncle was a good man."

Carrie's husband had also grown up in Magnolia but left town after high school. He'd returned just before Christmas along with Sam, who he'd gained custody of when the boy's family—Dylan's uncle, cousin and his cousin's wife—died in a plane crash. He and Carrie hadn't been in touch in the intervening years but had rekindled their relationship after a rocky reunion. Now Meredith couldn't imagine them not being together.

"Yes," Carrie agreed. "I'll tell him you said that. I'm sure it will mean a lot. Dylan has some funny stories about the adventures he got into with your sons when they were younger."

"Trouble is more like it," Carl said with a chuckle, then turned his attention to Avery as Carrie stepped into the house.

"My mom was just a faraway fling for Niall Reed," she said by way of greeting. "So I don't have any fun trips down memory lane to share."

Carl's eyes narrowed. "Do you like birdhouses?"

Avery inclined her head. "Do I look like a Hitchcock heroine?"

Meredith was so used to working through her own bitterness about the situation that she sometimes forgot that Avery had arrived in Magnolia last summer with a glacier-size chip on her shoulder. Raised by a single mom, Avery had been possibly the most shocked to discover her ties to the small coastal town. She'd made the cross-country trek because she needed a change from her life on the West Coast but hadn't planned to stay for more time than it took to collect whatever inheritance Niall had left her.

When it became clear that the estate was in worse shape than any of them could have imagined, Avery's plan to turn things around had begun to forge the bond between them. She still hadn't intended to stay, but thanks to falling in love with Gray and finding her place in the town, she was in Magnolia for good.

Avery's edges had softened quite a bit over the past several months, but she retained some of her spunk. Meredith just wished it wasn't on full display with her dad.

To her surprise, he threw back his head and laughed long and loud at Avery's comeback. "You've actually got a bit of Grace Kelly in you," he said, wiping at the corners of his eyes. "I can tell you right now that I don't plan to take any trips down memory lane involving Niall. All that matters to me is my girl." He gestured toward Meredith. "You're important to her, so I wanted to meet you. Plain and simple."

"Works for me," Avery said, her grin widening. "Meredith is one of a kind."

"Damn straight," Carl whispered, then winked at Meredith. "You don't look like you want to puke your guts out the way you did when you got out of the truck."

"Yeah," she agreed. "I think I'll make it through lunch without hurling at this point."

With another chuckle, her father led them into the house. Despite their small group being a strange mix and the nerves that still flitted through her, Meredith realized it had been a while since she'd heard her dad laugh. Definitely not since she'd discovered her connection to Niall and maybe even months before that.

"Look at how cute you were." Carrie turned from the row of framed pictures lined up across the mantel.

"Did you cut your own bangs?" Avery asked as she studied a photo of Meredith, Theo and Erik.

"It took months for them to grow out," Carl said from the kitchen.

Meredith just smiled, not trusting herself to speak as emotions assailed her from all sides. This was the first time she'd been in her father's house since discovering the truth about Niall and her mother.

Although she hadn't known about her connection to the famous artist, she'd understood he and her mother had been close. When Meredith was only five, she'd walked home from the neighborhood pool one hot summer day after Erik pushed her off the diving board and she'd needed to be rescued by one of the cute lifeguards on duty. Her brothers were supposed to be keeping an eye on her, but they'd been horsing around with friends and hadn't cared that she was too little to walk the mile from the community swimming pool back to their house.

She'd been angry and embarrassed, and all she'd wanted was to grab an orange Popsicle from the freezer and to watch game shows on the television. Her mom had gone back to work as a receptionist at a local insurance agency by then, so she expected to have the house to herself.

Instead, there had been a sleek black sedan parked in the driveway, although the house was quiet when she entered. At least she'd thought it was quiet until she'd heard a sound coming from her parents' bedroom like someone was in pain.

Her mom had been acting weird recently, so Meredith's first thought was that she was home sick. She took two Popsicles from the freezer, excited at the prospect of having her mother to herself for a quiet afternoon, even if she was feeling ill.

But when she'd opened the door to the bedroom, the scene in front of her had shocked and confused her in equal measure. Thinking back on it, she wasn't sure how long she'd stood there before backing away and shutting the door again.

She must have made a sound because her mother came charging out a minute later, reading Meredith the riot act for leaving the pool on her own. She remembered that she continued to stand in the hallway, Popsicle syrup dripping down her hand. Then Carrie Reed's father had emerged from the room, tucking in his shirt and looking annoyed but not quite as angry as her mom.

"You've got your father's sense of timing," he told her with a chuckle. The words still burned in her mind, and she'd wanted to tell the man to shut up. She knew he was important but also that he shouldn't have been in her parents' bedroom. He shouldn't be anywhere near her mother, and he definitely shouldn't feel so free to talk to Meredith about her daddy.

Now that she got the inside joke he'd been making, she felt even angrier about his tasteless humor.

"You okay, Pup?"

She blinked back into the present moment, turning to see her sisters and her dad gathered around the kitchen table. All of them stared at her with the same questioning look. Avery and Carrie knew that Meredith had caught her mom with Niall when she was a girl, but she'd never told her father.

Her mom had left for Florida six months later, and Meredith had blamed herself. Things had changed with her mom after that afternoon. Meredith guessed that Niall had broken things off. He was a slimeball, but at that point, he was still in his prime. His standing in Magnolia society and the regional art community as a family man mattered. Maybe if she hadn't come home that day and the affair had continued, her mother wouldn't have left.

Maybe everything that went bad in her family was, at its core, Meredith's fault. Her existence a constant reminder to Carl about his wife's infidelity. Her temper the reason she and her brothers had grown up with no mother. No wonder she'd never fit in.

"Your dad made chicken salad." Carrie gestured her forward. "You're hungry, right?"

"Chicken salad was always your favorite," Carl said, looking ten kinds of uncomfortable at her behavior. "If you want something else, I've got cold cuts in the fridge." Meredith's heart broke all over again. Her dad—the father of her heart—had always tried his best. He'd been too strict and emotionally distant most of the time. He hadn't understood the first thing about raising a girl, but he'd tried. Knowing she wasn't his daughter, he'd still tried.

That was the least she could do in return. With a forced smile, she approached the table. "Chicken salad is still my favorite, Dad." She took a seat across from him. "Thanks for having us to lunch. I want to hear all about your time up at the cabin and how Erik and Theo are doing."

CHAPTER THIRTEEN

It was nearly seven on Wednesday night, the sky streaked with tendrils of purple and orange, when Ryan heard the truck rumbling down the driveway. His heart stammered, and he did his best not to leap over the raised garden bed he'd just finished, in his excitement to see Meredith.

Instead, her trio of dogs stampeded toward him after she let them out of the back seat. They greeted him like a long-lost pack member, then trotted off to investigate their new surroundings.

"Hey, stranger," Meredith said as she approached with more caution than her herd.

He recognized the accusation in her tone. He hadn't seen her for a few days, other than when he stopped over to help with chores at the rescue. It was as if they'd come to some silent agreement to pull back before things between them got too serious. Like their connection wasn't already more than either of them could handle.

"Hello there, beautiful," he said, earning an eye roll. It was the same reaction he got every time he tried to pay her a compliment. How could she truly not see how gorgeous she was? Tonight she wore a V-neck T-shirt and faded jeans, her dark hair tucked behind her ears.

"Thanks for stacking the new shingles near the barn," she said as she kicked one booted toe into the dirt. He'd gone over to the rescue yesterday while she was at the vet clinic and organized the supplies that had been dropped off. Whatever he could find that needed doing. "I've got one more load coming tomorrow, and then I'm ready to start on the roof."

"I'll be there to help," he offered automatically. "Unless I can convince you to hire a professional."

She held up her hands for him to examine. "These two are the only crew I need."

"Ouch." He mimed a knife in the chest. "And here I thought I was making myself indispensable."

Her breath hitched, and her green eyes went stormy. Ryan wished he could take the words back. They settled in the air between them like smoke, thick with all the things they hadn't spoken to each other. Physical intimacy was easy enough, but with this woman nothing felt simple.

"How's your leg?" she asked. "No cane, I see."

He automatically stood a little straighter. Normally he hated even acknowledging his injury, but if he had a choice of discussing his leg or his feelings for Meredith, he'd take the damn gunshot wound every time. "Stronger every day. Well, not every day but most of them."

"You're still doing too much," she said, but there was no judgment in her tone.

"Probably, but I need to push myself. Makes me feel not so feeble."

She laughed at that. "You are anything but feeble."

"Weak," he said instead. "Damaged."

Her gaze softened. "Aren't we all?"

"I've missed you," he blurted, then immediately wished he could take back the words. He bent to pick up some of the leftover materials from the garden bed. "Forget that. It's only been a few days and we don't owe each other—"

"Me, too." She stepped closer to him and went up on tiptoes to brush her mouth over his. He breathed in the scent of vanilla lotion and fresh hay.

"You've been cleaning stalls," he said into her hair.

"Are you telling me I smell?" she asked as she pulled back to look into his eyes.

"Amazing," he murmured. "You smell amazing."

"You're weird."

"Better than feeble."

She ran her fingers through the short hair at the base of his neck. "I took my sisters over to meet my dad a few days ago." A shiver passed through her.

"Did it go badly?"

"Not at all. Things were awkward at first, but then they got along great."

"Is that a problem?" He splayed his hands on her hips, his thumbs grazing the waistband of her low-slung jeans.

"Only for me. It makes no sense." She tugged her lower lip between her teeth, and he could see the distress on her face, hating it even though he didn't understand what made her feel that way. "I don't know why it freaked me out so much. It's what I wanted, but somehow seeing the dad I thought was mine with the sisters I just discovered…it made me feel like I have no real place to belong. Nothing that is truly mine without layers of complications."

"All of them love you," he told her, tucking a stray lock of hair behind one ear. "Isn't that enough common ground?"

"That's the worst." She pushed away, turned and placed her hand on the cool dirt he'd scooped into the garden bed like she needed the earth to ground her at the moment. He understood the sensation. "It makes me feel like a horrible person, but I don't know how to deal with being happy." Her eyes were stricken as she glanced over her shoulder at him. "I want to pick a fight with someone or start trouble just so I can come back to my center."

"No takers here." He held up his hands.

"You haven't been around much…" Her voice trailed off as her gaze sharpened. "At night, anyway."

"It seemed prudent for both of us. We've been busy with our crappy thoughts," he said with a laugh. "I'm definitely not looking for an argument. Unless you need a punching bag."

"You're going to volunteer to be my punching bag?" She sounded doubtful.

"If that's what you need me to be." He could be a lot of things for Meredith. Lover, friend, confidant and even punching bag. He was afraid, however, that the one thing he couldn't be was a man she could depend on long-term. It shamed him how much the thought of that both tantalized and terrified him, but he wouldn't offer it. Some things were beyond even his abilities.

"Want to go for a walk on the beach?" she asked suddenly, like she could sense that his thoughts had gotten as maudlin as hers. He didn't doubt it. She had a sensitivity about her, not that she'd ever admit it.

"I haven't taken many beach walks," he admitted, absently rubbing at his leg.

"We have about an hour until dark, but if it's too much…"

"Too much is becoming my new favorite thing," he said, shaking his head. "Let's go."

She whistled for the dogs, and they headed down the driveway, then turned on the dirt road that led to the ocean.

The smell of sulfur and salt became more pungent the closer they got, and the dogs seemed to realize they were on a new sort of adventure.

"They love the beach," she said as they pranced and circled. Buster was in the lead with Gracie and Marlin following close behind.

They came to the end of the road, and Meredith led the way through a cluster of sea grass down a narrow path that turned from dirt to sand. As he crested the dune, Ryan's breath caught at the wide expanse of slate-gray water.

"The fact that I haven't taken enough advantage of this view is just one more thing to give myself crap about."

Meredith shot him a curious glance. "Why haven't you come down here before now?"

"I thought my leg wasn't strong enough," he said honestly. "I didn't want the reminder of how far I had to go in my recovery."

"And now you're not using the cane, and I barely see you favoring your other leg."

"It's getting there. I feel better than I have in a long time." Even before the shooting, he realized. A bullet had ripped through his flesh, but he'd been damaged long before that.

They made it to the edge of the sand, and he followed Meredith's lead in taking off his shoes and socks. The horizon stretched in front of them, the sky a kaleidoscope of burnt colors, and the pounding surf breaking and then receding on the shoreline sounded like a chant. The dogs ran down the beach toward the water, thrilled at a potential game of chase with the waves. About a hundred yards down, he could make out two other people walking along the water's edge, but otherwise the beach was deserted.

They tucked their shoes near the closest beach marker, then rolled up their jeans as they headed toward the water.

"I can't believe I avoided this for so long." He inhaled the salty air and turned his head so that the breeze whipped his hair. Stupid pride. He didn't want to stop and consider all the ways his foolish pride had prevented him from truly living.

"You're here now." Meredith nudged him as they walked through the sand that was still warm from the day's sun. "You might try giving yourself a break."

It seemed the most natural thing in the world to link his fingers with hers. "Are you going to show me how?"

"Doubtful." She grinned at him. "I can tell you, but leading by example is definitely not part of my makeup."

"How was your statistics test?" he asked, knowing she'd taken a big online exam the previous day.

Her fingers squeezed his. "I got a ninety-two."

"Congratulations."

He gasped and tried not to wince as a wave rolled up the wet sand and cold water covered his bare feet, both biting and refreshing. Meredith laughed as Gracie galloped by, sending up a spray of water and sand in her wake.

"I can't believe you remembered to ask about my test." She wiped sand off of the front of her shirt. "I still haven't told my sisters or my dad that I've gone back to school."

"Why?"

"It belongs to me," she said simply. "I don't want to hear from anyone that I don't need a degree or that I'm wasting my time."

"I don't think they would tell you that."

"I'd see it in their eyes, and it would confirm what I already believe."

He turned to her. "Which is?"

For several long moments she didn't respond, until eventually he thought she might not answer. He could see the emotions swirling in her gaze and wished he could find a way to calm whatever turmoil clamored through her.

"It doesn't matter what I accomplish on the outside," she said finally. "I still won't be enough."

"Of course you're enough." He reached out and laced their fingers together.

"Spoken like a person who has a successful career and checked all the right boxes for family, school and life in general. May I remind you that my actual father didn't even acknowledge me until after his death, and my mom walked away and hasn't looked back? I'm not actually the poster child for reasons to have faith in myself."

"You should be." He drew her closer until she was pressed against him. "Because you've been through more than most people, and you're achieving every goal you set for yourself."

Before she could argue, he leaned in to kiss her, then lifted her off her feet into his arms when another wave broke at their feet. She tasted like new beginnings and second chances and everything that he'd never realized he wanted but wasn't sure he'd be able to live without.

THREE DAYS LATER, Meredith waved to the busload of elementary schoolkids as the vehicle pulled down the driveway. Avery had helped her arrange to have Violet's class out for a field trip to learn about caring for rescue pets. She loved introducing kids, especially the ones who were naturally skittish, to the animals. Now she had to get back to the endless preparations for the foundation's site visit next week. The new barn roof was the biggest item on her to-do list.

Ryan had asked her to wait until tomorrow morning when he could begin the project with her. Today was his first day volunteering for the mobile medical clinic, and as happy as she was for him to be getting involved, a small, selfish part of her didn't like that she'd be sharing him with the rest of Magnolia when his time here was so limited.

Because of the circumstances, Meredith couldn't help but feel like he belonged to her, even when she knew on a rational level that wasn't the case. The women of Magnolia might be lining up with lists of nonexistent ailments for a chance to meet the eligible doctor.

Not that it mattered. He was going back to his life in the city at the end of the month. Which was for the best, or at least that's what Meredith kept telling herself. Never mind that her heart didn't seem to want to get with the program.

Her wayward emotions made her even more determined to start the new roof today. She needed to prove to herself as much as anyone else that she wasn't dependent on Ryan Sorensen. She didn't need anyone.

Of course, she couldn't deny that his help tearing off the old roof had made the project go far more smoothly than it would have if she'd tried to handle all the work on her own.

They'd climbed up on the barn together yesterday and worked in companionable silence as they ripped off old shingles. It had taken almost the entire day and her arms burned by the end of it. Ryan hadn't seemed to get tired at all, although she'd noticed him favoring his injured leg when they'd headed to her house for a shower as the sun went down. She could imagine him running a busy emergency room, all boundless energy and focus.

For so many reasons, she appreciated his help and presence in her life, even if it was temporary. The site visit for the grant was scheduled for early next week, and Meredith wanted the new roof on and a myriad of other projects completed by then.

Plus there were still last-minute details for Avery's wedding the following weekend and the continued work on Niall's house so that they could get it on the market by the middle of next month, which had always been the goal. They had a tax payment due, and a quick sale on the house would help ease the pressure she knew all three of them felt.

If the house sold quickly. Avery and Carrie had backup plans if it didn't, but deep in her heart Meredith knew that making the animal rescue financially solvent was a necessity. She hated that she'd assumed Niall was giving her a break on rent for the property out of the goodness of his heart when he'd been her landlord. Like other people in town, she'd willfully ignored the signs that he was teetering on the verge of financial ruin because it served her purpose.

Carrie had been doing her best to manage Niall's negligible savings while he continued to squander money on trying to keep up appearances. Even more, she'd wanted to stick it to Niall Reed for that long-ago afternoon when she'd caught him with her mother. She didn't know for certain that it precipitated her mother's abandoning their family, but to Meredith, Niall would always be tied to one of the worst parts of her life.

Yet discovering her connection to him had also led her to some moments of intense happiness, derived from the bond she shared with her sisters.

But she yearned to feel as though she'd found a way to turn the situation with their inheritance into something positive, both for herself and for Magnolia, the way Avery and Carrie had managed. At this point the farm was the one property that still was a financial suck on the estate. Carrie's growing popularity as an artist had put the gallery back on solid footing, and Avery was well on her way to making downtown Magnolia a viable and thriving coastal destination, no longer dependent on Niall's largesse. She'd even managed to convince Dylan Scott to modify the real-estate development he was planning so that it would add to the small-town resurgence she and the town council wanted to create. There was an energy within the community, and Meredith wanted to do her part. At this point, although her sisters might argue with her, she still felt like a burden.

The rescue barely broke even and wouldn't be able to cover the back taxes they owed. She'd fielded enough calls from developers and spoken at length with the estate's probate attorney regarding options for the property if the sisters wanted to sell. Avery had even met with one aggressive Realtor when she'd first arrived in Magnolia. To her credit, she'd abandoned the plan for selling once she realized what the property meant to Meredith.

Meredith couldn't stand the thought of losing her home, so she needed to find a way to keep it without anyone needing to bail her out.

She drew in a deep breath and began to climb the ladder with a load of the waterproof underlayment and shingles. The temperature had climbed to a balmy seventy degrees, but dark clouds loomed overhead, promising more rain if the weather forecast could be trusted.

Who was she kidding? She didn't need a Doppler radar to know what those swirling clouds meant. If her luck held,

Meredith would have maybe an hour before the rain started, and it wasn't supposed to let up for two days.

Most of the roof would have to manage with the big plastic tarps she'd affixed over the sections they'd already ripped off. But she at least wanted to get part of it done. She needed to feel like she was making some progress.

The roof was pitched at nearly forty degrees, and she started to unroll the first tube of adhesive underlayment. A gust of wind blew several strands of hair out of her braid, and she quickly tucked them behind her ears. The last thing she needed was to lose her balance and end up...

A loud crash from inside the barn had her pausing to listen. The sound of pounding hooves followed, and a moment later the three goats, Monica, Rachel and Phoebe, came charging out of the barn, followed by Marlin, who clearly thought he was playing a great game of chase with his new friends.

The goats were bleating as they ran toward the open field, not at all amused by the game. Damn.

This was exactly why Meredith's to-do list was in a constant state of not getting done. With another furtive glance at the darkening sky, Meredith tucked the hammer into the tool belt she wore and scooted to the edge of the roof. She placed a foot on the top step of the ladder. The property was fenced in, but if the goats headed down the driveway and the dog continued to chase them, no telling how far the animals could get before she found them. Meredith had no desire to be out in a thunderstorm.

As if on cue, a fat drop of rain hit her face. The echo of Marlin's barking got louder again, and she was two steps down the ladder when the goats came thundering around the barn's outer edge.

Maybe she'd get lucky and the little dog would herd them back into the barn. A few more raindrops fell from the sky, letting her know that her hour of productivity was over before it had started.

She called to Marlin, trying to distract him from the goats but catching Rachel's attention instead. A small yelp escaped her mouth when the farm animal changed directions and began barreling right toward the ladder. Meredith was still too high to jump so tried to scramble down, keeping an eye on Rachel. Instead her shoelace caught on one of the rungs, and she lost her balance, careening backward at the same time that Rachel butted her head against the ladder.

The seconds of her fall ticked by with exquisite slowness. Her stomach pitched, giving her a sense of weightlessness as if she were a baby bird launched from a nest and ready to take flight.

Only she had no wings. With a gasping breath, she shifted and reached out a hand to break her fall. Like that would work. She heard the snap in her wrist at almost the same time the sensation of burning pain shot up her arm. Then she landed in a crumpled heap, the wind knocked out of her lungs. Was it the pain or the impact that kept her from drawing in a full breath?

Either way she struggled to take in air, worked to not heave up the handful of Goldfish crackers one of the schoolchildren had shared with her. Then the ladder landed on top of her: more pain, although nothing in comparison to the stabbing ache of her arm.

She didn't even have the strength to push the metal off her, let alone to drag her body up and to the house to call for help. Of course she'd left her cell phone on the kitchen counter so she wouldn't be distracted on the roof.

Marlin got to her first, whining and pacing. Gracie showed up next, alerted to her distress, and showered her cheeks with doggy kisses like that would make her all better. Those two were soon joined by Buster, and Meredith cursed herself for not locking up the dogs before she'd started on this project. Who in their right mind climbed a ten-foot ladder with three dogs running loose below them?

She managed to roll to her back as the rain started in earnest. She struggled to pull air in and out of her lungs, telling herself she had to get up.

In a minute.

The dogs stayed with her, still whining, clearly aware something wasn't right. Thunder cracked overhead. Gracie, who'd always been afraid of storms, cowered close to Meredith's side.

Get up, she ordered herself, even as darkness crept along the edge of her vision. She couldn't just lie in the dirt with a metal ladder on top of her during a thunderstorm. It didn't take a college degree to know that was a bad idea.

This whole thing had been a bad idea. She should have listened to Ryan and found a way to hire a professional. She should have listened to her dad and brothers back when they'd told her that managing the farm would be too much on her own. To the estate attorney who'd explained that if she would just move her operation to a small property away from the beach, they could make the money to pay off most of Niall's debt. She should have listened to her inner voice—the one that sounded like her mother—when it said that giving up was easier.

She gave a half-hearted push at the ladder with her legs.

She managed to slide it to one side but stayed on the ground when the effort to move more proved too painful. Then she heard the rumble of a car coming closer. It was the most beautiful sound she'd ever heard. With a silent prayer of thanks, she closed her eyes.

CHAPTER FOURTEEN

RYAN NEARLY SAGGED with relief when Meredith's eyelids fluttered open a few moments later as he picked her up to carry her through the pouring rain.

"Hurts," she whispered.

"I know, honey." He dropped a kiss on the top of her head but didn't break his pace. He opened the passenger-side door and then positioned her inside as gently as he could manage. She moaned softly, and the sound cut through him like a scalpel blade.

"I fell."

"I gathered that," he told her. "And your wrist needs some attention. We've got to get you to the hospital. Will you be okay here for a few minutes?"

"The goats…"

He nodded, not surprised that in the midst of her obvious pain, her thoughts still went to taking care of the animals. "I'm going to put away the animals, and then we'll be on our way. You good?"

"Never better," she said, glancing down at her wrist. "My phone…kitchen counter."

"I'll grab that, too." One benefit of having a goat half in love with him was that Rachel, who'd taken shelter inside the barn with her partners in crime, was happy to follow him to the stall. Monica and Phoebe followed. He closed the door on the goats, then led the trio of wet dogs into the house and shut them in the laundry room. He plucked her phone from the counter and jogged back to his car, then climbed into the front seat and started down the driveway.

Meredith rolled her head to the side to look at him. "I'm sorry to be a pain in the—"

"Stop. No apologies. You're going to be fine." He placed a hand on the wet fabric of her jeans, noticing when a shiver ran through her. "How bad is the pain?"

She managed a wan smile. "I think the adrenaline is keeping it at bay. Or maybe it's not actually broken. Could be a sprain."

"I'm almost positive it's broken," Ryan told her, pulling out his phone when they got to the end of the driveway. "That's what happens when you take chances on your own with a ladder and a rainstorm."

"You have a sucky bedside manner," she told him with a frown.

"Duly noted." He punched in Paul Thorpe's number, grateful when the other doctor picked up on the first ring. Paul assumed Ryan was calling to discuss the mobile medical clinic but switched gears without missing a beat when Ryan explained what had happened—or what he thought had happened to Meredith.

Obviously a fall from the ladder, but he didn't know how high up she'd been and wasn't going to ask until later when his emotions weren't so chaotic. He was an emergency-room physician and had dealt with horrendous injuries, but pulling up to the barn and seeing Meredith sprawled on the ground had been a shock.

Based on Ryan's explanation of the situation, Paul promised to have an exam room ready and have the on-call orthopedic surgeon prepped for a consult.

Meredith's eyes were closed when Ryan ended the call. "I don't want surgery," she said, her voice hoarse. "No time for that."

"You're going to have to make time if the hand surgeon says it's necessary. From the look of it, I don't think the fracture is displaced, so surgery might not be necessary. How is your head?"

"Pretty good other than the herd of horses stampeding through it."

"I checked, and there are no bumps, but that doesn't mean you weren't concussed in the fall."

"Didn't hit my head," she said, her voice tight. "Knocked the wind out of me, but my head is fine."

"You're still going to get a CT scan as well as the wrist X-ray."

"That sounds expensive, and I have a crazy-high deductible."

"Don't worry about that," he said, taking a turn when the GPS prompted him. He'd punched in the hospital's address after Paul gave it to him.

"Easy for you to say. You're rich and probably have great benefits."

His gaze darted to hers. "I'm not rich."

"Come on. All doctors are rich."

He blew out a breath. Of course, she was talking about his profession, not his family money. Ryan wasn't sure why it mattered to him that she didn't know the wealth he'd come from, but it did. "I do okay," he said by way of answer.

"Can't you just give me a sling and some good pain meds? I'll heal up just fine."

"Do you want me to call your dad or your sisters?" he asked. No point arguing the right course of treatment for her wrist. He'd seen plenty of people deny that they needed medical attention due to fear. The hospital staff would take care of her.

"I'd rather no one know. Can we say I was attacked by a gaggle of postapocalyptic beach zombies and fought them off with my bare hands? Falling off a ladder because I lost my balance at the same time a goat knocked into it doesn't quite have the same ring."

He pulled into the hospital's parking lot and headed for the ER. "Beach zombies? If this is your train of thought now, I can't imagine how bad it's going to get when you have drugs in your system."

"I don't want drugs." She shook her head, then let out a low groan and winced. "As soon as things dry out, I need to be back on the roof, so we stay on track for the site visit."

"You aren't going back on that roof." He parked the car just outside the entrance to the hospital's emergency room.

"You aren't the boss of me," she countered, but there was no fight in her words.

Meredith was a smart woman, and no doubt she understood what this injury meant for her ability to work around the rescue as her wrist healed. He also understood not wanting to deal with the harsh truths of reality. Hell, he'd run away from his own life to the beach in order to distract himself from a recovery that was taking too long for his taste.

"Don't I know it," he answered, then climbed out of the car and greeted Aimee Baker, who approached with an empty wheelchair.

"I can walk," Meredith insisted when Ryan opened the passenger door to help her out.

"Humor me," he said, then sucked in a breath when she seemed to have trouble balancing. She gave a small whimper of pain, and he didn't hesitate before scooping her into his arms again.

"Wheelchair," Aimee said in a wry voice.

"Show me where to go," Ryan answered.

To his surprise, Meredith didn't protest or insist that he put her down, which told him all he needed to know about her level of pain.

Aimee led Ryan through the double doors that opened with a swish. Paul was waiting at the registration desk. "Send the paperwork back to exam three," he told the receptionist. "We'll get her checked in while I examine the wrist. The X-ray tech is on his way."

Meredith shook her head. "Just so you know, I don't want surgery."

"Hopefully it won't be necessary," Paul said.

"She'll have the surgery if she needs it," Ryan muttered.

"Bully," she snapped.

"Sticks and stones," he countered and tightened his hold on her. She sighed and rested her head on his chest. A few seconds later, Aimee opened the door to an empty exam room, and Ryan strode in behind Paul and then deposited Meredith gently on the examination table.

"We're going to take good care of you," Aimee promised, her voice soothing.

Paul nodded. "I'm guessing Ryan wouldn't have it any other way."

MEREDITH WOKE SLOWLY, like swimming to the surface after a deep dive in a shimmering lake. Her head felt fuzzy, and she drew in a deep breath, confused by the unfamiliar medicinal scent in the air.

She blinked several times to clear the cotton from her mind as flashes of memory rushed back. The ladder, the goats, her fall and Ryan. Most of all Ryan with her through the pain and fear. Despite everything else, she'd had no doubt that he'd take care of her.

He had without hesitation, and it had felt strange to let someone else take over for a time. Even when Meredith was in no shape to be in charge, that was what she was used to…her familiar place.

"Welcome, back," a kind voice said, and Aimee, the nurse who'd greeted them at the hospital entrance, stepped into her line of vision. "How are you doing?"

Meredith did a quick assessment of her body. The stabbing pain from earlier was gone, and she lifted her left arm to find it encased in a cast from the base of her hand to her elbow. "Fine, I think. Better."

"Dr. Barthel is the best," the nurse told her. "He did the reduction with no problem. You'll heal up better than before."

Right. The orthopedic surgeon had diagnosed her with a distal radius fracture, typical after falling on an outstretched hand. He'd determined that she didn't need surgery but suggested something called a closed reduction to manipulate the fractured fragments back into alignment before casting the wrist. They'd given her a sedative, and that was the last thing she remembered until now.

"Are you nauseous?" The nurse wrote something on the chart she held.

"No." Meredith glanced around the hospital room. "What time is it?"

"Almost seven," the nurse answered.

"I need to go." She tried to force her heavy limbs to move. Ryan had called Avery when they'd arrived at the hospital, and she'd asked him to call Shae as well, to take care of the animals. She couldn't for the life of her remember if the girl had answered, and the idea that her babies had been left alone for most of the day made her chest tighten with anxiety.

"Ice chips, and then the doctor will check in with you," the nurse said calmly. "After that you'll be discharged."

"You don't understand. I need to go."

"Would you like to see your family?" Aimee ignored Meredith's plea. "They'll want to know you're awake."

"Yes," she answered automatically, even though she had no idea who would be waiting to see her. Her father? Had Ryan called him, too?

As the nurse stepped out of the room, Meredith did her best to control her breathing. The door opened not more than a minute later, and her dad, Avery and Carrie filed in, all of them sharing the same look of concern.

A pang of disappointment pierced Meredith's chest when the door shut behind Carrie. Obviously Ryan had gotten sick of babysitting her and dealing with her high-maintenance adventures.

She smiled as her sisters flanked the bed with her father at the foot, looking worried and relieved in equal measure. "Tell me you didn't climb on the barn roof in the rain," he said, his voice gruff.

"I didn't." She picked at the edge of the cast with one finger. "It started raining after I was on the roof."

Carl muttered a curse, earning twin smiles from Avery

and Carrie. "How do you feel?" Carrie asked, placing a gentle hand on Meredith's arm.

"Like I need to get out of here and feed the animals. The puppies—"

"Are fine," Avery assured her. "Ryan called a few minutes ago for an update. He said everyone at the rescue is good."

"Ryan?"

"Hot doctor," Avery clarified. "From all reports, he carried you into the hospital with the same intensity as Heathcliff striding over the moors."

"The nurses are all atwitter," Carrie added, squeezing Meredith's arm.

"Ridiculous," Meredith's father grumbled. "Both that you weren't just wheeled in like a normal patient and that a trip to the hospital was even necessary. I thought we agreed that you'd hire out the roof."

"I never agreed," Meredith said. "Especially not after an unexpected litter of puppies and the vet bills that came with it. I twisted my ankle in the fall, which is why Ryan was helping me." She raised her injured arm. "At least the ankle is just a mild sprain. I'll deal with the wrist, and I'm plenty capable of putting a new roof on the barn. If the dogs and the goats and—"

"Dogs and goats," Carl interrupted. "That's exactly my point. No one with a lick of sense does a roofing job with dogs and goats running around."

Meredith's cheeks burned. She understood her father was worried and his harsh tone came from fear. But she was already embarrassed about the stupid decision she'd made not to lock up the dogs. "I didn't think about it," she said quietly.

"We're just glad you're okay," Carrie said with a pointed look toward Carl. For someone who was sweet as apple pie, Carrie could level a disapproving stare like a professional.

Her dad scrubbed a hand over his scruffy jaw. "Of course we're glad. You scared the hell out of me, Pup. I'm an old man. My heart can't take your escapades. It was bad enough when you were a girl. I thought you had more sense now."

Somehow her father could make a declaration of love sound like a judgment. "I have plenty of sense. I have to get that roof on before the site visit from the foundation next week. The whole place needs to look perfect. Or as perfect as I can make it." She waved her arms in front of her, or tried to, then winced at the pain.

"Take it easy," her father said. "Things will work out. What's most important right now is making sure you're on the mend."

"I'm fine," she insisted, frustrated by the attention. She hated feeling like a burden to people who already did and gave her so much.

"Your dad is right," Carrie said. "Your recovery is most important. I can help cover the cost of hiring out the roof."

Meredith shook her head, trying to swallow back the tears that clogged her throat. "I don't want you to help."

At Carrie's frown, Meredith sighed. "I appreciate it, but this is my problem."

"I'm your sister." Carrie said the words softly, like it pained her to have to remind Meredith of that fact.

"We both are," Avery added. "Don't leave me out in the cold, here."

Meredith's father cleared his throat from the end of the bed. "I have first dibs on her, ladies. She's my baby girl."

Meredith swiped at her cheeks. "Stupid pain medicine is making my eyes water," she said through her tears.

"That's exactly right." Avery handed her a tissue just as the nurse walked back into the room.

"Am I interrupting?" Aimee asked, one brow raised. "Or can we start the discharge process so you can go home?"

"Home for sure," Meredith answered.

"Clear the room, then," the nurse told her sisters and father. "She'll be out in a few minutes after the doctor sees her."

"Will you call Ryan and tell him he doesn't have to stay?" Meredith asked Avery as she backed away from the bed. "If he's checked on the animals, they'll be fine until I get home."

"Sure," Avery said slowly, then motioned for Carrie to follow Meredith's dad out of the room before turning back to Meredith. "Do you have any memory of how our favorite cutie-pie doc was acting with you when they were prepping you for surgery?"

"He found me after I fell," Meredith said, glancing between Avery and the nurse. "And drove me here. He called Dr. Thorpe to help coordinate everything. Why do you two keep looking at each other?"

Avery shrugged. "I don't think Ryan is looking for an excuse to ditch you at this point, Mer."

"I've seen a lot of people come through those ER doors," the nurse said, "when someone they love has been hurt. Ryan was as protective as any boyfriend I've witnessed."

"He's not my boyfriend," Meredith muttered, but the nurse just laughed while Avery gave her a *Whatever you say, girl* look and left the room.

She wasn't sure exactly what Ryan was in her life at

the moment, but she knew she wanted to keep him for the weeks he remained in Magnolia. She couldn't allow the way he'd taken care of her today to mean something other than him being a good doctor. Then, she might have to admit that her heart longed for more than a temporary arrangement. There was no way to force him into becoming a man he wasn't willing or able to be for her, no matter how much she might want it.

CHAPTER FIFTEEN

"YOU SHOULDN'T BE ALONE."

"Carrie will be here within the hour." Meredith lifted her casted arm as if that range of movement would prove to Ryan she could handle herself.

They'd been arguing for the past thirty minutes over whether he was going to leave for his shift at the mobile medical clinic or cancel so he could stay with her after her coworker from the vet office called to say he couldn't help her at the rescue due to a stomach bug.

"What if something happens between now and then?" he demanded, pacing back and forth in front of her kitchen table.

"Like what?" Meredith popped the last bite of bacon into her mouth.

"Like you decide to climb up on the roof now that the sun is out and start hammering shingles with one good arm."

"I could do it," she said, narrowing her eyes. "Do you doubt that I could manage?"

"It wasn't a challenge." Ryan drew in what looked to be a calming breath. "You are the most infuriatingly stubborn woman I've ever met."

"Determined," she corrected. "I prefer the word *determined*."

He looked as though he wanted to throttle her, but then

one side of his mouth quirked into an almost smile that set her pulse racing.

Meredith might be stubborn in a lot of areas, but she couldn't force her body not to react to Ryan even in her weakened state. He'd been a fixture, more than usual, at her house and around the rescue since her accident two days earlier. He'd taken on the bulk of the work with the animals in addition to acting as her personal chef and all-around right-hand man. He'd even helped her wash her hair over the kitchen sink the previous night. She hated being dependent on anyone, but Ryan made it seem like she was doing him the favor by allowing him to feel useful.

"Determined," he repeated, "to send me over the edge of reason."

"You sound like a tut-tutting grandma fussing over me."

"I don't tut." He took a step closer and smoothed a hand over her cast, then lifted her fingers and brushed a soft kiss across her knuckles. She worked not to sigh with pleasure. "But I do worry."

"I'm fine," she said for what felt like the millionth time in the past couple of days. It amazed her how fast news about her injury had spread, leading to a steady stream of people who'd called or shown up to offer help. From the mayor to her fifth-grade teacher, Mrs. Bales, to at least a dozen people who'd adopted animals from Furever Friends, Meredith's life had never felt so crowded.

Up until Avery and Carrie, she'd felt like a loner in town. Sure, she had her dad and brothers, although Erik and Theo had rarely returned to Magnolia once they moved away. But other than her work colleagues, she didn't have many friends in town. Or so she'd thought.

The outpouring of support and a fridge filled with food

overwhelmed her. She had trouble believing that so many people really cared about her.

"Promise you won't push it too much," Ryan said, and it grated on her nerves how well he knew her. In the back of her mind, she had thought about tackling a small fence repair when she had a moment alone on the property.

She was used to doing things for herself, although she had to admit that most of her to-do list had been or was in the process of being checked off. In addition to covered casseroles, many of the visitors who came by also stayed to help with various projects.

In her normal, überorganized way, Avery had made a list of what needed to be handled before next week's site visit, and she'd rallied the community to pitch in where they could.

Meredith's first instinct had been to turn away the short-term volunteers who'd suddenly materialized. But when it became clear that people were bound and determined to contribute, she breathed a slow sigh of relief and let them.

The last major hurdle was the roof. Meredith's father had commandeered the managing of that project and assured her without any trace of judgment in his voice that he had a plan. She almost believed that her father wanted her to succeed at raising the funds she needed to expand the rescue.

"I'm not sure there's such a thing as too much pushing when twenty-five grand is on the line."

"No amount of money is worth you being hurt again," Ryan said.

"Spoken like a man who's never struggled to pay the bills."

"How do you know I haven't struggled?" His gaze shuttered. "Plenty of people are poor in med school."

She laughed. "You don't give off vibes of ever having been poor, even as a med student or resident."

"There aren't vibes for that sort of thing."

"It's called desperation. You don't have it."

He looked like he wanted to argue but shook his head. "The point is not whether I've been desperately poor. You aren't desperate, Mer. You've built an amazing organization that has done good things for people and animals in this community. The never-ending line of people wanting to pitch in and help is proof of that."

"It's a slow time in town." She shrugged, uncomfortable with the thought of being the center of attention. "The weather's unpredictable at best, and festival season won't really kick off until next month. They don't have anything better to do."

"They came because they want to help you. I do, too. In fact, I could finish the new exercise pen out back today if I didn't have to go in for the peds clinic. I'm sure Paul could find someone else to cover for me."

"You can't use me as an excuse." She knew she'd hit on the truth of his reluctance to leave when he looked away from her, jaw clenching.

"Stubborn and too smart for your own good," he said softly. "That's a dangerous combination."

"Dr. Thorpe needs your help." She straightened from the table and placed her palm on his cheek, forcing him to look at her again. "The pediatric clinic is going to help a lot of kids within the community."

"I know. I've just gotten out of the habit of being Dr. Sorensen. It was hard enough with the urgent-care clinic last week. Kids are a whole different ball game. I'm not sure how to…how to act like a normal doctor again." He frowned, as if he'd revealed too much. She understood his reluctance to open up, but something had changed between them since her accident. A deepening of their connection, like her injury bound them together in some strange way. It was stupid. She understood that without a doubt. He'd be gone—returned to his life in the big city—before her cast came off.

Yet despite the shocking outpouring of assistance from the town and the unwavering support of her sister and father, it was Ryan's presence that she relied on the most. Ever playing a silent game of quid pro quo in her mind, she wanted to do something for him. To support him in the way he did her. No, that wasn't exactly true. She wanted to support him because she cared. She'd care even if he didn't reciprocate the feeling. Even after he was gone.

"One patient at a time," she advised. "Trust me, you haven't shed your doctor persona, despite what you might think. You're bossy and demanding, and I need you to have someone to fuss over besides me."

"You weren't complaining about my demands last night." His eyes darkened as he leaned in to kiss her.

Meredith's skin heated at the memory of sharing her bed with him. The night of her accident, he'd insisted on staying with her—on the couch—in case she needed anything or the pain got out of hand. She'd refused to fill the prescriptions the surgeon had given her because she didn't want to experience the side effects of the pain pills. But even though she was already feeling much better, she'd asked him to stay last night as well, this time in her bed.

"Stop trying to distract me." She pushed away, wagging a finger at him. "You need to leave so you won't be late for your shift."

"Who's bossy now?"

"I'll walk you out," she told him with a wink.

He grabbed his phone and then his white lab coat. He'd gone to the cottage earlier and brought over a change of clothes. Meredith could imagine women flinging themselves into the ER just for the chance of being seen by Dr. Sorensen. He looked almost too handsome to be a doctor in real life. TV-doctor handsome, like he should have some sort of Mc-Something nickname.

"I feel you checking out my butt," he said as she followed him out the front door.

"Just wondering if the mamas who have appointments for their kids today know what awaits them."

He kissed her again. "My phone will be on silent, but I'll check for messages when I get a break. You have the number for the mobile clinic if there's an emergency."

"The only emergency might be Rachel's temper tantrum when she realizes you've left." The goat had become even more smitten with Ryan in the past couple of days, if that were possible. Meredith had an appointment scheduled for a family who'd just purchased a farm a few miles away to visit the three goats tomorrow morning. She worried that Rachel's bond with Ryan would make it tough to adjust to life without him. Meredith knew the feeling.

"Tell her I'll be back soon." He waved and headed for his car.

"Have fun storming the castle," Meredith called, quoting from one of her favorite movies. She'd always wanted to use the line but never had an opportunity since she lived alone.

To her surprise and delight, Ryan glanced over his shoulder and said, "As you wish."

He got her reference? A man with a medical degree who

looked like a movie star, had cantankerous goats falling in love with him, was a world-class kisser and could quote Buttercup's beloved Wesley. How was Meredith's heart supposed to stand a chance?

AN HOUR LATER, Meredith walked out of the barn with two of her newer canine-rescue residents on leashes. She'd heard a car pulling down the drive and assumed it was Carrie, even though her sister texted shortly after Ryan left to say she was running late.

The dogs, Labrador mixes, cowered as gravel sprayed from the unfamiliar truck. The pups were nearly nine months old, brought to her by a shelter in Raleigh because they needed more socializing than the facility could handle. The dogs had been, at best, ignored for most of their young lives, and based on their behavior, she suspected abuse. She'd videotaped her training sessions to submit as an addendum to her grant application for the Howard Family Foundation. She hoped that if the dogs had a breakthrough before the site visit, it would help prove that while she might not have the degrees or formal training of an experienced shelter manager, her success with animals was enough to earn the foundation's support.

There were no appointments scheduled for the morning, so she wasn't sure who she expected to climb out of the truck. Her heart skipped a beat at the familiar tousle of caramel-colored hair, shorter than he normally wore it but still thick and standing up in all directions.

"Theo," she breathed, her fingers trembling.

Her oldest brother slammed shut the door, took in the house and the barn before turning to her. He wore a denim shirt, faded jeans and aviator sunglasses over eyes she knew were brilliant blue. The color of a perfect summer sky.

"Pupsqueak," he said with the easy smile she remembered from childhood. A smile she hadn't seen in far too long.

She wanted to run to him and throw herself into his arms. Meredith had spent most of her childhood tagging along behind Theo, Erik and their friends, wanting desperately to fit in with her oh-so-cool older brothers. They'd been patient with her—mostly—until puberty hit and they got wilder and started to drive and wanted nothing to do with their pesky younger sister. She'd been an annoyance at best and in the way more times than she could count.

Then there had been the awful night her sophomore year, at a party she had no business attending with a boy who'd played football with her brothers for years. Someone she'd known for most of her life. After that, things had changed. She'd changed, of course, and she'd vowed that neither of her brothers would ever know the details. Her reputation had turned south, and she hadn't bothered to worry about that, either. She'd worn her rebellion like a badge of honor. If she made the lies into truths, then the awful things boys said about her couldn't hurt.

But she'd almost buckled under the weight of her brothers' disappointment. She'd stopped answering their calls and texts, stayed in her room when they came home to visit, then gone off to college and tried to forget everything about her past. That had been a colossal failure.

By the time she returned home, the rift between them felt vast, and none of them bothered to bridge the distance. Theo joined the Marines, and Erik moved to Wilmington to build a life away from Magnolia. That hadn't stopped her from missing them.

"Nice dogs." Theo took a step closer.

"I think they were mistreated and have a ways to go before they're ready for adoption." The two animals cowered behind her legs. "Issues with men for one. You can help me socialize them." The smaller of the two suddenly tugged on the leash, and Meredith took an unsteady step to her right.

"For the love of God, don't go down again." Theo rushed forward, which only served to whip the dogs into more of a frenzy. They pulled, and the leash twisted around her legs. Meredith steadied herself by digging in her heels. "Watch your arm, Mer."

"I've got it." She held up her cast. "Just don't come closer. Let them get used to you." She talked softly to the dogs, making sure they knew she was in control, until they started to relax.

"Meredith, this is too much. You're doing too much. Dad said you were going to take it easy." Theo lifted his sunglasses onto the top of his head so she could read the disapproving stare he was sending her. As if she couldn't hear the censure in his voice loud and clear.

"I'm resting plenty. Half the town has been out here with offers to help. I've had more people wanting to scoop poop in the past forty-eight hours than you could shake a stick at."

"They're your friends," Theo said, and she almost laughed at the absurdity of that statement. Her brothers had always had such an easy time with popularity. They were handsome and charming, and everyone loved them, even when they got into trouble.

She hadn't made friends easily, and she couldn't exactly explain why. Maybe it was the scars from her mother leaving or being raised in a house bursting with testosterone. Meredith didn't seem to understand the cadence of female friendships. She pushed too hard or too far, spoke too bluntly. She'd been one of the boys and then the girl all the boys wanted to date once her reputation got out of hand. Girls didn't seem to trust her, and until Avery and Carrie, she'd never felt like she had true friends. Her brother knew this. Or maybe he didn't. Maybe the men in her family never realized how alone she felt.

"What are you doing here, Theo?" she asked, crouching down to give the two dogs a confidence-bolstering nuzzle. "Come closer, slowly, and put out your hand so they can sniff you."

He did what she said without question, which felt like a strange sort of victory. She was used to her brothers ignoring her requests and having to force them to take her seriously. One of the dogs, Brodie, whined softly but moved forward, pushing his wet nose against Theo's outstretched fingers.

"I'm here to see you," Theo answered, grimacing slightly when the dog licked his palm.

"That's good. He likes you." Meredith straightened. "To see me and give me crap about taking care of myself? Dad has that angle covered."

"To see you and to figure out how much manpower we need to bust out your new roof."

Meredith's mouth dropped open. "No."

Her brother had the nerve to look affronted. "What do you mean, *no*? You need a roof, and I've got men ready to work."

"Dad said he was going to hire a crew."

"I'm the foreman of that crew."

"No," Meredith repeated, then let out a string of curses that had her brother grinning.

"I taught you most of those words," he said proudly.

"Not the point. How much is he paying you for this?"

Theo's blue eyes narrowed. "Why can't I volunteer to help like the rest of the town?"

"You don't even live here anymore. What about your actual life?"

"Don't worry about me, and I can't believe you're fighting me on this." Theo scratched Brodie under his chin. The dog leaned in, although Benji remained unconvinced about Theo and retreated behind Meredith's legs.

"I'm not a charity case," she said through clenched teeth.

"That isn't what this is about."

"You think the rescue is stupid," she reminded him. "I remember clearly your opinion of me opening the organization, especially because of renting this property from Niall Reed." She lifted her casted arm again to point a finger at him. "You knew, Theo. You and Erik, both. Why didn't you tell me?"

Her brother stared at her for a long moment, then sighed. "We didn't know for sure because Dad wouldn't talk about it. But we had suspicions. Why would we tell you? It wouldn't have changed anything. We had no reason to believe Niall was ever going to say anything, let alone drop that bombshell in his will."

She kept her expression neutral as memories from the days after discovering the truth about Niall Reed assailed her. Her dad's anger, her anger, the way her brothers seemed to turn on her like she'd done something to purposely hurt their father. How alone she'd felt until she got to know Avery and Carrie.

"I'm sorry, Pup," Theo said, like he read her thoughts, anyway. "None of us handled it very well."

"You told me I was hurting Dad."

Theo's jaw clenched. "He ended up in the ER with chest pains."

"I didn't do that," she insisted despite her lingering guilt. "I didn't ask for what happened, and neither did Avery or Carrie."

"Your half-sisters," he said, and the sadness in his voice cut across her chest like a knife. "Dad says you've gotten close to them. I remember when you hated Carrie Reed like it was your job."

"I've grown up," Meredith answered simply. "They weren't anymore at fault in this situation than me." Benji whined softly. "It's not my fault, Theo."

"I never knew having sisters was that important to you. Brothers weren't enough?"

"Don't do that."

He scrubbed a hand over his jaw, a gesture so like their father's it made the dull ache in her chest expand like a balloon. "I didn't come here to fight with you."

"Yet, here we are again. I'm not going to apologize for getting to know my sisters."

"Half," he mumbled.

"They don't take away from how I feel about you and Erik."

"How do you feel?" he demanded. "Because I have at least a dozen unreturned calls and texts to you. Christmas was awkward for all of us. It seems like you've moved on to your new, better family."

"That's not true, and it's not fair. I miss you, Theo. Both of my brothers. But I know you blame me and—"

"For what?" He inclined his head. "Are we still talking about Niall?"

"Mom," she said softly, then looked down, unable to hold his gaze and unwilling to see the judgment there. The dogs had settled, both of them lying at her feet, happy to sun themselves and seemingly unaware of the tension radiating from the woman holding their leashes. That was good. She needed them to be able to relax in whatever circumstances they encountered.

"What does any of this have to do with Mom?" Theo took one of the leashes from her hand. "Show me the property while you explain your convoluted logic when it comes to our mother."

The animals hopped up, and Brodie glanced between Meredith and Theo and then clearly decided it was okay for him to be holding the leash. More progress. Too bad Meredith was so emotionally mixed-up she could barely register the win.

"It always comes back to her," she said, not bothering to hide the bitterness in her tone. "Her leaving. Dad not being my real father."

"He's your father," Theo countered. "In all the ways that count. Just like I'm your brother."

She turned fully to face him. "You have no idea how much I want to believe you."

"Then, believe me." He looped an arm around her shoulder. "No more fighting. Show me your place and the animals and, most importantly, the roof. You might be stubborn, but you learned it from me."

CHAPTER SIXTEEN

"THAT'S OUR LAST patient of the day," Megan said as the door to the clinic shut behind a mother and her twin toddler boys. The pediatric nurse had been working alongside Ryan for the day, and he was grateful for her assistance and her knowledge of the community.

Paul, who'd arrived about fifteen minutes earlier to check on things, looked up from his laptop and nodded at Ryan. "You two did good work today."

"Megan gets all the credit." Ryan finished washing his hands. "She has a way with kids. I probably would have had them all in tears if I'd been left on my own."

"We make a great team." She winked, and Ryan wondered—not for the first time today—if the pretty nurse was flirting with him.

"Let's celebrate." Paul glanced at his watch. "It's game night at the brewery in town. Aimee and a few of our friends are meeting there for a drink and a shuffleboard tournament. I'll introduce you to more of our team."

Ryan smiled past the tightening in his gut. "I'm not much of a team player."

"Come on," Megan urged. "One drink. It won't kill you."

"Unless you need to rest your leg," Paul said. "Is it bothering you?"

Ryan felt his temper spike at the question but then realized he was unconsciously pressing two fingers to the back of his leg. "No," he answered honestly. "It might be sore later, but right now, I feel completely normal."

Physically, anyway. In contrast, his emotions pinged like a pinball shot off a spring-loaded rod. He hadn't known what to expect from today. Staffing a pediatric clinic was 180 degrees from his normal caseload in the ER, but he'd actually liked the slower pace and the chance to interact with parents and their kids.

It was progress. More than he'd made hiding away in the cottage by himself. He felt useful in a different way than he did working around Meredith's property. That was a physical and mental distraction, but seeing patients—even for routine vaccinations—made him feel like he was truly doing something that fulfilled his purpose in life.

"I think a couple of those mamas were excited to be face-to-face with our big-city hero," Megan said as she packed up her things.

Ryan blinked. "What are you talking about? No one around here knows my background."

"Oh, Doc." She patted his arm in the same way she might comfort a nervous child. "Welcome to life in Magnolia. Everyone here knows all about you."

Ryan darted a glance at Paul, who shrugged. "I put the word out at the hospital that we had a real expert volunteering with the clinic for the next couple of weeks. Thought it might help encourage more people to make appointments."

"I'm no more of an expert than anyone else from the local medical community," Ryan answered.

"You're still a draw." Megan blew out a laugh. "You didn't think it was odd that we got so many plates of baked goods and casseroles?"

"I figured it was Southern hospitality." Ryan massaged a hand along the back of his neck. Meredith had gotten food after returning from the hospital, so he thought it was simply custom in a small town. "Do you know that one of the moms had her number written on the aluminum foil along with the baking instructions?"

"That's bold," Paul said with a chuckle.

"Evelyn Cusma," Megan clarified. "She makes a mean tater-tot casserole."

"Stop." Ryan shook his head, then pointed at Paul. "I didn't think you were a Magnolia native. How do you know so much about people around here?"

"Like Megan said, it's a small town." Paul placed a stack of flyers on the counter. "A close-knit community. We take care of each other, and part of that is getting to know people."

"That's not how medicine works in DC," Ryan told them. "At least, not in my hospital."

"You liked today." Paul pointed a finger in Ryan's direction. "Admit that you liked it."

"I did."

"And you'll have a drink with us," Megan insisted with a coaxing smile. "It will be fun."

"Let me just check and make sure Meredith isn't alone."

Megan frowned at that and then looped her bag over one shoulder. "I'm going to head over to the bar. I expect to see you both there. Bring your girlfriend if you want."

Ryan blinked. "She's not my girlfriend."

Megan studied him for a long moment. "Even better."

The call to Meredith went straight to voice mail, so Ryan left a message, then sent her a quick text.

"You've got dibs on the dog lady, a gaggle of mommies

swooning over you, and our best pediatric nurse sending googly eyes across the exam table." Paul grinned. "You work fast, Sorensen. It took me ages and a ridiculous bachelor auction to work up my nerve with Aimee."

"You lost me at bachelor auction." Ryan shook his head. "Megan wasn't giving me any kind of eyes. Meredith and I are friends, and I'm no match for any of your local moms."

"Come on." Paul flipped off the lights, then held the van's door open for Ryan. "Megan is definitely into you."

"Not interested." Ryan had no intention of telling the other man how he couldn't stop thinking about Meredith and the way he felt when he was with her. Paul seemed to accept Ryan's claim of friendship, and it was best to leave it at that, for his sake as well as Paul's.

"Let's grab that beer," Paul suggested with a knowing smile, "and you can tell me all about why you're not cut out for a relationship."

"I'll go for the beer, but I draw the line at talking about feelings. I'll take a dozen more screaming babies over the thought of that."

"Fair enough." Paul nodded. "I'll see you at the bar."

Ryan checked his phone again before heading downtown, but still no response from Meredith. Worry snaked along the back of his neck, but he pushed it aside. She was probably busy in the barn or hanging out with her sister. Hell, for all he knew she was glad to have a break from him. The fact that she'd practically pushed him out the door this morning hadn't escaped his notice.

He wanted to believe she'd been supporting him, but what if she was just happy that he wouldn't be underfoot for a few hours? Ryan had never felt dedicated to anyone the way he did Meredith, and it probably wasn't healthy for either of them.

His thoughts continued to swirl around the drain as he drove through town. He parked behind Paul's SUV in a lot around the corner from the bar. "Quite a crowd," he said, surveying the crowded tables on the enclosed patio out front and the steady stream of people moving in and out.

"Things are picking up around here," Paul told him. "Your friend Meredith and her sisters have had a lot to do with it. When I first arrived almost three years ago, Magnolia was like a ghost town. But in the past six months, a different energy has emerged. Apparently there's some new outdoor company looking to move its headquarters here. That's good news for the local economy, which means the hospital and the mobile clinic will be able to get more funding."

"Glad to hear it."

"In fact…" Paul stopped on the sidewalk a few doors down from the bar's entrance and turned to face Ryan. "Maybe you could put in a good word for us with your family."

Ryan felt his stomach drop. "What do you mean?"

"The community health-care grant," Paul clarified. "We're applying for it."

"Nobody in Magnolia knows about my ties to the foundation." Ryan forced his expression to remain neutral.

"Is it a secret?" Paul studied him. "I heard Furever Friends had been short-listed for their annual local-business grant."

"I don't want to talk about the foundation," Ryan said. "It's a family obligation, nothing more."

"Hey, I get wanting to make your own way, but you've

done that. I'm just saying that if you happen to talk to anyone in your family, you might mention the clinic."

"I will," Ryan said. How else was he supposed to answer? He knew he couldn't explain his feelings about the Howard Family Foundation to someone who hadn't been raised by Duffy Howard's bitter son-in-law. "But…uh… who else knows?"

"Just me." Paul raised a brow. "Are you worried the ladies will flock to you even more if they know how much you're worth?"

"My family's financial situation doesn't change how much I'm worth." Ryan said the words through gritted teeth. He'd done all he could to distance himself from his grandfather's legacy. If there was one thing his father had drummed into him from a young age, it was that he shouldn't want, need or expect to ride on the coattails of his grandfather's success. It was why he'd chosen a career path that had nothing to do with his family.

But he could make that argument until he was blue in the face. Once people knew about his family money, everything changed. If Meredith found out that he'd been the one to submit the rescue for consideration…well, he had no idea how she'd react, but his gut told him it wouldn't go over well.

"No more shoptalk," Paul said, clapping him on the back.

They entered the busy bar, and Paul immediately headed for the back. "We're meeting by the shuffleboard tables," he said over his shoulder.

Ryan followed, feeling his shoulders relax as the festive mood of the place infused him. He'd only taken a few steps when his gaze snagged on a group of people near the far end of the scuffed wood bar. He recognized Carrie and

Dylan, but his breath caught when he realized the woman being pulled into a playful headlock by the man standing next to Dylan was Meredith.

"Guessing you didn't know she'd be here," Paul said. He'd turned around and followed Ryan's gaze.

"Doesn't matter," Ryan said, running a hand through his hair. "We're here for a beer with coworkers. Let's go."

"ISN'T THAT YOUR handsome doctor?" Carrie asked, staring at a spot over Meredith's shoulder.

"I don't have a handsome doctor," Meredith said even as she turned around to search the crowded bar, her stomach fluttering at the mere mention of Ryan. Despite her sister's warning, it shocked her to see him amidst a group of people, laughing at something a pretty woman said into his ear. "Ryan isn't mine." Meredith turned back to Carrie. "Clearly."

"What's up?" Theo asked, elbowing her. "You want to play shuffleboard?"

"No." She shook her head and picked up the margarita she'd been nursing since they arrived at the bar and downed half of it in one swallow.

"Damn," her brother murmured. "Good thing I'm driving."

"Help me choose some songs on the jukebox." Carrie linked her arm with Meredith's.

She allowed herself to be led through the groups of people toward the jukebox. The old machine had sat against the far wall since she used to come into the bar with her dad after community softball games when she was a kid. The Watering Hole was a local institution, although with the new influx of tourists and younger residents, the longtime owner, Ned Miller, had begun updating things. The bar now hosted karaoke and Jenga tournaments and served on tap regionally brewed beers and handcrafted liquors.

Meredith appreciated the renewed energy of the place, even if sometimes she felt like she wasn't quite cool enough to hang out there anymore.

It had been Theo's idea to invite Dylan and Carrie to meet them for a beer after he'd outlined his plan and time-line for replacing her roof. Apparently, Dylan had suggested that Carl call Theo to help with project. She knew Carrie's fiancé had been friends with her brothers back in high school but hadn't realized that they'd also been in contact since Dylan returned to Magnolia.

She tried not to let it hurt her feelings that Carrie hadn't mentioned it. According to her sister, Dylan had reached out to both Meredith's brothers when it became clear that he and Carrie were serious. Despite the tension within her family, she dearly loved both her brothers and wanted them to know Avery and Carrie.

Once Theo stopped giving her grief about overextending herself, they'd fallen back into the comfortable teasing and banter that had made her idolize him so much when she was a girl.

"You should go and talk to him." Carrie deposited quarters into the machine and chose her first song. "You said he called earlier."

"Yeah." Meredith blew out a breath. "I didn't answer. I didn't want him to think I needed him."

Carrie nudged Meredith's arm with her own. "Do you need him?"

"No," Meredith lied, pulling her casted arm closer to her body. Her first thought after Theo's arrival was to call

Ryan. To have his steady support calm her nerves and help her work though her complicated feelings about her family. But he didn't belong to her. They were friends. They had chemistry. Nothing more. It would be foolish to pretend it was anything else.

"Most of that group works at the hospital. It's not like he's gone out and made a whole new set of friends."

"Not my business if he has," Meredith grumbled. She recognized Paul Thorpe, his girlfriend, Aimee, and several of the other people in the group, so there was no reason for the jealousy that ricocheted through her. Ryan didn't owe her anything, and he had called and texted.

But the way her heart leaped at seeing his name on her screen and the intensity with which she'd missed him today scared her. She knew she needed to pull back before she fell for him. That wasn't a smart idea for either of them.

"You like him," Carrie said. "Your turn to pick a song."

Without thinking, Meredith punched in the code for an old Patsy Cline song.

"Fits my mood," she said when Carrie chuckled.

"You're not crazy," her sister told her.

"You know my history with guys." Meredith bit down on the inside of her cheek. "The reputation I had back in high school."

"A long time ago. For all of us. You like him, and there's nothing wrong with that."

"There is when he's leaving in a few weeks. I'm not going to let myself fall for someone who's not only here temporarily but also so far out of my league it's not funny."

"What does that mean?" Carrie turned to her as the first strains of the country song Carrie had chosen began to play over the bar's ancient speaker system.

"It's embarrassing how much you like Garth. You need better taste in music, Care-bear."

"I'm not going to be distracted by you trying to bait me. Why would you think Ryan's out of your league?"

Meredith threw up her hands. "Um, he's a successful doctor and also some kind of reluctant hero because of how he helped stop the gunman after his friend was shot." She ticked off the reasons she wasn't good enough for him on her fingers. "He doesn't talk much about his childhood, but I can tell he grew up with money. He's educated and refined, like you." She pointed a finger at her elegant sister. "He'd be perfect for you."

"Dylan would beg to differ." Carrie frowned. "All of those are excuses, external rationales that have nothing to do with how the two of you feel about each other."

"He feels like I'm a casual fling. That's all there is between us."

"I don't believe you. Go talk to him." Carrie glanced over Meredith's shoulder. "He keeps looking this way."

"I'd just embarrass him or myself." Meredith wanted to turn to see if her sister was telling the truth but forced her gaze to remain forward. "Did you notice Julie Fowler over there? She works in accounting at the hospital."

Carrie shrugged. "So what? We went to high school with her. It's a small town."

"I stole her boyfriend senior year," Meredith said. "He was looking for fun, so we hooked up at a party the weekend before prom. They broke up, and she skipped both prom and graduation because she was so distraught. She hates me."

"That was a long time ago."

"You weren't the only person I was awful to back then."

Meredith lowered her gaze, shame seeping through her like poison. "I had issues, and I took them out on nice girls."

"You're not the same person you used to be."

Meredith sighed, as always amazed by her sister's capacity for compassion. "Not everyone is as forgiving as you."

A couple walked up to the jukebox, and they headed back to Dylan and Theo. Or at least they would have, but a burly man stepped in front of Meredith. "I was hoping I'd see you around town after I spotted that article in the paper," he said, and bile rose in her throat. "Do you remember me?"

She shook her head even as recollection clung to her like a spiderweb. "Did you adopt an animal from my rescue?"

One side of his mouth curved into a nasty smile. "No, darlin'. That sounds a little G-rated for how we're acquainted."

Damn it. The way he called her *darlin'* made the fuzzy clouds of her memory solidify into a clear picture. A weekend in Charleston, a seedy dive bar and too many shots of tequila. Meredith was nothing if not an expert at the poker face. She gave him a cool once-over and shook her head. "I guess you're not that memorable."

She made to move past him, but he grabbed the biceps of her injured arm, tight enough to pinch. "Oh, but you are, firecracker. I think I'd like to get reacquainted, unless you want your friend with the stick up her butt to hear all about how good you are on your knees." He gave Carrie a leering grin. "Or maybe she'd like to join us."

Temper snapped in Meredith. It was one thing to insult her. She'd done plenty to deserve it. Carrie, on the other hand, was bright and pure, and if it took every ounce of strength Meredith possessed, her sister would remain untainted by this dirty piece of her past.

She rounded on him, then stumbled when he was yanked back, taking her with him a step until she tugged free of his grasp. A moment later he was on the ground with Ryan looming over him.

"You don't touch a woman who doesn't want to be touched," he said through clenched teeth.

"She wants it, pretty boy," the man—Meredith still couldn't remember his name—shot back. "Me and her got history."

"Not anymore."

"What the hell's going on?" Her brother appeared at her side at that instant, because this moment couldn't get any more humiliating. "What's your problem?" he demanded of Ryan, whose murderous gaze took in Theo, his arm wrapped protectively around Meredith.

"Break it up," Ned commanded, elbowing his way through the crowd that had gathered around them. "We don't want trouble."

"I was just having a friendly conversation." The man on the floor climbed to his feet. "And this guy came after me for no reason."

Ned eyed Ryan, clearly suspicious of the accusation, then turned to Meredith. "He needs to go." Meredith pointed to the man from her past.

"Slut," the guy hissed. "I'm not standing in line for you, anyway. Even a fantastic lay isn't worth that."

Meredith's cheeks burned.

"Another word, and I'll deck you myself," Ned said. "Get out."

The stranger stalked away. Meredith met Carrie's concerned gaze, then shook her head and looked up at Theo. "I'm fine," she said.

He pulled her in closer. "I thought you were done with trouble," he said, then dropped a swift kiss on the top of her head.

She glanced toward Ryan, but he was already turning away.

"Do I need to kick his ass, now?" Theo asked, inclining his head toward Ryan.

"No, he's…" Meredith wasn't sure how to describe Ryan to her brother. "No," she repeated. The people watching had lost interest now that the show was over.

Carrie grabbed her arm and pulled her into a tight hug. "What a horrible man. Are you okay?"

Hysteria threatened to overtake Meredith, but she managed a steady nod. "I'm going to the bathroom. I just need a minute."

"Do you want company?" Carrie asked.

"I'm fine. I'll be back in a few minutes." Without waiting for an answer, she wove through the crowd trying to locate Ryan. He wasn't with his friends, and she wondered if he'd already left. She made her way down the dim hallway that led to the bar's restrooms. Instead of stopping, she continued out the door at the end of the hall that led to the alley.

The air was fresh, and she pulled a deep gulp into her lungs, hoping to relieve some of the pressure that had built there. So much she felt like she might suffocate from the weight.

She pressed a hand to the cool brick as the door to the bar slammed shut, leaving her in blessed quiet. She turned toward the street to make sure the jerk from her past hadn't come around from the front of the bar.

A throat cleared behind her, and she gasped, then whirled to see Ryan leaning against the brick exterior, his gaze intense on her. Her heartbeat picked up speed, and she forced herself not to move toward him. He was more dangerous than any man from her past. Although Ryan offered no threat to her body, Meredith's heart was in serious trouble when it came to him.

CHAPTER SEVENTEEN

FOR AN INSTANT, Ryan wondered if he was imagining Meredith. Had his deep longing willed her to appear in the dark alley where he'd taken refuge after the altercation in the bar?

His blood still ran hot, not completely cooled after that redneck biker put a hand on Meredith. He hadn't been close enough to see the look in her eyes, but her ramrod posture told him everything he needed to know. She hadn't wanted the guy's hands on her.

"I owe you another round of thanks," she said, breaking into his thoughts and making him understand that not only was she really standing in front of him but she was as upset by the encounter as he'd guessed.

He could hear it in her voice, the thread of shame and residual panic.

"The dude shouldn't have touched you," he answered simply. "Or called you a name. I had half a mind to follow him out of the bar and finish what I'd started."

"I'm glad you didn't," she said, shaking her head. "You don't have to fight my battles."

"Because the guy who's been hanging on to you tonight can fill that role?" He cringed at the petty jealousy in his tone. "Never mind. It's none of my business who you spend your time with."

She stared at him like he'd grown two heads. "What guy?" She looked genuinely confused. "Wait. Do you mean my brother?"

The truth hit Ryan like a sharp uppercut. "I thought your brothers weren't local," he muttered.

She took a slow, almost tentative step toward him. "My dad called Theo and told him about the accident and my arm. He's here to help with the roof."

"Your brother," Ryan repeated, rubbing a hand over the back of his neck where embarrassment continued to tickle his skin. He'd been jealous over her brother. What the hell was wrong with him?

"Theo and Dylan were friends in high school. He wanted to meet my sisters. Avery and Gray had plans tonight, so Carrie and Dylan met us here."

"You didn't answer my calls or texts."

She closed her eyes for a few seconds, and he could almost see her struggling with whether to reveal whatever truth she was hiding. "I didn't want to admit how badly I wanted to talk to you about Theo," she said as if she resented the feelings. "I figured as you spent more time doing your doctor business, you'd realize how much time you've been wasting with me."

"You're not a waste of time, Meredith."

"I hate needing people," she said softly, looking away from him.

"Do you need me?" The thought of it made his chest tighten.

She laughed without humor. "More than is smart for either of us."

He reached for her, but she backed away, holding up a hand. "Tell me about Megan whispering in your ear."

"Who is…" He thought about the group he'd been with at the bar. "The nurse? She and I worked together today."

Meredith gave a shaky nod. "I met her at a hospital fundraiser a couple of months ago. She seemed nice and very friendly. Tonight in the bar looked very friendly. It was definitely more than working together." She emphasized the last two words with air quotes, so adorably perturbed that it made Ryan grin. "Don't laugh at me," she said, wagging a finger at him. "I'm not jealous. This isn't jealousy."

"Good," he answered. "Because I'm not interested in Megan. She's a great nurse. End of story—or at least the end of my story with her."

"Okay," she murmured. "I guess we're clear. You're just friends with the cute nurse, and I'm not on a date with my brother."

"Yeah," he agreed with a laugh, unsure of what to do next. This was uncharted territory for Ryan, the feeling of longing and possession that gripped him every time he was near this smart, beautiful, infuriating woman. It would be wise to let tonight's misunderstanding serve as an excuse to take a step back. His feelings for her were too much— too raw, too overwhelming, too addictive.

They were thundering along on thin emotional ice, and he knew if he fell through he was a goner. She had her sisters and this community, a full life with people who cared about her. People who would see her through anything. He had his career and a handful of colleagues who wanted him back to work because he was useful to them.

"Your day was good?" she asked, her tone gentle, and all the prudent thoughts he had about cutting and running disappeared like a puff of smoke. It didn't matter what the future held for either of them. That simple question undid him because it reminded Ryan that she was the only person he wanted to share his day with. She was the person who mattered to him—to his heart.

"It's better now that I know you weren't on a date tonight." He stepped forward and reached for her. This time she didn't back away but let herself be drawn to him, although she remained stiff in his arms.

"With my brother," she said, eyes rolling heavenward. "How much of a small-town hick do you think I am?"

"I think you're a woman who sells herself too short." He smoothed a hand along the edge of her cast. She never complained about the injury or made excuses to do less work around the rescue. Her determination to take care of herself was admirable, even though he wanted the chance to do more for her. "I wanted to kill that guy who grabbed you in the bar."

"He's somebody I used to know," she said, then dropped her gaze. "I have plenty of mistakes in my past, and most of them have tattoos and drinking problems. It's not important."

"You're important," he countered, and her chin trembled ever so slightly. "That's why I just stewed in my petty jealousy instead of coming to you earlier. You were with your sister, so I knew the guy at your side had to be okay. If you were out on a date with a decent man, I figured that was my signal to back off. To let you have your chance with someone who can give you what you need."

"What if what I need is you?"

He sucked in a breath as he watched her let down her guard and emotion filled her stormy eyes. It humbled him and made him want her all the more because he understood that she was giving him a rare gift. Meredith was strong and sometimes standoffish. She'd built walls around her heart as tall and wide as his own, and for her to give him even a glimpse of the vulnerability behind them…the staggering power of it almost brought him to his knees.

"For as long as we have," she clarified, and her gaze became guarded again.

"I'll do everything in my power not to screw it up."

Her mouth quirked at the edges. "That's romantic, Doc. Really knocking my socks off over here."

"I have plans for knocking your socks off," he said, pitching his voice low. He liked the smile in her eyes and welcomed the good-natured teasing. And when she rose to press her mouth to his…well, he liked that even more. It was so easy to lose himself in this woman—her taste and scent and the way her body fit perfectly against his.

He wrapped his arms around her waist and deepened the kiss. The dim alley felt like their own private sanctuary, although his body commanded him to get her back to his house or her house or anywhere they could have more privacy.

They were so consumed with each other that neither of them noticed when the door to the alley opened. Ryan vaguely registered the muffled sounds from the bar's interior but with Meredith clinging to him and her tongue doing wicked things to his senses as it swirled with his, it was easy to ignore anything else.

A throat cleared. "Don't make me have to bleach my eyeballs, Pupsqueak," a male voice said, and Meredith tore herself away from Ryan in an instant.

She whirled on the interloper. "Seriously, Theo, enough with the nickname. It's embarrassing."

Meredith's older brother only shrugged before turning to Ryan. "You took care of that jackass from earlier."

"Right before you were going to take care of me," Ryan answered.

"Instinct. I'm Theo Ventner." Theo stepped forward and held out a hand, which Ryan shook without hesitation.

"Ryan Sorensen."

"I take it you and my sister are…"

"Friends," Meredith said, and Ryan tried not to be disappointed at the classification.

Theo didn't look like he believed her any more than Ryan did. "Carrie is worried about you," he said instead of arguing. "I'm heading back to Dad's house. You ready to go?"

"I'll drive her," Ryan offered. Actually less of an offer than a statement. No way was he letting her walk away from him tonight. Too much adrenaline still buzzed in his system, and he knew the only way to take the edge off was with Meredith.

Theo cocked a brow at his sister.

"I'll go with Ryan," she said and stepped closer to him.

Without thinking, Ryan laced their fingers together. He might only be in the picture temporarily, but he had a soul-deep need to make sure Theo—and anyone else who was interested—understood where he and Meredith stood for the time he was part of her life.

To his great relief, she didn't shake off his touch but squeezed his hand. Nice to know he wasn't alone in this. He'd spent far too much time alone.

"Will you tell Carrie I'll call her tomorrow?" Meredith asked.

Theo glanced between the two of them as if searching for something. Ryan wasn't sure if the man found what he wanted, but he nodded. "I'll be over early with a few guys to start on the roof."

"I can help," Ryan told him.

"Your leg," Meredith protested, and Ryan felt the back of his neck burn.

He didn't break eye contact with Theo. "I can help," he repeated.

"The more hands the better," Meredith's brother answered. "I'll see you at seven tomorrow."

Meredith groaned. "Seven? Good lord, Theo. Is that really necessary?"

Her brother laughed. "I'll bring doughnuts, Pup. You make coffee."

Then he turned and went back into the building.

"It must be hard to give shots to those babies and toddlers." Meredith looked down at Ryan's hand on her knee, then out at the two-lane road that stretched in front of them.

She was trying her best not to be distracted by the warmth of his touch or the way lightning bolts of sensation seemed to radiate up her body. Trying to tamp down her instinct to ask him to pull over onto the shoulder so she could climb across the console and into his lap.

It had only been fifteen minutes since they'd walked out of the alley behind The Watering Hole, hands linked together. She'd tried to tug away when she saw his work friends gathered in front of the bar's entrance, but Ryan had held on to her.

He'd introduced her like it was the most natural thing in the world and she hadn't just been accosted by a rude redneck in front of half the bar. If anyone was surprised to see her with him, they hid it well. Even Julie Fowler gave

Meredith a friendly smile despite their history. She knew one of the nurses, Aimee Baker. Aimee had adopted a cat from Furever Friends when she first moved to town, so she gave Meredith an update on the animal.

Paul thanked Ryan for his work at the pediatric clinic that day and confirmed his next shift for the following week. To Meredith's surprise, much of the tension Ryan had exhibited before he'd left that morning seemed to have dissipated, and he sounded like he was actually looking forward to continuing his work with the local community.

She tried and failed to stop her foolish heart from reading more into his new attitude. Just because he was willing to continue to pitch in with the mobile medical clinic didn't mean anything would change for good. He'd still leave Magnolia and return to his real life when his leg had completely healed. Based on the way his limp had all but disappeared, the end would come sooner than later.

She shouldn't expect anything different.

After all, he'd only told her he wanted to enjoy what was between them for his remaining time in town, not that he wanted to extend his stay or continue their relationship for longer. Her feelings for him didn't change anything, and she'd do well to remember that.

"The nurses do most of the heavy lifting for those kinds of appointments," he told her. "Doctors get to come in and play good cop. But I liked seeing the young patients and talking with their parents."

Meredith bit down on her bottom lip. She must have it really bad if hearing him talk about his work was a turn-on. Down girl, she commanded her frenzied lady parts. No need to make a bigger fool of herself than she already had.

"That's nice," she said, then inwardly cringed. "I mean,

it's good that you enjoy your work. It would be a waste if all that training was for nothing."

"My dad made it pretty clear to my sister and me that we had to choose careers that made a difference in people's lives. He was big on service to our fellow citizens."

"Admirable," she murmured.

"I guess." He sighed. "It always felt like pressure to me. Nothing I did could be for fun. Vacations were spent building houses or volunteering in far-flung countries. Major holidays at soup kitchens. I sound like a complete jerk. I appreciate that we got to help, and I understand that it's important. But it felt like we were never really off the clock. I would have loved a weekend with just my family, even camping or going for a hike that didn't involve trail maintenance for the park service."

"Clearly the lesson stuck." She picked up his hand and cradled it between both of hers. "You're on leave from your job and still volunteering with my rescue and the mobile medical clinic. The whole reason you're here is because you were injured helping to take down a raging gunman."

"That's not how it happened. You make me sound like I did something right. I allowed a friend of mine to be killed."

He fisted his hand, and she slowly unclenched his fingers, tracing small circles on the center of his palm until she felt him relax. "You didn't allow anything," she said, keeping the emotion out of her voice. She knew that her getting upset wouldn't convince him otherwise. "I'm sure that without your intervention, more people would have been shot or even killed."

"Other people would have intervened if I hadn't." He pulled his car down the long gravel drive that led to her property.

"I'm not here to argue your hero status." She moved her hand up his arm and gripped his biceps. "After all, I don't want to give you a chance to get distracted from the task you're about to undertake."

The car rolled to a stop, and he shifted into Park, then turned to her. "Tell me you don't have more poop to scoop this late at night."

She grinned. "No, but I appreciate the thought. I was talking about you and me and the knocking-off of my socks."

"That I can handle." He leaned forward and kissed her, a gentle tease of his mouth against hers, but when he pulled away, Meredith had trouble catching her breath.

Would she ever become so accustomed to this man that her body didn't react like he was her drug of choice?

She certainly hoped not.

They exited the car and started toward the house before Meredith stopped and turned toward the barn. "Something's wrong," she said. "The animals are too quiet."

"They're probably asleep. Even goats need their beauty rest."

"I need to check." She glanced in Ryan's direction, expecting impatience or irritation. If he was anywhere near as turned on as her, a detour into a dusty barn was the last thing he'd want at the moment.

"Let's go" was all he said as he pulled his phone from his pocket and flipped on the flashlight.

If she hadn't been so preoccupied with making sure the animals were safe, she would have kissed him. Instead, they were silent as they approached the barn. In truth, there might be nothing out of the ordinary. Half the time she was already curled up in bed with a book or studying at the kitchen table at this time of night.

She pushed open the door enough that she and Ryan could enter. She didn't want to get all her babies riled up if there was nothing wrong. Following her gut, she went immediately to the stall that housed Sugar and her pups. The little ones were snuggled against their mama's belly, and the dog lifted her head when Ryan shined the light into the stall but looked calm. Nothing amiss with them.

"Maybe I'm imagining a problem," Meredith whispered, frowning.

Then a low, pained whine came from across the aisle.

She and Ryan followed the sound, and the flashlight shined on Brodie and Benji, the two young Labs. Brodie was on his side, panting and fidgeting like he couldn't get comfortable.

"Oh, no." Meredith let herself into the stall, and Benji immediately came to her side and nudged her as if to let her know there was really a problem.

"What do you think is going on?" Ryan asked, crouching down next to her.

"I don't know. He was fine earlier tonight. I let all the dogs out into the fenced-in pasture after dinner. They ran for a while but seemed great when I left."

"What do we do?" he asked.

She ran a hand over the dog but found no obvious sign of injury. "If we don't know what's wrong—"

"Hold on." Ryan moved from her side and shined the flashlight on a pile of vomit. "Did you feed them a different kibble tonight?"

"No." Meredith kept one hand on Brodie's side, feeling his labored breaths as she followed the beam of light. "I guess he could have gotten into the goat food or something out on the property."

"The food Brodie threw up hasn't been digested. It looks like normal kibble but not the kind you use." Ryan shook his head and bent closer to ground. "It smells almost sweet, like antifreeze. I think someone poisoned him."

That sentence spurred Meredith into immediate action. Cases of deliberate poisoning were rare, but she'd seen a few in her years as a vet tech and knew time was of the essence.

"Will you check the other dogs?" She had nearly a dozen at the rescue at the moment. Most of them had been out in the field earlier.

Ryan nodded, and she followed him out of the stall to get the hydrogen peroxide and a syringe. She needed to induce more vomiting in the animal as soon as possible. If Meredith couldn't get the dog to throw up again, she'd have to take him to the emergency vet clinic in Raleigh, which was an hour away, or wake one of the vets from her local practice. Either way, she had no time to waste.

CHAPTER EIGHTEEN

MEREDITH OPENED HER eyes hours later, unsure whether the insistent knocking was coming from the door or inside her head. Sun streamed in from the picture window, and her three dogs wagged their tails as they sat in front of the door but surprisingly didn't bark in greeting. It was as if somehow they knew her exhausted brain couldn't take any more noise at the moment.

She moved to get up from the sofa where she'd fallen asleep only a couple hours earlier and then realized she was pinned under Ryan's arm.

"Wake up," she said, nudging him. "Theo's here."

He groaned low in his throat but lifted his arm. She climbed off the couch and hurried toward the door. Buster, Gracie and Marlin sniffed her brother in greeting, then trotted out to do their morning business.

"Damn, Pup." Theo gaped at her. "Did the party keep on raging after the bar? You look like hell. Are those the same clothes you were wearing yesterday?"

"Shut it, Theo. It was a rough night."

His eyes narrowed at something beyond her, and she turned as Ryan straightened. "I'll check on Brodie," he muttered before heading toward the spare bedroom, not bothering to greet Theo.

"Seriously, Meredith? I don't need to bear witness to

your sex buddy getting ready to do the walk of shame. The rest of the guys will be here soon. Let's not give them a show either, huh?"

If Meredith wasn't so physically and emotionally spent, she'd find her brother's indignation almost funny. Theo was the last person in a position to judge.

"Someone left tainted food on the property." She stepped back to let him into the house. "One of the rescues got into it, and we spent most of the night up with him. Luckily, he seems to be doing okay, but it was touch and go for a while." She swore under her breath and elbowed past her brother to call for Buster, Gracie and Marlin. Until she did a sweep of the property to make sure there was nothing else out there, she didn't want any of the animals straying far.

"Why the hell would anyone try to poison your animals?" Theo demanded.

All three dogs came running, motivated by the promise of breakfast. She herded them into the laundry room at the back of the house and scooped kibble into their bowls.

"I don't know," she said as irritation and panic warred within her.

"A bitter ex-boyfriend?" Theo followed her to the spare bedroom, where Ryan was on the floor, both Brodie and Benji snuggled against him, their tails wagging happily.

The sight made the tightness in Meredith's chest loosen. The dog clearly felt much better. "I don't have ex-boyfriends," she said over her shoulder, not even bothered by the suggestion that someone would want revenge on her. She was too relieved that Brodie appeared healthy to care about anything else at the moment.

"I'll take them out, then head to the barn to start the

feeding routine." Ryan stood and ran a hand through his rumpled hair.

Like Meredith, he wore the same clothes from the previous day, but even wrinkled and in need of a shave, he looked far too handsome.

He turned to Theo. "Once things are settled with the animals, I need to change clothes, then I'll be back to help with the roof."

Before her brother could answer, Meredith stepped forward. Brodie approached, and she scratched the dog's ears. "You have to be as exhausted as me. Theo and his guys can handle the roof. You should rest. Your leg—"

"It's fine," Ryan said. His gaze shifted to Theo. "I'll be ready in about an hour."

"Sounds good," Theo said. "I'll save a doughnut for you."

Meredith got the impression that the guys had come to some silent understanding that she couldn't quite follow.

Ryan picked up the two leashes that sat on the bed and fastened one to each of the dog's collars. "See you in a bit." He squeezed Meredith's arm as he walked by, and she rounded on her brother.

"What did I miss there?"

"Nothing. We need to figure out who would want to sabotage the rescue."

"Theo, don't brush me off." She gestured to where Ryan had been standing moments earlier. "Something happened. Like *doughnuts* was some kind of code word for *bromance*."

"No bromance." One side of Theo's mouth curved. "But I like your doctor, Pup. He seems like a stand-up guy. What's the deal with you being worried about his leg?"

She blew out a frustrated breath at the realization that

different parts of her life were converging in ways she couldn't control. Meredith hated feeling out of control. "He's not my anything," she said, even though her heart told a different story. "He's in Magnolia recovering from a leg injury. He was shot when a gang fight broke out in his ER and is on leave, so I don't want him to overdo it."

"He seems capable of making his own decisions on what he can handle."

"He pushes himself too hard."

"And you say he isn't yours." Theo reached out and ruffled her hair. "Silly, Pup. Go help your man in the barn. I'll make coffee and get things rolling. The guys should be here soon. Dylan and Gray are coming, too."

She swatted at his hand, but her heart filled. She'd missed both of her brothers, and it made her happy to have Theo here, even if he was annoying as all get-out. "Thanks, Theo," she whispered. She gave him a quick hug, then headed out the door.

RYAN WAS USED to functioning on little to no sleep, but by the end of a day spent hammering in roofing shingles after a night of keeping watch over a sick dog, he wanted to weep with exhaustion.

His leg, which he'd thought had healed almost completely, throbbed as much as his head. But he didn't allow himself to take a break until the last shingle was in place.

Despite his physical fatigue, he'd had more fun than he would have imagined for a day of manual labor. The guys Meredith's brother had rounded up for the project were hardworking and high-spirited. He already liked Dylan and Gray, and the crew fell into an easy camaraderie as they completed the project.

Even the town's mayor stopped by to lend a hand, or at least to play the part of honorary supervisor. It was a testament to the community of Magnolia—and Meredith's place in it—that so many people seemed willing to help when she needed it.

Her sisters had arrived a few hours earlier, along with Gray's daughter, Violet, and Dylan's teenage nephew, Sam. Ryan grinned as the boy followed Shae around the property like a lovesick puppy. Their group had combed the edges of the property looking for more tainted food, and a deputy had stopped by to take an official statement from Meredith. Two of the vets from her clinic also visited to check Brodie and the rest of the animals. Luckily, the dog had indeed recovered, and no other animals showed symptoms of poisoning.

Ryan was glad they were taking care of the roof today. It would keep Meredith's mind off the fear that someone wanted to harm her furry charges. He just hoped law enforcement could figure out who was behind the poisoning. The deputy had made it sound like it might be teenagers and a prank gone wrong, but Ryan didn't quite believe that.

"Nice work today." Theo clapped Ryan on the back as they headed toward the tables of food set up in front of the house. It had been Meredith's idea to feed the crew at the end of the day. Ryan could tell that she struggled with accepting assistance and her limited ability to pitch in due to her casted wrist.

"Glad to do my part. You deserve the credit for rounding up enough guys to bang this out in a day."

"Dad's instructions were pretty clear on the matter." Theo inclined his head toward his father, who stood nearby talking to the mayor. "It about killed him when his baby girl got hurt trying to take care of it herself."

"She likes to do things on her own," Ryan murmured, shaking his head as he watched Meredith heft an oversize pitcher of iced tea onto one of the tables.

"It's a family trait." Theo's jaw tightened when Avery and Carrie hurried to either side of Meredith and helped situate the container on the table.

"The three of them are close," Ryan observed. "Is that hard for you?"

Theo blew out a breath. "It makes me feel like a prick to say yes, but it's not my favorite part of this situation. Actually, there's no great part, as far as I can see."

"Meredith has more people who care about her." Ryan glanced at the other man. "That's a positive."

"Yeah," her brother conceded. "I don't think Erik, Dad or I realized how tough it was on her when Mom left. We were all dealing with it in our own way. None of us handled things well. But we're guys. It's simple enough to ignore the hard emotions. I guess we didn't realize that made Pup feel like we were also ignoring her."

"Family dynamics are always complicated."

"Are you close to your family?" Theo asked, and Ryan's first instinct was to change the subject. The last thing he wanted to talk about was his family, especially when he didn't want anyone else in town to discover his connection to the potential grant money.

"Not exactly." He shrugged. "But if they needed me, I'd be there."

Theo pointed to the barn roof and nodded. "Exactly."

They joined the rest of the group, and Ryan loaded his plate high with barbecue, potato salad and corn bread.

The temperature was beginning to cool now that the sun had dipped below the horizon, but it was still comfortable enough to enjoy the fresh spring air.

A couple men approached him while he ate to ask about various health conditions and the hours for the mobile medical clinic. It amazed him that the clinic appeared to serve a huge need in this community. He wondered how many more people could be helped in his part of the city if there were similar initiatives. More often than not, the population that his hospital served were the under- or uninsured, people who ignored health issues until they became an emergency problem.

Because his work was in the ER, Ryan hadn't given much thought to preventative care or wellness programs. He regretted that shortsightedness. He understood there was more to medicine than simply treating symptoms or full-blown emergencies, but he didn't pay enough attention to the world outside his tiny scope of vision.

As the sky began to darken to gray, most of the crew packed up their tools and headed out. Meredith had taken her sisters and Violet to visit the puppies in the barn, so Ryan joined the other men in cleaning up the leftover food.

He couldn't remember the last time he'd felt so at peace. The pace of life in this small town, which at first had seemed ridiculously slow compared to what he knew from life in the city, had grown on him. He liked having time to think about things beyond himself. Time to enjoy the setting sun and the simple sense of fulfillment that came from real connections with other people. He'd miss more than just Meredith when he returned to his regular life.

The thought of leaving made a band of frustration cinch around his lungs. Of course he would leave. His life—his career—was in DC. He'd achieved what he set out to, although compared to the richness of life in Magnolia, his world felt as sterile as an exam room.

Meredith and her sisters rejoined the group after most of the crew had left. Ryan saw her gaze flit between the two branches of her family, and he could feel her agitation. As if on cue, her sisters took turns praising Theo for his coordination of the roof project and then Carl for reaching out to his son in the first place.

Ryan noticed that Dylan and Gray seemed to be trying to hide their smiles as Meredith's brother and father accepted the admiration with twin expressions of wonder. It would be difficult to remain standoffish in the face of the sisters' combined charm.

Meredith visibly relaxed, and the group spent a few more minutes chatting before everyone other than Ryan left.

"Anything for you, Pup," Carl said as he gave his daughter a tight hug.

Her smile looked a tad watery as her father walked away. Ryan wrapped an arm around her shoulder. They both waved to the cars pulling down the driveway.

She sagged against him with a heavy sigh. "I'm sorry," she whispered.

He looked down at her. "For what?"

"You must be counting the hours before you can escape me and my nutty life. Between crazy guys in bars, poisoned dogs, hours of hard labor and my family putting the *fun* in *dysfunctional*, you've gone above and beyond. I know this isn't what you signed up for when you came to Magnolia."

How was he supposed to explain that it was so much better than what he'd expected from his time in town?

"You have no reason to apologize," he said, the words

coming out testy even to his ears. He wanted to tell her just how much being with her meant to him, how happy he felt with her tucked at his side. But he knew she didn't see him as a long-term arrangement. If he gave her an indication of his feelings, would she end things before he was scheduled to leave? Instead of some flowery profession of emotion, he settled on a lame "I'm not complaining."

"I know." She looped her arms around his waist despite her cast. "I appreciate it. You don't have to stay with me tonight. I'm sure you want a break."

I never want to leave. The words bubbled up in his throat, and he choked them back before they could escape. "Are you trying to get rid of me?" He made his tone light, but she hugged him tighter.

"Not one bit."

He breathed a sigh of relief, imagining the fool he'd make of himself if she tried to push him away again.

She glanced up at him. "But you could use a shower, and I'm sure I could, too. My bathroom is kind of small, but…"

"I think we'll manage." He pressed his forehead to hers. "In fact, I can imagine lots of ways we could fit."

"I like the sound of that." She stepped away and took his hand to lead him up the front porch.

Ryan followed—at this point he'd follow Meredith anywhere—and tried to ignore the hammering of his heart, which seemed to beat with the message that he'd found the place he was meant to be.

CHAPTER NINETEEN

THE NEXT FEW days sped by in a flash. Although the cast was a hindrance, Meredith got used to working around it as she prepared for the foundation's site visit.

People she knew and some she barely recognized from town continued to stop by or call with offers to help so that by the day of the site visit, her rescue looked better than she could have imagined.

The only lingering issue was they still had no leads on who had left the tainted food in the pasture. Ryan insisted on installing motion lights around the property and a game cam on one of the trees near the edge of the fence line. Shae and the other volunteers made regular sweeps of the open space to make sure there were no other suspicious activities and the animals remained healthy.

Meredith tried to put the whole incident out of her mind and to convince herself it was a random prank, as the police suspected. But she couldn't shake the feeling that she'd been targeted for a specific reason she didn't yet understand.

She put that worry aside when the rental car pulled up with the program director from the Howard Family Foundation. Nerves danced across her stomach as she watched a woman get out of the car and survey the property before approaching her. Meredith smoothed a hand over the buttondown shirt and cargo pants she'd chosen to wear for the appointment, after trying on almost every article of clothing she owned. She'd thought about wearing a dress or something suited to a business meeting but realized that would make her even more self-conscious and out of her element.

She ran an animal shelter not a multinational corporation, although this was a time she wished she had a mom to call and ask for wardrobe advice. She'd FaceTimed her sisters instead, and they'd patiently given feedback on her multiple outfit changes until they all agreed on one.

The woman offered a friendly smile. "You must be Meredith Ventner. I'm Ann Baltman from the Howard Family Foundation."

Meredith's mouth went dry, and all she could do was nod. She wanted to kick herself or run in the other direction. The woman had offered a simple introduction and every doubt Meredith had about whether she was worthy of being awarded such a large amount of money came rushing at her like a tidal wave. She willed herself to get a grip. This wasn't about her. It was bigger than her overwhelming self-doubt.

If she couldn't believe in herself, she needed to channel her sisters' faith in her. Carrie and Avery had each given her their version of a pep talk earlier, Carrie in her soothing mom voice, and Avery in the clipped tones that demanded Meredith sit up straight and pay attention. And Ryan had reassured her before he left for his scheduled shift at the mobile clinic, his soft words helping to convince her she deserved this chance.

Ann inclined her head. "Is everything okay?"

"I'm nervous," Meredith blurted, then felt her cheeks heat with embarrassment. "Forget I said that. It's nice to meet you, and I appreciate you taking the time to visit Furever Friends."

She expected the foundation's representative to give her attitude about her lack of professionalism, but the older woman only smiled again. "You have no reason to be nervous, Ms. Ventner. Your application was extremely impressive, and with the personal recommendation from…" She broke off.

"Personal recommendation?" Meredith asked with a frown. The woman made it sound like she had an inside connection with someone at the foundation, but Meredith couldn't figure out who that would be.

"What I mean is your references had glowing things to say about the work you do here. Several families who've adopted pets from the rescue and both of the local vets. In fact, we received more testimonials about your work than from both of the other finalists combined. Either you're skilled at drumming up support, or your fans are legion."

"I appreciate that." She studied the woman, her curiosity piqued. It made her feel good to know that people had gone out of their way to speak up for her, but it didn't explain the other woman's comment about some connection to the foundation. "I'll admit I was surprised to learn I was in the running for such a prestigious and generous award. The past recipients have been much larger operations than mine."

Ann nodded, then pulled a notebook out of the tote bag she carried. "We want to support organizations of all sizes, and the plan you submitted convinced us that you weren't going to remain small for long."

That bit of news made Meredith relax slightly. She was proud of her business plan and the application she'd submitted to the foundation. Plus, she'd turned in that same plan as part of a project for her nonprofit-management class and gotten some great feedback plus an A from her hardest professor. Suddenly she was struck with the realization that she'd worked hard for this moment and she was ready.

"I'd love to show you around," she said, feeling the tension slide out of her shoulders. Nothing made her prouder than sharing what she'd built here. She had no doubt that if she was awarded the grant money, she could do something truly meaningful with it.

RYAN WALKED INTO the Italian restaurant across from the Reed Gallery just after six, surprised when several people greeted him by name. Hell, he'd been going to the same coffee shop around the corner from his apartment in the city for years and still barely got a nod of recognition from the rotating pool of ubiquitous hipsters mixing up overpriced drinks.

He'd never given his lack of connection with the neighborhood where he lived much thought. His hometown was small, and everyone had known him or at least known his family. That had seemed like a drawback growing up. He'd craved anonymity and a chance to make his own way in the world without the weight of his grandfather's legacy on his shoulders.

Being recognized in Magnolia didn't feel heavy. It made him happy to be connected, even if he knew it was only temporary.

He saw Meredith in a booth near the back of the restaurant, her head bent over her laptop. His heart gave a tiny leap, shifting and then settling like a puzzle piece that had found the place where it fit.

Stupid heart, he thought, trying his best to ignore the sensation.

She didn't notice his approach, so he placed the bouquet of flowers he'd purchased after his shift ended on the table next to her computer.

Her eyes widened as she looked at the flowers and then up at him, a smile curving her pretty mouth. "What's this for?"

"You," he answered and bent to kiss her before sliding into the seat across from her. "We're celebrating your success today, right?"

She rolled her lips together, trying and failing in her attempt not to beam. "Nothing is certain yet, but the lady from the foundation really seemed to like my operation."

"Of course she did." Ryan kept his features neutral. He'd had to force himself not to text his sister for a debrief on the site visit. Emma had sent one of her program officers to meet Meredith because Ryan insisted it would be too weird for his sister to be the one to evaluate Meredith. He might have suggested Furever Friends as a candidate for the foundation's biggest community grant, but he had faith that Meredith would be awarded the money on her own merit, not because he exerted any influence in the process. Not that Emma would allow him to interfere. She took impartiality to a new level, as conscious of the advantages she'd been given based on their birthright as Ryan was.

"Thanks for all of your help over the past few weeks." She trailed a finger along the edge of one of the flower petals. "I should be buying you flowers. Will you settle for dinner?"

He shook his head. "No way. This is me taking you out. It's a date."

"Oh, that's cute." She scrunched up her nose as she flipped closed her laptop. "But you know I'm a sure thing."

"Hey." He reached across the table and took her hands in his. "I'm planning to woo you tonight. Don't give me a pass." He squeezed her fingers. "Don't give any man a pass, Meredith."

Her chest rose and fell as if she was struggling to catch her breath. "I'm used to giving passes," she whispered, almost as much to herself as to him. "I don't expect much."

"Not nearly enough."

She huffed out a quiet laugh. "I'm not sure it's necessary for you to agree with me."

"I'm a supportive friend that way."

She frowned and then opened her mouth to respond, but a waitress arrived at the table at that moment. Meredith tugged her hands out of Ryan's grasp, which was both understandable and disappointing.

The older woman looked between the two of them and then at the flowers. "Pretty," she murmured. "Let me guess. Six-month anniversary celebration?"

"Not exactly," Meredith answered.

"A year," the woman amended.

"Just a date," Ryan said, unsure what to think about a stranger assuming they were a long-term couple. His heart didn't seem to have any question in the matter. It beat a rhythm in his chest that felt like a chant of *yes* over and over again. But the rest of him was freaking out.

If the waitress thought they were a real couple, maybe he was getting too close. So close that it would hurt like hell to walk away when the time came. The time was getting closer every day. His boss at the hospital had called yesterday morning to check on his progress.

He was scheduled to drive up to DC the following week—after attending Avery and Gray's wedding as Meredith's date—to be cleared to return to work with no restrictions. At the start of his stay in Magnolia, it felt like the weeks would drag along at an interminably slow pace, but now he just wanted to stop the clock altogether.

"Well, can I get you something to drink to start the date off right?" the waitress asked. "You're cute together. I've seen a lot of couples over the years. I have an instinct for the ones who are doomed and the ones who are destined."

Meredith lifted a brow. "Don't keep us in suspense," she said wryly.

"Destined, without a doubt," the waitress answered, then glanced over her shoulder as the hostess led a family of five to a nearby table. "Getting busy in here. How about drinks?"

Blood roared in Ryan's head, which was stupid. A random waitress made a prediction about his destiny, and he reacted like someone just whispered a winning lottery number into his ear. Pathetic.

He studied the beer list without really seeing any of the selections, then cleared his throat and said, "Whatever's on tap."

"We have a nice IPA," she suggested, seeming not to notice that he was having a mini panic attack right before her eyes.

"Sure."

He glanced up at Meredith, somewhat relieved to see that she looked just as poleaxed as he felt. "Wine," she said, sounding numb.

"Red or white, hon?" the waitress asked.

"Wine," she repeated as if that was all her brain could manage.

"How about a pinot grigio?" Ryan managed with an encouraging nod.

To his great relief, Meredith nodded in return.

"Got it." The waitress tapped her pen on the pad of paper she held, looking just a touch impatient. "Any appetizers?"

"Your favorite." Ryan nodded again, beginning to feel like a bobblehead doll. "We'll have your favorite."

"Bruschetta with the olive tapenade." The waitress looked between them again, a faint frown line forming across her forehead. "I'll be back shortly. You look like you could use those drinks sooner than later."

She walked away, and without looking at Ryan, Meredith began to pack up her laptop and the notebook open on the other side of it.

"How's class?" he asked, feeling ridiculous that one off-hand comment had put them into this awkward space where they could barely make eye contact.

"Fine." Her voice sounded wooden. "We're mainly getting ready for finals."

"If you want a study buddy..." He broke off, covered his face with one hand, then dragged it over his jaw. "Did that sound as stupid to you as it did to me?"

She looked at him, all earnest confusion. "Can we meet in a dark corner of the library?"

He wasn't sure how to answer until he realized the corners of her mouth were twitching. She kept her features steady, then gave up trying to hide her amusement at his expense and let out a peal of laughter.

It broke through his shock, and he grinned. "Our waitress is getting the worst tip ever. Who says the things she said to us?"

His obvious distress made Meredith laugh even harder. "It was like we were being punked," she said, struggling to draw in a steady breath.

"Or like a woman neither of us know thought she could predict our future."

That sobered her, which wasn't his intention, but he couldn't help it. The stranger's words had affected him. Maybe they confirmed what he wanted to believe.

"I don't put much stock in destiny," Meredith said. "Based on my past, that would make my future appear pretty dismal."

"Your future is incredibly bright," he told her, starting to reach for her hand again, then pausing as the waitress brought their drinks.

"You sound so sure." Meredith twirled the stem of her wineglass between two fingers. He loved her hands—the dichotomy between the elegant, slender fingers and the calluses on her palms that told of the physical work she did each day. "You're like my own personal cheer squad. The truth is we don't really know each other well. How can you be so certain I'm not going to mess up my chances—either with my degree, the grant or even with you? I'm kind of an expert at self-sabotage."

"You couldn't mess up what's between us if you tried." He lifted his glass and took a long drink of beer. "And if you don't have enough faith in yourself, I'll have it for you."

"Until you leave," she clarified, then sipped the wine, her gaze dropping to the table.

Another server brought their appetizer at the same time the waitress returned to take their dinner orders. Hope buzzed through Ryan as Meredith spoke to the waitress. He could have sworn he heard something in Meredith's tone of voice that hinted maybe she didn't want their temporary arrangement to end.

But he knew he couldn't say anything until after the grant was awarded. He might not be involved with his family's foundation, but he wouldn't do anything that might jeopardize Meredith's chances at winning or risk any hint of impropriety.

"You have a lot of people who care about you," he told her when they were alone again. "I'm just one in a long line. You're like a shining star. People can't help but gravitate into your orbit."

She smiled and lowered her wineglass. "You've been working on your wooing skills. I'm impressed."

If you only knew, Ryan thought. Meredith was the only woman he could imagine wooing, but he was out of his element. How could he share his feelings when he had yet to name them? He needed to wait until she heard back from the foundation and until he sorted through these unfamiliar emotions. He needed to think about what he wanted and what he was able to offer her. He drew a deep breath, assuring himself he had plenty of time to figure out what came next.

CHAPTER TWENTY

IF SOMEONE HAD told Meredith nine months ago that she'd be standing with a group of single women at a wedding reception, waiting to catch a bouquet thrown by one of her two best friends in the world, who also happened to be her half-sister, she probably would have punched that person in the throat for being a liar.

The revelation of Niall Reed being her father had brought so many changes to her life, not the least of which was that Meredith had lost some of her edge. Maybe *lost* wasn't the right word. The bond she'd formed with Avery and Carrie had softened her rough edges, so much so that she'd had to dab at her eyes through most of the ceremony. The vows Avery and Gray spoke to each other tugged at her heartstrings, just like they did for every other sentimental woman in attendance.

The wedding had taken place at a local inn with only thirty or so people attending. Avery wanted a small celebration since allowing others to share in her emotional life wasn't easy. If Avery had had her way, they probably would have penciled in an hour at the courthouse between town events and Gray's shifts with the fire department.

But Gray's daughter, Violet, had been desperate to walk down the aisle as a flower girl, so Avery coordinated the entire day around making Violet happy. The girl, who wore her hair in an elaborate braid, had beamed as she scattered rose petals over the white runner that led to the arbor where Gray had been waiting for Avery along with Malcolm, who performed the ceremony.

Meredith still couldn't believe how much she'd enjoyed helping to plan the event, from flowers to seating charts. Even Avery's little Chihuahua mix, Spot, had a role in the festivities. The dog had pranced down the aisle at Violet's side like she knew the importance of the tiny pillow strapped to her back that held the two rings.

"You're not paying attention." Carrie elbowed Meredith in the ribs, bringing her back to the present moment. "She's about to throw the bouquet. It could smack you right in the face."

"I'm counting on you to dive in front of me so that doesn't happen." Meredith glanced around, then tried to take a step back. Somehow she and Carrie had ended up at the front of the group, which included several of Meredith's former classmates who Avery had gotten to know since moving to town, as well as the more seasoned bachelorette, Josie Trumbell, who owned the local dance studio.

"I have a fiancé," Carrie reminded her. "I shouldn't even be out here."

"You can't desert me now." Meredith forced a smile and purposely did not look to where Ryan stood with Mayor Mal and Dylan near the side of the dance floor. "I hate having people look at me."

"Are you ready, ladies?" Josie leaned forward, the scent of White Diamonds perfume wafting toward them. "You know she'll be aiming at you two."

Indeed, Avery winked at the sisters and then turned around. The guests counted to three, and then she tossed the bouquet of spring flowers over her head. It soared through the air, and Meredith realized with a start that it was headed directly at her.

"All yours," Carrie whispered.

The bouquet began its descent. It felt like time slowed as Meredith's gaze slid to Ryan. She expected to see him smiling at her, but he'd turned away, talking to Aimee and Megan from the hospital. She could see Megan batting her eyelashes at Ryan.

Without thinking, Meredith stepped to the side and then watched as Josie held out her hands and caught the flowers.

"Oh, my." The older woman grinned broadly. "This is unexpected."

"It's an omen." Meredith squeezed Josie's arm. "A sign that it's never too late for love."

Avery approached and hugged Josie before slanting an arch look at Meredith.

"Miss Josie." Violet bounced up to them and threw her arms around her dance teacher's waist. "Does this mean I get to be a flower girl at your wedding, too?"

As the girl and the older woman walked away, Avery turned to Meredith. "You totally dodged the bouquet."

"There's no sense in me catching it."

"Come on, Mer-Bear," Carrie said, looping an arm over Meredith's shoulder. As bridesmaids, they wore similar cocktail-length dresses in a pale blue hue. Meredith's had a simple boatneck collar and a lace overlay, while Carrie's was a sheath to highlight her slim frame. "We're trying to give you and your hottie doc a little nudge."

"He's leaving Magnolia soon. That's more like a shove out the door." She reached out and touched a fingertip to the lace veil cascading down her sister's back. "You're a beautiful bride. I'm happy for you, Avs. Let's not discuss my soon-to-be nonexistent love life. This moment is all about you."

Carrie squeezed Meredith's shoulder as Avery flashed a sentimental smile. "I honestly had no idea I could be this happy." She looked over her shoulder. "Even my mom is having a good time."

"I saw her talking to my mom earlier." Carrie grimaced. "I have a feeling they were bonding over Niall-bashing."

"Whatever works," Avery said with a laugh. "It's almost time to cut the cake. I know Meredith won't sidestep that."

"I'll be right there," Meredith answered as she shifted out of Carrie's embrace. She kept the smile on her face as she moved toward the hallway that led to the women's bathroom. At the last second, she ducked around a corner into the empty coat closet, squeezing shut her eyes and pressing her back to the wall as emotions threatened to overtake her.

She was happy for her sisters. They'd found love and new beginnings in Magnolia. She knew they had strained relationships with their respective mothers growing up, but both of them had managed to mend those fences over the past few months. It only seemed to highlight Meredith's lack of connection with her own mother.

She didn't begrudge them yet couldn't help but compare her own circumstances. As usual, she came up lacking. Theo had actually admitted that he'd reached out to their mother after Niall's death to inform her that her dirty little secret was now public knowledge. According to what he told Meredith, there had been no response.

It stung to know their mom still wanted nothing to do with any of her children. Meredith wished she could give up blaming herself for the division that had ripped apart their family.

And bearing witness to the fullness in both Avery's and Carrie's lives made her own feel hollow in comparison. She pressed the heels of her hands to her forehead, which had suddenly started to pound. This train of thought would lead to nowhere useful.

She needed to remember Ryan's words from the other night. She had friends and family who loved her. She had a bright future with a job that meant the world to her. Things were so much better than they had been before the revelation about her parentage. So what if she didn't have a relationship with her mom? Her father and brothers were all she'd ever needed.

Did it really matter that the man she'd fallen for was planning to leave in a matter of days? She'd be busy with the rescue and selling their dad's house and working with her sisters to settle the remainder of the estate. She wouldn't even have time for love for quite a while. When she did, she'd be ready to open herself up to a good man.

If she could find a way to abandon the memory of the most perfect man she'd ever met.

"You're missing out on the cake."

She drew in a shuddery breath at the familiar voice and swallowed back the emotions that moved deep within her like the ocean's swell.

"Anything but that," she said and opened her eyes to find Ryan standing in front of her holding a small plate with a generous slice of cake.

"My thoughts exactly."

He held out a bite, the sweetness of the buttercream icing bursting on her tongue. She savored it, allowing herself to put aside thoughts of the past and worries about the future and just enjoy the moment.

"Wow."

Ryan's eyes had gone dark, and his chest rose and fell like he was having trouble catching his breath.

"I never considered that eating a piece of cake could be sexy," he told her, his voice a low rumble.

"Then, let me rock your world." She straightened and took the fork from his hand, scooping up another bite and feeding him in the same way he'd done for her moments earlier. His gaze never left hers as he chewed. She had to admit watching him enjoy the cake was sexy as hell.

"Everything about you rocks my world, sweetheart." He leaned forward and captured her mouth for a long, insistent kiss, holding the plate out to the side as Meredith fitted her body against his. He tasted like the strangest combination of vanilla and mint—sweet and slightly tangy. Every one of her nerve endings seemed to be singing a Hallelujah Chorus.

The tiny part of her brain that was still functioning amid the onslaught of desire gave off warning bells, but her body silenced them. It didn't matter what the future held. She would savor every minute she could get with this man, potential broken heart be damned.

I LOVE YOU.

Those three little words called out like a refrain in Ryan's head as he and Meredith swayed to a slow song surrounded by other wedding guests on the dance floor. He told himself it was just the spirit of the celebration that was making his emotions attempt to bludgeon his good sense.

Everyone felt sentimental at a wedding, especially when

the bride and groom were as obviously meant for each other as Avery and Gray.

It was hard not to look at the blissful couple dancing a few feet away and want some of that magic for himself.

He'd been running on all cylinders for so long. It never occurred to him that slowing down might actually make him happier in the long run. His childhood had taught him that service was more important than any sort of personal gain and the only path toward fulfillment for someone who'd been given as much as he had.

His life was the one he'd wanted. Or so he'd thought. He'd worked his ass off to prove that he wasn't the rich-boy trustafarian his father had implied he was destined to become. But in the process, he'd forgotten to be happy. Maybe because happiness felt indulgent and admitting that he craved something for himself beyond what he could do for others would prove his selfishness.

Contentment had found him anyway, in the arms of a beautiful, independent woman and a friendly community far from the life he'd built.

"Look at Josie." Meredith's voice tickled his neck as she spoke.

He followed her gaze to the far side of the dance floor where the bouquet-catching dance teacher had her arms wrapped around Phil Wainright of the hardware store.

Ryan smiled. "They make a cute couple." He'd gotten to know Phil on his frequent trips into town. His daughter, Lily, had returned to Magnolia along with her boyfriend, some kind of big-name Hollywood screenwriter. That was the unique thing about this community. Magnolia opened its arms to people from disparate walks of life. Anyone willing to embrace the town as home seemed welcome.

Ryan knew he couldn't always view life through the Norman Rockwell–esque lens that seemed to frame Magnolia since he'd come to know its residents. There were problems everywhere, evidenced by the fact that Magnolia was pulling itself back from the brink of ruin after Niall Reed had made a mess of things for so many years.

But compared to his lonely, sterile existence, Magnolia felt like a utopia.

He leaned back to study Meredith. "You jumped away from Avery's bouquet like she'd hurled a live grenade at you."

Her delicate brows drew together. "How do you know?"

"I was watching," he said with a frown.

She looked almost shocked. "I saw you talking to Nurse Megan right before Avery tossed the flowers. The two of you seemed deep in conversation, and she should have been out with the rest of us single ladies."

"I'm not sure what to think of your jealous streak." He placed a kiss on the top of her head.

She sniffed. "I'm not jealous. I'm a realist."

"Mainly I'm flattered," he continued, ignoring her protest. "For your information, Megan was telling me about the follow-up visit of a boy I'd seen at the mobile clinic. And she figured she didn't have a chance with the bouquet."

Meredith frowned. "How did she know she didn't have a chance?"

"It was obvious to everyone Avery was aiming for you."

"I freaked out," Meredith whispered, making a face. "Catching the bouquet felt like I was publicly saying I wanted to find a man and get married."

"Would that be so bad?" he asked softly.

"I'm not sure," she said, and he heard the thread of vulnerability in her voice.

"What if I told you I don't want this to end when I leave?" His chest pounded as he said the words. What he truly wanted was to tell her he wanted to stay, but that felt like too much of a risk.

If catching a wedding bouquet made her nervous, he could only imagine what an outright profession of his devotion would do to her.

In a lot of ways, Meredith reminded him of the animals she cared for, although he wasn't fool enough to compare her to a dog or cat and especially not a goat. But she was hesitant and shy about giving her affection. Her past had taught her not to trust and particularly not to trust men. At the same time, she had so much love to give. She just needed someone who could value her and show her the respect she deserved.

He wanted to be that man.

"Okay?" she whispered, and although the one word was uttered as a question, he saw everything he needed to in her eyes. That was the greatest gift he could imagine—the fact that she opened her gaze to him—sharing her vulnerability, her desire and, most importantly, her hope.

He knew that same hope was reflected in his own eyes. A month ago it seemed impossible that he might feel hopeful about anything. The shooting in the ER, his friend's death and the utter helplessness he'd felt at not being able to do more had left him with an unbridled sorrow in his soul. He'd pressed forward because that was all he knew. That was what everyone expected of him. But his heart had remained melancholy. He'd come to Magnolia broken in so many ways. More than his leg had been damaged by that fateful night.

But Meredith had given him hope, and he wanted to try to be the man she deserved. She helped him believe that happiness was within his grasp.

"Okay," he agreed. He didn't say anything else. Not the three words that continued to race through his mind. Not any of the flowery professions that beat in his heart, making him feel like he'd healed into a different man entirely. He squeezed her hip. "Would it be inappropriate for a bridesmaid to sneak out of the reception?"

She smiled. "Probably, but let's go." She took his hand and led him from the dance floor. They passed Carrie and Dylan, and Ryan saw a look pass between the two sisters.

"Did she just give you a pass?" he asked when they made it to the parking lot.

"Yep." She turned to him. "How fast can you get us out of here, Doc?"

He wanted to pull her close and kiss her until she couldn't remember her name, but that would have to wait.

"Did I tell you that before I decided on a career in medicine, my goal was to be a professional race-car driver?"

She laughed as they got into his car. "You'd be a horrible race-car driver."

He made a show of gunning the engine but pulled out of the parking lot at a normal speed. He wasn't about to take the chance of delaying what came next on this night by getting a speeding ticket.

"That hurts." He pressed a hand to his chest. "I'm a stellar driver. Where's your faith, woman?"

"It has nothing to do with your driving skills." She reached across the console and ruffled his hair. "I just figure you'd be constantly disqualified. I know you'd stop to help anyone who needed it. Someone has a hangnail in the stands, and it would be Doc Speed Racer to the rescue."

He snorted. "Are you saying I wouldn't be able to focus?"

"I'm saying you're dedicated. It's a compliment."

"Well, thank you." He glanced over at her, then turned onto the road that led to the beach. "I'd tell you I was going to prove to you how fast I can go, but I plan to take tonight very slow."

"Yeah?" The word came out on a low huff of air, and his body immediately reacted. Just listening to her breathe could elicit a reaction from him.

Damn, he had it bad.

"I promise."

They were silent for the rest of the short drive and then walked into her house hand in hand. Staying over had become his routine of late, and as much as he liked the little cottage, he couldn't imagine a night without Meredith.

And when she unzipped her dress and let the silky fabric fall to the floor, he couldn't imagine anything but touching her.

"I'm going to hold you to your promise," she said as she slid her arms around his neck.

"I sure as hell hope so."

CHAPTER TWENTY-ONE

"ARE YOU SURE you're okay with this?" Meredith placed a hand on Carrie's arm the following Saturday morning as they watched a dozen strangers circle around the front yard of Niall's home. Today was the estate sale. Most of the furniture and belongings they hadn't already given away were being sold. Meredith couldn't imagine her childhood home being emptied in this way. "If you don't want to be here, I can handle it."

"We can handle it," Avery added, coming to stand on Carrie's other side.

"I'm fine." Carrie's voice sounded hollow but steady.

They'd finally gotten the go-ahead to put the house on the market from the probate judge, and the first step was this weekend's estate sale. They'd talked about hiring someone to help with pricing and to handle the actual transactions. Carrie'd insisted that she knew more about the items than a professional would, and they could avoid paying a percentage to an outside agent if they did the work themselves.

"Are you sure?" Avery drew in a deep breath. "It's weird to see people going through his stuff. And I didn't grow up with it."

They'd advertised the sale online, and Meredith couldn't believe how many people had shown up. It helped that the day was perfect, the rain of the past few weeks giving way to a bright spring morning with the fresh smell of new grass and budding flowers filling the air. The scents evoked memories of riding her bike through these streets as a girl and imagining herself living in one of the grand houses that encompassed the neighborhood. Sometimes she'd stayed out for hours, the only way to be ensured of privacy. Her house had always been filled with boys and their games.

She'd known this was the Reed house. Everyone in town knew where Niall and his family lived. At the time, it had been one more thing to make her resent Carrie—her life as the pampered daughter of Magnolia's most illustrious resident. It never occurred to Meredith that a perfect facade might hide just as much discontent as she felt in her life. She also was coming to understand that her childhood had been a happy one despite the pain of her mother walking away. It may not have always felt like it, but she realized her father—the man who had raised her—had done his best.

As the only girl, it seemed to Meredith that she felt the loss in a particularly deep way. But each member of her family had suffered and coped with the abandonment as best they could.

Theo had remained in town even after his crew finished the roof. He was helping their father with a few projects around the house, and Meredith enjoyed spending more time with him. Erik was scheduled for a visit with his family in a few weeks. It would mark the first time all of them had been together in Magnolia in years.

"I like the idea that everything is going to homes where people will treasure it." Carrie sighed. "Most of it holds memories I'd prefer to forget. Or maybe that's what I'm telling myself." She turned to survey the house's exterior.

"Everything about this place feels distant to me now. I'm not the same person as the girl who lived there."

Meredith cringed as one of the shoppers picked up a vintage clock that had fascinated her since she'd first seen it. "I know I've said it before, but I'm sorry I was such a jerk to you when we were younger."

"You weren't that bad," Carrie said, always ready to forgive.

Avery barked out a laugh. "Even you can't sell that line of bull."

"Hey." Meredith reached around Carrie to flick Avery's shoulder. She wore a pair of dark pants and a silk shirt that would probably be ruined by the end of the day. Carrie was dressed in one of her usual floral-print skirts and a fitted white T-shirt, looking both boho chic and pulled together. Meredith couldn't compare to either of them on the style front, so she didn't bother. She'd spent the early morning out with the dogs and still wore the faded jeans, baggy T-shirt and hikers she'd put on for the daily chores.

"Don't deny it," Avery said with a laugh.

"I'm not." Meredith crossed her arms over her chest. "But it's rude of you to mention it when Carrie is being so magnanimous."

"Big word," Carrie murmured. "I like it."

Meredith flicked her arm, as well. "I use plenty of big words. In fact, my lit professor…" She broke off as both women turned to her.

"What professor?" Avery demanded, arching a brow.

"What kind of lit class?" Carrie echoed.

Meredith had forgotten that she'd kept her college courses a secret. Embarrassment washed over her at the thought of her sisters thinking her stupid for working toward her degree.

"I'm taking a few classes through an online program."

"What classes?"

"What program?"

"Stop with the interrogation." She threw up her hands, then crossed them again only to lower them to her sides, nerves pinging along her spine. "I'm going for a degree in business—nonprofit management to be specific." She turned her gaze to a new crop of shoppers. "Those ladies look like they're ready to start a fistfight with anyone who gets in their way."

"No changing the subject," Avery said, then nudged Carrie. "But have your phone set to video in case an estate-sale brawl breaks out."

"No fights on the front lawn," Carrie said, making Meredith want to smile despite her tension. "Mer, that's so great about your degree program. How far along are you?"

Meredith shrugged. "It's an accelerated program, so if I stick with it, I'll graduate in two years. I had a few credits that transferred from when I was away at school, which has helped. It's not a big deal."

"It's a very big deal." Avery frowned. "I don't understand why we're just hearing about this."

"Why would you care?" Meredith asked with an eye roll. "I'm not even sure why I'm bothering. It won't change the fact that I clean up poop for a living."

"Enough." Carrie turned to face her, hands on her hips. "Enough of this selling-yourself-short routine, Meredith. You are talented and smart and have built an amazing rescue organization. A national foundation has short-listed you for its biggest grant. Everyone knows you do way more than scoop poop, and it's past time you start accepting what we all know. You—" she jabbed a finger at Meredith "—are a badass."

Avery nodded. "What she said."

Meredith's heart pounded, both hopeful and self-conscious at her sister's assessment. She wanted to rebuff the claim. Denial was her go-to reaction to most things that made her uncomfortable. Compliments definitely made her uncomfortable. "Compared to the me who made self-sabotage into an art form, yes. I'll give you that. But I don't hold a candle to either of you." She pointed at Carrie. "You're already becoming one of the most acclaimed new artists on the East Coast." Her gaze switched to Avery. "And you came here knowing no one and in less than a year have almost single-handedly been responsible for a miraculous turnaround in town. Downtown businesses are thriving, and new companies and potential residents are flocking to Magnolia. If that outdoor retailer really moves its head-quarters here, you're going to put us back on the map."

"Remind me to hire you as a publicist if I ever want one," Avery said, flashing a crooked smile.

"It would be an easy job," Meredith said. "You're amazing."

"We think the same thing about you," Avery answered.

Sudden and unwanted tears pricked the back of Meredith's eyes. "What's wrong with me?" she asked, then wiped her nose on the hem of her T-shirt.

"Other than the fact that you just snotted all over your shirt?" Carrie grimaced. "Nothing."

Meredith chuckled. "Why can't I manage to see myself the way other people do? I feel like such a fraud. Like at any moment someone is going to call me out on wanting more than I can handle."

"It's called impostor syndrome," Avery said with a nod. "We all have it."

"You two don't."

"Are you joking?" Carrie snorted. "Every time I pick up a paintbrush I wonder if that will be the day my creativity runs dry."

"I keep waiting for Mayor Mal and the rest of the town council to escort me out of my cute little office in city hall." Avery made a face. "I love that office."

Meredith felt her mouth drop open. "Come on. You're both saying those things to make me feel better." She growled low in her throat. "Which you totally shouldn't have to do."

"We're not," Carrie promised. "But we have your back. It's what women do for each other. You never experienced that because you grew up with men."

"Men suck at talking about emotions," Avery confirmed. "Even the good ones."

Meredith thought about Ryan and his comment that he wanted things to continue. She still didn't know exactly what he'd meant, and he hadn't expanded on the topic. Oh, he'd told her plenty with his hands and his mouth. They'd spent the whole night after the wedding reception—and every night since—wrapped in each other's arms. He could communicate plenty without saying a word.

Or at least that's what she thought. In truth, he could mean that he wanted to continue having sex with her when he got a free weekend. He could mean any variety of setups, and she was too scared of having him walk away to ask for what she wanted.

More.

"Is that true, or is it what we tell ourselves to give them a pass?" Meredith posed the question but wasn't sure if she was asking her sisters or herself.

"Good point," Avery conceded. "No passes."

"I didn't give Dylan a pass." Carrie tapped a finger to her chin. "I gave him a few chances to fix the mistakes he made, and I accepted responsibility for my part in what kept the two of us apart for so long…"

"I was perfect with Gray," Avery said, then dissolved into a fit of giggles. "Hardly. That's the thing, Mer. No one is perfect, but somehow you manage to see only the good in everyone else and the bad in yourself. It's not that black-and-white."

Carrie leaned in. "You have to believe you deserve the life you want if you're really ever going to get it."

"I believe…" Meredith began, then broke off. What did she really believe about herself? That she was someone who could easily be discarded or used? That she'd done something—just by being born—that had driven her mother away? That she was the type of woman men slept with but not the type they would ever choose if they wanted to truly build a life with someone? "I want to believe in myself the way the two of you do." The way Ryan did.

"It's not always easy, but you'll get there." Avery turned as one of the shoppers called to her. "I'm going to see what she needs, then do some mingling. A little talk about Niall's legacy might drive sales, and I'm all about the Benjamins right now." She did a little shimmy as she walked away, like she was dancing to hip-hop music that only she could hear.

"*Niall's legacy,*" Carrie repeated, her voice barely above

a whisper. "How those words have changed for me in the past year."

"We're his real legacy," Meredith said suddenly, linking her arm with her sister's. "Even if he was too self-absorbed to see it. You with your art, Avery's spunk and…"

Carrie glanced at her. "And you?"

"My determination and resilience." To Meredith's surprise, her chest loosened as she spoke the words. They didn't ring false or make her feel like she was trying on a mask. Despite everything she'd faced and the times she'd given up on herself, she knew those things to be true. She might not have all the confidence she needed, but she had a start.

"That's right," Carrie agreed with a smile.

RYAN WALKED OUT of the grocery store late that afternoon and drew in a deep breath, appreciating the sweet scent of spring on the air. He'd spent a few hours that morning helping with an urgent-care clinic and then taken Meredith's three dogs, along with several of the current rescues, for a beach walk.

She'd texted that the estate sale at her father's house was going well and keeping all three sisters busy, so he'd decided to stop by the market so that he could make dinner for her later.

In addition to her updates via text, he'd received another message from David Parthen at the hospital in DC. That message, along with the several before it, he ignored. He had an appointment with several members of the hospital board early next week, and Ryan had no doubt they'd want him to return to work.

His leg was almost back to full strength, and he felt as

rested as he had in years. Of course, there was no way of knowing whether to attribute his reinvigorated attitude to the time off work or the way Meredith and life in Magnolia seemed to renew his spirit.

Maybe that was why he couldn't bring himself to answer his boss with a specific date for when he'd be back to work.

Part of him didn't want to return.

"Small-town life has turned you domestic."

He whirled at the sound of the familiar voice.

"Emma?"

"Hey, bro." His sister smiled a cheeky grin as she walked toward him.

He couldn't believe he was really seeing her. She wore a striped T-shirt and dark jeans with sneakers and a ball cap covering her brown hair. She'd come to see him when he was discharged from the hospital after the shooting. Things hadn't gone well during that visit. He'd been surly and gruff, snapping at her as she cleaned up his condo and prepped food so he'd have healthy meal options. He'd been an ungrateful ass and owed her an apology, although she didn't seem to be holding on to any lingering resentment.

"Is that fresh cilantro?" She nodded toward the bunch of leafy greens peeking out over the top of the brown bag he carried. "I'm impressed."

He laughed, then shifted the bag so he could wrap an arm around her. "You don't even know what I'm doing with it."

"Salsa, I assume." She squeezed his shoulders, and it felt good to hug her and be surrounded with the citrusy fragrance she'd worn since they were teenagers. "What's for dinner?"

"Shrimp tacos," he told her, then pulled away. "Don't try

to distract me with small talk. What are you doing in Magnolia? Why didn't you tell me you were coming?" He arched a brow. "How did you know I'd be at the grocery store?"

Her grin broadened. "The tracking device the family implanted in you during the last board of directors' meeting. Didn't you notice the croissants tasted a little off?"

He fake-laughed at her obvious joke, although he wouldn't put it past his mother to attempt to keep tabs on his every move. Her overbearing desire to give her opinion on all aspects of Ryan's life was part of what kept him from wanting to be more involved in the family foundation.

He'd needed a clean break from his mother's side of the family.

He knew—or thought—that Emma felt the same way. She'd chafed under the pressure of the family expectations just as much as he had. But then she'd shocked him by returning to the fold after graduate school to run the Howard Family Foundation.

Slowly they'd grown apart as she began to toe the family line more fully and he continued to distance himself. It still surprised him that the little sister who'd tagged along with him everywhere when they were kids had grown into a woman who wore designer pantsuits and kept her normally curly hair tamed into a sleek bob.

He missed Emma's wildness and sense of whimsy. He was glad their mom and the rest of the stuffed shirts at the foundation hadn't managed to force her to abandon her sardonic sense of humor.

"Seriously, Em. Is everything okay?"

Her smile dimmed the slightest bit. "Never better. I had a free weekend and wanted to check out the town that has captured your attention so fully. Really, Ry. When you told me you were coming down to the North Carolina coast to rest and recover, I figured you'd be crawling out of your skin with boredom within the first few days. Instead, it looks like you've gone native. When was the last time you shaved?"

Ryan scrubbed a hand along his stubbled jaw. "A few days ago. Don't make this a bigger deal than it is." Annoyance crawled along the back of his neck. "I had to take time off work for my leg to heal. It was easier to do it out of the city, so I wasn't tempted to sneak in for a shift."

She studied him for a long moment. "I don't think that's it. You actually look good despite needing a shave and a haircut. Way better than I expected."

"Is that supposed to be a compliment?"

"And you're volunteering as a doctor and then working at an animal shelter as a side hustle? I wanted to see it for myself. It's hard to believe you could survive without the adrenaline rush of the city and the ER." She waved a hand in the general direction of the parking lot. "This meeting is pure coincidence. I stopped by the store for snacks for the drive home."

"You're already leaving? Why didn't you call to say you were driving down?"

"Because you would have told me not to come."

He opened his mouth to argue, then shut it again. That's exactly what he would have said. Ryan loved his sister but having her here was a shot of reality he wasn't ready to handle. Not yet.

"It's good to see you, Em," he answered instead.

"Of course it is." She winked. "You missed me, even though you acted like an ass the last time we were together. By the way, I met your Meredith."

"How?" Ryan choked out the word, trying and clearly failing to keep his features neutral, based on the knowing look Emma gave him.

"Niall Reed's estate sale."

He narrowed his eyes. "That's why you came this weekend."

"She's adorable."

"She's not mine." He started walking toward his car, remembering all the reasons he stayed away from his family. Both Emma and his mother were too nosy for their own good, and his father could find fault in anything Ryan did.

"Then, you're a fool," she answered simply, falling into step beside him.

He opened the door to the back seat and placed the grocery bag on the floor. "Did you introduce yourself?" He couldn't keep the worry from his voice. "Does she know who you are?" And about our connection, he added silently.

"I bought a really cool clock." She inclined her head toward her Toyota SUV, parked a few spaces away. "It was a great deal."

"Don't play games, Em." His sister had always loved to goad him. "Meredith can't know about my affiliation with the foundation."

"What if she gets the grant?" Emma's smile faded, and her gaze sharpened. "We have one more site visit to do, but she's got a good shot at it. Her rescue is exactly the type of organization that fits with our mission."

"There's no reason for her to find out," he argued.

"You're on the board of directors," Emma countered.

"She'll have the money by then." He shook his head. "It won't matter."

"Do you believe that?"

"Just don't tell her yet." He looked up at the water tower that sat over the town like a watchdog. "I like that she doesn't know, and I figured that by the time she discovered my involvement with the board that I'd be back in DC."

"You don't seem to be chomping at the bit to return to your old life."

"I get cleared next week, so it's only a matter of time."

"Unless you don't go."

The words made his blood run cold. "That's not an option. The hospital needs me."

"People need doctors down here, too." Emma threw up her hands. "Obviously since you've been seeing patients on a volunteer basis."

"Get a hobby, Em. You know way too much about my life."

Her eyes darkened as she took a step back, like his words had landed a physical blow. Immediately he regretted them, although he wasn't sure why. The backbone of their sibling bond felt like it was wavering. Neither liked to talk about the dysfunction of their childhood, but it was always a part of their bond nonetheless.

"I'm too busy being the dutiful daughter for a hobby. Someone in the family has to toe the party line." He heard and ignored the thread of resentment in her tone.

"No one is forcing you."

She moved farther away. "Great to see you, too, Ry. Call me when you're back in the city. I'll be there for a few days next month to visit a shelter we're funding."

"Emma, come on. I'm sorry. Don't go away mad. You came all this way. Do you want to have dinner or something?"

She shook her head. "Not a good idea since you want to hide who you are with your girlfriend."

"Not my girlfriend," he felt compelled to point out.

"Whatever you say." She leaned forward. "Remember, dear brother. Denying something doesn't make it less true. You're a member of our family as much as me, and I know you like this woman. Fool yourself as much as you want. You aren't fooling me."

He clenched his jaw but didn't answer because there was no adequate response to that truth.

"Seeing you is a bonus, but I came to Magnolia for some time alone. It's a great town, and I'm a little obsessed with Niall Reed's house. You know it's going on the market in a few weeks?"

"Are you looking to relocate?" He studied his sister, noticing for the first time the tension around the edges of her mouth. "It would be a challenge to be the favorite child from several states away," he pointed out.

"I know," she whispered, then patted his shoulder. "Good to see you, Ry. Stay happy."

He grabbed her arm. "Emma, I'm really sorry I made you mad. I'm here if you need me."

She smiled, but this time it didn't make it all the way to her eyes. He hated the sadness he saw there. Hated that he'd contributed to it by insensitive behavior. "I know. I'm spending one night in town. You free for breakfast tomorrow?"

"Yes. Eight at the diner across the street?"

"See you then."

She walked away, waving over her shoulder, and Ryan still couldn't quite believe she'd shown up in Magnolia, another reminder that the life he'd created these past few weeks wasn't real.

He sighed and climbed into the car. The temperature

hovered in the mid-seventies and sweat dripped between his shoulder blades as soon as he closed the door. He turned on the ignition and pulled his phone out of his pocket. Cranking up the air with one hand, he dialed David Parthen's number with the other.

As much as he wanted to, he couldn't avoid his life forever.

CHAPTER TWENTY-TWO

"SHE'S ABSOLUTELY PERFECT."

Meredith smiled at the young couple who stood next to her booth at the Sunday Magnolia Farmer's Market the next morning. "Ginger is a sweetheart," she agreed.

The woman laughed when the tan-and-white mutt flipped onto her back and wriggled on the grass like a worm. "Are you sure, Mike?" she said to the man at her side. "I know we agreed we wouldn't look at dogs until you were done with graduate school." She glanced at Meredith. "Everything about this weekend has been a surprise. I thought we were going out to dinner, and instead he whisked me away for a couple of days. He even arranged the time off with my boss."

"You needed a break," Mike said, and the way he looked at the pretty brunette made Meredith's heart clench.

"Which is why I'm wondering if the time is right for a dog." She bent to rub the animal's belly. "We're both so busy."

"Ginger is around four years old," Meredith said. "She's got a mellow personality. As long as you can give her some exercise each day, she won't need much more than a good home with people who love her. No pressure, of course."

The woman flashed a sheepish smile. "I feel like I love

her already. How can I know she's the one in just a few minutes?"

The man crouched at her side to love on the dog. "I knew that about you the second I saw you," he told his girlfriend.

"You're making me blush." The woman, who'd introduced herself as Anika, glanced up at Meredith. "We met on a blind date. I came this close to canceling." She held up two fingers, only centimeters apart. "I'd dated so many losers that I'd almost totally given up on love."

"The fact that she showed up is the best thing that ever happened to me," Mike said with a wink.

"That's so sweet." Emotion clogged Meredith's throat. Normally the cynic in her would be repulsed by that sort of sappy emotion. A month ago she would have said she didn't believe in the type of love these two displayed. But something had changed inside her. She recognized the unfamiliar sensation that had been pinging around her chest like a loose pinball for what it was—hope. Hope that she could one day find this kind of connection and happiness for herself. Could she have this kind of future with Ryan?

"In fact…" Mike cleared his throat and returned his gaze to Anika. "I have something I've been meaning to ask you, but I've been too nervous." He pulled a small velvet box from his jacket pocket. "But if we're going to be parents to this gal…" Ginger snuggled against his side as he ruffled her fur "…we should make our family official."

Anika and Meredith let out twin gasps of surprise when he opened the box to reveal a small, sparkling diamond set in a thin gold band.

"This isn't exactly how I planned it," Mike said with a sheepish laugh. "Anika, I can't imagine my life without you. You are my everything. I want to spend the rest of my life with you. You're the best person I know, and you have my heart forever. Would you marry me?"

Anika flashed a watery smile and nodded. Tears streamed down her cheeks. "Yes," she whispered, sinking to her knees next to Mike. They both laughed when the dog lifted her head to lick Anika's face. "What took you so long?"

With a wide grin, Mike slipped the ring onto her finger. "I don't know." He leaned forward and kissed her. "I was ready to ask you the night of our first date, but I thought you'd think I was crazy."

"All I know," Anika told him, "is I'm crazy in love with you."

Meredith felt her mouth drop open as she took a dazed step back. She lifted a hand to her face and realized she was crying almost as hard as Anika. She'd just witnessed the sweetest, most romantic proposal she could imagine, and it made her want…so much.

She watched as the happy couple embraced again and then brought Ginger into their little circle of love. As Meredith congratulated them and filled out the adoption paperwork, they promised to invite her to the wedding.

"Maybe you can catch the bouquet," Anika told her with a wink.

"I doubt it," Meredith answered, thinking about Avery's reception. Had it really been necessary that she avoid the bouquet like it carried the plague?

Probably not.

She couldn't fail if she never put herself out there to try.

Up until the past month, that had felt like the smartest and safest path.

Now it seemed as though she was taking the coward's way out.

Anika and Mike walked away arm in arm with Ginger happily following. Only two dogs remained in the temporary pen Meredith had set up behind the booth. Brodie and Benji were learning to be more social, but they still had work to do. Because they were bonded, the two would need to be adopted together. Meredith knew that limited the potential families but felt that it was important for the dogs' emotional well-being, especially Benji, who stuck to Brodie's side.

Luckily there had been no more instances of tainted food being left on the property since the night Brodie became ill. Meredith wasn't sure if it was her heightened vigilance about walking the perimeter of the pasture or the cameras Ryan had installed, but she appreciated the sense of peace.

She started to pack up when a young woman approached the booth.

"You must be Meredith," the woman said. She wore leggings and a fitted athletic top. "I'm Heather from the Howard Family Foundation."

"Oh." Meredith paused in the act of packing up the pamphlets she'd created about animal care. "I didn't realize the foundation was doing another site visit."

Heather shook her head and adjusted her high ponytail. "I'm not here in any official capacity." She flashed a sheepish grin. "In fact, I'm just a program assistant, so I don't have any real say in awarding money. But my mom came to visit from Minnesota for a week." She glanced over her shoulder. "She's buying goat cheese at the moment. We wanted to get away for a few days, and both Ann and Emma spoke so highly of Magnolia, I thought I'd check it out."

Meredith relaxed slightly although she wasn't sure who Emma was. "I hope you're having a great time."

"It's beautiful, especially all the cherry blossoms."

"They're lovely." Meredith glanced around at the trees blooming along the path that ran through the town square. Sometimes she got so caught up in her own life that she took for granted how special this town was. "I don't think I met anyone named Emma."

"She was here after Ann's official visit." Heather shook her head. "She came to see Ryan, I guess. She's recused herself from the decision process this round since she knew he had a connection with Furever Friends."

A sliver of unease snaked along Meredith's skin. "Who exactly is Emma?" She kept her tone neutral and tried to offer Heather a friendly smile as she asked the question.

Based on the look the other woman gave her, it might have come across a bit on the intense side. "Our executive director." Heather frowned. "The granddaughter of Duffy Howard, who established the foundation."

"Right." Meredith nodded like that information wasn't a shock to her, and she inwardly chided herself for not doing more research on the foundation's staff. She'd filled out the grant application and other requested paperwork without much thought beyond making the best use of the money for her organization.

"We know your qualifications have nothing to do with being friends or whatever with him."

"Whatever," Meredith repeated woodenly. Obviously this woman was somehow acquainted with Ryan. Was that how he described their relationship to people in his life—*friends or whatever*? The thought made her stomach turn.

She still didn't understand Ryan's relationship to the

foundation's executive director or what he had to do with the organization. She felt too embarrassed to ask outright, afraid of revealing herself as the ignorant, small-town bumpkin she felt like at the moment. "Have you seen Ryan?" she asked instead.

"Unfortunately, no." Heather grimaced. "I haven't seen him since our meeting at the end of the fiscal year. He probably wouldn't recognize me. He's so handsome it kind of takes my breath away, you know?"

Meredith sighed. "I do. Tell me about the meeting." What the hell was this woman talking about?

"Just the foundation's annual board of directors' meeting. I didn't get to go to the staff retreat last year, but Ryan usually doesn't show up for that, either. I don't think he gets along with his mom so does the minimum expected for the family."

"Good to know." Meredith grabbed another stack of pamphlets and shoved them into the tote when she realized her hands were shaking.

Heather looked past her to Brodie and Benji. The dogs were dozing on the grass, Benji's paw resting on Brodie's back.

"Those two are adorable," Heather said cheerily. "If my landlord would let me have pets, I snap them up in a heartbeat."

"If your living situation changes, give me a call. If not these two, we'll find the perfect furry companion for you." Meredith thought her face might crack from smiling so hard, but she didn't stop. If she stopped, she might descend into a full-blown panic attack.

"I will." Heather reached out and grabbed her hand,

squeezing gently. "A final decision won't be made until next week, but Furever Friends is my pick for the money."

"Thank you." Meredith returned the handshake, then waved as Heather walked over to join an older woman who looked just like her.

Meredith finished packing the marketing supplies and the table sign and then put Brodie and Benji on their leashes. She folded the travel dog pen, and when everything was packed, she pulled out her phone and dropped to the grass between the two dogs.

She'd searched for information about the shooting at Ryan's hospital when he first came to town but hadn't dug any further into his personal information.

Now she typed in his name along with the foundation name and then sucked in a harsh breath at the images and articles that popped up in her newsfeed. She scrolled through a couple; her heart seemed to sink to her toes. Ryan had more than a passing connection to the Howard Family Foundation. He was Emma Sorensen's brother and the grandson of the man who'd started the charitable organization.

From everything she could find, his sister ran the foundation. He had little involvement other than attending a few board meetings and a gala event on occasion.

But he was part of it.

And he hadn't told her.

"You and the pups taking a rest?"

She glanced up sharply.

Mayor Mal frowned down at her. "I don't know what's caused you to look like that, but I know it's not good." He tipped his straw hat in her direction. "What can I do to help?"

"Do you know who Ryan is?" she asked, her throat dry and her heart heavy.

"I thought he was a visiting doctor and perhaps a man who has a chance at capturing your heart."

"No." She whispered the word. "Do you know?"

Mal shook his head and then bent to scratch Benji between the ears. Meredith registered that the dog didn't flinch, but her pride in his progress was marred by the emotions flooding through her. "Is there something we should know about him? A dark and mysterious past?"

"This is serious, Malcolm." She scrambled to her feet. "He's rich."

The mayor shrugged. "Most doctors I know do pretty well, and he's from the city so—"

"His grandfather was Duffy Howard."

Mal's dark brown eyes widened. "The billionaire?"

Meredith felt like her whole world was spinning. "The foundation that approached me about applying for the grant was started by Ryan's family. His sister runs it."

"Maybe he recommended you for consideration. That's great."

"It's not great," she practically shrieked. "I didn't even know about it. I thought I'd earned this chance on my own."

"Meredith." Mal reached out and patted her shoulder. "You earned it. You've built a fantastic organization with a reputation for doing amazing things for animals in need. So what if you got a foot in the door for funding? They won't give it to you if you don't deserve it."

"I'm pulling my application," she said, more to herself than the mayor.

He whistled under his breath. "You can't mean that."

"Why?"

"Because it's a stupid idea."

"He didn't tell me," she said, looking away.

"Is it possible he knew you'd react like this?" Mal shook his head. "Come on. It's not a big deal."

"It is to me," she insisted and blinked rapidly so she wouldn't start crying. No way was she going to cry over this, even though it felt like a soul-deep betrayal.

She thought she'd finally done something on her own. That a renowned foundation had singled her out for their short list because of her accomplishments. All she'd ever wanted was to finally make it on her own without having to be bailed out by her father or brother and more recently her sisters. Yes, she'd had to accept help with the barn roof, and she'd allowed her friends and neighbors to volunteer around the property.

But what Ryan had done was different. Too much. It felt like a handout, and the thought of accepting money from his family's foundation—essentially allowing him to rescue her—made her skin crawl.

"You could ask him why he didn't tell you," Mal suggested with his usual calm. "Maybe he has a good reason."

"Maybe he didn't believe I could find funding or raise money on my own."

"Don't sell yourself short, Mer. We're proud of you around here. You're our own Dr. Doolittle."

Before the chance encounter with Heather, Meredith would have agreed. Now she just felt like a pathetic charity case. Again.

RYAN STARED AT the clock on the oven in the cottage's small kitchen. Five more minutes until he was scheduled to talk to David with an update on his progress and a date when he'd be returning to work. He'd called his boss after seeing Emma in town but had hung up as soon as David answered.

He hadn't seen Meredith last night because he didn't want to have to lie outright to her about his sister. Emma met him for breakfast in town, and he'd actually admitted how happy the changes in his life made him. She hadn't argued or questioned his sanity. Instead, she'd calmly told him to leave DC and move to Magnolia permanently. Somehow her effortless support had been the push he needed, and he'd texted David to set up a call.

He still couldn't quite believe what he was planning to do: turn in his resignation. Glancing around the cottage, he marveled at how much had changed since he'd first arrived in Magnolia a month earlier.

He'd been a shell of a man—hurting, broken and drinking way more than he should. The physical healing had been easy enough to accomplish—physical-therapy exercises and time were all his leg needed to return to its full capacity.

But he hadn't expected the mental and emotional healing that came with it. The guilt that overwhelmed to the point of choking him in the days after the accident had all but disappeared. In its place was a sorrow for the loss of his friend and colleague, but the blame was gone. He understood that it wouldn't bring Kevin back and only paralyzed Ryan, preventing him from moving forward.

He wanted to move forward.

In Magnolia. With Meredith.

She'd changed things for him. Hell, she'd changed him.

He had no plans to share all of that with his boss, but that didn't change the truth of it. What he knew for sure was that he had no desire to go back. Either to the adrenaline rush of the ER or the empty life he'd had outside of work.

Volunteering at the mobile clinic over the past couple of weeks had made him appreciate the opportunity to really get to know patients. To learn their names and their stories.

He hadn't told Meredith his plan yet, but in his heart he believed she'd be happy. He wanted to talk to David first so she knew he was all in. He was ready to risk everything for a chance with her and planned to do everything he could to make sure he earned his place in her world.

A loud knock came from the front door a moment later, and for an instant he was transported back to that first night and the rainstorm that had brought Meredith into his life.

With a quick glance at his watch—David should be calling any minute—he walked to the door and opened it to reveal Meredith glaring at him.

"Hey, sweetheart." He reached for her. "What happened?"

She stepped away from him. "Your grandfather is Duffy Howard."

A pit of dread lined with spikes of panic extended across Ryan's gut. "How did you find out?"

Her green eyes blazed. "Not the point."

He nodded past the emotions roaring through him. "Agreed. I was going to tell you."

"When?"

"When the grant came through."

"The grant that you arranged," she said, her voice sharp as the edge of a blade.

"No." He shook his head. "It wasn't like that, Meredith." His phone began to ring, and he cursed under his breath. Although it was a slow Sunday morning in Magnolia, David Parthen was on call and apparently slammed in the ER. If Ryan didn't speak with him now, he wasn't sure when he'd get another chance for a few uninterrupted minutes. But he couldn't leave things so muddled with Meredith. His finger trembled as he declined the call.

"Don't let me stop you." She gestured to his phone. "Probably your sister calling to have a good laugh over all the work I've put into the grant process when you were pulling the strings all along."

"I'm not pulling any strings."

"How did the Howard Family Foundation find me?"

He ran a hand through his hair as he thought about all the different ways he could have handled this situation. With Meredith's temper blazing, he understood that he'd made some huge missteps by trying to keep his connection to the foundation a secret.

"I mentioned Furever Friends to my sister," he admitted. "But it was before anything happened between us. I knew about the community grant, and it was clear you'd make a great candidate."

She continued to glare at him. "Then, why not tell me from the start?"

"The money comes from my mom's side of the family." He sighed. "My dad always made it clear that he expected Emma and me to create our own success. When people find out where I come from, it tends to change how they view me. Like I'm not just a regular person or something. I didn't want that with you."

Her pert nose wrinkled. "I don't think you're a regular person, Ryan. I think you're a liar." She stepped closer, and her sweet scent filled the air around him. Somehow breathing her in made his chest burn like someone was trying to rip it apart. "You knew how important it was for me to do this on my own." She held up her casted arm. "Everything

I was willing to go through to ensure that I won the award on my own merit. Now I don't even want the money."

"Don't say that." He closed his eyes as the urge to mutter a string of colorful curses clogged his throat. "You deserve that funding."

"I know," she whispered, and her tone was so miserable it was hard to hear, knowing he'd been the one to cause her that pain. "But everyone will think that you arranged the whole thing. Once again, it will be like someone had to bail me out because I couldn't manage my life on my own."

"No one thinks that about you."

"Everyone knows that about me because it's been true up until now. This was my chance to prove them wrong and show them I could succeed on my own. You stole that from me."

"What would have changed if you'd known?" he demanded, feeling desperate.

She studied him for a long moment. "I wouldn't have gotten involved with you."

"You don't mean that." His phone rang again, and he muted it without a second thought. "Neither of us could have stopped this thing." He waved a hand between the two of them. "It was destiny."

"No," she said. "It was a mistake. I knew we came from different worlds, but I didn't realize how far apart they were. You and I aren't even in the same solar system, Ryan."

"Where we come from doesn't matter," he insisted, panic clawing at him. "Where we're going—"

"No place." She crossed her arms over her chest. She wore her usual uniform of a T-shirt and faded jeans. Wisps of dog hair clung to the soft fabric. He loved her realness and the fact that she cared more about what she was doing than how she looked. It made her even more beautiful to him. "We're going nowhere together."

"Don't say that."

"Call your sister or whoever you need to and tell them your little charity-case relationship is over. No reason for them to consider bankrolling me anymore."

"The grant has nothing to do with you and me."

"It does. It means everything."

"You're scared." Frustration welled inside him, blotting out his regret until all he could feel was the pain of her turning away from him. "You're terrified because you know this is real between us."

"I'm angry because you lied to me," she countered, color flaming on her cheeks. "I can't trust you. You're just another grown-up rich boy who thinks that his money and privilege excuse him from doing what's right."

"Is that what you really think of me?"

"That's who you've shown me you are."

It amazed him that he could go from feeling so much to complete numbness in an instant. All the walls that had dropped over the past few weeks shored themselves up in seconds, leaving him hollow.

"Then, we have nothing more to say."

She stared at him, started to take a step forward like she might ignore everything complicating what was between them and let her heart guide her. But just as quickly she moved back. "Goodbye, Ryan," she said, and he watched her walk away.

His phone vibrated in his pocket, and he pulled it out, unsurprised to see his boss's name on the screen. He answered the call without emotion and made a plan for returning to his old life.

CHAPTER TWENTY-THREE

MEREDITH CLOSED HER laptop as she heard a car pull up the driveway the following week. She'd been working in the office inside the barn for the past several hours, applying for new grants and contacting potential funders even though what she really wanted to do was sit on the sofa eating ice cream and binge-watching movies with sad endings. She'd done a tearjerker marathon the first couple of days after her confrontation with Ryan. Anything that would give her an excuse to cry out some of the emotions pummeling her.

Avery and Carrie had brought food and then sat with her while she railed on how much she hated men. They'd both tried to convince her not to pull her application out of the running for the funding from the Howard Family Foundation, but Meredith had emailed Ryan's sister, anyway. She'd explained that she'd just learned about his connection with the foundation and didn't want anyone to think she'd used undue influence in order to be considered for the money.

Emma Cantrell had responded almost immediately that she appreciated the concern but everyone at the foundation respected what Meredith had built with her rescue. The range of services Meredith provided so that pets and their adoptive families made the rehoming transition more successfully was special, according to Emma. The testimonials, as well as the site visit, made it clear the rescue deserved the grant money.

Meredith wished she could believe the woman.

Her sisters had insisted Emma must be telling the truth. What point was there in lying, especially since Meredith had told Emma that she'd cut off all communication with Ryan because he was a first-class jackass? That seemed like it should be enough to sour the executive director. Instead, Emma had offered a thumbs-up emoji in response to that piece of information.

Several people, including the mayor and Dr. Thorpe, had stopped by to check on her after hearing about her breakup with Ryan.

The dogs who'd been let out in the back pasture barked a greeting, and Meredith exited her office to welcome whoever had stopped by the rescue. That was happening more often than not these days. There was already a waiting list for the puppies, who were getting bigger every day, but Meredith couldn't look at them without thinking of Ryan.

She smiled as a woman approached, a stranger but one who looked vaguely familiar to Meredith. "Welcome to Furever Friends," she offered. "Do we have an appointment?"

"No." The woman smiled as she looked around. "I'm hoping you could spare a few minutes. I'm Emma Cantrell." She held out a manicured hand, which Meredith shook even as shock bubbled up inside her.

"This is unexpected."

Emma arched a brow. "I thought you might refuse to see me if I called first. It's nice to meet you."

Meredith knew the right response. She understood manners and how to be polite. She might be known for her sass, but that didn't mean she was a complete half-wit. Yet she only stared at the elegant woman with caramel-colored hair. Ryan's sister was just as beautiful as he was. Emma's resemblance to Ryan was obvious, from her blue eyes to the gentle slope of her nose. Clearly their family not only had money but also good genetics on their side.

That only irritated Meredith, which made her feel petty, which irritated her more. God, she was a train wreck.

"What can I do for you?" she asked, unable to offer anything more.

If Emma noticed Meredith's abrupt manner, which she must, she didn't bat an eye. "The Howard Family Foundation is announcing the winner of our community-outreach grant tomorrow."

Meredith's breath caught. "Congratulations in advance to the winner."

"I'm here to make sure you aren't going to refuse the money," Emma continued without missing a beat.

"I pulled out." Meredith kept her voice even, although a riot of emotion flooded through her.

"Our email exchange didn't go any further than the two of us," Emma explained. "I understand you were upset, and I don't agree with my brother not revealing to you his connection to the foundation." She gave a small shake of her head. "Ryan has always tried to distance himself from the family. It was a survival technique for a while, and now it's his habit. Or at least, that's what I tell myself."

"Why would he distance himself?" Meredith crossed her arms over her chest. "I still don't understand that part. Your grandfather was one of the most successful men in this country. The foundation does amazing work. It's a legacy to be proud of."

"He doesn't want people to judge him for his privilege."

"That's dumb," Meredith said.

Emma laughed. "Maybe. But is it any smarter to remove yourself from the possibility of receiving funding that would allow you to expand your operation in several areas?"

Meredith stilled.

"I've spent a lot of time reviewing the finalists for the award, and you're the best fit, Meredith. You have a solid plan and have accomplished a lot with very little." Emma glanced past Meredith's shoulder. "In fact, I'd love to meet your current residents. Ann couldn't stop talking about the puppies after the site visit. I'm guessing they're even cuter now."

"Definitely more active." Meredith led Emma into the barn. "It's not fair to the other finalists that I have a personal connection to Ryan."

"Why?"

Meredith's mouth dropped open as her brain scrambled for how to answer that question. When she'd first learned that Ryan was the grandson of the organization's founder, her anger at him for keeping that detail from her, coupled with the heat of embarrassment thinking he was the reason she'd been chosen as a finalist, had seemed like a valid reason to pull out. She'd spent so much time feeling like a charity case and her one big chance of making something happen all on her own had been stolen from her.

But now she wondered if she'd been falling back into her old pattern of self-sabotage again. It killed her to admit it.

"I had an advantage," she muttered, knowing that didn't fully explain the situation.

"So you think the only way you had a chance at winning was because Ryan mentioned Furever Friends to me?" They'd stopped in front of the stall that housed Sugar and her pups. At almost four weeks old and weighing between six and eight pounds, they were five balls of wriggly, spastic energy unless they were piled up together sleeping like their lives depended on it.

"Oh, my gosh." Emma's voice had gone an octave higher, which was a typical reaction to the onslaught of puppy cuteness. "Can I go in?"

Meredith nodded and slid open the stall door. "They still have a few more weeks before they're ready to be weaned. They're alert and aware of their surroundings now, so we're working to socialize them."

"I didn't see them featured on your website."

"Not yet, although people around here know about them so there's a waiting list. I'll put photos up on Facebook in a few days. Puppies are popular, especially in the spring. I want to focus on some of our older dogs."

"Ryan sent me a picture of his favorites. Brodie and Benji?"

Meredith's heart tugged. The two dogs were still with her and as strange as it was, she could tell they missed Ryan almost as much as she did. Especially Brodie. Every morning the dog came out of his pen and trotted up and down the aisle like he might find Ryan hiding in wait. Meredith could relate since she checked her phone far too often for potential missed calls or texts that never materialized.

Emma sat down on the hay cross-legged and laughed as two of the pups immediately scampered into her lap.

"The one with the purple collar is a girl, and the other is our blue boy. He's the runt."

"I love him," Emma answered without hesitation. "I've always been a fan of the underdog."

Meredith smiled. "Me, too." She liked Ryan's sister even though she didn't want to. It would help if the woman would be snarky or judgmental about Meredith or her ragtag operation.

"We didn't pick you because of Ryan," she said, her attention still focused on the dogs. "It would be a shame if you let this opportunity pass because of your pride."

"Pride?" Meredith sputtered. "This isn't about pride."

"Fear of success?" Emma asked conversationally.

Meredith groaned. "You remind me of my sister Avery. It's not a compliment."

"You do realize I'm actually the one you need to suck up to?" Emma laughed. "I run the foundation and lead the committee that makes the decision about funding."

"So are you going to take it away?"

Emma looked up, her gaze sharp. "Do you want it?"

Anticipation moved through Meredith like a slow wave. She could do so much with that money. A grant from a high-profile foundation like Howard would give her the legitimacy she craved and might open the door to other sources of funding.

Yes, she had a deep desire to take care of things on her own. It came from years of feeling like she was a burden. But she'd never considered that her pride might actually get in the way of the success she wanted for herself and for her animals.

"Yes," she whispered. Instead of the uneasiness she expected, there was an almost overwhelming sense of serenity.

"Excellent." Emma smiled. "We'll have a small ceremony when we officially award you the money. You'll be expected to mix and mingle with our other grant recipients and people who support the foundation."

"I won't show up with dog poo on my shoe," Meredith promised, her mind already whirring at the possibilities of what she could do with the funds.

"I'm not worried about that. Our board of directors attends."

"Ryan." Meredith drew in a breath.

"Does the fact that you're accepting the award change what you think about him?"

"He lied to me."

Emma nodded. "If it helps, he thought he was justified and doing what was best for you and the rescue."

"I know," Meredith replied softly. "I'm not sure if it makes a difference."

"I've never seen him talk about a woman the way he did you. He really cares about you."

"Cared," Meredith corrected. "Past tense. Trust me, your brother wants nothing to do with me after the things I said."

"I'm not sure I agree with that," Emma countered. "But that's between the two of you. And I really have no room to give relationship advice."

"Aren't you married?" Meredith asked. "I figured, with your last name."

"Divorced." Emma shoved her hands into the front pockets of her dark pants. "A spectacular crash and burn of the perfect marriage."

"Doesn't sound so perfect, then."

"That's on me," the other woman said, and the sadness in her voice made Meredith want to know more, although she wouldn't ask.

"How do you feel about goats?"

"I'm not sure how to answer that."

"Let's go meet Monica, Rachel and Phoebe. I have a feeling they won't be with me much longer. There's a family moving to town that's bought a small farm nearby. My goats might be just what they're looking for."

"Those names are funny. Ryan used to love *Friends*," Emma said as they started down the aisle.

"He told me he watched it for your benefit."

Emma flashed a smile. "No way. He had a huge crush on Jennifer Aniston."

"Well, my Rachel happens to have a huge crush on him. She's been depressed ever since he left." She looked away. "Everyone around here has."

"He's back to work in the city," Emma said. "Pushing too hard and taking on too many shifts."

"Your brother has a deep sense of service." Meredith reached down to pet one of the barn cats as it wrapped itself around her ankles.

"You two have a lot in common." Emma clapped her hands. "Oh, my. Goats. They're so cute."

"Intelligent and inquisitive as well, which leads them into trouble more often than not." Meredith knew she needed to change the topic away from Ryan before she completely lost her composure.

She and Emma walked around the rest of the property as they discussed Meredith's plan for expanding the operation. She explained that she and her sisters were hoping for a quick sale of their father's house in town, and her share of any profits from that would also go toward paying off the land. Emma mentioned that she'd stopped by the estate sale and loved the architecture and spirit of the neighborhood.

Meredith had finally reached a point where she could discuss Niall's house without a knot of bitterness forming in her belly. A small win, but she'd take it.

Emma asked perceptive questions and gave a few suggestions based on previous experience helping rescue organizations. Meredith wasn't sure whether realizing she'd achieved one of her ultimate goals made her feel better or worse. She was proud to be receiving the funding, but the happiness bursting in her chest also made her miss Ryan more.

He'd been the one to help her have the confidence to believe in herself, and he remained the person she most wanted to share her success with. The idea of never having that opportunity dulled her joy, and she had no idea how to make it better.

"SOMETHING'S WRONG."

Ryan frowned as David took the seat across from him at the table in the doctors' lounge.

"They're serving a Chinese special on Taco Tuesday?" Ryan guessed as he forked up a bite of fried rice. "I guess the food-service staff wants to keep us on our toes."

"With you," David clarified.

Ryan shook his head, ignoring the way his shoulders tensed. "I met with the surgeon and the psychologist. Both of them gave me the all clear. I've been working my ass off, and my leg is holding up fine. It's sore at night, but otherwise—"

"It's the working-your-ass-off part." David grabbed an egg roll from the plate in front of Ryan. "You're working like you have something to prove. What's the deal?"

"Wow." Ryan sat back, laced his fingers together over

his stomach. "I have to admit I didn't see that coming. The chief of staff complains because one of his docs is working too hard. Don't you have anything better to deal with other than harping on me for doing my job?"

"No need to get defensive. I'm concerned about you. Not just as a doctor but as my friend."

Ryan's jaw went tight. He wanted to deny the problem and the friendship. Not because he didn't consider David a friend as well as a respected colleague. But Ryan didn't want to care about anyone at the moment. To risk opening his heart and having it stomped on again, especially when he was nowhere near over the pain of losing Meredith.

"I'm making up for lost time," he said. "No need to be concerned. I'm glad to be back."

"You might be the worst liar I've ever met," David said with a soft laugh.

Not according to Meredith. She'd called him out on lying, and the pain in her eyes during that confrontation still played over and over in his head. She'd had every right to be angry. In hindsight, he realized that he'd used the excuse of wanting to protect her and ended up hurting her instead. All he'd done was to delay the inevitable because of his own convoluted feelings about his family and his role in the world.

Keeping that information to himself wasn't something that had been solely for Meredith's benefit. It was selfish, motivated by fear that if he shared the truth with her, she'd look at him differently. He would have given her a reason to choose his family's money and influence over him, the way so many other people had in his life.

Ryan hated people knowing about his family because he could never tell if they wanted to be with him because they cared about him or because of what they thought they could get from him.

He'd underestimated her because of his own stupid fears.

"I'm here," he said when David continued to stare at him, his dark gaze far too knowing. "And I'm doing a good job."

"Not arguing that point. From what I hear, you've gone into beast mode. It's freaking out the nurses."

"Stop."

David leaned forward, reached for another egg roll, but Ryan smacked away his hand. He sure as hell wasn't going to endure a grilling and then share his food. "What happened while you were away?" David asked as he drew back.

"I healed. Isn't that what you wanted? It's why I got put on medical leave in the first place."

"You healed," David repeated thoughtfully. "I'm actually thinking you did, which is why you're having such trouble readjusting now."

"No trouble." Ryan placed his fork on the table. "The trouble is in your head."

"I think it might actually be in your heart," his boss answered.

Ryan bit down on the inside of his cheek. He forced himself to continue to meet David's measured gaze. "You're wrong."

"Paul Thorpe called from Magnolia Community yesterday. He told me what a great job you did with the mobile medical clinic. Mentioned that you also got involved with a local animal rescue down there."

"I had a lot of time to kill."

"He also told me about the woman who runs it. She's the daughter of that famous artist?"

"Yeah." Ryan choked out the word. There was so much

more to Meredith than being one of Niall Reed's three daughters. She was amazing all on her own. He understood that part of the reason she'd reacted so strongly to him not telling her the truth was because she had a history of being hurt by people she trusted. She'd trusted him, and he'd broken that faith.

His last girlfriend had accused him of being so wrapped up in his family issues that he couldn't pull his head out of his ass long enough to figure out how to make an identity separate from his past. He thought he had done that. All his work in college and med school and the fast track on the hospital career path to prove he wasn't riding the coattails of his grandfather's success. It meant nothing now.

"It sounds like you were happy in Magnolia." David studied him.

"You got this insight from a man who knew me for a month." Ryan scoffed. "Paul has his own reasons for wanting me in Magnolia."

"I get that. Are you saying he's wrong?"

Ryan started to shake his head, then stopped. If nothing else, he was done lying—to himself or to anyone else. "It was a good break."

"You know, it wasn't just what Paul told me. I could hear it in your voice. In fact, I was surprised when you told me you were coming back. I got the impression our phone call was going to be so that you could turn in your resignation."

That's exactly what was going to happen until it didn't. Ryan spread his hands wide. "Yet here I am."

"I hate to say it, but you don't belong here anymore."

Ryan blinked as disbelief clouded his vision. "What is that supposed to mean? Can't have damaged goods mucking up the place? Because you know—"

"Don't get your panties in a bunch. You're a good doctor, Ryan. Possibly better because of what you've been through. That night changed everyone who experienced it, but it's those kinds of situations that sometimes spur real change. Like the kind you experienced in Magnolia."

Ryan couldn't deny it. He hadn't expected life in a sleepy Southern small town to fit him, but it did. It fit who he wanted to be. Meredith fit.

"I screwed things up with her," he said slowly. "So I'm not sure I belong there at this point, either." He huffed out a harsh laugh. "I don't belong anywhere."

"We both know that isn't true. Is the only reason you liked Magnolia because of the girl?"

"Meredith," Ryan whispered. "Her name is Meredith."

"She's obviously special."

"You have no idea. But she wasn't the only reason. I liked practicing small-town medicine."

"You understand you don't owe us anything."

"I owe Kevin's memory," Ryan argued. "He loved this place and the work he did here."

"Exactly." David tapped a finger on the table. "Kevin was happy, and he'd want you to be, too. It had nothing to do with the hospital. He loved working with patients. The best way to honor his memory is not to kill yourself and everyone around you by going on overdrive. He'd want you to be the best doctor you could—to make people's lives better."

Ryan looked away as familiar grief washed over him. "I hate that he's not here anymore."

"We all do." David sighed. "But you can't pretend things are the same as they used to be. They're not. You're not."

"So do I just insert myself into the world of a woman who doesn't want me?" Ryan asked.

"Uh, no." David shook his head. "That sounds a tad stalkerish. But have you thought about asking her for another chance?"

"Which might be the perfect way to get kicked to the curb all over again."

"Spoken like a man who's never had to work to earn a woman's love."

The truth chafed at Ryan's nerves. "I work plenty hard."

"Not in relationships." David held up his hands when Ryan would have argued. "I'm not saying it's easy. But is she worth the risk?"

"Yes." Ryan breathed out the word without even realizing it.

But it was true. He'd tried to walk away without looking back, and he was miserable. It was time to admit he wanted another chance with Meredith more than he wanted his next breath. How did he convince her he deserved one?

CHAPTER TWENTY-FOUR

MEREDITH PRESSED A hand to her rapidly beating heart as she looked around at the family and friends who'd gathered outside the barn two weeks later. Spring had come fully to Magnolia with the trees in bloom, and the pasture shimmered with the brilliant green hue of the new grass.

It had been Carrie and Avery's idea to host a potluck to celebrate the grant she'd won, and despite her still-aching heart, Meredith had agreed. Several dozen people milled about, talking and enjoying the tables full of options. Southerners liked nothing more than sharing food, and there was a spread that included barbecue chicken and pulled pork, mayonnaise-based salads of all varieties and so many baked goods her teeth ached just looking at them.

The outpouring of support overwhelmed her. Theo and her dad were near the pen Ryan had helped her update, which had been turned into a sort of petting zoo for the goats. She was happy to see Monica, Rachel and Phoebe getting so much attention and even happier that Mayor Malcolm's granddaughter and her husband had decided to adopt them after doing a goat meet and greet last week.

Sometimes Meredith lost sight of how much she and her sisters had done to reinvigorate the community. It wasn't as though anyone wanted the town to continue the slow decline that started when Niall's popularity waned and visitors stopped coming to see the well-known artist. But no one had realized they had more to offer than just his dubious fame.

Meredith could relate to that. She'd sold herself short for far too long. The past—her mother's rejection and the way she'd devalued herself through her relationships with men—had shaped her into someone who couldn't seem to trust herself or others. Niall's death—as much as a shock as it had been—had shaken her out of her troublesome comfort zone. Forging a bond with Avery and Carrie offered the proof she hadn't even known she'd needed that she had more to offer.

But she knew it wasn't just them. Being with Ryan had changed her, as well. He'd broken down her defenses, and in doing so, he'd helped her see that she didn't need them anymore.

It's why she kept to herself today. Oh, she'd talked to people. Even Emma Cantrell had made the drive down after Meredith invited her.

Meredith couldn't help that her gaze kept sliding to the winding driveway—over and over—hoping to see Ryan's car, even though she knew he'd returned to DC and his regular life. He'd probably forgotten all about her.

The thought made her chest ache.

"Hey, Shae?"

The teenager paused as she carried a tray of cookies from the house toward the food tables.

"I'm going to take Brodie and Benji on a short walk along with my three dogs." She smiled when the girl gaped at her.

"In the middle of your party?"

"People won't even notice I'm gone, and I'll only be a

few minutes. I didn't have a chance to do the regular scan of the fence line this morning, and I want to make sure it's all clear."

The dogs trotted around her excitedly as they began the trek across the field. She took a deep breath, her lungs filling with the tangy, fragrant scent of springtime on the coast. It still amazed her that almost overnight the world around her had gone from brown and dreary to green and blooming with new life.

She hadn't allowed herself to concentrate on anything beyond the present moment because she'd lived for so long with the fear of losing her property or somehow failing the animals she cared for. Even when Niall had been alive, she'd always worried that he would decide to rescind the great deal he gave her on rent, which afforded her the ability to make a go of her organization.

In some strange way she owed her biological father for the state of her current life. If he hadn't agreed to rent her the property for such a low monthly amount, she didn't know if she would have found another way to start Furever Friends. Even more, she owed him a debt of gratitude for revealing what he did in his will. It had felt like a blow at the time, but the revelation had brought Avery and Carrie into her life. Now, she couldn't imagine a world without them in it.

About halfway toward the fence line, Brodie's fur bristled, and he started barking incessantly. The dog tore across the field and the rest of the pack joined him almost instantly. Meredith's hair stood on end as she realized the dogs were running toward a figure standing near the gate that led out of the far side of her property. She glanced over her shoulder but was far enough away from the barn that no one at the party noticed the ruckus.

She jogged forward, calling for the dogs, but only Benji obeyed her shouted commands. The other four dashed through the open gate to surround a man who'd climbed onto the hood of a shiny Tesla SUV. A strange car to find on this empty stretch of beach road.

The man looked vaguely familiar, although Meredith couldn't quite remember where she'd seen him before. He was as out of place in the pasture as she would have been in a five-star restaurant. He wore a pale gray suit with a bright pink button-down shirt and matching tie.

As she got closer, he hollered at her to control her blasted animals and kicked out a foot when Brodie placed his front paws on the shiny hood of the Tesla. Anger bubbled up inside of Meredith. Something had set off the dogs, and she had no tolerance for physical violence against animals.

She was about to shout that at the stranger when her gaze snagged on a container sitting a few feet away from the front of the car. Through the clear plastic she could see that the bin was filled with what looked like dog food. The same size and shape of the tainted kibble that had been left on her property a few weeks earlier.

"Who the hell are you and…wait…you're the Realtor who Avery fired. Jacob. I remember you. I remember how slimy I thought you were."

The dogs settled as she moved to the other side of the fence with them but continued to mill about the vehicle. Jacob Martin slid to the front of the hood but didn't climb down. "I guess that makes us even because I thought you were a crazy bit—"

"Don't say it."

Meredith startled at the familiar voice and turned to find Ryan striding toward her from the direction of the cottage.

Benji let out a yelp of delight and rushed toward him with Brodie following. Meredith's three dogs wagged their tails but stayed in position guarding the Realtor.

At Meredith's questioning stare, Ryan shrugged. "I heard the racket from the dogs…"

"All the way from DC?" she asked, crossing her arms over her chest.

"I'm staying at the cottage again." Something flashed in his gaze that she recognized but didn't dare put a name to.

"Since when?"

"Do you mind calling off your fleabags?" Jacob demanded. "The hood of the car is hotter than blue blazes right now."

"I got in last night." Ryan ignored the flustered real-estate agent. "What's going on here?"

"The dogs found the guy who poisoned Brodie." She hitched an arm toward Jacob. "I need to call the cops."

"You don't have proof," the guy said with a sniff. "It could be coincidence that I'm out here. I was heading for the beach and had car trouble."

"What the hell kind of monster tries to poison animals?" Ryan turned his attention fully toward the other man, and his anger on behalf of her babies melted Meredith's heart.

As if she weren't already a puddle of goo upon seeing him. She'd discovered that Ryan had sent a letter to the other members of the foundation's board of directors detailing his experience with Furever Friends but expressing his opinion that the rescue deserved to be funded regardless of his involvement. Emma explained that he hadn't wanted Meredith to have any doubt that she'd been awarded the grant on her own merit. With a little time and perspective, she understood that she'd overreacted to what he'd done. Yes, he'd lied and kept a secret, but that didn't change how much he'd helped her and believed in her dream. She'd come to understand the lie had more to do with his issues and not his feelings about her.

But she hadn't believed she'd have the opportunity to make it right again.

"I wasn't trying to hurt the damn dog," Jacob said, sounding oddly affronted for a man who'd just been caught. "It was a message for her." He pointed at Meredith. "Your sister would have sold me this land if it wasn't for your stupid animal rescue. It's prime real estate. You can scoop dog poop from any location."

"This farm belongs to me," Meredith said, her eyes narrowing. "It's not for sale. Avery told you as much."

"I could make the three of you rich," Jacob answered. His shrewd gaze took in the swath of open space surrounding them. "I have big plans for this part of the coast, but I need land to develop."

"So you tried to chase her away by poisoning the animals?" Ryan shook his head and took a step closer. "I have half a mind to shove that tainted kibble down your throat."

"It wasn't enough to kill an animal." Jacob held up his hands. "I researched the amounts. You need to realize this property is too much for you to manage. Sell the farm and set up whatever kind of rescue you want in another location. There's plenty of crap land for sale in the area. What we're standing on is too valuable to be wasted on dogs and cats and goats and whatever else you're hoarding."

Rage made Meredith's hands tremble. "What I do isn't a waste." As much as she'd questioned her ability to succeed, she'd never doubted the importance of working with the animals who needed her. Hearing this man trivialize it was an unwelcome shock.

"Say the word and I'll kill him," Ryan muttered.

"He's not worth the effort. Call the cops instead," she responded. "We'll let them deal with it."

"Oh, hell no." Jacob started to climb down from the hood, but the dogs still blocked his way. A couple of them growled, and Jacob scrambled back a few feet. "Call off the mutts."

"I don't think so." Meredith crossed her arms over her chest again and took a step forward as Ryan placed the call to local law enforcement. "You're going to stay right where you are."

"Just let me go," Jacob said through clenched teeth. "I'm done with you and your stupid land. It's not worth the trouble."

"It's worth more than you could ever imagine," she countered but didn't call off her dogs.

Jacob glared at her. "I hope a damn hurricane tears through here next fall."

"Well, I hope you're prepared to never sell a property in this part of the state again." Meredith pointed a finger at the man. "I'm a part of this community, you big jerk. I have friends here, and I guarantee you'll never be welcome anywhere near Magnolia again."

She turned to Ryan. He nodded at her as he pocketed his cell phone. "The department has a deputy in the area. He'll be here shortly."

Meredith glanced over her shoulder at Jacob. "You're done."

Ryan moved to stand beside her, and her heart hammered

against her ribs. Not from the confrontation with Jacob but because of Ryan's return and what it might mean.

RYAN WATCHED MEREDITH as the deputy drove away with Jacob Martin in the back seat of the squad car. She looked both tense and determined, and he wished he knew what to do to take away the last half hour and the pain of knowing that someone had wanted to harm her.

He couldn't stand the thought of anyone hurting her. Not on his watch. How the hell had he ever thought he could walk away from this woman?

"Are you okay?" he asked, shutting the gate that led from her property to the beach road.

Her chest rose and fell as she drew in a deep breath before turning to him. "Yes," she answered after a moment. "I am."

Brodie trotted over to him and nudged his leg. He automatically bent down to scratch between his ears. "You're a good boy."

"He missed you."

He glanced up at Meredith. "Was the dog the only one?"

One side of her mouth curved. "Rachel was pretty depressed at first, but then she transferred her affections to Theo. Fickle animal."

"I'll remember that."

She tucked a stray lock of hair behind one ear. "I should get back to the barn. I skipped out on my party. I texted my sisters and asked them to cover for me, but I need to go home."

"Mind if I walk with you?" He held his breath as he waited for her answer, afraid she might say no.

Something flashed in her eyes, but it was gone before he

could name it. "I'd like that." She whistled, and the crew of dogs came running, and they all started back across the field.

The silence between them was heavy but not uncomfortable. The dogs were entertaining as they scrambled across the pasture, and he caught the salty scent of the ocean on the breeze. It smelled like home.

"I didn't expect to see you again," Meredith said with a furtive glance in his direction. "Shouldn't you be saving lives in the city?"

He shrugged and tried to look nonchalant, even though nerves skittered along his skin. How would she react to his news? "I'm not going back," he said simply.

She stopped walking but continued to look straight ahead. "But you did go back. You returned to your old job. Dr. Thorpe told me."

"You talked to Paul?"

"He and Aimee adopted two cats from me last weekend. They were only planning on taking one, but Paul fell in love with a bonded pair."

"Paul is becoming a cat lady? I can't wait to mention that to him."

Meredith squeezed shut her eyes, then turned to him. "Why are you here, Ryan?"

He heard the vulnerability in her tone, and it made him know that he had to allow himself to be unguarded as well if this was really going to work. "Magnolia feels like home."

Her brows drew together as she tried to make sense of that. Before she could respond and before he lost his nerve, he added, "You're my home, Meredith."

Her mouth opened and closed as color flooded her cheeks. She gave a barely perceptible headshake, and he wasn't sure how to interpret her response. She had the power to ruin him, but he refused to give up. Not when he was so close to having more than he would have believed possible.

"I understand that I screwed up." He fisted his hands at his sides to keep from reaching for her. "I understand if you don't want to give me another chance. But I'm here for you." He massaged a hand over the back of his neck. "Not just you, though. I'm here because being with you changed something in me. You made me see that there's more to life than other people's expectations or chasing a goal that doesn't truly mean anything to me. I can't go back to how I was living before. I want a chance to build something more. I want that chance with you."

"You do?" Her voice trembled as she met his gaze, hope blazing in her eyes.

"I love you so damn much," he whispered and didn't bother to hide the tremble in his voice. "I love your heart and your intensity, and I love that you never give up. You're the best person I know."

"I doubt that," she said with a self-deprecating laugh.

He stepped closer until the toes of his sneakers and her boots almost touched. "You're my person. You always will be. Even if you don't want me."

His heart hammered in his chest as he waited for her reply, wondering if she would open her heart to him again or walk away. He could barely stand the thought of that— the loneliness of the last two weeks had been worse than he'd thought possible.

She closed her eyes, and he held his breath. The sound of the dogs investigating the world around them made for a soothing background noise, but he couldn't take his eyes off Meredith.

When she finally looked at him, her eyes glittered with tears. "I want you, Ryan. I love you. Always."

Then she launched herself at him. He wrapped his arms around her, and his world was right again.

MEREDITH TRIED TO choke back her tears. She didn't like crying, but the joy that flowed through her at Ryan's declaration of love seemed to be too big to contain. It had to be let out or else she might explode with happiness.

"I love you," she said into the crook of his neck, thrilled at how the words continued to sound so right each time she said them. "If you ever walk away from me again, I'll kill you."

He hugged her tighter. "Wild horses couldn't drag me away, sweetheart. Don't cry. I don't ever want to see you cry."

"These are happy tears." She lifted her head with a sniff. "The good kind."

"I'll take your word for it," he said but dashed the sleeve of his shirt across the corner of his eye.

She grinned. "We're quite a pair. Both of us hate sloppy emotions, and now we're a blubbering mess."

"Speak for yourself. I have allergies."

"Liar," she whispered, then winced when his expression sobered.

"I'll never lie to you again," he promised. "I'm sorry, Meredith. I've been struggling with conflicting feelings about my family and where I came from for years. I should have believed you wouldn't judge me for that."

As much as she appreciated his apology, Ryan wasn't

the only one who'd acted like a fool. "You were right. If you'd shared your connection to the foundation with me at the beginning, I would have judged the heck out of you. I would have missed getting to know you." She leaned in and brushed a kiss across his lips. "Falling in love with you."

"And now…" The vulnerability in his blue eyes made goose bumps erupt across her skin.

"It's too late." She gave a purposefully casual shrug. "I'm hopelessly devoted to you, and I'm going to make the best use of your family foundation's money. Also, I think your sister and I are going to be great friends."

"God help us all," he muttered, then captured her lips.

"So you think you can be happy as a small-town doctor?" she asked when they finally broke apart.

"I can be happy wherever you are," he answered without hesitation. "But, yes, I'm looking forward to working in Magnolia and becoming a part of the community. This place is special."

He took her hand as they began to walk toward her house once again. "It is," she agreed, still amazed at how long it took her to realize it, but content knowing she finally had.

With this man at her side, the future would be better than she'd ever imagined.

* * * * *

A CAROLINA VALENTINE

CHAPTER ONE

PAUL THORPE WATCHED the woman approach, but even when she met his gaze and offered a tentative smile, he couldn't believe she was headed toward him.

He glanced over his shoulder although he knew there was no one sitting behind him in the almost empty hospital cafeteria. Nine o'clock on a Saturday night wasn't exactly a high traffic hour.

"Hey, Dr. Thorpe." Aimee Baker balanced her food tray in one hand and gave him a tiny wave with the other. "Mind if I join you?"

He stared at the pretty nurse for several long moments, mesmerized as always by her beauty. Aimee's blond curls framed her face like a bright aura, and her almond-shaped, sky blue eyes and luminous skin made her seem like a throwback beauty from the age of classic movies.

Yet Paul knew she was thoroughly modern. Her manner with patients and coworkers deftly straddled the line between command and comfort. She regularly made people in the hospital laugh, putting her adorable dimples on display. She never joked around with Paul, much to his chagrin. Obviously she took his silence as a repudiation. She glanced at the laptop open in front of him, her smile faltering.

"Or maybe you're busy," she said on a rush of breath,

color flooding her already rosy cheeks. "Sorry. I won't bother—"

"You're not a bother," he said, then cleared his throat and pushed back from the table to stand, snapping his laptop closed. "Please sit down. And call me Paul. You know you can call me Paul, right? I mean we've…"

His voice trailed off at the alarmed look she gave him.

"Worked together for over a year," he finished quickly. She nodded with what looked like relief.

Did she really think he'd mention anything else and embarrass them both? His heart stammered at the memory from a few weeks earlier. The stroke of midnight on the roof of Magnolia Community Hospital and an innocent New Year's kiss between two overworked, exhausted colleagues that had quickly turned into something more. A spark of desire had flamed into a brush fire of need and longing and rocked him to his core.

It ended before things got out of hand, or so he told himself. His heart and his body might disagree with his rational brain.

"Right." She sat her tray on the Formica tabletop and slid into the chair across from him. "Slow night." She picked up a fry, then pushed the plate toward him. "Want one?"

"No carbs," he answered with a shake of his head.

Her gaze rolled toward the ceiling. "I should have known. I bet you do CrossFit, too."

"Occasionally. What's wrong with CrossFit?"

"Nothing. It just explains why you look the way you do." She pointed a fry at him. "I'm more a body by pasta type of person."

His mouth went dry because her body was perfect as far as he could tell. Not that he'd ever seen her in clothes other than scrubs or had any business fantasizing about what she might look like out of the shapeless uniform. "I don't have anything against pasta," he told her. "It's not my thing."

"What about cake?" she asked, one delicate brow lifting.

He leaned forward like he was about to reveal some universal secret. "I might have a thing for cake."

She bit down on her lower lip as she tried to hide her smile. His body tightened in response. Holy hell, he needed to get out more. How could talking carbs in a hospital cafeteria make him this hot and bothered?

But he knew the answer. It wasn't the conversation. It was Aimee. He'd noticed her immediately when she came to work at the hospital a year ago, but he had a strict policy against dating coworkers. In truth, he hadn't dated anyone since his former fiancée had winged her engagement ring at him over two years prior. The look of pain in Kimberly's eyes—and knowing he'd been the one to put it there—had been enough to convince him he wasn't cut out for love.

"Then I'll bake you a cake," Aimee said, leaning back and pressing two fingers to her chest like she might be having the same trouble catching her breath as he was. "If you agree to a date."

Paul felt his mouth drop open, but she continued before he could answer. "With the highest bidder at my bachelor auction."

He blinked. "You're auctioning off bachelors? Is that some new side hustle?"

She laughed, a husky rumble of sound that made him think of evening thunderstorms on a hot summer night. "It's part of the hospital's fundraising gala at the end of the month. We're partnering with local restaurants. Attendees will bid on eligible bachelors from Magnolia. They'll get an evening with their date of choice, and all the money raised will go to funding the mobile health-care clinic."

"That's a worthwhile initiative," Paul said. As head of emergency room medicine at the hospital, he was involved in planning for and staffing the facility's newest offering. "The mobile clinic has the potential to make a big impact in a community like ours."

"Exactly." Aimee sipped at her water. "If we can raise enough money, the clinic should be able to start making rounds by early spring."

"I didn't realize you were so engaged in the project."

"I grew up in a rural community on the Tennessee border. If my town had a mobile health-care van, people would have had access to better medical care and early detection for cancer and other diseases."

"That sounds personal."

"My mom died when I was in high school," she said quietly, her eyes darkening. "Stage four breast cancer. By the time she went to the doctor for treatment, it had metastasized."

"I'm sorry, Aimee." Her fingers tightened on the plastic cup, and he had the strange longing to reach for her. He didn't, of course. It wasn't his place to offer her comfort as much as he might want to.

"So you'll do it?" she asked.

"No."

Her features went slack. "But we need you, Dr. Th— Paul."

"I'm not a good candidate for a bachelor auction."

"The women of Magnolia might disagree." She held up a small hand and ticked off a list of attributes. "Single, check. Good hair, check. Nice teeth, check. Popular with the ladies, ch—"

"Uncheck," he interrupted, resisting the urge to run a hand through his brown hair. Did he have good hair? He'd never considered it an asset. "I don't date. I haven't been on a date in years. I don't know what I'm doing anymore."

"You know what you're doing," she whispered, her gaze intent on the plate of fries on her tray.

Was that a reference to the kiss they'd shared? It had to be, and the thought sent pleasure snaking along his skin.

"Are you planning to bid?" he asked before he thought better of it.

She squeezed her eyes shut for a moment before raising her gaze to his. "No."

Well, then. That was definitive. She might remember the kiss but didn't want to revisit it. Good to know.

"I've had requests," she continued, looking as uncomfortable saying the words as he felt hearing them. "For you. It hasn't gone unnoticed that you seem to be almost aggressively single. Apparently, there are several women who think the bachelor auction might be their chance to change that."

"It won't change," he told her.

"It's one date," she countered. "I'll bake you a cake. Whatever flavor you want. It's for a good cause."

He felt one side of his mouth curve up at that. There were a lot of things he wanted from Aimee, but cake wasn't on the list.

His cell phone, which sat on the table next to his laptop, pinged with an incoming text. He read the short missive from his brother and inwardly groaned.

"Do you have plans for Valentine's Day, Aimee?" he

asked suddenly. "Cupid's favorite day of the year is almost upon us."

She shook her head. "It's a fake holiday. I don't celebrate fake holidays."

"A true romantic," he said with a chuckle. "I like that. Unfortunately, I do have plans. My brother's wedding is this coming weekend outside of Asheville."

"Congratulations to him," she murmured.

"Come with me."

She let out a small gasp, which wasn't the worst reaction he could have imagined. "You're joking. You just told me you don't date."

"Right," he agreed. "And you don't believe in romance. I don't want to deal with the event on my own. It's complicated, but the arrangement I'm proposing is simple. Go with me to the wedding and I'll be your bachelor."

"That's extortion," she muttered, her eyes narrowing.

"Maybe, but that's my proposal. I'll make it worth your while, I promise."

"Excuse me?" she stammered.

"The auction," he clarified. "The fundraiser is in two weeks, right?"

"Yeah."

"I'll turn on the charm, and you can let everyone know how much I'm looking forward to being a part of it. How I'm ready to be leg shackled and all that jazz."

"You make it sound so appealing." She rolled her eyes.

"It could be."

"Have you ever been married, Paul?"

"No." He thought about explaining exactly why he wanted a date for his brother's wedding but didn't want to freak her out more than he already had with his proposition. "Close, but no. You?"

She took another drink and he thought he might have pushed her too far. "Five years," she said. "Turns out, it wasn't for me."

That surprised him. Aimee seemed like the type of woman any man in his right mind would want as a life partner. "We'll raise a lot of money if you say yes." He flashed what he hoped was a charming and not desperate smile. "Word on the street is I'm quite the catch."

"What street?"

He drew in a breath. "I don't actually know. You're the one who thinks that."

"Not me." She wiped her fingers on a napkin. "Other women. I'm not much of a fisherman so I'm not looking to catch anyone."

Too bad. He clamped his lips together before the words popped out.

She studied him for a few long seconds, then pushed back from the table. "Okay, Paul. I'll go to your wedding, but you better live up to your end of the bargain. The mobile clinic is important. I expect you to do your part to get it funded."

He nodded, unable to read her expression but relieved and strangely excited that she'd agreed. He'd been dreading next weekend since Peter had called him about the wedding date. Suddenly the prospect of spending the weekend with his family—including his ex-fiancée, who'd married his father only months after they'd called off the engagement—didn't bother Paul quite so much.

CHAPTER TWO

"YOU'RE CRAZY. What if he's some kind of creep?"

Aimee paused in the act of packing her compact roller bag early Saturday morning and turned to her roommate. Megan sat on the recliner in the corner of Aimee's bedroom, a silky black cat perched in her lap. "You work with Paul Thorpe, too. Do you think he's a creep?"

Megan shook her head, dark eyes going wide. "Well, no. I think he's hotter than sin and, quite frankly, I'm jealous. I wish I'd been the one he'd made the bargain with. Valentine's Day at a fancy resort with a smokin' doctor. Where do I sign up?"

"Stop." Aimee tried to will away the heat rising in her throat and inwardly cursed her fair complexion. Her tendency to blush made it difficult to hide her emotions, something she'd definitely need to manage spending so much time with Dr. Thorpe.

Paul. She had to start thinking of him as Paul, even though she'd relegated him to a more formal distance after the New Year's kiss they'd shared. It had been a mistake, stupid and impulsive—two things Aimee rarely let herself be anymore.

She hadn't told anyone about the kiss, not even Megan, a pediatric nurse at the hospital and Aimee's roommate since she'd moved to Magnolia a year earlier. Secrets were hard to keep in a small town, and she understood that the hospital gossips would go crazy if they thought she was making a play for everyone's favorite doctor crush.

In fact, Megan had been the one to insist that Aimee convince Paul to take part in the bachelor auction. She wasn't the only nurse interested in bidding on the ER doctor, just the most determined. Given the way Megan cycled through men, Aimee had no doubt that her friend would pursue him aggressively if given the chance.

Aimee didn't care who won the date with him. Not one bit.

"It's not like that," she insisted, unsure if she was trying to convince herself or her friend.

"Are you packing lingerie?"

Aimee shut her suitcase and zipped it. "I don't own actual lingerie. Unless cotton bras count."

"Lord, girl, no." Megan stood, dumping the sleek cat onto the floor. Mo trotted over to Aimee and rubbed up against her leg. She'd adopted the cat from a local rescue, Furever Friends, right after moving to Magnolia. Reeling from her divorce and the understanding that she'd never have the life she dreamed of for herself, she'd needed something to love. After the rescue's owner explained that black cats were often ignored by potential adopters, Aimee had chosen the inkiest kitten in the group. "Do you want to borrow a negligee?"

Aimee sputtered out a laugh, not just at the general thought of wearing lingerie but also because her well-meaning roommate was two inches taller than Aimee and a good fifteen pounds lighter. "No, thank you. I'd look like a stuffed sausage in anything of yours."

"Men like curves."

"It isn't like that," Aimee repeated, then checked her watch. "I need to go. I told Avery Keller I'd drop off flyers for the auction this afternoon."

"Why isn't he picking you up here?"

"I don't know. It seemed easier to meet at the hospital." Aimee bent down to scratch between the cat's ears. "Don't forget to feed Mo."

"Got it." Megan saluted her. "Text me if you get lucky. I know I would if given the opportunity."

Exactly the reason Aimee hadn't wanted Paul to come to the house. What if Megan started flirting and he decided to switch his impulsive invitation from Aimee to her outgoing roommate? Megan made no secret of her feelings for Paul, although her interest was purely physical, which worried Aimee even more. According to Megan, he'd so far ignored her subtle suggestions about getting together. Yet something had made him desperate enough to want a date for this wedding. Aimee shouldn't be looking forward to it, but she was.

"I'll see you tomorrow night," Aimee said, then left the house.

She took a quick detour through downtown and parked at the curb outside town hall, which housed the sheriff's department, the county's health and human services division as well as the offices for local government. She knocked on the open door to Avery Keller's office and smiled as the polished blonde gestured her inside.

"Let me finish this email," Avery told her, "and I'll be right with you. Have a seat."

Holding the envelope of flyers in front of her, Aimee lowered herself into the leather chair across from the desk. The office was small but welcoming, with botanical prints on the wall that looked nothing like the paintings of Niall Reed, the famous artist who'd been Avery's biological father.

Aimee didn't know Avery or her history well, although she appreciated the other woman's attention to detail and willingness to help promote the hospital fundraiser. Avery had arrived in town at the end of last summer after Niall, who'd been Magnolia's most famous resident, named her in his will. From what Avery had told her during their brief meetings, she hadn't been planning to stay in town long-term, but she'd fallen for the community and for a local firefighter, Grayson Atwell.

Magnolia had been struggling before Avery's arrival, but she and her sisters—one of whom was the woman who'd helped Aimee adopt Mo—had quickly turned things around. Aimee was grateful because new residents and visitors meant more potential support for the hospital, and specifically for the mobile clinic.

"Done." Avery turned from the monitor toward Aimee. "Thanks for dropping the flyers to me. I don't usually work on weekends but took yesterday off for a field trip with my soon-to-be stepdaughter. I'll distribute them to local businesses when I finish here. How are plans for the event going?"

"Good," Aimee said with a nod. "I got another bachelor for the auction." That portion of the event had actually been Avery's idea, inspired by something she and her fiancé's daughter had watched on a TV movie.

"Is he cute?"

"Yes." Aimee cleared her throat when the word came out as a croak. "He's a doctor."

"I can tell he must be very handsome by the way you're blushing."

Aimee bit back a groan. Stupid complexion.

"Are you planning to bid?" Avery leaned forward in her chair with a smile. "I do enjoy a good start to a love story."

"No love story for me." Aimee put the envelope on the desk. "Been there, done that. I have the scars to prove it."

Avery's gaze softened. "Don't we all. I thought the same thing a few months ago, but don't give up on love. It can find you when and where you least expect it, especially since it's Valentine's Day."

"Fake holiday," Aimee muttered, then cringed. "Sorry. You're happy and that's great. Ignore me and my bad attitude."

"Yours doesn't come anywhere near to how bad mine was before Gray. You never know what might happen."

"I guess," Aimee agreed, because she knew that's what Avery wanted. But Aimee did know. She knew the issue that had led to the end of her marriage was hers, and there wasn't a thing she could do to change it. She was, quite literally, broken. And she wasn't about to take a chance on allowing another man to remind her of what she couldn't have.

"Have a good weekend, Avery," she said as she stood.

"Happy heart's day." Avery grinned. "Watch out for Cupid and his arrow. I'm telling you that guy has a wicked sense of humor."

Aimee chuckled. "I'll keep my guard up." She walked out of town hall, wistful after Avery's words but knowing she didn't have anything to worry about. Aimee's heart was impenetrable to arrows.

CHAPTER THREE

"I THOUGHT MAYBE you weren't going to go through with this."

Aimee smoothed a hand across her seat belt as she glanced toward Paul. "Have a little faith, Bachelor Paul. We made a deal, and I always keep my word."

"Good to know," he murmured, and something about the timbre of his voice sent a shiver through her.

She adjusted her purse on the floor and sat back against the plush leather interior of the Audi sedan. Her ex-husband had liked fancy cars, so this should be a strike against Paul, but as he maneuvered the vehicle onto the highway that led west through the state, she appreciated the smooth ride.

"The town's marketing director is putting up flyers about the event this weekend. We're going to draw a big crowd." She lifted a hand, her fingers fluttering between them. "You're going to draw a crowd."

He laughed softly. "What a letdown for some unsuspecting woman. Since when does Magnolia have a marketing director?"

"Since people are interested in breathing new life into the community. It's a great place to live."

"Agreed."

"By the way," she said before she lost her nerve. "I doubt you'll be a letdown to anyone."

His fingers tightened on the steering wheel. "Don't be so sure. Doctors are notoriously bad partners. We work too much and neglect our personal lives for our professions. We thrive on stress and are known to be selfish. Not traits that make great partners."

She couldn't help the snort that escaped her mouth. "You might actually be describing my ex-husband."

"You were married to a doctor?" Paul slanted a glance in her direction, and she regretted sharing that tidbit of information.

"We met in college and got married just before he started his residency. Turns out we wanted different things in life."

She crossed one leg over the other. "The decision to separate was mutual. I'm not trying to paint him as the bad guy. He wasn't, and I wish him lots of happiness with his new wife."

"He's remarried already?"

She shrugged. "He was ready to start a family so didn't waste any time. The last I heard they've got one baby and are trying for another."

"Why didn't it work out with the two of you?" He held up a hand when she would have answered. "Different things doesn't tell me much."

Aimee couldn't explain why she wanted to tell him anything about the breakup of her marriage. Very few people in Magnolia even knew she had an ex-husband, let alone the heartbreaking, humiliating reason things hadn't worked out. It had nothing to do with her current life or who she was now. Who she'd become after two years of trying—and failing—to conceive.

Maybe it was her visceral reaction to Paul Thorpe that

made her willing to share the details. She needed to remind herself that there was nowhere to go with her attraction.

"Do you see yourself with a family someday, Dr. Thorpe?" she asked instead of answering the question.

A muscle ticked in his jaw, and he didn't take his eyes off the road. "Paul. You have to call me Paul. No one is going to believe that I'm the kind of prick who would make a date refer to me so formally."

She nodded. "Right. What about that family, Paul?"

"I guess." He shrugged. "Someday. Maybe. Once I get over the selfish and self-centered bits."

"I don't believe that about you," she told him.

"That I want a family?"

"That you're selfish."

"Talk to my ex-fiancée."

His voice held a combination of pain and bitterness that cut across her chest. He might make the claim of being selfish, but she'd bet her last dime that this man's heart had been broken. "My ex wanted kids and I can't have them," she said on a rush of breath. Nothing like revealing her deepest secret to a man she barely knew to really get things rolling. Megan would have been horrified. Her friend would have taken the opportunity of being alone in a car with a handsome man for an hour's drive to their resort destination to flirt and bat her eyelashes and generally set the mood for where the weekend might lead.

Aimee's revelation seemed to suck all the air out of the Audi's rich interior.

"Can't," he repeated, darting a questioning glance toward her.

She pressed a hand to her stomach. "Endometriosis."

"There are medical options."

"My ex is an ob-gyn." The irony of it made her gut clench. "We exhausted all the options."

"What about adoption?"

The word sent a maelstrom of emotion pouring through her. "He wasn't interested in adopting. That wasn't part of the plan."

"Plans change," Paul muttered, sounding disgusted.

She appreciated his outrage on her behalf. So much so that tears pricked the back of her eyes. That was the problem with never sharing the personal details of her life. She'd shoved all the emotions from that awful time into a dark corner of her soul and then ignored them. Exposing that shadowed place to light made the pain fresh again, and it had almost killed her the first time around.

"Christopher pivoted to a new path," she explained, working to keep the hurt out of her voice. "Without me."

"Asshat," Paul said after a few tense moments.

"It's not that simple," she argued although once again she appreciated his support.

"Yes, it is."

To her shock—and maybe his as well—he reached across the console and took her hand in his. His hand was so much bigger than hers, his skin warm and strangely comforting. He squeezed her fingers gently as his thumb traced circles on the center of her palm. "I don't need to know your ex-husband to know he's a complete son of a…" He released his hold on her. "I've been to enough weddings to know the 'for better or worse' part is pretty standard. The inability to conceive naturally isn't anywhere near the worst thing a couple could face."

"Thanks." She forced out a laugh. "I bet you're regretting our little bargain at the moment. This can't be the fun start to the weekend you imagined."

"You can't know how grateful I am to have you with me, Aimee. *Fun* is the last word I'd use to describe how I imagine things going. By the end of this, I'm going to owe you far more than an auction."

"You should probably tell me more about your family. I know it's your brother's wedding. Older or younger?"

"Younger by three years," Paul said, but offered nothing more.

Okay, then. They had approximately forty-five more minutes until they reached the hotel. She could play investigative reporter for a bit.

"Just the two of you?"

"I have an older sister. She turned forty last year."

"And how old are you? I should know that if we're dating."

"Thirty-five." He glanced at her. "You?"

"Thirty-one. Are you close with your siblings?"

Paul shrugged. "We're all busy. Gretchen is a neurosurgeon in Boston. Mass General."

"Two doctors in the family." Aimee whistled. "What about your brother?" She held up a hand. "No, let me guess. US Senator," she said with a grin.

"Congressman," Paul corrected, one side of his mouth curving up.

She burst out laughing. "I was joking. Holy buckets. Your parents must be so proud."

"The bar was set pretty high. My dad is the former governor."

Aimee felt her mouth drop open. "Of the state of North Carolina?"

"For two terms." Paul flashed a smile. "I wish I wouldn't have told you. It would kill my dad to meet a resident not aware of his legacy."

"I'd look like an idiot." She wagged a finger at him. "Not good for you to be dating a fool."

"I should warn you, I'm the black sheep."

"I don't think a doctor can be the black sheep," she argued.

"They had bigger plans for me. As the oldest son, I was supposed to go into politics. If not elected, then at least some high-ranking medical position. An ER doctor at a small community hospital is a disappointment."

"You're the chief of staff."

"Magnolia's barely a dot on the state map. It doesn't count."

She sat up straighter, upset by the resignation in his voice. Did Paul actually believe he hadn't achieved enough in his life because of some arbitrary standards set by his family? She didn't know him well, but they'd worked together for over a year, so she could say without question he was a talented physician. He cared about his patients, the hospital staff and the community. She wanted to reach for his hand again but kept hers in her lap. Suddenly, she was glad that she'd come with him.

Aimee knew what it was like to be judged for something that couldn't be controlled. No way would anyone at the wedding make the man sitting next to her feel less. Not on her watch.

CHAPTER FOUR

BY THE TIME they pulled up to the elegant hotel, Paul wasn't sure what he needed more—a drink or a cold shower. When he'd made the impulsive bargain with Aimee to be his date at the wedding, he'd only been thinking about having someone at his side during the actual ceremony and reception. A distraction and excuse for avoiding his family, particularly his ex-fiancée.

He hadn't thought about the fact that he'd be spending so much time with a woman who intrigued him more than he cared to admit. It would have been easier if she'd been obnoxious or had some kind of strange hyena laugh.

But no. She was sweet, funny and gently persistent, coaxing details from him that he hadn't shared with anyone in years. His sadness about the strained relationship he had with his brother and sister since their father remarried two years ago and memories of happier times when Paul's mom was alive and managed to make even the little moments of life seem special.

In turn, Aimee had told him about growing up on a dairy farm in central Tennessee, the first of her family to attend college. She'd explained that after her divorce, she'd wanted to get away and had applied for the nursing position at Magnolia Memorial on a whim.

"I'd never seen the Atlantic Ocean," she'd explained with

a smile. He could tell she appreciated the small town and all of its quaint charm as much as he did.

They'd discussed lists of favorite things and details a significant other would know—from preferred drink to favorite food to a story of how they started dating. In the span of an hour, much of his curiosity about Aimee had been satisfied, except he wanted more.

He would have liked to continue driving past the exit, maybe head to Nashville or Gatlinburg. They could spend the weekend exploring the kitschy town nestled in the heart of the Smokies. Saltwater taffy and mountain slides seemed like a lot more fun than what they were about to face.

Paul hadn't told her everything about his family. There was one particular detail he'd omitted. As the valet took his keys and a bellman pulled their luggage from the trunk, he turned toward the hotel and realized that detail was walking straight toward him.

"Paul." Kimberly Thorpe held out her arms, gold bracelets jangling on her wrist. "Your father has been asking when you were going to arrive. You didn't respond to his texts."

"No texting while driving," Paul answered, instinctively stepping closer to Aimee as he avoided Kim's proffered cheek. "State law."

Kim's laugh tinkled in the reserved quiet of the hotel portico. "Always a rule follower." Her impeccably made-up hazel eyes narrowed on Aimee. "Who do we have here?"

"My girlfriend," Paul said without hesitation. "I told Peter I was bringing a date."

"Last minute," Kim said, giving Aimee a not-so-subtle once-over that made Paul want to bustle her back into the car. They could make it to the state line in a few hours and he'd buy Dollywood tickets for tomorrow. "Aren't you going to introduce me?"

"I'm Aimee Baker." Aimee held out a hand toward Kim even as she wrapped her other arm around Paul's waist, her fingers curling into his side in a gesture that felt oddly proprietary.

"Kimberly Thorpe." Kim took Aimee's hand like someone would grasp a dead fish. "Paul's stepmother."

"Stop it, Kim." Paul stiffened but Aimee only snuggled closer. He realized he'd made a huge tactical error in not telling her about this critical piece of his past. No one could deny Kim was beautiful, in the glamorous way of Southern beauty pageant contestants. Her dark hair hung in glossy waves over her shoulders and her skin had the sun-kissed glow of an impeccably applied spray tan. In comparison, Aimee looked natural and real and so appealing it made Paul wonder how he'd ever thought Kim would be a good match.

"Your ex-fiancée seems inappropriate under the circumstances," Kim countered, crossing her arms over her chest. The five-carat diamond ring his father had given her sparkled in the afternoon sunlight. "Water under the bridge and all that."

Interesting that she made the reference to water because at the moment Paul felt like he was drowning.

"It's nice to meet you, Kim," Aimee said without missing a beat. She went up on tiptoe to brush a kiss against Paul's jaw. In an instant, he surfaced from the murky water threatening to pull him under. "I don't really give a rat's backside about your history with Paul or your current role in the family." She wagged a finger in Kim's direction.

"But if you ask him to call you 'mommy,' we're going to have an issue."

Kim's glossy mouth opened and shut several times. "I prefer to be called Kimberly," she said after an awkward moment.

"Good for you." Aimee linked her fingers with Paul's. "Let's check in, sweetie. I'd love a bit of a rest—" she gave him an exaggerated wink "—before dinner tonight."

Mind reeling at her audacity, Paul allowed himself to be tugged up the steps of the hotel and into the elegant lobby. Next to him, Aimee blew out a breath. "She's a real piece of work."

He could only nod.

"Any other pertinent family dynamic details you forgot to mention?" she asked, annoyance clear in her tone. He couldn't decide whether she was annoyed with him or his ex-girlfriend at this point. "Tell me you didn't date the bride, as well."

"No."

Paul glanced up as a familiar voice called out his name.

"You made it," his brother said as he approached with a relieved smile.

Aimee laughed under her breath, probably greatly entertained by the fact that even the groom doubted whether he'd show.

"I wouldn't miss your big day, Congressman." Paul enveloped Peter in a tight hug. It had been too long, and he immediately regretted letting bitterness affect the relationship he had with his siblings.

"That's good to hear." Peter patted him on the back. "Because I couldn't imagine waiting at the altar without my big brother at my side."

Before Paul could answer, Peter turned to Aimee, giving her his thousand-watt politician smile. "You must be Paul's mystery woman. I'm so glad you could join him."

"Aimee," she said, and shook Peter's hand with considerably more warmth than she'd shown Kim. No one could resist Peter's easygoing charm. "Congratulations. Paul has told me so many great things about you and your bride-to-be. He's thrilled for you, and we're both excited to be a part of your celebration."

Paul breathed out a relieved sigh. Truly, she really was the most amazing woman.

"I'm the luckiest guy on the planet." Peter cleared his throat when his voice cracked on the last word. Somehow, Paul knew that hadn't been a staged show of emotion. Peter really was that happy to be marrying his longtime girlfriend, Grace. He glanced at a spot over Aimee's shoulder and his smile dimmed. "Have you already talked to Kim?"

"Kimberly," Aimee corrected him with a teasing smile. Once again, she'd defused any potential tension before it could even take hold. "We did have the pleasure."

"You're the first person this weekend who's used *pleasure* to describe an interaction with our father's wife," Peter told her.

"This weekend is about you," she answered gently.

Gratitude filled Peter's dark gaze, and Paul realized he hadn't been the only one affected by their dad's whirlwind courtship and marriage to Paul's ex.

"It's going to be a wonderful weekend." Paul couldn't resist dropping a kiss on the top of Aimee's head. She smelled of lemons and cinnamon, an unexpected combination that seemed to wind around his senses.

"Yeah," Peter agreed with a nod. "I'll let you two get

checked in and settled. I managed to have your room up-graded to a suite, bro. Wicked good view of the pool."

"Two rooms," Paul corrected, and felt Aimee stiffen next to him. "You got my text, right? I've been having trouble sleeping and hate keeping Aimee awake so—"

"Sorry." Peter glanced between the two of them, confusion clouding his features. Paul understood that two rooms had been a strange request, but he thought he'd given his brother a convincing rationale for it. "The hotel is completely booked. A sitting room with a couch was the best I could do."

Tension knotted Paul's stomach at the thought of sharing a room with the woman who consumed his thoughts, even for one night.

"It's fine." Aimee nestled closer again. Damn, she should have been an actress. "I'm used to him by now."

Peter reached out and gave her a quick hug. "I like you, mystery woman. I can already tell you're good for my brother."

Paul couldn't hear Aimee's response from the rush of blood to his head. Hell, yes, she was good for him. Even as a fake girlfriend. He just hated the fact that he wished it could be real.

CHAPTER FIVE

AIMEE SIPPED HER champagne as she looked around the elegant ballroom later that night. Her stomach was in knots and her jaw hurt from smiling for so long.

Not that the wedding ceremony and reception hadn't been everything she'd expected. Other than Paul's snarky ex, everyone in the family was lovely, even his rather gruff father. As she'd imagined from Paul's description, Grace, his new sister-in-law, welcomed her with enthusiasm, making Aimee feel as though their celebration wouldn't have been complete without her presence at Paul's side.

Gretchen, Paul's older sister, was serious and intense but also wickedly funny with her running commentary about how each person in attendance was part of the dysfunctional family dynamic. She had a quiet husband, Max, who clearly adored her, and two well-behaved elementary-school-age children.

Aimee loved weddings, and the personal touches Grace and Peter had added to their vows had her dabbing at the corners of her eyes. For all her talk to Avery about not caring about Valentine's Day, she couldn't help but be touched by the obvious love between the bride and groom. Several times during the short ceremony, her gaze had snagged Paul's, and the intensity in his hazel eyes made her breath catch.

Part of her wished they were still in the car, which had felt like their own private sanctuary. She'd loved getting to know him, his sense of humor and inherent kindness confirming her good taste in being intrigued by him from the start. She actually hadn't seen much of him since they'd first gone to their room. It had been obvious that he didn't like the thought of sharing a room with her for the night. She hadn't even thought to ask about separate accommodations, but of course he had.

She told herself he was being a gentleman. This was a business arrangement of a sort, and she'd never been the kind of woman to indulge in meaningless intimacy anyway. Especially not with a coworker.

She sighed and smiled at the waiter, who handed her a fresh glass of champagne. Who was she kidding? She had no desire for a fling with Dr. Paul Thorpe because she liked him. More than the general crush that most of the female hospital staff had on him. Yes, he was good-looking but now that she'd seen behind the curtain of his formal physician facade, she liked him even more.

It was going to be horrible if Megan indeed won him in the bachelor auction. The last thing Aimee wanted to do was hear about her roommate going on a date with Paul. Even worse, what if he spent the night at their small house or he and Megan actually got serious? Would Aimee have to move out just to save herself the reminder of what she'd never have?

"Is it as awful as all that?"

She blinked as Paul lowered himself to the empty chair next to her. He'd been seated at the head table with the rest of the bridal party. Aimee had enjoyed the group she'd ended up with for dinner, consisting mostly of Peter and Grace's college friends.

"It was a lovely ceremony," she said, and took another drink of champagne. The bubbles tickled her throat. Was this glass number three or four? She'd lost count, although the fizziness in her head told her it should be her last. "What could be more hopeful than a wedding on Valentine's Day?"

"My brother has always been an idealist," Paul said with a half smile. "It makes him a great politician. I have no doubt he'll be a devoted husband, as well."

"I hope so," she whispered, resenting the emotion that clogged her throat. She thought her divorce had made her a cynic when it came to love, but she'd been holding back tears most of the night.

"You don't look like you're having fun," he said. He reached out and traced a finger along the top of her hand. She felt the featherlight touch all the way to her toes. "Would you like to dance?"

The music had just changed from an up-tempo tune to a slow ballad. It would be smart to decline the invitation. She felt fragile at the moment, like her defenses were made of nothing more than tissue paper.

"Yes, I would."

He offered his hand and a megawatt smile that did all kinds of crazy things to her insides. Then she was in his arms and the feel of it was everything she could have imagined and more.

She hadn't dated since her divorce, hadn't been with a man since her ex-husband. By the end of their marriage, intimacy had been so fraught with tension and the pressure to conceive, there'd been no real pleasure in the act.

One simple dance shouldn't affect her this way. But she

knew it was more than the dance. It was the man holding her, his body rock-hard under the tux he wore, yet also comforting, like a favorite pillow she wanted to snuggle closer to. He smelled of soap and spice, and it was all she could do not to press her nose to the base of his neck and inhale.

Neither of them spoke as they swayed in a gentle rhythm to the song, and Aimee wondered if Paul could feel the current of attraction that threaded between them. As if he'd read her mind, his hand squeezed her hip. Her knees went weak with longing.

She wasn't the one-night stand type, but maybe she could make an exception. Just this once.

The thought and all the potential land mines that went with it had her stepping away from him as soon as the music ended. The DJ announced that it was time for the bouquet toss, and through her muddled mind, Aimee registered the single women making their way onto the dance floor.

Paul gave her a curious look and then laced his fingers with hers. "Let's get out of here," he said, and she nodded, unable to put words to the gratitude rushing through her.

His ex-fiancée—now stepmother—shot her a glare as they passed, and his sister smiled. "You're going the wrong way," Gretchen called, but Paul either didn't hear her or chose to ignore the gentle admonishment.

Aimee just wanted to get away from the reception. She needed to catch her breath, to set her tumbling thoughts to rights. To get a damn hold of herself.

Paul led her out of the ballroom and across the lobby. He jabbed the elevator button, then breathed out a ragged puff of air when a chime immediately dinged. The doors swished open and he pulled her in. As the doors closed, he went to hit the button for their floor, paused and pressed the stop lever instead.

Then he turned, pulled her closer and kissed her, his mouth hot and demanding as he coaxed apart her lips. She met his need with hers, giving herself over to the moment. She groaned when the tip of his tongue touched hers. He spread his hands around her waist, and his thumbs grazed the soft flesh of her breasts through her thin dress. His touch practically set her body on fire. She leaned into him, winding her arms around his neck. He lifted his mouth from hers and kissed a trail along her jaw and neck, goose bumps erupting in his wake.

"You're even softer than I imagined," he said against her skin. "So damn beautiful."

Aimee sucked in a breath. She felt beautiful at this moment, pliant with desire. She'd spent so long thinking of herself as broken after her divorce, and even with desire stealing her thoughts, she still managed to recognize that this moment and this man were a revelation.

He knew the worst thing about her and wanted her anyway. Before she could truly process the ramifications of what it might mean, all of her doubts came crashing in around her. He wanted her physically. It couldn't be anything more. He'd told her he wanted a family. She couldn't give him that.

Yes, she could take the pleasure he was willing to offer—almost believed it would be worth it. The sharp ache that sliced across her chest told a different story. She cared about Paul. More than was smart for either of them.

Deep inside she knew she wouldn't be satisfied with a fling. Despite understanding that she could never be a long-term possibility for a man like him, that was exactly what she wanted.

And exactly why she'd kept herself cut off from relationships.

She wanted too damn much.

He pulled back and cupped her face in his hands. "I'm sorry," he whispered, his gaze intense on hers. "I had no right to—"

"We got caught up in the moment," she told him, and stepped away, pressing herself to the corner of the elevator. "But it can't go any further, Paul. I'm not..." Her voice trailed off.

"I know." He reached out for the elevator's keypad, and less than a minute later the doors opened to their floor.

He followed her into the empty hall. It made no sense how much she missed holding his hand. She'd known what this date was when they'd made their agreement. Stupid to want something more.

And now she had to share a hotel room with him. Oh, lord. Could it get any worse?

He placed his room key in front of the sensor and opened the door for her.

"Aimee."

She turned. He still stood at the threshold.

"I'm going to head back down for a little while. I need... some space."

"Okay," she agreed, biting down on her bottom lip. "I'm sorry I wasn't more fun as a date." She tried for a smile, but her facial muscles refused to cooperate.

"You're perfect," he said, his expression unreadable, then disappeared into the hall.

CHAPTER SIX

"THANK YOU AGAIN," Paul said, clearing his throat when the words came out harsher than he'd intended.

He'd just pulled to a stop next to Aimee's car in the hospital parking lot. The hour drive from the resort had seemed to stretch on for days, mainly because he'd spent the whole time wanting to touch her and knowing he had no right.

What in the hell had made him think that taking the woman he'd had a crush on for the better part of the past year would be a good idea?

It wasn't just that he'd invited her as his date. He'd bribed her into going with him, not an auspicious start to any potential relationship. Not that she'd given him any indication she wanted more from him than his help with the bachelor auction next weekend.

He didn't even know her ex-husband's name but could easily envision himself planting a fist in the guy's face. Paul couldn't imagine hurting Aimee in the way her ex obviously had. Sure, he saw himself with a family someday, even though Kim's betrayal left him with the sense he couldn't trust women or his own judgment about them. But if he had a woman like Aimee in his life, nothing could force him to give her up and especially not the inability to conceive when there were so many kids in the world who needed a good home. She'd be a fantastic mother. Based on her dedication to patients, he could clearly see that she had so much love to give.

It killed him to know she didn't believe that about herself.

"You have a great family," she said with a forced smile. "All except for Kim, anyway."

He laughed. "It's hard for me to believe I ever saw a future with her. She seems to make my dad happy, though. I guess I can be happy for the two of them."

"That's very mature," she murmured.

"I don't plan on buying her a Mother's Day gift anytime soon," he clarified, and felt a strange sense of relief when Aimee's smile relaxed.

"Awkward."

"Yeah."

She placed a hand on his arm. "I'm glad I went with you to the wedding."

"Me, too." He covered her hand with his, grateful for an excuse to touch her, even if it was just for a few short moments. "You made everything better."

She shook her head. "I doubt that. You would have been fine no matter what. It's obvious you and your siblings are close, even if it hasn't felt that way."

"We are. I appreciate you giving up your Saturday for me. I promise I'll live up to my end of the bargain."

As soon as the words were out of his mouth, he regretted them. He didn't want to think about the hospital fundraiser or being auctioned off for a date with another woman. Yes, he and Aimee had an arrangement, but it was so much more than that. He wanted a chance with her—a real chance. Not just something she'd agreed to because she needed his help.

Walking away from her last night had been one of the

hardest things he'd done. She'd looked so damn irresistible, standing in the doorway of the quiet hotel room, cheeks flushed and her mouth swollen from his kisses. He knew it had been the right thing to do. He'd returned to the reception, hanging out with a few of his brother's single friends. Then he'd crashed on the couch in his high school friend's room until morning. One-night stands didn't interest him in general, and he had a feeling that if he took Aimee to his bed, he might not have the strength to let her go. She'd been showered and dressed by the time he returned to the room and had left almost as soon as he walked in, retreating to the lobby until he'd found her at the family brunch his sister arranged.

Although she'd publicly played the role of his doting girlfriend, she'd made it clear she had no interest in a relationship. And he wasn't sure he was ready to open his heart to a woman he knew had the potential to break it. He'd spent a long time patching himself back together after Kim's betrayal. He couldn't imagine risking that kind of pain again.

As he watched Aimee's blue eyes cloud over, he regretted letting the moment slip away.

Her gaze cleared, and it was as if he could see her mentally rebuilding the walls that kept people at arm's length. She withdrew her hand and pointed a finger at him. "I expect to see lots of charm out of you this week." She laughed, and he wondered if he imagined how hollow it sounded. "Just remember it's for a good cause."

"Right," he agreed. They exited the car, and he retrieved her suitcase from his trunk and transferred it to hers. What was the correct protocol for saying goodbye to your fake-for-one-night girlfriend?

"I'll see you around," she said, gesturing toward the hospital's brick facade.

"Maybe we could grab dinner sometime," he blurted. "After the fundraiser when you're not so busy or—"

"Maybe." Her mouth thinned. Paul could tell she had no intention of seeing him again, but somehow he couldn't give up.

So much for not being willing to risk his heart.

"I like you, Aimee," he said quietly, and stopped trying to shutter the emotions from his gaze. "I want to see you again. Not just at work. I want to—"

She shook her head. "That's not...I'm not..." Her gaze dropped to the ground in front of her. "I've explained how things are with me, Paul. I'm not a good candidate for... anything."

"I want to try. I really like you," he repeated, unsure of what else to say. "I think you like me, too."

She closed her eyes like she couldn't bear to look at him.

"Nothing else matters," he told her, and lifted a hand, wanting to pull her to him.

She stepped back and opened the door to her car. "It matters to me," she whispered, and climbed in.

He watched her drive away, wondering how one night managed to change everything for him.

CHAPTER SEVEN

"Oh, don't you look lovely." Avery made a small circle with one finger. "Give me a spin."

Aimee laughed and then did the requisite turn in the shimmery cocktail dress she'd bought for the fundraiser. "I'm feeling a bit like a princess." She smoothed a hand over the front of the red-lace overlay. "I even shaved my legs."

Avery shifted the candle centerpiece on one of the round tables that filled the banquet room where they were hosting the event. "You must be planning to bid on one of the bachelors," she said with a wink.

"No." Aimee worked to keep the smile fixed on her face even as a sharp ache sliced across her chest. In the past week she'd gotten used to smiling through her pain. Each time she saw Paul at the hospital, leaning over the nurses' station in the ER with a gaggle of swooning women surrounding him, the ache was fresh again, like ripping a bandage off a wound that hadn't quite healed. It was exactly what she'd asked him to do, yet it was still difficult to watch. "But I'm counting on raising buckets of money for the mobile clinic."

"We will." Avery took a step closer to her, tucking a strand of blond hair behind one ear. "Are you okay? You kind of look like a princess who's been punched in the gut."

"Then I need to fix my face before the event starts,"

Aimee answered, scrunching up her nose. She checked the time on her phone and sucked in a breath. There was a notification of a message from Paul. She glanced up at Avery. "I'm fine. Promise."

"I recognize that lie," Avery said gently. "But it's not my business, although my sisters would tell you that normally doesn't stop me from butting in. Just know I'm here if you need a friend."

"Thanks," Aimee whispered. She didn't have many friends in Magnolia outside of her coworkers and appreciated the other woman's offer. Even though there was no way she was planning to share her muddled feelings at the moment. She'd spent way too long on her makeup just to have it run down her face before the guests arrived. "I'm going to make sure everything's ready at check-in. I really appreciate all your help."

"It's good for the town." Avery nodded. "You're making a big difference in the community with the mobile clinic initiative, Aimee. You should feel proud."

Heart thumping wildly, Aimee walked toward the lobby and opened the text from Paul.

Good luck. I hope it's everything you wanted.

Tears sprang to her eyes, and she furiously blinked them away. Tonight was on track to exceed her expectations as far as the hospital's fundraising goal. It was more than she thought she could achieve when she'd first arrived in Magnolia. At that point, all she'd wanted was to be a good nurse and work to forget the dreams she'd had for her future.

She'd given up the dream of sharing her life with a husband and raising kids, until they were beyond the scope of even her wildest imaginings. She'd left behind those girlish hopes when she signed the divorce papers because she'd believed her ex-husband when he told her she would never be enough.

Paul Thorpe made her feel like she might be more than enough.

HE SHOULD HAVE gotten drunk.

Paul rolled his shoulders as he waited behind the curtain at the side of the stage that had been erected in the ballroom. Logan Hughes, a local firefighter stood next to Avery Keller, who was acting as the auctioneer for the event.

He'd met Avery and her fiancé, Gray Atwell, another firefighter, earlier in the evening, as well as Logan, who seemed much more comfortable with being auctioned off to the highest bidder than Paul. The man had even worn his uniform, flexing his impressive biceps to the delight of the crowd.

Paul's gut clenched. What in the hell had he gotten himself into?

He'd seen only brief glimpses of Aimee since arriving at the event and couldn't decide if she was truly busy or just avoiding him. She hadn't responded to his text from earlier, a clear message but one that he still didn't want to accept.

The tables were filled with his coworkers and people he'd met around town. The mobile clinic was a worthwhile cause, yet he couldn't help but think they would have found a way to raise the money without his involvement. Hell, there had to be more single first responders in town besides the one strutting his stuff onstage.

He thought about his dance with Aimee and knew without a doubt that whatever humiliation he endured tonight was worth it. One dance shouldn't have made such a difference but holding her in his arms had changed everything. At least for him.

Now he just had to convince her.

Before he could work on that, he had to get through the next several minutes. There was a high-pitched whoop of delight from the audience as Avery pointed to the highest bidder. The firefighter did a few Magic Mike–inspired hip thrusts before she swatted him on the arm and then shooed him offstage.

"That was a trip," the firefighter said as he passed Paul. "Have fun out there, Doc."

Paul plastered a good-natured smile on his face as Avery introduced him. Heat crept up his cheeks when a chorus of cheers greeted his arrival next to the podium. Avery explained that his date would include an afternoon of sailing, generously donated by a local charter company. He wondered if Aimee liked being on the water even though he shouldn't care at this point.

Then the auction started. He tried not to look as uncomfortable as he felt as the bidding increased at a remarkably fast pace.

Avery gave him an exaggerated once-over and then leaned in. "You must have a great bedside manner, Dr. Thorpe," she said into the microphone.

He laughed at her joke as the crowd applauded. Out of the corner of his eye, he could see the table of nurses where most of the attention on him came from. Aimee wasn't among their group.

When the bidding got to six hundred dollars and stopped, Avery glanced around the room and Paul let out a small sigh of relief. The firefighter had gone for five hundred so at least Paul had kept up without having to shake his moneymaker.

"Going once." Avery looked out to the crowd. "Going twice."

"A thousand dollars."

Anticipation pulsed through Paul when he recognized the voice of the high bidder, and he hoped to hell he wasn't imagining the moment. Avery's eyes widened as she nodded. "A cool grand for the good doctor." She grinned at him and covered the microphone with one hand. "I hope she's going to get something better than a pelvic thrust for that."

He barely registered her teasing as he watched Aimee wind her way through the sea of tables. Her hands were clasped tightly in front of her. He couldn't decide whether she looked like she was going to laugh or throw up. She looked beautiful in a fitted red dress and her blond hair curling around her shoulders.

Avery didn't waste any time pounding the gavel, but he'd already hopped off the stage. He met Aimee in the center of the room, and she gave him a tentative smile. "I like you, too."

"You have no idea how happy I am to hear that. And thank you in advance for your generosity."

She raised one brow, joy sparkling in her sky blue eyes. "I would have gone higher. Just so you know. I wasn't going to lose you."

His heart filled, and he leaned in and brushed his lips over hers, not caring that they had an audience.

"How come she gets a kiss and I just got some booty shaking?" a female voice complained loudly.

Aimee smiled up at him. "I've changed my mind about love. I'm willing to take a chance if you are, especially now that I've officially won you."

He reached for her hand and pressed it to his chest. "You had my heart long before tonight, Aimee. For you, I'll take every chance."

* * * * *

Sergeant Hayden Mitchell's mission: give every canine veteran the perfect forever home. But when it comes to Sierra, a sweet Labrador, Hayden isn't sure Lizzie Vega fits the bill. When a storm leaves her stranded at his ranch, the hardened ex-military man wonders if Lizzie is the perfect match for Sierra...and him...

Read on for a sneak peek at
The Rancher's Forever Family,
the first book in the Texas Cowboys & K-9s miniseries
by USA TODAY *bestselling author Sasha Summers.*

His fingertips traced the curve of her jaw.

"This is the strangest day of my life," she whispered, entirely focused on him. His touch. His gaze. His proximity.

"Agreed." His voice was low, gruff and toe curling.

"I'm not complaining." She wasn't breathing. Was she? Did it matter?

"Agreed." He stepped closer, his hand resting against her cheek. "But that's not going to stop me from asking if I can—"

"Kiss me," she finished, sliding her hands up his chest, his impossibly warm, wall-like chest, and around his neck. "Yes, please."

It was the softest sweep of his lips against hers, but potent enough to induce a full-body shudder from her and a ragged— bone-melting—hitch in his breath.

He lifted his head, just as caught off guard as she was…

But then her hands gripped his shoulders, his arm slid around her waist and she was pressed against him. Being wrapped up in Hayden Mitchell's arms was just as intense as he was. His lips met hers and every single fiber of her being was alive with want. Every sensation seemed magnified. The firmness of his mouth against hers. The cling of his lips, seeking… And when she opened for him, the sweep of his tongue against hers.

No breathing. No thinking. Just this. Just him.

Don't miss
The Rancher's Forever Family *by Sasha Summers,*
available soon wherever
Harlequin Special Edition books and ebooks are sold.

Harlequin.com

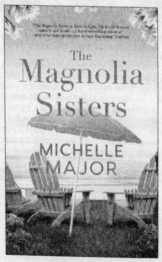

Praise for Michelle Major's
Magnolia Sisters series

"A dynamic start to a series
with a refreshingly original premise."
—*Kirkus Reviews*

"A sweet start to a promising series,
perfect for fans of Debbie Macomber."
—*Publishers Weekly* (starred review)

"*The Magnolia Sisters* is sheer delight,
filled with humor, warmth and heart....
I loved everything about it."
—*New York Times* bestselling author RaeAnne Thayne

Also by Michelle Major

The Magnolia Sisters

A Magnolia Reunion
The Magnolia Sisters
The Road to Magnolia
The Merriest Magnolia

For a full list of titles by Michelle Major,
please visit www.michellemajor.com.